Darcy Comes to Rosings

Darcy Comes to Rosings

Andrea David

Darcy Comes to Rosings

© 2018 Andrea David

ISBN-13: 978-1-942198-17-8

ISBN-10: 1-942198-17-5

All Rights Reserved Worldwide

The author has asserted her rights to be identified as the author of this book. Duplication or distribution via any means is illegal and a violation of international copyright law, and subject to criminal prosecution. No portion of this literary work may be sold, manipulated, transmitted, copied, reproduced, or distributed, in any form or format, by any means or in any manner whatsoever, without the express written permission of the author, except for brief excerpts used for the purpose of review. To request written permission, contact Artesian Well Publishing at www.ArtWellPub.com.

All trademarks used herein are the property of their respective owners.

Published by

Artesian Well Publishing

www.ArtWellPub.com

Learn more about Andrea's books at AndreaDavidAuthor.com

This book is a work of fiction. All names, characters, locations, and incidents are the products of the author's imagination, are used fictitiously, or are based on the public domain works of Jane Austen. Any resemblance to actual events, locales, organizations, or persons, living or dead, is entirely coincidental.

Published in the United States of America

First print edition, October 2018

This book is set in England and uses predominantly British spelling.

Table of Contents

Table of Contents...7

About this Book 9

Prologue 11

Chapter 1 19

Chapter 2 39

Chapter 3 57

Chapter 4 69

Chapter 5.. 88

Chapter 6 97

Chapter 7.. 108

Chapter 8 122

Chapter 9 136

Chapter 10...153

Chapter 11 169

Chapter 12... 181

Chapter 13..188

Chapter 14 197

Chapter 15.. 212

Chapter 16 225

Chapter 17..244

Chapter 18 252

Chapter 19 260

Chapter 20.. 284

Chapter 21..299

Chapter 22 314

Chapter 23 326

Chapter 24 338

Chapter 25 353

Chapter 26 372

Chapter 27 389

Chapter 28..407

Chapter 29 415

Chapter 30 430

Chapter 31..446

Epilogue...453

About the Author..457

About this Book

Elizabeth Bennet from Jane Austen's *Pride and Prejudice* is enjoying a visit with her newly married best friend in the idyllic countryside of Kent. Her pleasant holiday is interrupted when the arrogant Mr. Darcy appears at nearby Rosings Park. During their frequent meetings, her spirited retorts do nothing to deter his attentions to her. In fact, they only seem to encourage him.

Realizing Darcy is in love with her, Elizabeth is torn by an awful dilemma. With her father's estate entailed on a male heir, she and her sisters face the prospect of poverty if they do not marry well. Darcy's wealth could save them. But how can she marry a man she does not esteem simply for the material comfort he can offer?

Fitzwilliam Darcy is determined to forget the lovely Elizabeth, who stole his heart during his autumn sojourn in Hertfordshire. So naturally, when he learns she is spending the spring within walking distance of his aunt's estate at

Rosings, he goes for an extended stay. He finds Elizabeth even more enchanting than he remembered.

When Darcy discovers Elizabeth's rightful resentments against him, he seeks to make things right and court her properly. Can he convince her of his worth? Or have his past sins—and the machinations of an old enemy—sunk him in her opinion forever?

This Pride and Prejudice *variation is a full-length, sweet Regency romance. It includes kissing and a fade-to-black wedding night scene.*

Prologue

"Take that, you French rogue!" The fallen oak branch, which served as Richard's sword, clashed against Will's. "I'll run you through, I shall."

Will lowered his own branch and scowled at his cousin. "Why do I always have to be French?"

"Because when I am grown, I shall be a real soldier in His Majesty's army, whilst you will only be a gentleman."

Fitzwilliam Darcy, aged eight, puzzled at that. He had thought that being a gentleman was better than being a soldier, but he would have to ask his mama. She knew all about precedence. Will did not understand exactly what precedence was, but he knew it was important.

"*En garde!*" Richard commanded, and Will raised the branch again. It was not a fair fight, because Richard was two years older. Still, Will used all his strength, and Richard was careful not to knock him down.

They played a little longer, then ran along a path through a woodland, heading toward the manor house at Rosings Park. The building was no bigger than Will's home at Pemberley, but it was not a warm, friendly place. With Richard at his side, though, Will was happy.

Will sprinted as fast as he could, making his muscles work so he could keep up with his cousin. The breeze in his hair, the air coursing through his lungs, filled him with joy and wild abandon.

During this large family holiday at his aunt and uncle de Bourgh's, he was free from his tutor and could spend all day playing with his Fitzwilliam cousins. He liked his studies but did not care much for being confined to the nursery. It was full summer, the trees a leafy green, and his restless young body demanded fresh air and vast, open spaces.

Late afternoon sunshine cast dappled shade on the rich earth. Will slowed to catch his breath. When he and Richard reached the lawn, they fell into a walk, composing themselves and feigning the dignity of their elders.

Their aunt, Lady Catherine de Bourgh, insisted that despite their youth, they must behave like gentlemen. Since it was her house, they had to follow her rules. That's what Will's mama had told him. And he always tried to do what his mama said.

They strode into the house through the servants' entrance. The housekeeper called, "Go straightaway to the nursery!" as they bounded up the stairs. But they did not. Richard headed to his parents' rooms, and Will went looking for his own mother and father.

If he went to his nurse, she would get a wet cloth and rub it roughly over his face and hands, scolding him for getting dirty. His mama's touch was gentle, and she would tell him what a sweet, good boy he was whilst she washed him up. His mama was so pretty—it hurt his heart sometimes to look at her, like she was an angel from heaven.

When he reached the outer chamber of his parents' rooms, he heard their voices coming through the open bedroom door. "Can you believe Catherine," his mama said, "insisting that she has higher precedence now that de Bourgh has been knighted? We are daughters of an earl, and get our precedence from our father. As I am older, I outrank her."

"My love," his father said mildly, "is it worth spoiling this visit by arguing with her? She will never concede, and it is such a trivial thing."

"Trivial!" The pitch of his mother's voice rose on that exclamation. "The entire social structure of England rests on that hierarchy."

"I doubt very much that the kingdom will fall if the precedence of two earl's daughters gets reversed. Just be glad you are not French."

His mother turned silent at that, despite the laugh in his father's tone. Will was not sure what it meant to be French, except that they were dogs who had rebelled against their rightful king and queen. Will was very glad *he* was not French.

He stepped into his parents' bedroom, and they turned to him. They were dressed for dinner, his mother in a pale blue silk gown, his father in a dark suit with a gold waistcoat. They looked so dignified, whereas he was as dirty as a street urchin. For a moment he worried they might scold him.

Instead, his mother gave him a broad smile. "Why, look at you! Did you and Richard have fun?" She went to the wash basin and wet a cloth.

"Yes, except that he made me be a French soldier again, and the French are dogs."

She hesitated a moment. "Well, it is only make-believe. You do not mind, do you?"

Will thought about that. "No, I suppose not. I like Richard."

His throat tightened, and he pushed down the urge to cry. He was too old to cry. But soon, he would have to go back to Pemberley, where he would be all alone. He wished Richard were his brother. He did not have any brothers or sisters, and Richard had three of each.

It wasn't fair. Will had had a brother once, but the baby had gone to Heaven, and his mother had cried and cried. His father had not cried, but he had been sad. Will had tried to follow his father's example, but sometimes he had cried, too.

His mother gently caressed his face with the cloth, then his hands. "Goodness, you need a scrubbing. I shall tell Nurse."

"But she is so rough!" Will complained.

His mother's lips pursed. "Well, you are a big boy now. Perhaps you could wash yourself."

"She scolds me if I do. She says I get water everywhere."

"It is just a little water. It does not harm anything." His mother kissed his forehead and beamed. "If you get cleaned up and dress like a gentleman, you can dine with us instead of taking a tray in the nursery."

His father chuckled.

His mother turned. "What?"

"I can see Catherine's face now."

"It is a family dinner, and my son is the best-behaved child I know."

His mother's words filled his heart. He tried very hard to be good. When he was good, it made her smile, and her smile was the prettiest sight in the world.

"That will not stop her from chiding the boy for everything he does," his father remarked.

His mother narrowed her eyes, then looked at Will kindly. "Remember what I told you about not making Lady Catherine cross?"

"You said not to argue."

"That's right. Lady Catherine gets cross when she does not get her way, so we choose our battles. Do you understand what that means?"

Will nodded. He had heard it before. "We let her have her way if it doesn't matter."

"And if it does matter?"

Will thought a moment, then beamed. In a menacing voice, he said, "We battle to the death."

His father laughed and tousled his hair. "You sound like Richard."

Will's chest tightened, squeezing his heart. "Can Richard be my brother?"

His father knelt. "I am afraid not. But he can be your best friend, and he will always be your cousin."

Will nodded fiercely. "When Richard is a soldier, and I am a gentleman, will he have higher precedence than me?"

His mother laid her hands on his shoulders. "He will have higher precedence because his father will likely be earl by then, and your father will be a gentleman. But you will be a man of consequence. Always remember, you come from a noble family. Your grandfather is an earl, as your uncle will be after him, and then your cousin. And you will be master of Pemberley one day, one of the greatest houses in all of England."

His father chuckled. "In all of Derbyshire, at least." He stood and kissed his wife's cheek.

Will's mother stroked his arms. "You must always defer to those above you in the hierarchy—but in your heart, you must never think of them as your betters. Your father is the finest man in England, and if you emulate him, then you shall be, too."

"Anne," his father said in a soft voice, caressing his wife's back.

"It is nothing more than the truth. I defy you to find anyone who treats his servants and his tenants better, or who is a better husband and father. A title is not the only measure of a man's greatness."

His father rested a hand at his wife's waist and kissed her tenderly. Then, he turned back to his son. "Off to the nursery with you. And tell Nurse she must let you wash yourself, and any mess you make be damned."

"George!" his mother cried with a laugh.

"Say it for me, Will. Any mess be damned."

"Any mess be damned!" he said confidently.

"That's my boy. Now off with you."

Will skittered to the nursery, memorizing what his mother had said about his place in the world. It was important to come from a noble family, but it was also important to be kind, like his father was. That pleased Will. Because he wanted nothing more than to be like his father.

Chapter 1

Elizabeth Bennet stood atop a hillock a short walk from Hunsford Cottage in the countryside of Kent. Golden sunshine spilled down over the trees and open meadows. The cool morning air and sweet scent of wildflowers invigorated her senses.

She had planned her route with the purpose of avoiding Mr. Darcy, a handsome but aloof young man from Derbyshire who was staying nearby with his aunt. He often rode through the nearby fields in the morning. Encounters between the two were strained, as his excessive pride left him disinclined to speak.

From the high ground where she stood, she thankfully saw no sign of him. His aunt's home, the proud estate of Rosings Park, lay open to her view. The house was the largest and grandest she had ever seen. Its pale limestone walls gleamed in the sunlight, imposing towers reaching for the sky.

How strange that such a place had been built for people of flesh and blood, and not faerie princes and princesses! Lizzy could not imagine calling such a place home. Yet she had dined with the residents of the great hall more than once during her visit. Their manners were as imposing as the house, but their minds perhaps less impressive.

Surrounding the house was a wide lawn, cut through by a cobblestone lane flanked by tall cedars. Beyond the structure, a woodland sloped toward a stream that wound toward the horizon. In her mind she could hear the water babbling over smooth rocks, and could feel it cold and refreshing on her skin.

Lizzy breathed the spring air. April was her favourite month, with the bluebells dotting the forest floor and trees unfurling their new, translucent leaves. The forest was quickly greening, the birds undertaking the business of seeking a mate and building their nests.

During her weeks in Hunsford, she had come to love this walk. Besides the exercise and stunning views it offered, it also gave her a respite from the chattiness of her cousin. The reverend Mr. Collins had never encountered a silence he did not feel compelled to fill.

She had met Mr. Collins only recently, the two branches of their family split by an old feud. But upon the death of his father, Mr. Collins had sought to make amends. Whilst visiting Lizzy's family, he had procured the hand of Lizzy's best friend, Charlotte Lucas. It was for Charlotte's sake, and not that of Mr. Collins, that Lizzy had made this sojourn.

Older than Lizzy, with a practical nature, Charlotte had long been a steadying influence. Though Charlotte had never been pretty, she was patient and kind, and Lizzy had missed her terribly since she had left Hertfordshire. Lizzy's home life was not always felicitous, as one of five daughters in competition for the attention and affection of their parents—which were not always freely given.

Lizzy was visiting along with Charlotte's sister Maria, who was constantly amazed by the experiences she had in her sister's new home. From the French porcelain plates to the hand-carved woodwork to the beehives in the garden, everything she saw was fantastic and new. Lizzy loved Maria but could not share her enthusiasm.

Lizzy descended the hill in a dash, the fall of her boots sure against the soft earth. Perhaps when she arrived at the cottage, the post would have come. She longed for a letter from Jane. Her eldest sister was staying in London with their aunt and uncle, nursing a broken heart. Her attempts at feigning a tranquil spirit were transparent to her sister. Lizzy could hardly endure the separation, knowing Jane suffered.

Heading toward the woodland, she was startled to see Mr. Darcy emerging on foot from the dark shade of the trees. Her chest and shoulders sank. Fitzwilliam Darcy, of the great estate of Pemberley in Derbyshire, was a man of eight-and-twenty, as disagreeable as he was wealthy. 'Twas a pity he was consumed with pride—for in his person, he was as pleasing a man as Lizzy had ever beheld.

Since she was out in the open, in full view of him, there was no getting around it. She would have to greet him, and be as polite as their mutual stations required. Had she not disliked him so much, she might have admired his upright posture and earnest expression as he approached. But in a man for whom she held such an aversion, those physical enticements were unforgivable.

Drawing close, he bowed, and she curtsied. Since *he* said nothing, she began, "It is a beautiful morning, is it not?"

"Splendid."

She looked at him expectantly, and was about to break the silence when he added haltingly, "You are in the habit of taking an early morning walk, I think?"

She blinked in surprise. "Yes, but I have finished my exercise for today. I was just about to head back to the parsonage. If you will excuse me—"

"I would be happy to accompany you."

Good heavens! The man could not wish for her company, surely. This must be some gallantry on his part. "I would not wish to put you out—"

"Not at all. As you say, it is a beautiful morning. I can think of no better way to spend it than in the company of a beautiful woman."

Fire burned in her cheeks. It was not like Darcy to pay false compliments. Normally he was blunt in his appraisals; on the night they had met, he had dismissed her as tolerably pretty, but not handsome enough to induce him to dance.

And now he had the audacity to call her beautiful?

She was glad she had overheard his true assessment, or else his flattering words might have affected her. Instead, she held her head high, looking anywhere but at his face, and walked in a calm pace toward the parsonage, the home of Mr. and Mrs. Collins, where she was staying.

She would not look into those dark, intense eyes, nor gaze upon the high cheekbones, the firm jaw. She would not be tempted to notice how his sable hair framed his face, nor how his lips curved enticingly.

No. Elizabeth Bennet was sensible, and would not fall prey to a man who considered himself too grand for her. She would put Fitzwilliam Darcy out of her mind as soon as she was out of his company.

But for now, his proximity was torment.

"How do you find Kent?" he asked.

"It is quite fine, or at least this corner of it is. Did you spend a great deal of time here when you were a boy?"

He did not answer at once. She wondered if he would deign to speak at all.

Pride seemed to be a family trait. Darcy's aunt, Lady Catherine de Bourgh, was every bit as proud in her demeanour as her nephew. Unfortunately, she lacked Darcy's discerning mind, making her even more tedious than he. Enthralled with her own ideas, she rarely had time for anyone else's.

Darcy kept pace with Lizzy, walking at her side. "I did not spend as much time in Kent as Lady Catherine would have liked. My father considered it his duty to stay most of the year at Pemberley, and my mother her duty to stay at her husband's side rather than her sister's."

"And do you consider that the duty of a wife?"

"I hope that when I marry, my wife shall wish to be at my side out of affection rather than duty."

Lizzy raised her brows. "Why Mr. Darcy, I did not realize you were romantic. Hailing from a noble family, I would have thought you more interested in forming a beneficial alliance."

He coloured at that, which caught her by surprise. As diffident as he was, she had expected him to show no more feeling when talking about marriage than when talking about horseflesh. Indeed, Darcy was such an avid horseman, she would have expected truer ardour from him on *that* subject.

"What could be more beneficial," he said slowly, "than perfect domestic felicity? A home filled with the laughter of children? I am fortunate that I need not worry about my place in the world. I am independent and may marry whomever I choose. I intend to marry a woman who will make me happy."

A strange vibration stirred in Lizzy's chest, but she willed it away. "And how shall you find such a woman, Mr. Darcy? My friend Charlotte believes that happiness in marriage is entirely a matter of chance—that it is better to know as little as possible of your mate's disposition prior to matrimony."

"That says a great deal about your friend Mrs. Collins, but nothing at all about matrimony."

Lizzy laughed. It was the first time she had seen a spark of humour in Mr. Darcy, though she could not say whether it had been intentional.

"Mr. Darcy, you are unkind!"

"Come now, Miss Bennet, let us be honest. You give no more credence to Mrs. Collins' opinion on the subject than I do. I would be quite astonished if you were to marry for anything less than love."

Lizzy halted. She suddenly felt warm and could not breathe. The intensity of his eyes when he looked at her made her feel as if he had come upon her when she was wearing nothing more than her shift.

"You forget, Mr. Darcy, I am not independent. My place in the world is not settled. I do not have the luxury of marrying whomever I choose."

A stricken look came over his face. A long moment passed between them that she could not find voice to fill. She wished she could have prattled and teased, to make light of her plight; but in truth, her choices were poverty or marrying well. Given her meagre dowry, it was likely that any man who offered for her would be of a lower station than her father. Marriage would mean coming down in life, but if she was in love, she could endure it.

But what if marrying for love never became an option? If she were a spinster at twenty-seven, as Charlotte had been, would she be forced to take the same drastic measure, and marry a man she could not esteem for the sake of money?

The very idea was repugnant to her. Would not poverty be better than that?

"Miss Bennet, I believe I have distressed you."

"Not at all."

"I am afraid that anything I could say on the subject would sound impudent, but I hate to see your spirits dampened in this manner."

"My spirits dampened!" Ire shot through her veins. She blinked back tears, thinking how dependent she was on a husband for her very survival, whilst he spoke blithely of marrying for love.

"Forgive me, Mr. Darcy, if my company is not as entertaining as you would like. It was your choice to accompany me to the parsonage. I am capable of walking alone."

He was silent again for some moments before saying. "My apologies. I did not mean to be unkind. My only intention was to express concern for you."

Her anger did not lessen, but she could not ignore his apology. "Of course," she said. "I thank you for your kindness." Adopting a teasing air she did not feel, she added, "Perhaps these misunderstandings are bound to arise when you spend time in the company of someone as far beneath you as I am."

"Beneath me!" He stepped forward, his eyes searching hers. "Miss Bennet, that is nonsense. Except for the disparity in our fortunes, I consider you entirely my equal."

His words astonished her. Mr. Darcy, always so proud, calling her his equal! But it was preposterous. They both knew it was.

"The disparity in our fortunes is great."

He did not answer, but instead seemed to sink deep into thought.

They walked on, Lizzy as miserable as she had ever felt in her life. She did not doubt she could match him in a battle of wits. Given her circumstances, however, she could not hope to live in anything approaching the kind of luxury he took for granted.

No. They were anything but *equal*.

Her throat tightened, and she was glad he said nothing that required a response. She was unsure she could force out a word. Usually she was at peace with her lot—but she could not help longing for more, when the contrast between them was so great.

She was staying at the cottage, and he at Rosings, and that said all there was to say about their stations. Were he the most agreeable man in the world, she could not aspire to him. Not even if he pretended that the material differences between them were as nothing.

They soon reached the parsonage gate. He stopped and said, "As you are perfectly capable of walking on your own, I shall take my leave here. Good day, Miss Bennet." Turning, he walked quickly away.

Lizzy could only stare. Had she offended him? She thought, as she opened the gate, that she probably had. Why did that trouble her so? The man was intolerable.

He had shown kindness, though—she could not deny that. She had been less generous toward him than he toward her.

But then, Darcy could afford to be generous.

She stepped inside the parsonage and took off her bonnet. He had seemed to feel sympathy for her plight. His treatment of her sister Jane, though, had shown nothing of the sort. Lizzy could not prove that Darcy had persuaded Jane's suitor, Charles Bingley, to abandon her. Yet she had no more doubt of it than if she had been witness to the entire event.

No; no matter how sympathetic Darcy seemed, he had done material harm not just to Jane, but to her entire family. Bingley would have been a safeguard against destitution. But more than that, he and Jane had been deeply in love. In the five months they had been apart, Jane's devotion to him showed no signs of abating. Her heart was broken.

It was Darcy's doing. And it was unforgiveable.

Stupid, stupid, stupid! Darcy could not stop berating himself as he continued his walk back to Rosings. When he had encountered Elizabeth, he had determined to make an effort to be pleasing. Yet somehow, dolt that he was, he had distressed her.

This was what came of changing his routine. Normally he rode in the morning. But it was such a fine day, he had decided to walk along one of that paths that had been a favourite when he was a child.

Elizabeth had teased him often enough about being too silent in company. So he had forced himself to talk, and made a bungled mess of it. If she did not delight in teasing him, he would have thought her truly angry. Or perhaps she *had* been angry. Puzzle that she was, he could not tell.

What vexed him more was her ridiculous notion about the inequality between them. She, beneath him! The only way he could picture her beneath him involved a bed on their wedding night.

Yet it was lunacy to think of her that way. No matter how he ached for her, no matter how much he respected her, marriage between them was impossible.

He had been so careful, ever since he had left university, to avoid romantic entanglements. He had a list of criteria for the right sort of woman to be mistress of Pemberley. First, she must be a woman of fortune. How else could he ensure that her interest was in him and not his income?

He wanted a marriage like his parents had had, based on love and mutual respect. He knew well what Miss Elizabeth Bennet's circumstances were. It had been whispered about enough when he had been in Hertfordshire.

The Bennet sisters were pretty and were expected to marry well. But in their case, it was a necessity. He did not wish for a wife who saw him only as a safeguard against poverty.

When he had quitted Hertfordshire five months earlier, he had expected to forget Elizabeth in a few weeks' time. Instead, the absence had only proven how strong the attachment was. He was in love, body and spirit—violently, passionately in love.

The news that she was staying near Rosings had come as a shock to him. He had determined that this visit would rid him of his fever for her, once and for all. Instead, he found himself in a setting made for love. Trees bright with blooms. Birds singing their mating calls. Streams bursting their banks from the spring rains.

And Elizabeth, wild as a colt, traipsing through the countryside, her cheeks aglow. Could anything be more lovely?

He burned to make her his.

As he had said to her, he had the means to marry whomever he chose. And Elizabeth, though she might not be in love with him yet—surely, she could be persuaded?

But he had more to consider than her own fair self. There were significant objections to her family. He had saved Bingley from the greedy clutches of Mrs. Bennet. The family matriarch had sought out Bingley as husband for the eldest daughter, Jane, from the moment she had met him—possibly before.

Should Darcy have to endure such a woman as his mother-in-law? And the younger Bennet girls, wild and ignorant, as his sisters? What sort of influence would they have on his own sister, Georgiana?

No, it was unthinkable. And yet, so was life without his dear Elizabeth.

Ever since arriving at Rosings, he had come to think of her as his own. But it could not be. He must rid himself of this mad desire.

He reached the lawn and headed toward his aunt's house. The façade was beautiful but imposing, turrets framing the portico. As a boy, it had frightened him, even though he had grown up in a great house himself. His home at Pemberley was a jewel, not a fortress. The thought of Elizabeth as its mistress raised a longing inside him he could hardly bear.

The fawning of Bingley's sisters and their ilk—ladies who had attended one of those awful finishing schools that spent more time training their charges on how to win a husband than on improving their minds—turned him cold and cynical. But Elizabeth's lively spirit and irrepressible humour kept him rapt. He needed a woman who could challenge him and keep his mind sharp.

When he had quitted Netherfield back in November, he had been determined to forget her. To seek a wife who matched his own social standing. An earl's daughter, perhaps.

The fact was, Darcy had certain expectations to meet. He must think of his children. Their circumstances would be diminished if he married a woman of negligible fortune. Although Pemberley had no entail, he did not intend to sell off property to arrange a suitable dowry for his daughters.

His chest grew heavy. What a blackguard he sounded, even to himself. If another man had suggested a woman anywhere on earth was superior to Elizabeth Bennet, Darcy would have called him out.

He walked up the stone steps and entered the house. The wrath of Lady Catherine would be formidable if he married a woman who was virtually penniless, regardless of the lady's other qualities.

A brilliant match would benefit everyone in the family— and he was expected to make a brilliant match. An alliance with the Bennets would likely do his family no ill, but it would do them no good, either. It certainly would not help Georgiana's prospects.

He climbed the curving wooden staircase to his room. He could not bear to be in company, not when he was in such torment. How had he allowed this to happen?

He had seen other men besotted, and thought them weak. He had not understood how love could destroy all logic. How it could make every disadvantage seem desirable. Elizabeth Bennet was not an impoverished gentlewoman with country manners. She was an unspoiled jewel who constantly surprised him.

He had been a blockhead, thinking that if he came to Rosings and saw her again, she would not shine as bright— thinking that the longing of his heart had conjured up some idealized version of her.

On the contrary, his memories had been but dim imitations of the lady herself. She was even more delightful, more beautiful, more perfect for him than she had been in Hertfordshire. In the comfort of his aunt's home, without Elizabeth's country relations to distract, he could see even more clearly how poised she was, how playful, how she fulfilled every longing of his heart.

He entered his room and stirred the embers in the fire. What a damnable fool he was! He had got himself into this predicament, and he would have to get himself out. He ought to leave this place, go back to London and never see her again.

The prospect filled him with dread. He ought to, but he would not. His heart would not allow it.

No, he had three weeks to overcome this impossible desire before they would part forever. That was time enough to fall out of love, to discover her faults, to teach himself to feel disgust at her impertinence. He would—he must—forget her.

Lizzy sat down to dinner at the parsonage that evening, a simple meal of pork and mashed turnips. The aroma was heavenly. It made a nice change from the sumptuous feasts they enjoyed during dinners at Rosings, which could sometimes overwhelm the palate.

It was a quiet family gathering, just the four of them. Maria was in a state of distress after a letter from her younger sister earlier that day. She cried to Charlotte, "But how can my parents hold Hannah's debut ball two weeks before I return home?"

"I understand your disappointment," Charlotte said. "I was hoping to attend her debut as well. But with the officers decamping to Brighton—"

"To Brighton!" Lizzy cried. She should not have been surprised. The militia officers had been stationed in the town of Meryton for the winter, a short walk from her home at Longbourn. But of course they would head out to defend the coast now that the fair weather had rendered an invasion more likely.

The presence of the officers had created no little excitement amongst the gentlewomen of the town. Lizzy's youngest sisters, Lydia and Kitty, were quite mad for them. She herself had remained more circumspect, but had nevertheless developed a preference for one of the lieutenants. In the end, he had served as nothing more than a reminder of the inadequacy of her fortune.

"Oh, yes," Maria said. "The militia is leaving for the coast at the end of May. Hannah is determined to come out before they do. But surely she shall not find a husband from amongst them in the few weeks before they leave!"

"My dear sister," Mr. Collins said to Maria, "it is my experience that a long acquaintance is not required in order to discover that person who possesses exactly those qualities one most desires to ensure marital felicity."

Lizzy bit back a smile. That had certainly been true in his own case—for he had proposed to Charlotte but two days after Lizzy herself had refused him.

Maria sawed angrily into her slice of pork roast, metal clanging against china. "I think Hannah is coming out *now* because she fancies Mr. Wickham."

Lizzy berated herself for the little ache that rose in her breast at the sound of the man's name.

Charlotte's brows rose. "I do not think much of Mr. Wickham's constancy, given how his head turned when he learned of Miss King's inheritance."

Charlotte's cutting words only increased Lizzy's discomfort. Her cheeks burned at the memory. Wickham had seemed to prefer herself until Miss King unexpectedly came into ten thousand pounds. As he had no more fortune than Lizzy, she could hardly blame him. The pay of a militia officer barely sufficed to meet his expenses.

That did not stop George Wickham from being one of the handsomest, most agreeable men Lizzy had ever met. She could admit to *herself*, at least, that the loss of his attentions had been disappointing. She did not suffer a broken heart, though, as Jane did. Wickham had not played false with her affections. She could not lay that fault at his feet.

Had Charlotte misunderstood the situation between Wickham and Lizzy? "Perhaps such censure is too strong," Lizzy said to her friend. "To my knowledge, Mr. Wickham had made no promises to another."

Charlotte eyed Lizzy. In a gentle voice, she said, "Nor had he shown any interest in Miss King until word had spread of her sudden fortune."

That much was true. Lizzy had been his favourite. It had been a fine thing to be admired by the most sought-after of the young officers. The memory of losing his partiality gave her a pang—not least of all because her neighbours had observed how he had transferred his interest to Miss King.

But even if he had not, a match between him and Lizzy would have been disastrous.

"Miss King seemed most pleased by his attentions," Maria said. "One cannot help wondering why she removed to Liverpool."

"Liverpool!" Lizzy's mouth grew dry, and she sipped her spruce beer. The prospect of exciting Wickham's attentions to return to herself lifted her spirits, but only for a moment. He would be gone a fortnight after she returned to Longbourn. In any case, unless he miraculously came by a living, a union between them was impossible.

And here she had even more reason to despise Darcy. For he had once been honour-bound to bestow on Wickham a living in the church, yet had given the place to another. It pained her to think of Wickham in his now-reduced straits, when he might have had a comfortable situation. How different her own life might have been, if Darcy had behaved as he ought!

Forcing a calmness in her voice that she did not feel, Lizzy asked, "Why has Miss King gone to Liverpool?"

"Hannah's letter does not say," Maria replied. "Only that her uncle took her away."

"Perhaps he found her a wealthier suitor," Charlotte said.

Lizzy's eyes burned at the unfairness of it all. Poor Charlotte had married a foolish, obsequious man to protect herself against poverty. Lizzy could not permit a man she liked to court her, because of their mutual distressed circumstances. And yet a compassionless man like Darcy had the means to marry whomever he liked.

Bitterness grew in her stomach until she could not touch another bite. Her mother's machinations in seeking husbands for her daughters might have been unseemly, but one could not fault her for wanting financial security. She and her five girls were a heartbeat away from ruin.

Darcy had destroyed Jane's hopes, just as he had destroyed Wickham's. His sympathetic words to Lizzy that day rang hollow. Vain, selfish man!

In just three weeks, she would be back home in Hertfordshire, and would never have to see him again. That day could not come soon enough.

Chapter 2

The next morning, Elizabeth again spotted Darcy on her walk. This time, being on the woodland path, she managed to conceal herself before he could catch sight of her. How vexing that he had discovered this part of the countryside, which until now had been the perfect spot for her solitary ramblings!

She would almost suspect that he had taken this route with the intention of happening upon her, were she not convinced that he was as loathe to see her as she him. After the way they had parted the previous day, there could be no doubt he was incensed with her.

So be it. She did not desire Mr. Darcy's good opinion. In fact, there was nothing in the world she desired less. Even if, as she watched him, waiting for him to go, she could not help noticing his strong, upright posture, and the beautiful fit of his clothes. Her body flushed with warmth, and her breathing grew shallow. She hated herself for admiring him so, even as she despised him.

He walked back and forth a while, eyes scanning the horizon. She stayed well hidden, and she was sure he did not see her. He stopped and picked a bouquet of wild jonquils and bluebells—perhaps a nosegay for Miss de Bourgh? Lady Catherine would be pleased.

Lizzy could not help a bitter smile at the thought.

After what seemed like an age, he checked his pocket watch, then headed back in the direction of Rosings. For her part, she took the long route back to the parsonage, heading past a stream that opened into a peaceful meadow. Wildflowers waved in the breeze in tints of pink, blue, and white. The countryside of Kent was beautiful—a part of her would hate to leave it.

That evening, they were expected at Rosings for dinner. As Elizabeth dressed, she took extra care with her toilette. Darcy's cousin, Colonel Fitzwilliam, would be there after all, and she would be a fool if she did not at least try to make herself pleasing.

She did not love him, but she regarded him with affection. It would be an excellent match. The son of an earl—even a younger son—would give her mother raptures.

But even as she thought it, sadness filled her heart. She did not want a comfortable affection with her husband. She wanted a transporting, all-encompassing love. Was that even possible? Or was that only the stuff of novels?

She admired Colonel Fitzwilliam. Perhaps she could come to love him in time, if he took a fancy to her.

She quickly brushed away the tear that dropped from her eye. She was determined that love would be her only consideration, no matter how poor or wealthy the man might be.

Waiting for the dinner guests to arrive, Darcy sat at a long table in the library at Rosings reading a letter from Bingley. The dark wood might have given the place a sombre look if it had not been for the picture windows overlooking the green. Sculpted arborvitae stood like sentries at each corner of a goldfish pond, a low fountain gurgling from its centre.

Colonel Richard Fitzwilliam entered and picked up a volume. Darcy and his cousin bore a strong family resemblance—though Richard's build was more thickly muscled, as a man trained for combat. Of all his cousins, Richard was the closest to Darcy in age. They had been constant friends since boyhood.

Richard headed toward the door, giving his cousin a smile, then stopped when his eyes met Darcy's. "You look troubled, my friend. Not bad news from Pemberley, I hope? Or Georgiana?"

"Nothing like that." Darcy tapped the thick pages of the letter against the table top. "Bingley is in dull spirits, and has been ever since we left Hertfordshire. Now that I am here, he is stuck at Hurst's house." Darcy shook his head. "Whatever possessed his sister to marry that dullard, I cannot imagine."

Richard drew his brow. "Remind me again. Who is Hurst?"

"He is nobody."

"Ah." Richard nodded. "Probably why I can never remember."

Darcy held back a laugh. "He is second cousin to the Earl of Torland. Hurst himself has no land but apparently inherited enough from his mother for a life of leisure. The house he leases on Grosvenor Square is quite fine. But Hurst himself has nothing more to recommend him than a penchant for losing at cards and being amiable about it."

Richard chuckled. "Sounds like a good way to run through a small fortune quickly."

"His wife's fortune is tied up in trust, so he cannot touch the principle. Her father had that much sense, at least. Bingley was distraught when they got engaged. He knew she was throwing herself away. But Hurst runs in Beau Brummell's circle, and Beau Brummell runs in the Prince Regent's circle. No doubt, old Bingley had visions of his daughter obtaining a place at court."

Richard arched his brows and gave a wry smile. "And how has that worked out?"

"Much as you would expect," Darcy said drily. Even duchesses had to compete for a place at court. "Bingley claims his sisters are pestering him mercilessly about securing them an invitation to Almack's. He has asked me to persuade Adelaide to introduce them to Lady Jersey."

"Addie does not associate with that swarm of hornets," Richard said of his sister-in-law, Viscountess Astridge.

"No, but she and Lady Jersey are acquainted. I am tempted to ask her, to free Bingley of his sisters' harassment. The poor man is suffering enough without that."

"Is he still lovesick over the Hertfordshire maiden?"

Darcy set his jaw. "I've seen him in love before, but he has always recovered quickly. It has been five months now, and he is still pining."

"I believe you said there were some strong objections to the lady."

Darcy's face heated at the words. They were unfair to Jane, for whom he felt nothing but admiration. Like her sister Elizabeth, she was intelligent, beautiful, and well-mannered. He could find no fault in her.

"The lady herself is lovely," Darcy explained. "But she showed no genuine affection for Bingley. The strongest objection is to her scheming mama. The woman had apparently decided that one of her daughters would marry the man who let Netherfield, before she had even *met* Bingley. Had he been as dull-witted as the fawning Mr. Collins, he would have made a fine match in the eyes of that social-climbing mama."

Richard nodded. "In that case, one cannot help feeling sympathy for the young lady. She must have looked on Bingley as a saviour."

"Perhaps she did. Though her father is a gentleman, she has no fortune to speak of." A twinge of guilt settled in Darcy's chest. Certainly, Miss Bennet deserved to make a good match. If Darcy and Elizabeth married, he could help her find a man who better suited her temperament than Bingley. One more studious, perhaps, more quiet and thoughtful like the lady herself.

"Bingley is but three-and-twenty," Darcy added. "He need not rush to marry."

"True," Richard said, but the word did not match his tone. He sank into a chair next to Darcy at the table. "I cannot help thinking *I* have tarried too long. I am thirty now, and likely to be sent to the continent before the year is out. Yet I have no wife nor child to wait at home and miss me."

Darcy's brows furrowed. He hated discussing the prospect of Richard seeing military action again. He had been lucky so far, but how long could such luck hold?

He could not argue with what Richard said about marrying. A man ought to have children to follow after him. Richard would make a fine father, and imbue his children with his principles. But he would have to find a wife first.

"Have you someone in mind?" Darcy asked.

"No one at all. Is that not sad? I have guarded my heart to keep from falling for the wrong woman, and now I find I feel no *particular* desire for anyone at all."

"The remedy seems simple enough, then. Decide to fall in love, and it shall happen."

Richard grimaced. "You are mocking me."

"I am mocking love." Darcy let out a deep sigh. "Mrs. Collins has the way of it. Marry one who suits you as to fortune and respectability, and pay no mind to how ridiculous the match may otherwise be."

"When did you become such a cynic?"

Darcy stood. "Had you not noticed? Rosings always has this effect on me. Perhaps it is Lady Catherine's incessant hints that I propose to my cousin Anne. As if the shock alone would not be enough to kill the poor girl."

Richard chuckled. "Anne is a sweet girl, if you would bother to carry on a conversation with her."

"Fortunately, I do not have to. You are attentive enough for both of us."

Richard rose and walked up beside him. "You are unkind, Darcy."

"Better that, than reinforcing Lady Catherine's false hopes."

Richard did not argue.

Once his cousin had gone, Darcy wandered to the French doors. Warm sunshine streamed through the glass. High overhead, white clouds dotted the sky, whilst the new leaves of spring trembled in the breeze. A sudden fit of restlessness overcame him.

He stepped out onto the patio and down a wide stone staircase that led to the formal gardens. This was nature at its most civilized—urns bursting with pink tulips, square beds of blue larkspur edged with rosemary, boxwood topiaries shaped into swans.

He ambled along the path, white gravel crunching underfoot. The rigidity of this place discomfited him. Usually he found pleasure in order and predictability, but Elizabeth had taught him to see the world anew. Every moment with her was a surprise.

The thought of going back to London without her—of possibly never seeing her again—made him realize how hopeless the situation was. He had never been as happy as he had been at Netherfield, especially during the days she had spent there tending to her ailing sister.

Elizabeth had been so attentive to Jane, with so little care for her own comfort, that Darcy could easily imagine what kind of mother she would be. Caroline Bingley in the same circumstances? The thought made him shudder.

He considered his poor friend Bingley, nursing a broken heart whilst living with a cold woman like his sister. Darcy had no doubt that a deep familial affection existed between the two. But Miss Bingley had not the compassion, the empathy, to see him through a difficult period.

Nor did their elder sister, Mrs. Hurst. Bingley was likely being tea partied to death, his ears filled with the latest gossip. No wonder he was pining for Jane's sensible conversation and sweet disposition.

The sun peeked out from behind a cloud, bathing the landscape in the pink-hued light of late afternoon. He had half a mind to write Bingley and tell him Jane was in town, staying with her uncle and aunt.

Indeed, if Darcy had believed Jane capable of returning his friend's affection, he would have done so at once. But Jane had only been following her mother's instructions in allowing Bingley's advances—Darcy was sure of that.

He did not blame Jane. Her situation was precarious—indeed, all the ladies in her family faced an uncertain future should Mr. Bennet fall ill. Bingley was a pleasant, easy-going fellow, and Jane must have seen in him a man she could like and respect as a husband. Was Darcy wrong to want more than that for his friend? Was it wrong to hope Bingley would marry a woman who loved him as much as he loved her?

This temporary disappointment would be eclipsed by a lifetime of happiness once Bingley found the right woman. That was what Darcy would tell him in answer to his latest missive. The sadness would pass.

Just as his own sadness would pass at giving up Elizabeth, if it came to that. It was a silly dream, wasn't it, considering a future with her? Even if he could see his way clear to properly provide for their children?

That was hardly the only consideration. Allying his uncle, the earl, to a woman like Mrs. Bennet—it was unthinkable! Except...he could picture it. The man was so gracious, he could put her at ease, and she would be all smiles.

She was at her most ridiculous when she was crossed. Otherwise, she was almost amiable, if very silly. Noble families, too, had their share of silly people. Money and title did nothing to safeguard against that.

He crossed the lawn to a little pond edged with yellow irises. The leaves of a tall weeping willow stretched down and brushed the grass. With three weeks left before Elizabeth returned to Hertfordshire, Darcy must make up his mind soon. He must secure her, or give her up forever.

Falling in love with Elizabeth Bennet had not been part of the plan. Now that it was done, there was no going back. He would have to find a way forward.

He had just enough time before dinner to write Bingley and encourage him to be strong. Then, Darcy would see Elizabeth—and try to put his own advice into practice.

⚬৬৹

Darcy stood when the Collinses and their houseguests were shown into the parlour at Rosings. The room was decorated in a feminine French provincial style, Rococo paintings lining the walls. Cut flowers scented the air, phlox mixed with tulips and peonies, overflowing tall vases scattered about the room

Darcy startled upon seeing Elizabeth. She had never been more lovely. Her eyes shone, and her dark, upswept hair was decorated with a few small daisies. Delicate sapphires hung from her ears. Her pale-blue silk gown was cut low for evening, but not nearly as daring as he was accustomed to seeing.

At Netherfield, he had admired her for her fine eyes. Since coming to Rosings Park, he had become obsessed with her person. It was a source of consternation that she dressed more modestly than the fashionable ladies of London.

Pity, that. Although he supposed he would not mind her demure style once she was his wife.

Madness. He must not let himself think that way. It was weakness, self-indulgence. He had counselled Bingley to put Jane Bennet out of his mind, and Darcy would do the same with her sister.

Elizabeth took a seat by Colonel Fitzwilliam. Jealousy pierced Darcy's heart. His cousin had a knack for engaging conversation—which Darcy did not, especially when in the company of strangers. With Elizabeth, he was positively tongue-tied.

She rose and walked to the window. He hesitated a moment before joining her there. He looked out over the rolling lawn that disappeared into a woodland. "A pleasant view, is it not?" he asked.

She gave him a sad smile. "I am afraid I had not noticed the scenery. I was thinking of Jane. She was in poor spirits in her last letter. She tries to hide it, but I know her too well. She has been in misery since last November."

His spine straightened. Her meaning was clear: Jane had been low since Bingley had quitted Netherfield, the house he was leasing in Hertfordshire.

Had that been censure in Elizabeth's voice? Did she suspect Darcy was responsible for removing Bingley from Jane's grasp? But he had only been acting in his friend's interest. Jane had shown no partiality to Bingley. She admitted his advances, no doubt at the instructions of her fortune-hunting mother. But Darcy could not bear to see his friend taken in.

Bingley was of such an open disposition, trusting and looking for the best in everyone, that it fell to Darcy to watch out for his friend's interests. Bingley could not be happy in a marriage where he was not truly loved. And Jane had shown no signs of it.

No, Darcy could feel no shame on that score. He had done right by his friend. It was wrong for Mrs. Bennet to pin her expectations on Bingley as she had.

If Jane had been disappointed, Darcy felt sorry for that. She was a sweet young woman, and was no doubt attracting many a suitor whilst in London for the season. She would find someone more to her liking than Bingley, and forget him soon enough.

"I am sorry to hear it," he said. "Miss Bennet is one of the loveliest people I had the pleasure of meeting in Hertfordshire. I hope she will be herself again soon."

"I have lost all hope of that, I am afraid. Some disappointments are so great, one cannot recover."

If he did not know Elizabeth so well, he would suspect her of melodrama. Perhaps she did not refer to Bingley at all, and Jane was suffering from some other loss? Surely that must be the case.

"London must supply distractions for her, to ease some of her troubles."

"Oh, did you know she was in London? I do not believe I had mentioned it."

His face warmed. Bingley's sister Caroline had visited Jane in London. Darcy knew of it, but Bingley did not. To tell Elizabeth so would invite her censure. Instead of revealing the whole, he settled for a partial truth. "I saw her once at a distance, though I do not believe she saw me. I understand you have an aunt and uncle who live in town. Is she staying with them?"

"She is. They adore her, and are very kind to her. But then, it would be difficult not to adore Jane."

"I agree."

"Do you?"

He could not mistake the sharpness in her voice. Clearly she suspected him of overthrowing her family's plans. But Jane would make a brilliant match, he had no doubt of it. Beautiful, sweet-tempered, and intelligent, she would easily capture the heart of a man who could inspire more passion in her than Bingley had.

Poor Bingley. He had indeed been miserable since leaving Netherfield. Darcy grieved to see it. But Bingley had overcome a broken heart before, and he would do it again. Better to suffer the loss now than to live with a woman indifferent to him for the rest of his life.

He said to Elizabeth, "Your sister is a woman who easily captures the affections of others. Whether they can capture *her* affection is a different question."

"Are you suggesting she is cold?" Elizabeth's face flushed and her eyes darkened.

"I believe she is cautious."

"I assure you, Mr. Darcy, you could not be more deceived. Jane is the most kind-hearted person I know, predisposed to like everyone. I am constantly reminding her to be more circumspect."

"I beg your pardon." He bowed. "I am mistaken, then. I observed her to be aloof."

"Jane aloof? And what have you been, Mr. Darcy? Never initiating a conversation, barely speaking when spoken to? Aloof does not begin to describe it."

Her tone was steady but her words barbed. He should have known better than to speak so of her sister. Nothing could raise *his* ire faster that a word spoken against Georgiana, and he knew Elizabeth to be equally devoted to Jane.

"Indeed, madam, I should not have said so. I meant no unkindness, but clearly I have offended you. I beg your forgiveness. Now you see why I am reticent in company."

Elizabeth let out a quick laugh. "I do, sir. Perhaps it would be better if you were silent altogether." With a sly glance, she turned. Head high, she walked toward the sofa where Maria sat, leaving a rustle of silk in her wake.

Darcy watched her, unable to steal his eyes away from the gentle sway of her hips, or the dark curls that trailed down the curve of her neck. Her scent of sweet violets lingered behind.

Desire ached inside him. She had bewitched him, and there was no hope for him at all. How could he do anything other than make her his?

He was sick of this vacillation. The thought of life without her was unendurable. If he was going to try for her, he ought to work harder—become a more pleasing conversationalist, like his cousin.

The truth was, she was in no position to refuse him. She had hinted as much to him during their walk the previous day.

She wished to marry for love, though, and he wanted her to be in love with him. He wanted it very much.

She did seem piqued with him about Jane's disappointment. But surely, all would be forgiven if Darcy made Elizabeth an offer. All of Mrs. Bennet's ambitions would be satisfied. The loss of a prospective son-in-law of four or five thousand a year would be nothing after gaining one of ten thousand. And of course Darcy would ensure that his new sisters were provides for.

Elizabeth sat with Maria, and the two spoke in low tones. He tried not to stare, but his eyes kept wandering back to her. She met his gaze once or twice, and he ought to have been embarrassed. But where else should he look, when she was in the room? Why should he not pay her the compliment of admiring her? Surely it could not be unwelcome.

He ought to be more circumspect for Lady Catherine's sake. If he did propose, he could not do it whilst under his aunt's roof. She would make things uncomfortable for himself and Elizabeth both. It would be better to wait until the end of his stay.

Or perhaps he was waiting in hopes of a reprieve. He had never been so irresolute in his life. Decisions usually came easily to him. He looked at the facts, evaluated them, and came to the logical conclusion.

But where his heart was concerned, all logic was thrown asunder. Every fact in the matter told him that proposing to Elizabeth Bennet would be throwing himself away. Except for one small detail: he was convinced that she was essential to his happiness. How could he argue against that?

He had intended to walk her into the dining room, but she took Richard's arm before he got to her. Instead, Darcy accompanied Maria Lucas. No matter. They were a small party and would make an intimate group around the table.

Dinner was a grand affair, as it always was at Rosings. The first course started with leek soup and crimped cod. Next came the leg of lamb, haricots verts, potato mash, and chicken fricasseed with mushrooms. It was all delicious, but not as much as the sight of Elizabeth.

She was seated across the table, next to Richard. Lady Catherine had demanded that her nephews sit on either side of her, and Elizabeth had chosen her own chair. Darcy hated himself for being such a dull conversationalist that she sought the company of his cousin.

Did she truly prefer Richard, or was this designed to coax him into trying harder? He struggled for something witty to say, but his aunt's voice interrupted his efforts.

"Mrs. Collins," Lady Catherine said to Charlotte, "what do you think of our fine spring weather here in Kent? Surely Hertfordshire can offer nothing finer."

"Your ladyship is kind to ask. It has been especially lovely the past few days, warm and clear. In fact, if it continues without rain, I have been thinking it would be a fine thing to go on a picnic."

"What a splendid idea!" Richard said. "What think you, Darcy?"

Darcy considered how his cousin would respond if asked the same question, and said, "It would be a great pleasure to join the fair ladies from Hunsford Cottage on an excursion."

"Shall we do it, then?" Charlotte asked. "How would Saturday be?"

"But my love!" Mr. Collins cried, "I shall be preparing my sermon on Saturday. Surely tomorrow would be better."

"Oh, but my dear, we shall need tomorrow to prepare. And if we wait longer, this lovely weather might not hold. Lady Catherine, would you and Miss de Bourgh deign to join our humble party?"

"You are very kind, but I am afraid that with my rheumatism, I could find little comfort in such an excursion. And of course my poor Anne cannot tolerate a day in the sunshine."

"I am very sorry to hear it," Mrs. Collins said, though Darcy was certain she was not sorry at all. In fact, he suspected she had planned it that way.

She looked in his direction and met his eye, arching her brows ever so slightly before turning away. That expression, though brief, told him everything he needed to know. Mrs. Collins knew what he was about, and he had an ally in her.

Heaven knew he needed the help. This picnic would be his chance to win Elizabeth's heart.

Chapter 3

Once back at the parsonage, Charlotte joined Elizabeth in her bedroom to discuss the evening's events. The room was small but not cramped, with all the comforts Lizzy needed. The one exception was the closet, which had been inexplicably furnished with shelves at Lady Catherine's suggestion.

But Lizzy was making do. The mattress was firm, the blankets soft and warm. They were topped by a beautiful crown-and-star quilt, which Lady Lucas had made.

The homespun beauty of the place could not calm Lizzy's temper, however. She took the flowers from her hair and set them atop the oak vanity. "Mr. Darcy, calling Jane aloof! Can you imagine, Charlotte?"

"I see the irony, of course. But I cannot say I am surprised. Her serenity could be mistaken for indifference by a stranger."

"Why—because she does not have my sister Lydia's high spirits?" Lizzy asked.

"No one has Lydia's high spirits. I have never met anyone with more energy than she." Charlotte smiled gently, then touched Lizzy's arm. "Do not allow yourself to be blinded by anger with Mr. Darcy. The man is partial to you. I believe you could win him if you tried."

"Win him? I would rather win a prize pig at the county fair. He destroyed Jane's happiness because he considers his friend Bingley to be above her."

Charlotte sat on the bed, a composed expression on her face. She rarely showed emotion. Lizzy found it soothing at times, exasperating at others.

In a calm voice, Charlotte said, "Mr. Darcy did not destroy Jane's happiness. Mr. Bingley did. If *Jane* had been in the position of choosing, and you had suggested to her that Bingley was beneath her, would she have given him up? Of course not. If indeed Mr. Darcy did persuade him, the fault lies with Mr. Bingley for being persuaded."

Lizzy threw her hands up. "Why would you take Mr. Darcy's part in this?"

Charlotte rose and touched Lizzy's arm. "I apologize for being indelicate, my dear—you know I shall do all in my power to ensure that your family can stay at Longbourn for as long as necessary, should the worst happen. But we must prepare for that eventuality. Mr. Collins is happy here at Hunsford. His current situation is suited to his temperament. But I long to see you well-settled, so we need not fear the future."

It was the first time words had passed between them about Charlotte replacing Mrs. Bennet as mistress of Longbourn one day. The estate was entailed on a male heir, and would go to Mr. Collins on Mr. Bennet's death. It was painful to think of, but the fact that it was Charlotte and not a stranger made it easier.

"I know I must marry," Lizzy said, "and indeed I wish it. But I cannot marry a man I do not love, no matter how wealthy he may be."

"I would not wish you to make yourself unhappy. But if I can be content here at Hunsford Cottage, how content might you be at Pemberley? If you cannot like Mr. Darcy, then of course you should not marry him. But my dear, you have not even tried."

Ire rose in Lizzy's chest and heated her cheeks. Yet she could not deny the truth of her friend's words. Lizzy's animosity toward Darcy had been fixed from practically the moment she first saw him—he had insulted her before they had even been introduced. So no, she had made no attempt to like him. And everything she had learned about the man since that night had confirmed her initial assessment.

Lizzy unpinned her hair and brushed it through. Charlotte continued in a measured voice, "The night you met Mr. Darcy, he slighted you at a ball. Will you let that little bruise to your vanity get in the way of your happiness if he pays you the compliment of proposing marriage?"

Lizzy startled, then put down her brush and turned to her friend. The very idea sounded ludicrous. Mr. Darcy propose?

Charlotte clasped Lizzy's hands in her own. "You know I am not romantic. I do not incessantly imagine everyone is falling in love. I see the way he looks at you, the way his eyes follow you. Think of what you might throw away if you do not even *try* to like him. Ten thousand a year, possessed by a handsome, cultured, intelligent man. There are worse fates to be sure, Eliza."

Lizzy could not help wondering if Charlotte was thinking of her own circumstances. Considering Charlotte's suggestion about Mr. Darcy's feelings for her, Lizzy said, "I have never had any hint that he is smitten with me."

"Perhaps you misconstrue every compliment he pays you for an insult, because you doubt his motives."

"If he believes Bingley to be too good for Jane," Lizzy said heatedly, "how much more must he believe himself to be too good for me?"

"You must teach him to think with his heart."

Lizzy drew a breath, a whisper of hope rising in her breast. She forced it back down. "Charlotte, truly, this is madness."

"If you insist." Charlotte flashed her a knowing smile before departing.

Once the ladies of Rosings had gone to bed, Darcy and the colonel retreated to a small salon near the staircase. Richard poured them each a brandy. Sitting cattycorner to Darcy, he said, "Elizabeth Bennet is the most delightful creature I ever met."

Darcy startled. He knew Richard enjoyed her company, but surely there was no more to it than that? Cautiously, Darcy set his jaw and replied in an even tone, "Indeed?"

"If she had thirty thousand pounds, I would be half tempted to make an offer." He grinned widely. "But as she does not, and I am a younger son in need of a wealthy wife... Ah, well. I shall think no more of it. My circumstances forbid it."

Darcy picked up his glass from the end table. "Mine do not."

Richard arched his brows and blinked. His mouth fell open. "The devil you say! Hell, Darcy, that explains why you are so stupid around her. You are in love!"

The shock of those words rumbled through Darcy, stealing his breath. He sipped his brandy to regain his composure. "I would not go that far."

"I would. You are besotted. I do not know how I missed it before. If you want her, you had better propose before someone else does."

Hot fury washed over him. "Someone like you?"

61

"I like her well enough, but not so much as I'd like an heiress."

Richard's tone was light, showing he had no serious intentions toward Elizabeth. Darcy had no need to worry, then. The tension drained from his muscles. All would be well between him and his cousin if Darcy offered for her.

His eyes wandered over the dark wood of the coffee table, over the silk damask fabric of the sofa that reflected the glow of the candlelight. "It is an important decision. I shall not be rushed."

"What is there to decide? You love her. She is intelligent, lively, well-bred—she would make you an excellent wife."

"You have not met her family. Her father is gentlemanly enough, but her mother is the worst sort of country mama. An unabashed fortune hunter."

"And you do not wish to give her the satisfaction."

The words punched the air from Darcy's chest. Then, he gritted his teeth. "The woman has never made any overtures toward me. But she treated Bingley like a walking bank account. To align myself with such a woman!"

"Perhaps Miss Elizabeth Bennet is thinking the same of Lady Catherine. 'That Darcy,'" Richard said in a mocking tone, "'he would not make a bad husband, even if he is dull and silent in company. But that aunt of his! To marry into such a family!'"

Darcy grinned. "And what is wrong with my family?"

"Nothing, except Miss Bennet has seen the worst of it."

"Lady Catherine is not as bad as Miss Bennet's cousin Mr. Collins."

Richard scowled at him. "Is this a contest to see who has the most ridiculous relatives? Or are you trying to decide whether to marry the woman you love?"

Darcy stared into the fire. There was no denying it. The ladies of London had only made him think wistfully of her charms. Unlike them, she was genuine, not artful or studied. Her modest but impertinent demeanour seemed designed for him—as if she was the one he had been waiting for all his life, but he never knew it until he met her. She was nothing like what he thought he wanted, yet she was perfect for him.

And what was he to do about that?

Marry her.

The voice in his mind came unbidden. He would never rest easy until she was his. The thought of another woman sickened him, and the thought of her with another man filled him with an unendurable rage. She was his, as if their souls were joined together. He must make her so in fact.

Yet something held him back, something indefinable. Whenever he was close to her, he felt it, the knot in his stomach that kept him from approaching too close, from speaking too freely. He had seen her warmth toward her sister Jane at Netherfield—there was nothing of that in her demeanour toward him.

Of course she was cautious—a lady must be, under the circumstances. She could not show too much. And she could not but feel gratified by his attentions. Given the difference in their situations, she certainly recognized the tangible good he could do for her and her family.

It seemed petty to think in those terms. She was his equal in every way that mattered. She was a gentlewoman, lively and cultured, and he wanted—needed—her to be his.

The colonel's voice interrupted his thoughts. "You are a thousand miles away, Darcy."

He grinned. "No, only a mile or two." He rose and looked into his cousin's eyes. "I know little of love. I have been tempted by women, to be sure. But what I feel for Miss Bennet is of an entirely different order. I did not bid it, nor can I will it away. Heaven knows I have tried."

Richard smiled broadly. "Have you determined to propose, then?"

"My aunt will not be pleased."

"What has she to say about it?"

"Nothing, of course, but she surely will not stay silent." Darcy raised his brows. "She expects me to marry a woman of fortune, to add to the estate. Which of course I should. The truth is…"

Darcy looked out the window into the light of the full moon. "I do not wish to break up Pemberley. I wish to pass it to my eldest son whole, as my father did to me. If I marry Miss

Bennet, we will have to put aside a significant portion of our income to secure the future of our other children."

"Then you will have to give up your visits to the brothels and gaming hells during your frequent visits to London," Richard joked. "Darcy, you lead the most respectable life of any man I know. You live below your means and invest prudently. I would be surprised if you could not manage to save a sum each year equivalent to my entire income."

"A wife will be an added expense."

"Oh, yes, a vain woman like Miss Bennet could easily drive you to bankruptcy."

Darcy glared at Richard for his teasing. In truth, Darcy had noticed that Elizabeth seemed to favour a less ostentatious style of dress than her sisters (with the exception of Mary, who seemed to take pride in making herself as unattractive as possible, as a means of demonstrating her piety). Elizabeth would not, he was certain, desire the latest fashions from the Continent each season.

She was accustomed to a simple country life and seemed content in it. She might add no more than three hundred pounds a year to his expenses, if that. A fashionable woman like Miss Bingley would cost him at least a thousand. Elizabeth's lack of a sizeable dowry did not seem as significant when viewed in that light.

"She is not an entirely imprudent choice," Darcy observed.

"She is delightful. And will make you exceedingly happy."

"I have no doubt of it. Happiness is not the only consideration."

"Of course it is. Resist all you like, but it is only a matter of time. I wish you joy, cousin."

Darcy grinned wryly. "You can start by wishing me luck."

Once Richard had headed upstairs, Darcy went to the library and pulled out a sheet of paper. Sitting at the table, he calculated how much he would have to set aside each year, to settle a respectable sum on each of three children other than his heir. To his surprise, it was manageable. He would have to forgo other investments—but the expense would not lessen his style of living nor strain the estate in any way.

He stood and paced to stretch his muscles, stiff from sitting so long. Marrying Elizabeth was feasible. But what a mother-in-law he would have, as Miss Bingley had teased during their days at Netherfield. And what sisters-in-law, in the simpering Kitty and the wild Lydia.

He berated himself for the thought. Elizabeth was witty and beautiful and principled. She herself would never embarrass him. Her relations were merely foolish—they had no true harm in them.

He leaned one hand against the bookshelf and massaged the corners of his eyes with the other. Lady Catherine would be furious if he made such a match. A rift between them would not last long, however—perhaps a year or two. She was a proud woman who easily succumbed to flattery. He knew how to play her.

Richard had already become enraptured by Elizabeth's charms. He would convince his father, the Earl of Matlock, of the superiority of Elizabeth's mind and character. Where the earl went, the rest of the family would follow.

There was only one tangible disadvantage in marrying Elizabeth—a loss of opportunity to increase his standing by marrying the daughter of a noble family. A powerful political marriage had its advantages. A handsome dowry would provide an extra degree of security. But Pemberley was well-run, and Darcy cautious in his investments. Even with war looming, he had no fears about the state of his finances.

In his deepest heart, he knew that if he let her go, he would regret it. No matter how happy his life turned out, Elizabeth would always be a poignant memory. A reminder of what might have been.

When he thought of what a material difference he could make to her—and to her family—why should he resist? What was Mrs. Bennet's foolishness to him, if she was in Hertfordshire, and he in Derbyshire? He would not have to spend more than a few days a year in her company.

In the meantime, he would have Elizabeth in his life every day, and in his bed every night. Surely that was worth the humiliation of marrying into her family.

He paced, footsteps reverberating through the large room. She would make him happy—he had never admired a woman so much. For a man in his situation, was not happiness what mattered most? Had he not meant the words he had spoken to her about what he considered a beneficial alliance?

On paper, there were a thousand women better suited to him than Elizabeth Bennet. In his heart, she was the only one he wanted. Was that not the answer? Why was he resisting the inevitable?

His heart had already decided. It was time his mind caught up. Perhaps it was the brandy or the lack of sleep, but a sudden elation washed over him, and he saw the world anew.

He was determined to have her.

Chapter 4

"'T is a pity Miss de Bourgh cannot join us," Maria Lucas said as she, Charlotte, and Lizzy stood in the front hall of the parsonage tying their bonnets and buttoning their spencers. Lizzy turned toward the door and looked out the sidelights into the glorious April sky, a clear Prussian blue bathed in light.

"It is unfortunate," Lizzy agreed, "that her constitution is too fragile to endure fresh air and sunshine."

"Do you not think," Maria said, "that perhaps she is not sickly at all? That she is only pale and weak because she is hardly permitted to go out of doors, or take any exercise?"

"It is not for us to question Lady Catherine's pronouncements about her daughter's health," Charlotte said mildly, but her eyes gleamed and a faint smile touched her lips.

The housekeeper brought the baskets for the picnic, and each of the ladies took one to carry before heading off. As mistress of Hunsford Cottage, Charlotte had chosen the spot for their picnic: a pretty clearing by a stream, as she had described it to Lizzy. They would meet the gentlemen from Rosings on the road that ran along the two properties before following the woodland trail to their destination.

Lizzy was unsure about the wisdom of this excursion. She was glad for the chance to know Colonel Fitzwilliam better, since her mother would surely advise her to set her sights on him. But she was more wary of Darcy. He brought out such strong emotion in her—usually anger or outrage—but there was also an undercurrent of something she dared not name.

The path to the main road was edged with wildflowers in bright shades of yellow and pink. Finches flitted overhead, chipping a cheerful song. Lizzy was enjoying her visit to Hunsford, but it was not without its awkward moments.

Charlotte's husband, the reverend William Collins, heir to Longbourn, had sought to make amends for his fair cousins' plight by proposing to Lizzy. Unless she and her sisters married, they would be destined to live off their share of their mother's fortune, amounting to a mere forty pounds per annum each. She could not, however, accept his kind offer, as she believed the two of them to be utterly incompatible.

Put more precisely, Mr. Collins was one of the most ridiculous men in England, an odd mix of obsequiousness, narrow-mindedness, and self-satisfaction. Elizabeth would find life with such a man unendurable.

Charlotte, with her unromantic attitude toward marriage, had not been deterred by these qualities. Mr. Collins was respectable, and he doted on his new wife. She was adept at managing him so they spent as little time together as possible. Charlotte seemed happy with her new life, so Lizzy could not feel disappointment at her friend's circumstance, but neither could she feel truly happy for her.

Charlotte had married for money and position rather than love. The idea seemed a horror to Lizzy—more so because, if Lizzy found herself twenty-seven and unmarried as Charlotte had, she might be forced to make the same decision. Fortunately, she still had seven years before such an event might occur, and hoped instead to marry for love in the meantime.

Charlotte seemed intent on helping her move in that direction.

When they reached the road, they did not have to walk far before they spotted the gentlemen. Colonel Fitzwilliam was tall with agreeable features. Darcy was taller and astonishingly handsome. But where Darcy wore a serious expression, his cousin smiled and greeted the ladies enthusiastically.

"What a fine morning you picked for our outing, Mrs. Collins," the colonel greeted. He and Maria flanked her as she led the way through the woods, leaving Lizzy walking behind with Darcy. A hot flush of consternation washed over her—it seemed even the colonel was conspiring to thrust Darcy and Lizzy together.

What a horrible coincidence, that he had come to visit his aunt at the same time she was visiting her friend! After he and Mr. Bingley had quitted Netherfield, the estate Bingley had rented near Longbourn, Lizzy had expected never to see him again.

Yet now, they were walking together through a dark wood in an uncomfortable silence. He hardly found a word to speak to her, and she little wished to tax her brain searching for a topic that would interest him.

"Are you a fan of Gothic novels, Mr. Darcy?" she ventured.

"I cannot say that I am. Why do you ask?"

"Because if we did not have Charlotte to lead the way, I might think we were walking into a deep and dangerous forest, destined to lose our way and become prey to highwaymen or vicious wild creatures."

He deigned to grin at her. "I did not think, Miss Bennet, that you were one to put much store by lurid tales."

Twigs crunched beneath their feet, and sunlight filtered through the leaves, casting them in dappled shade. "I confess that I am more a fan of Mr. Fielding than of Mrs. Radcliffe."

Darcy raised his brows. "Indeed?"

"Are you shocked?" Perhaps she should have been more circumspect. Fielding's work did have a hint of scandal about it.

"I have found you to be fonder of humour than melodrama," Darcy observed, "so I cannot say I am surprised, no."

"And what about you, Mr. Darcy? Who do you favour? My guess would be Swift."

"You consider me a misanthrope?"

"Not at all. Colonel Fitzwilliam assures me you can be quite amiable, in the company of your closest friends."

He had the good grace to flush at that. "You are forever rebuking me for my reticence in company. I must improve myself for your sake."

Her heart thrilled at that assertion, but quickly sank again. His words were gallant, but certainly they meant nothing. "I am surprised you should endeavour to do anything for my sake. After you leave Rosings, and I leave Hunsford, we are likely to never see one another again."

He grew stony, then said at last, "I hope that shall not be the case."

She arched her brows. "Surely, Mr. Darcy, you cannot long for the company of one who scolds you as relentlessly as I do."

"On the contrary. The fault is all mine. I should like to have the opportunity to prove that your influence has made me a better man."

Lizzy's stomach twisted. On the surface, the conversation seemed playful and courteous. But Mr. Darcy was not playful by nature. She had the unsettling feeling he was utterly sincere.

She did not wish him to show so much regard for her. Lizzy had cause to feel wary of Mr. Darcy—and not only because of the harm she believed he had done to Jane. No, her suspicion ran deeper.

Wickham, her friend from the _____ shire militia, had been the son of old Darcy's steward. He had known Darcy his whole life—the two had played together as boys. Darcy's father had planned to offer Wickham a living in the rectory that was in his gift, but had passed away before he could see this intention through.

Darcy had known of his father's wishes. But when the position became vacant, he gave it to another, passing over his childhood friend. It was the most abominable sort of betrayal, both of his friend and of his father's memory. All this Wickham had confided in Lizzy, and Darcy's coldness toward the man seemed to confirm the story.

Darcy's behaviour, and every account she had heard of him, demonstrated him to be an arrogant sort of man, and lacking in integrity. Yet here he was, deferring to her, saying he endeavoured to better himself due to her influence.

She could make no sense of it, and that troubled her. The only logical conclusion, given what she knew of his character, was that he was mocking her. And yet, that was not in his character, either. He was proud, not petty, and did not tend toward humour nor false courtesy.

She changed the topic. "Do you find your cousin Miss de Bourgh much changed since you saw her last?" She had heard that Darcy was destined to marry the heiress of Rosings, although they did not seem to be formally engaged.

His brows drew together a moment. Then, he said, "She is taller, to be sure."

Taller! Why, even a casual observer might notice that much. Should not a cousin's feelings run deeper? "I imagine you must be fond of her."

He spoke carefully, a look of regret in his eyes. "Lady Catherine is protective of Anne, and we are not as close as I would like. I suspect she is a little afraid of me."

Lizzy could not help but smile. "Afraid of you! What cause could she have to fear a man who exudes such warmth and generosity of spirit?"

Darcy set his jaw, yet the lines on his face did not grow hard. "You are teasing me again. Which proves that you, at least, are not afraid of me."

"Which may only prove a decided lack of sense on my part."

"You are the last person on earth I would accuse of lacking sense, Miss Bennet."

His words stopped Lizzy in her tracks. They could not be construed in any way but as a compliment, and a great one at that. Surely Mr. Darcy did not...admire her? It seemed quite impossible. But could there be any other way of interpreting his words?

He stopped and turned back toward her. "Is something wrong, madam?"

"Either you have paid me a great compliment, or made a great joke at my expense. I am puzzling out which one. Since you have never looked upon me but to laugh, I cannot help thinking it is the latter."

"When have I ever laughed at you, Miss Bennet?"

"The night we met," she said coyly, "you were not altogether gallant, especially when I was in want of a dance partner."

He stiffened, and in the faint light of the woodland, he seemed to pale. "Forgive me. I behaved abominably that night. I was distraught over a letter I had received from my cousin's wife, with unfortunate news regarding my sister Georgiana. I do not offer that as an excuse, for nothing can excuse my behaviour toward you that night. But I hope at least it provides an explanation."

She could not speak at once. "Indeed, sir," she said, her voice unsteady, "I am grateful. Your sister is not unwell, I hope?"

"No, not unwell. The moods and afflictions of sixteen-year-old girls pass quickly, but it was troubling at the time."

Lizzy nodded thoughtfully. Could this be true—could Darcy's incivility that night have been caused by worry over his sister? She had no cause to doubt him. It certainly explained the foul mood he had been in all evening.

She did not like seeing him in this new light. If he was a disagreeable man, it was easy to ignore the fact that he was the most handsome she had ever met. And that his fine, tall figure drew her eye whenever they were in company.

Thinking well of him simply would not do.

The woodland opened into a meadow crossed by a stream. It was a fine sight, as lovely as anything Lizzy had seen so far in Kent. The stream widened into a depression and formed a small pond, rushes growing at the edges, wild ducks skimming the surface.

Lizzy sighed. "My father's manor cannot boast so pretty a sight as this."

A smile touched Darcy's lips. "It makes me homesick for Pemberley. The pond on the approach to the house is much like this." His face reddened. "You must think me boasting. Is it wrong that I am so fond of my home, as to consider its beauty unsurpassed?"

Lizzy's heart ached. *Pemberley.* The sound of the word conjured idyllic pictures in her mind—rolling hills, flowering meadows, a herd of fluffy white sheep dotting the countryside. A place she had heard so much about, but that she would never have occasion to visit.

"Not wrong at all," she answered at last, holding back a sigh. "You are a man who has seen the world. Who better to judge?"

He turned his eyes to her, still wearing a jovial look. "You are mocking me, I think."

"Perhaps a little," she confessed.

"And what about you?" he asked gently. "Have you travelled much, Miss Bennet?"

"I have been to Bath a few times with my family. My mother loves the activity, but my father hates the crowds. He refuses to go again. It is a source of great anxiety to Mama, as you can imagine."

"She does have five daughters," Darcy said with a quirk of a smile, but a wary look in his eyes.

He was teasing her, she guessed, and she ought to let him. After all, he tolerated her treatment.

"Bath is well-known for its efficacy in ridding oneself of daughters," she replied.

"I cannot imagine your father eager to be rid of you."

"No, but my mother is. I am too like my father, and try her nerves."

He looked at her intently, then turned away. "I know I should think about finding a match for Georgiana, but I still regard her as a child. She is a pretty girl, and sweet, like your eldest sister. I have no doubt of her marrying well. But I would like her to make her own choice, once she is old enough to choose wisely."

"Has she finished her schooling?"

His face changed, and his mouth grew thin. "I have not found much satisfaction in schools for girls. They seem universally deficient in offering intellectual pursuits. I want to bring her back to Pemberley, perhaps hire a companion for her. Ideally, though, I ought to marry first—a woman who can help develop Georgiana's mind to be less romantic, without crushing her spirit."

His words effected such a dejected feeling in Lizzy's chest, she hardly knew what to make of it. Of course Mr. Darcy would marry. It was surely nothing to Lizzy if he did. She struggled for a breath, then rushed to say, "I have heard rumour of an intention between you and your cousin Miss de Bourgh."

He paled. "Nothing to it, I assure you."

She bit her lip. "Forgive my impertinence. I should not have mentioned it. Perhaps there is hope for Miss Bingley, then, after all."

Miss Bingley had flirted with him outrageously whilst he and the Bingleys had been at Netherfield. Lizzy expected him to smile. He did not.

Rather, he coloured, and his eyes shone with some emotion she could not name. "Is that what you wish for me?"

She felt abashed for a moment, but then ire seeped into her veins, sending heat through her. Why did it matter what *she* wished? She was nothing to him—he was paying her far too much notice. There might be a dearth of gentlewomen in Hunsford, but that was no excuse for his singling her out in this way.

A more foolish woman might think he was courting her.

Chiding herself for ever scolding his reticence, she said in a cross tone, "You and Miss Bingley certainly *appear* compatible. You are both so tall, you find it easy to look down upon your company."

Certain her face was glowing red, she strolled toward Charlotte. She ought not to have said such a thing to him. Yet she was not sorry she had. No good could come from any friendliness between herself and the infuriating man.

Catching up to her friend, she helped lay down the blankets so they could unpack the picnic baskets. She chatted with Maria but dared not look behind her. She could not meet Darcy's eyes.

Darcy stood with his mouth agape, watching Elizabeth set out the picnic. Her cut did not miss its mark. Nor could he argue with her. She had seen him at his worst, and truly his treatment of the people of Meryton had not been as amiable as it ought to have been. But he had come to Rosings intent on showing he could be a better man.

Since his arrival, his admiration for her had only grown. She was as pretty a woman as he had ever seen, especially now, with the ribbons of her bonnet blowing in the breeze, and her white muslin gown showing off her figure enticingly. He hardly knew what to make of her impudence. They had both spoken too freely, to be sure. He could not help thinking, though, that her comfort with him seemed encouraging.

And the discussion of whom he might choose for a wife—certainly, that was intended to reassure herself that he was free. That his heart was not attached to someone else.

Caroline Bingley, indeed. He liked her, enjoyed her intellect, but there was no warmth in her. She was hardly the right sort of companion for Georgiana. No, Giana was too sensitive. The kindness Elizabeth had shown toward Jane at Netherfield—that was what Giana needed.

Once the food was set out, Elizabeth sat on the blanket next to Richard, and Darcy took her other side.

"Have you heard from your sisters at Longbourn?" Maria asked Elizabeth. "How are they faring, now that the officers are to remove to Brighton for the summer?"

The officers removing to Brighton. That was good news. The good people of Meryton would be safe from Wickham at last.

"Lydia claims to be inconsolable, of course," Elizabeth said. "But I do not think she is seriously attached to any of them. They were an interesting addition to our society for a while, and they will be missed."

"And there is one in particular that *you* will miss, I think," Maria said.

Elizabeth smiled and said lightly, "I shall indeed, but alas, I am not wealthy enough to tempt him."

Darcy stiffened. He had never noticed Elizabeth's attention being engaged by any of the officers in particular. At the ball at Netherfield, she had seemed quite indifferent to them.

"Some men," said Charlotte, "are ruled by considerations other than money. What say you, Colonel Fitzwilliam? Which is a more important consideration when marrying—love or money?"

"Charlotte, that is unfair," Elizabeth protested. "He is the second son of an earl. Of course money is a consideration for him."

"I can easily see myself falling in love with a woman of means," Richard said. "I have no plans to choose between the two."

"But what if you fall in love with a woman of more modest fortune first?" Elizabeth asked.

"I believe I can control my heart better than that. What think you, Darcy?"

Darcy had no desire to hold this conversation in front of Elizabeth. Yet he had even less desire to stay silent and seem indifferent, or worse, proud. He knew that if he took pains to construct an intellectual answer, it would come out stilted and wrong. Instead, he let his words flow unencumbered.

"Controlling one's heart is an illusion. A man who would give up love for money is a fool." His face heated, and he avoided looking at Elizabeth.

"I have never heard you profess such a thing before," Richard taunted. "Is this a new conclusion on your part?"

Darcy worked his jaw, fighting through his embarrassment. "Of course one must choose a partner who is compatible—one with similar breeding. But as long as one has the means to live comfortably, love should be the first consideration."

"That is easy to say," Richard countered, "when one has grown up as heir to a great estate."

"Is Pemberley very fine?" Maria asked. "As fine as Rosings?"

Richard scoffed. "Rosings cannot compare to Pemberley."

Elizabeth's eyelashes fluttered. "Indeed?"

Richard looked at her with a broad, easy smile. "It is not that Pemberley is *vastly* superior to Rosings. Simply that it is superior in every way."

Darcy eyed his cousin wearily. "When you come to Pemberley, you have the run of the place. No aunt to answer to."

"Excellent point."

"Do you visit there often?" Elizabeth asked.

"As often as I can," Richard said. "I do have a regiment under my command, however, so I cannot always be idle. I shall rejoin them in a few weeks."

"Is there likely to be an invasion, do you think?" Maria asked.

A puff of air rushed through the trees. Leaves scattered, falling from their branches. A raven cawed a distant warning.

"Our navy is far superior," Richard reassured her. "Bonaparte is a military man. He is unlikely to overestimate his strength in that area. But we must prepare for anything, I am afraid."

"It is all very frightening," Maria said.

"You must not be afraid," Richard said. "Be prepared. Be cautious. But do not give him the victory of destroying your peace of mind."

Maria gave him a sweet smile.

"You are far braver than I would be," Elizabeth said, "were I in your position."

Richard looked at her intently. "My men are well trained. I have confidence in them. Besides, it is too fine a day to think of such things."

There was never a day when Darcy wished to think of such things. Richard was virtually a brother to him. Never before had a military career held such danger. Darcy had wished his cousin to go into the law, where all his battles might have been fought in a courtroom. But alas, Richard was a man of action, not words.

"Do you prefer the countryside to town, Colonel?" Elizabeth asked.

"Very much so. When I am in town, I am my father's representative. My role is to inspire a sense of patriotic duty, to win him favour in the House of Lords. I am happy to support him, but I am not my own agent. Here in the country, I am free."

"I suppose any woman you marry must take on that role as well," Elizabeth said. "She must be diplomatic and above reproach."

He grinned. "Do you know of such a one?"

Elizabeth's eyes roamed the countryside. "I am sure there are many. I had not thought before, though, how ill-suited I might be as the daughter-in-law of an earl. I speak my mind too freely."

Richard tipped his hat at her. "I have observed, madam, that you are perfectly civil in company, and that your witticisms go generally undetected by those at whom they are directed. With the exception of my poor cousin, who feels the full brunt of them, but is entirely deserving."

"I confess," Darcy said, "I am accustomed to flattery. It gives one too great a sense of one's importance. Miss Bennet does a fine job of keeping me in check."

"You are too generous, Mr. Darcy," Elizabeth said. "My treatment of you borders on unkindness."

"You have not said a word to me that I have not deserved. You are my instructor, madam, and I am grateful."

"Then by all means, I shall abuse you without restraint."

Darcy arched his brows. "Have you been restraining yourself till now? I would not have known it."

"Eliza," Maria protested, "I have never known you to be anything but kind. Indeed, Mr. Darcy, she is all goodness and patience. She is playful to be sure, but she has the gentlest heart."

"Miss Lucas," Darcy said, "you know her to be so, for you are all goodness yourself. If she points out my faults, then I am to blame for failing to recognize how inconsiderate I have been to others. My behaviour in Hertfordshire was not what it ought to have been."

"Now I *am* curious," Richard said.

"I behaved with indifference, and it was perceived as arrogance. Miss Bennet, I have never considered another person beneath me. That I have left you with such an impression fills me with shame."

"Darcy is not proud," Richard said. "He is simply a misanthrope. He would prefer to sleep in the stables with the horses."

Elizabeth raised her eyebrows. "I had already guessed he was an enthusiast of Mr. Swift."

Maria looked at them blankly.

"Gulliver's Travels," Elizabeth explained.

Maria's face fell. "I did not get past the Lilliputians. I am hopeless at satire."

"That is a compliment to the sweetness of your disposition," Richard said.

"I am not clever the way Elizabeth is."

"Then I wager you are clever in your own ways," Richard added.

Maria looked at him with a beaming smile.

Darcy wished he had Richard's ease with the fair sex. Such a simple thing, to treat a girl like Maria kindly. Why had Darcy never learned the importance of courting the goodwill of others?

He would have to do better if he wished to win not only the hand of Elizabeth Bennet, but also her heart.

Chapter 5

It was not an overly suspicious mind that led Lizzy to think others were plotting against her. During the picnic, Charlotte ensured that Lizzy and Darcy spent as much time together as possible. Lizzy was tempted to simply give in, to do her best to learn to like Darcy, in case Charlotte was right about his intentions. But she could not forget his treatment of Jane, or poor Wickham.

On their walk back to the road, Charlotte, Maria, and the colonel managed once again to get ahead of Lizzy and Darcy. She was forced, once again, to be civil. It was trying her nerves.

"Miss Lucas is a sweet, ingenuous girl," Darcy said.

Lizzy startled, then comprehended his meeting. "You mean Maria, of course. I am afraid I cannot get used to Charlotte being Mrs. Collins. You are right, Maria is very sweet, and more romantic than her sister. I hope the colonel will take care."

Darcy nodded thoughtfully. "I shall mention it to him."

"I hate to bring it up—I have heard nothing from her on the subject—but your cousin is quite dashing, and the sort of man to turn the head of an inexperienced young woman."

"But not yours?" he asked.

"I have no illusions." She grinned wickedly. "I may be tolerably pretty, but not enough to tempt a man of any social standing."

She continued a few steps before realizing Darcy was not at her side. She turned to see him standing and staring, mouth agape as if dumbstruck. She almost laughed aloud to see the man, normally so dignified, now at a complete loss.

He clearly recognized her words as those he had used to describe her on the night they had met. There had been a shortage of male partners at the ball. Yet Darcy would not deign to dance, and told Bingley that he would not be induced by women who were slighted by others.

Since then, he had been so fixed in her mind as a proud man above all his company that it was strange to watch a deep flush of embarrassment overtake his cheeks.

"Good heavens!" he cried. "I knew you must have felt slighted by my behaviour that night. I had no idea you had heard my words. You must think me beastly."

"Not at all. It is not your fault that your sentiments fell on ears not meant to hear them."

"I could not be more ashamed. You have my deepest apologies, madam. And whilst it may be of little consolation, I confess that I have long since thought of you as one of the most beautiful women of my acquaintance."

Her pulse quickened, and a strange fluttering rippled over her body. "Your flattery is unnecessary, sir." She struggled to hide the quivering in her voice. "I have never sought your notice, and so had no reason to take your words to heart. We are but passing acquaintances."

"You must allow me the chance to regain your favour." His jaw worked, and his lips tightened. He stared at the ground, shaking his head. "I have never *had* your favour, have I."

Lizzy remained silent, her eyes surveying the landscape.

"What a fool I have been!" He paced, the dried leaves rustling under his feet. "I imagined...well, never mind what I had imagined. May we start again? I ought to have behaved better, and instead I gave offense to the most enchanting woman I ever met."

She drew her brow. "Surely you cannot mean me?"

"Can you doubt it? A woman of wit and intelligence, who constantly challenges me instead of fawning as others do—of course I am enchanted." He leaned against a tree, hat in his hand as he stared at the ground. "While you must think me insufferable."

Until that moment, she had. But now, he looked so perfectly miserable, it was difficult not to feel for his discomfiture. Without meaning to, she gave out a little laugh.

He met her eyes. "Do I amuse you?"

She walked up to him. "Humility becomes you."

He looked at her with hard eyes, but otherwise his expression was one of consternation.

She placed a gloved hand on his arm. "Come now, Mr. Darcy, we must all be ridiculous at one point or another. Our neighbours would not like it if we were infallible." She looked around. "We are falling behind. We had better catch up to the others."

"Of course." He walked mechanically, the downcast look still on his face. Lizzy's attempts to cheer him could not evoke even a smile.

When they reached the main road, with the ladies heading back to Hunsford Cottage and the gentlemen to Rosings, the wistful look he shot her gave voice to the thought that had been creeping through her mind all day.

Mr. Darcy was in love with her.

⁓ↀ⁓

Lizzy wandered aimlessly about the parsonage, hardly knowing what she was about. Charlotte and Maria were in the kitchen, which was just as well, because it was impossible for her to endure company at that moment. Her mind was too jumbled.

It could not be true. Mr. Darcy, nephew of an earl, with an income of ten thousand pounds a year, could not be in love with her, Elizabeth Bennet.

How could Darcy esteem her, when she had never spoken a word to him except to tease? And yet, he had praised her wit. He had called her enchanting. And he was mortified to learn she had overheard his insult.

Mr. Darcy, whom she had every reason to dislike. Who had separated Jane from Bingley. Who had deprived her friend Wickham of the living promised him by Darcy's father. No, she could not respect him. It was unthinkable that she could entertain any hopes in that quarter.

Yet, what a comfort it would be to her mother, to have a daughter so well settled! To know that their future was no longer in jeopardy!

And Jane—surely she and Bingley would be reunited. A match between Lizzy and Darcy would bring happiness to everyone she knew.

Everyone except herself.

The sweet scent of rhubarb pie baking in the oven wafted through the house. Lizzy could not think of food at that moment. Her entire world had shifted.

The fact that Darcy had fallen in love with her—if, indeed, he had—was not evidence that he was a man of good character. In fact, his manner of speaking might have been too familiar, if looked at in a certain light.

Really, a man ought not to go about calling a woman enchanting. She might get ideas.

A more romantic person might have thought he was on the brink of making an offer. She might have felt herself at liberty to fall in love. Not that it mattered. Darcy was the last man on earth Lizzy could love.

She stepped out into the garden for solace, knowing that Mr. Collins would be working on his sermon and unlikely to disturb her. Instead, it was Charlotte who joined her there after a few minutes.

Lizzy looked out over the even rows. The leaf lettuce was full and robust, happy in the cool spring air. The strawberries were in full flower. But the carrots were coming to the end of their season, their tops starting to yellow.

Charlotte spoke. "You and Mr. Darcy seemed to have had a serious conversation as we were walking home this afternoon."

"Oh, Charlotte. This is madness, but I think you must be right. Mr. Darcy is in love with me!"

Her friend nodded serenely. "I am glad you finally see it. I was worried he had made you an offer this afternoon, and you had refused him."

Lizzy shook her head. At least it had not come to that. "Nothing so serious, thank goodness."

"But you must consider the possibility. I cannot help thinking that he came to Rosings to see *you*. From what I have been able to tell, he usually visits in the summer."

Elizabeth stared. She had hoped Charlotte would talk her out of this delusion. Instead, here was more evidence of his intentions. "If that is true...what am I to do?"

"Everything in your power to secure him, I think."

Never in her life had Lizzy missed Jane so much. Jane would understand Lizzy's struggle. Charlotte seemed to think Lizzy's feelings were beside the point.

Lizzy said in a sharp whisper, "I do not even like him."

"If I were in your position, I could come up with ten thousand reasons a year to like him."

Lizzy smiled in spite of herself. She could not begin to comprehend his fortune, and in truth, it hardly mattered. A husband who could keep her from poverty was all she required—as long as he was a man she could esteem. "I know nothing of his character. The people of Meryton were of one mind in considering him a proud, disdainful man."

"Do *you* think so of him, after all this time?"

Her cheeks heated at Charlotte's words. She could not deny that Darcy had proven himself far different than the sort of man Lizzy had thought him to be when she first met him.

"To be sure," Charlotte continued, "he is a man of wealth and breeding who knows his position in the world. Is that such a terrible quality in a husband? I have never heard any suggestion that he is a vicious man—"

"Certainly not!" The vehemence of her own expression surprised Lizzy.

"Well then, perhaps I might observe that a man in love is easily led if you appeal to his vanity."

"Charlotte!" This was not at all what Lizzy needed. She wanted her marriage to be an honest partnership.

"Now, Mr. Darcy seems to be a man of superior intellect," Charlotte continued. "He will not be easily deceived. But as a husband, he might well be persuaded to align his desires with yours."

Elizabeth laughed. "And this is the marriage advice you give me!" But of course it was. It was exactly how she was managing Mr. Collins.

Charlotte smiled affectionately. "Remember when we read *The Taming of the Shrew* together? You complained that Petruchio had destroyed Kate's spirit. And I said he had taught her to rein in her passions, as a means to secure her own happiness. I would never suggest that you marry a man you do not love. But your dislike of Mr. Darcy is based on nothing more than his slight of you the night you met, and the report of a man you barely know. Mr. Wickham seems personable, but do you really know any more of his character than you do of Mr. Darcy's? Do you not think you should at least get to *know* Mr. Darcy before you determine you cannot marry him?"

DARCY COMES TO ROSINGS

Lizzy looked toward the sky, watching the birds fly overhead and listening to their song. "It is unimaginable."

"Oh, I doubt that. You are quite clever. I believe you could imagine it down to the last detail. Mistress of Pemberley, which is superior to Rosings in every way. You were thinking of it during the picnic today—do not deny it. You may not like him now, but my advice to you is to *try harder*."

Chapter 6

After the service on Sunday, Lizzy stepped out of the grey stone church with Charlotte and Maria. The tall steeple and heavy wooden doors were expertly carved. The building was modern with beautiful stained glass, modest in size yet splendid in detail. There could be no doubt that this was the result of Lady Catherine's patronage.

For all her officiousness, Lady Catherine was generous to the parish. She took her *noblesse oblige* seriously, as she did all things. She gave, and she expected loyalty in return. Nonetheless, she did seem truly concerned with the welfare of those within her sphere of influence—even if that concern was not always wanted or needed.

Lady Catherine stepped into her barouche to head back to Rosings, along with Miss de Bourgh, her companion Mrs. Jenkinson, and Colonel Fitzwilliam. Darcy, however, approached Charlotte.

"Mrs. Collins," said he, "might I accompany you and your fair friends home?"

Charlotte gave him a bright smile. "I would be obliged, sir. My husband has much to do after the service, as you can imagine."

"Of course."

Whilst Charlotte informed Mr. Collins, Lizzy bit her tongue. Apparently Darcy had recognized an ally in Charlotte. Yet the last thing Lizzy wanted was another awkward conversation with this man, so tall and handsome and proud.

And tall.

And handsome.

Lizzy's opinion was unswayed by the effects of his person, though his nearness as he walked by her side toward the parsonage caused a fluttering in her heart and a quickening of her breath. In all the months she had known him, she had found his company barely tolerable. He was not handsome enough to tempt *her*.

Never mind that he had called her enchanting the day before, and apologized profusely for his slight of her at the Meryton ball. Nor that his behaviour in Kent had shown him to be a different sort of man than the one she had imagined in Hertfordshire.

Kinder. Less cold.

The man had his charms—she could not deny it. Yet it was not his actions toward *herself* that she blamed him for. The harm he had caused to Jane and to Wickham remained foremost in her thoughts.

Soon Charlotte and Maria began to lag behind. No coincidence, that. Darcy did not hesitate to put their time out of earshot of the others to good use.

"Miss Bennet, I hope you will indulge me. I have been uneasy since we spoke yesterday. I shall not be at peace until I have said these words. The night we met, my behaviour was beastly—"

"Mr. Darcy, this is entirely unnecessary." Cold blossomed in the pit of her stomach. She did not want to rehash that night—she wanted to forget it had ever happened. Had he not already explained himself?

Consternation crossed his features. "I do not expect you to excuse me for it. Yesterday I made light of Georgiana's situation, and I should not have done that. Not with you. When you hear the full story, I know I can count on your discretion."

She wanted to protest—he ought not entrust his secrets to her, when she was no more to him than an acquaintance. He was singling her out again. The thought twisted her stomach into knots.

Yet she did not interrupt. Clearly, speaking these words was important to him. Lizzy could indulge him that far, at least.

He looked off into the distance. A twig crunched under her foot as she waited for him to gather his thoughts. She had come to realize that he valued precision and did not rush.

After nearly a month listening to Mr. Collins' prattling, she was beginning to appreciate Darcy's judiciousness.

At last, he set his jaw and continued, "At the time of the ball, my sister was suffering the worst sort of heartache. She had nearly fallen prey to a scoundrel."

"Oh!" She stopped short, the revelation taking her breath away. How dreadful—no wonder he had been preoccupied. If anything like that had befallen one of *her* sisters, she would have been beside herself with grief.

She looked down and realized that without knowing or meaning to, she had grasped his gloved hand in hers. Her gaze travelled upward and met his eyes, pain evident in their dark pools, in the tight crease between his brows.

That expression undid her, liquefying her resolve. Darcy was not a beast. A tender heart beat in his chest, and in that moment she felt a strange pull to place her hand there, to feel its rhythm.

But the mere fact of his love for his sister did not excuse the coldness he showed toward those not connected to him. Even if she recognized his good qualities, she could not forget the bad. Steeling her spine, she forced herself to release his hand, and walked forward again.

"I considered last night whether I ought to confide in you," he added. "You have said that I am a puzzle, and perhaps this will provide one of the missing pieces. I wish you to know my heart, Miss Bennet. I trust you will tell no one what I am about to impart."

She ought to deny him. She had no desire to increase the intimacy between them. In the end, her curiosity won out. "Of course—I would not betray a confidence."

He nodded, walking at a slow pace. "On the day of the ball, I received a letter from Lady Adelaide—my cousin's wife, with whom my sister was staying at the time. Georgiana was in poor spirits, and Lady Adelaide was considering an excursion to the Cotswolds to cheer her. She wanted my opinion."

He coloured and grew silent a moment before continuing. "About six months earlier, Georgiana had fallen under the spell of a man courting her for her fortune of thirty thousand pounds. She was but fifteen at the time and besotted."

He tugged at the hem of his glove, clearly uncomfortable. "The man is as worthless as they come. I immediately removed her from his influence, and from the school where she was staying."

Lizzy nodded. She could sympathize with the girl, but also saw how a guardian would have to take such actions to protect her. "Most girls that age would be unhappy at such treatment."

"Georgiana is a sweet, obedient girl. She accepted that I was acting in her best interest. Still, her heart was broken. The letter from Lady Adelaide confirmed my fears that she was pining for him. A man not fit to set his foot in the dirt where she trod," he added with a growl.

Elizabeth saw true sorrow in his eyes. At the same time, she could not forget how Darcy had separated Bingley from Jane. Might this have been the same kind of situation? "Poor girl. To have a brother who disapproves of the man she loves—"

"I assure you, these were not star-crossed lovers. I have known the man all my life—he is dissolute and unscrupulous, a dozen years her senior. If you were in the same circumstances, would you not do anything in your power to protect your sister? Would your heart not grieve the harm he had done her?"

Lizzy grew thoughtful. With so little information, it was impossible to tell whether Darcy was the hero or villain in the story. "Indeed, sir, I know well the pain of seeing a beloved sister suffering a broken heart. I have been in that predicament since a mutual friend of ours departed Hertfordshire. My sister protests that she will forget him, but every letter is as full of his name as the last."

Darcy stopped. "Miss Bennet—"

"Oh, do not trouble yourself. She has not seen him. His sisters have made sure of that. He is quite safe."

She moved quickly, putting space between them. With his long strides, he easily caught up. They continued in silence a while before Darcy said, "Perhaps I have been mistaken."

She stopped and stared. "You have been quite mistaken, sir, where my sister Jane is concerned. You have overthrown her best chance for happiness." Her face warmed, and tears prickled at her eyes. She had said too much, but she was not sorry. Darcy ought to feel the force of the damage he had done.

"I had no idea of her harbouring any serious feelings. She was quite serene in his company. It was your mother who showed all the eagerness—"

"Mr. Darcy! Whatever you may think of her, she is my mother. I shall not hear her disparaged."

"Pardon me. I meant no disrespect." He straightened his coat. "It seems I have made an error in judgment."

She scoffed. "Have you indeed?"

"You have every reason, every right to be angry. I confess I saw no ardour in your sister—"

"You are not the only one uncomfortable showing strong passions in public." With the cottage now in sight, she continued walking on.

He fell into step beside her and was silent a long time. At last, he said, "I shall remedy this."

"Some things, sir, cannot be remedied." They reached the gate, and she went inside without another word to him.

∼◇∼

On her walk the next morning, Lizzy found herself nearing the path back to Hunsford Cottage with her mind still unsettled.

The pale leaves of spring were giving way to their summer colours. Primroses were fading, and honeysuckle just starting to release its delicious fragrance. The grasses were full and thick, alive with bees and butterflies.

Darcy's confession about his sister had made Lizzy both more sympathetic and more wary. Was this a habit of his? Separating lovers he found unsuitable? Who was he to judge?

In the case of his sister, of course, he was within his rights. With Georgiana at such a tender age, perhaps the man in question *had* been preying on her. Elizabeth did not know what to make of it, and until she had puzzled it out, she was in no mood for the noise of the cottage.

She followed a route she had tried only once before. Meandering between a wildflower meadow and a tall hedgerow, she came upon more genial company than she had encountered during her previous outings.

"Taking your morning exercise?" Colonel Fitzwilliam asked.

"I have been out a bit longer than usual. Preoccupied, I suppose."

She had barely slept the night before, her mind filled with the most distressing thoughts. Whatever the circumstances might have been with regard to his sister, Darcy had all but admitted his responsibility for separating Bingley from Jane. The audacity of the man, inserting himself into a situation that did not concern him! How could she ever respect him after he had done such harm to the dearest person in the world to her?

"No bad news from home, I hope?" the colonel asked

"Nothing unexpected. The news has been...the usual."

He walked in step with her. "Your family is well?"

"Oh yes, quite well. Truly, it is nothing to concern yourself with." She gave him a grateful smile. "You have the fate of the nation on your shoulders."

"Not on mine alone. At least I hope not, or the nation might be in terrible danger."

She chuckled. "I have no doubt of your abilities, but I appreciate your modesty. You are so different from your cousin in that way."

He lifted his brows. "I have not known Darcy to be a braggart."

Her lips parted in confusion. "No, of course not. I apologize. I do not mean to speak ill of him."

"Perhaps your preoccupation this morning has to do with him?"

They approached a copse of trees, and the tapping of a woodpecker interrupted the stillness. The sun was bright, the sky cloudless, the air comfortably warm for late April. She could not imagine a more pleasant day for walking. Yet her thoughts troubled her.

She pressed her gloved fingertips together. "I cannot make out Mr. Darcy's character. He says he considers no one beneath him, yet in Hertfordshire, he acted as though *everyone* were beneath him. And in some sense, everyone was, certainly with regard to breeding and fortune. He showed not the least interest in making himself amiable."

The colonel gave a thoughtful nod. "He is cautious, and does not make friends easily. To those who *do* manage to win his favour, he is generous and loyal. I hope that grants him some measure of approbation in your eyes?"

Did it? Kindness toward one's friends was hardly an uncommon quality. "He has described himself as resentful. Is that his greatest fault, do you think?"

"He is not the sort of person you can fool twice. I am not certain that makes him resentful."

She quirked her lips into a wry smile. "So even his flaws are strengths in your eyes."

He grinned and shook his head. "I have known him his whole life. He is amongst the best of men. You have not seen enough of him to really know him, Miss Bennet. I pray you, get to know him better before you reach any conclusions."

"For your sake," she said, "and yours alone, I shall try. Perhaps at dinner tonight."

"Unfortunately, he left at first light with business in London. We expect him back tomorrow."

Lizzy's heart sank at the news. It ought to have filled her with joy. In truth, it would be better if she *never* saw Darcy again—never looked into those intelligent dark eyes, never heard the flattery in his smooth baritone, never felt her breath hitch when she caught sight of his tall figure and aristocratic bearing.

She could no longer deny that she felt drawn to him. But he was the wrong sort of man. She ought not to consider marriage to him, but her imagination kept running away with her. The weeks until her return to Longbourn would be interminable.

But she would stay strong. She would not succumb to Mr. Darcy.

Chapter 7

Darcy had been inside few homes in Cheapside and usually found them drab and cramped. This one, however, was like an exhibition hall. As the maid led him toward the drawing room, he noted the décor. It included fashionable pieces from around the world: teak elephants from India, silk tapestries from China, porcelain figurines from Dresden. Mr. Gardiner's business must be profitable indeed.

The maid opened the door to the drawing room, announcing him to the ladies of the house. Miss Jane Bennet looked up with astonishment in her eyes. Her beauty was still breathtaking—eyes a deep sapphire blue, blond ringlets framing her face. But the pallor in her cheek confirmed the suffering she had endured in the months of Bingley's absence. If Darcy had indeed caused her harm, he would make amends.

He bowed to the lady with her, whom he assumed to be Mrs. Gardiner. He was surprised that she was perhaps only five years older than himself, a red-headed beauty with a contagious smile.

"Miss Bennet," he said to Jane, "delightful to see you. Will you do me the honour of introducing me to your companion?"

"Of course," she said in a rushed voice. "This is my aunt, Mrs. Gardiner. Mr. Darcy of Pemberley."

"Pemberley! Good heavens!" Mrs. Gardiner said in a refined but enthusiastic voice. "I grew up in Derbyshire, and have ridden through the park there many times. What a pleasure to make your acquaintance, sir." She motioned for him to sit.

"The pleasure is all mine." He took a chair near Jane and said to Mrs. Gardiner, "You must excuse my coming unannounced, madam. I have arrived today from Kent, where I have had the pleasure of seeing your niece, Miss Elizabeth Bennet. She is quite well. The air there seems to agree with her."

He winced. This was why he did not converse with strangers. He sounded stiff and insipid.

"I am pleased to hear it," Mrs. Gardiner said, looking gratified.

He turned to Jane. "Miss Bennet, how do you find London?"

"I find the quiet here soothing."

He blinked. "London quieter than the country?"

"You obviously have not lived in a house with four sisters, sir."

He smiled at that. "But you must find the variety of social events here more stimulating."

"In truth, we hardly go out in the evening."

He blinked, taking in that information. "I am surprised." Then, Elizabeth's voice sounded in his mind. "I can imagine what your sister Miss Elizabeth would say, were she here. She would declare that you lived in such retirement, you had not been to Almack's above three times."

Mrs. Gardiner laughed. "That is precisely what dear Lizzy would say."

But Miss Bennet did not smile. Miss Bennet looked deeply unhappy. And it was his doing.

Jane was a beautiful and accomplished young woman whose circumstances required her to marry well. Yet she chose to stay hidden away here during the London season. That told of a deep melancholy.

Elizabeth had not exaggerated. Jane's heart was broken.

He hated what he was about to say, but he had to know. "Have you seen the Bingleys since you have been in town?"

Jane blanched, then rose and walked to the window. "I have seen Caroline twice."

Darcy rose. "And you have not seen her brother at all?"

"No, sir." Her voice was exceedingly weak.

"Then he must not know you are in town."

She turned and looked at him, the expression in her eyes almost wild. "Caroline assured me that he knows."

"I assure you that he does not." He watched her carefully, heart aching at the confusion in her countenance. "Given that you have been in town nearly four months, and Caroline has endeavoured to see you no more than twice, I think you can observe that she is no friend to you. It pains me, because you deserved better from her."

He stuffed his hands into his pockets, then took them out again. "And you deserved better from me as well. It was not my intention, but I have wronged you, Miss Bennet. And I intend to put it right."

⁓⊶⧽⧼⊷⁓

Darcy went to Grosvenor Street. There, Bingley lived at the home of his brother-in-law, Mr. Hurst. Darcy had sent word ahead when he arrived in town, and was expected for dinner. As it had taken him some time to discover the direction of the Gardiners' home, he was shown in just before the meal was to start.

"Mr. Darcy, how lovely to see you," greeted Mrs. Hurst, née Louisa Bingley. "It has been too long."

It had been two weeks.

Still, in one sense, she was right. Two weeks in Kent had purged London from his system. He had become accustomed to the less fashionable mode of dress at Rosings—so much so, he was tempted to ask, *Madam, are you aware of the dead ostrich on your head?* But he refrained.

Darcy could not say whether Bingley's sisters were pretty. Their mode of dress was such that one saw their clothes and coiffures—one did not see *them*. It was as if they were costumed for a masquerade ball, and were only missing the masks.

Bingley entered in a rush, combing his fingers through his unruly dark-blond hair. "Darcy, pleased you could join us." He gave Darcy's hand a boisterous shake. "How is your aunt?"

"Quite well, thank you."

"And your cousin, Miss de Bourgh?"

"Her health is no worse. I wish I could convince my aunt that more time in the sunshine would do Anne good."

"So nothing has changed, then."

Darcy joined in Bingley's laugh. In fact, *much* had changed, for both of them. But Darcy could not say so until they were alone, which would not be until after dinner.

Caroline Bingley stepped forward, red silk swishing. "You are looking well, Mr. Darcy. The country agrees with you." She offered her hand.

He kissed it—or rather the air above it. "Indeed it does. I look forward to settling in at Pemberley for the summer."

"Will Georgiana join you? Lady Adelaide keeps her so busy, I have hardly had the chance to see her here in town."

Darcy suspected Lady Adelaide had her reasons for that. "Yes, Georgiana will spend the summer at home with me."

"How delightful," Miss Bingley said in a cultured but insipid tone. "It will be good practice for her to serve as your hostess."

Unless I marry first. He was tempted to say the words aloud, but knew no good could come of it. Miss Bingley would quiz him incessantly. The path was certain to lead to Elizabeth, and he had no desire to hear Miss Bingley's jealous barbs.

Dinner was announced, and Darcy processed into the dining room with Louisa on his arm. She was dressed in a sort of orangey silk—apricot, he supposed the ladies would call it— with a bouquet of tall, white plumes sticking out of her very fashionable hat.

Hurst, accompanying Caroline, was of course dressed in whatever Beau Brummell had been wearing the previous week. He likely kept his tailor in business with the constant alterations to keep up with the latest trends.

As they sat at the table, Darcy could not help noting the décor. It looked as if they expected the Prince Regent to arrive at any moment. Tall porcelain vases in the Neoclassical style, crystal candelabras, and gilded everything. He suspected that all the ostentation was rented, like the house.

The first course was an herb soup with potato dumplings, the tarragon a little strong for Darcy's taste. Then, as the duck was served, Caroline asked him, "How is the company in Kent? I imagine that outside your aunt's household, it must be as savage as Hertfordshire."

"As it happens, some of our acquaintances from Hertfordshire are visiting. Miss Lucas has come to see her sister at the parsonage, along with Miss Elizabeth Bennet."

In the candlelight, Darcy could not see whether Caroline had paled, but the lines of her face went rigid.

Bingley's countenance was easier to read. The mention of the name Bennet had driven away all semblance of good humour. He stared a moment, then cast down his eyes, his brows deeply furrowed.

"And how is Miss Eliza Bennet?" Caroline asked. "Are her eyes as fine as you recall?"

"Quite. For all her beauty, however, I find her wit to be her most enticing quality."

"Yes." Bingley sipped his wine. "Miss Elizabeth Bennet is most clever. I say, has she mentioned...are all her sisters still at home?"

"All but one," Darcy said. "The eldest is...visiting her aunt. I believe she returns to Longbourn soon, however."

Louisa shot him a hard look across the table, which he ignored.

Bingley nodded. A deep sadness filled his eyes, but his lips pursed thoughtfully.

"And what does your aunt think of these visitors to the parsonage?" Caroline asked. "Does she receive them at Rosings?"

"Twice a week or so."

Caroline lifted her chin. "She must be aflutter with hope that Miss Elizabeth Bennet might one day become her niece."

"I think that unlikely." Darcy sipped his wine. Then, he realized his statement was ambiguous, and she might misconstrue his meaning.

Though he had not come with the intention of baiting Caroline, she had thrown down the gauntlet. "By that I mean, I think it unlikely my aunt is hoping for it—not unlikely that it might happen."

"Why, should we wish you joy, Mr. Darcy?" Caroline's tone was icy.

"My aunt has more than one nephew. My cousin Colonel Fitzwilliam also finds Miss Elizabeth Bennet delightful."

"Colonel Fitzwilliam! Indeed!" Louisa cried with an arch look at Caroline. "I can picture it now, the earl and countess welcoming Mrs. Bennet and her daughters into the family." She let out a simpering laugh.

"As can I," Darcy said in an even tone that hid his rising ire. He dabbed a slice of duck into the accompanying fruit sauce. "My uncle and aunt care more about their son's happiness than they do about rank. Unlike the ladypatronesses of Almack's, who care about rank above all things."

He resisted using terms like *nouveaux riches* and *sons of commerce*, because that would be gauche. Surely the ladies needed no reminder that their fortune had come from trade. Even a stranger's ticket to Almack's was likely beyond them.

Darcy endeavoured to engage Hurst in conversation. Darcy's temper would not hold if he continued in his discourse with the ladies. They had been his co-conspirators in separating Bingley from Miss Bennet, an action he now fervently regretted.

He had trusted Caroline when she had agreed that Miss Bennet's heart had not been much involved. He had done so because the ladies had been friends. Caroline had quite attached herself to Miss Bennet whilst they were in Hertfordshire. She had dropped the friendship once they removed to London. It was badly done.

Now she was ridiculing his admiration of Elizabeth. It was not the first time, but it had ceased to be amusing months ago. Caroline might have thought that her fortune and fashionable education made her Elizabeth's better, but Elizabeth came from landed gentry—something Caroline could not boast.

Caroline knew nothing of dignity or true elegance. She was as crass a social climber as Mrs. Bennet. Did she really think that her barbs against the woman he loved would raise her in his estimation, and lower Elizabeth? He had never heard

Elizabeth speak an unkind word about anyone (except himself, to his face, when he had behaved like a fool).

The more he thought of it, the more his anger grew. So he talked with Hurst, asking which of the dishes he preferred, and what successes he had recently had playing cards at White's. The man never had anything of substance to say, but at least he was not a viper.

Finally—after a ridiculous amount of time for a family meal—the ladies retreated to the drawing room. As usual, a half glass of port sent Hurst into slumber. Darcy invited Bingley into the study where they could speak in private.

The small room was lined on one side with dark bookshelves; across was a sitting area of upholstered furniture. A table with a decanter of spirits sat in front of the window. Darcy poured them each a fortifying drink.

He did not belabour the facts. He spoke gently but without emotion, taking care to avoid overwhelming his friend. If Bingley's feelings were all Darcy supposed them to be, the news would give him quite a jolt.

Indeed, Bingley's consternation seemed to grow with each word, and he paced about the room. "You are saying Miss Bennet is *here*, in town, and has been since the new year?" His countenance showed more intensity than Darcy had ever seen in him.

"She has. And I am ashamed to admit that I conspired with your sisters to keep it from you."

Bingley sank into a chair, his brow creased. He said in a voice laced with pain, "It is for the best that I have not seen the lady. You said yourself she had no sincere interest in me. Better that I should not be tempted again."

Darcy refilled their glasses. He had to own up to what he had done, even if it cost him Bingley's friendship. "I may have been deceived in that."

Bingley sat forward, face pale, his eyes animated.

Darcy took the chair next to him. "Her sister, Miss Elizabeth," Darcy continued, "assures me that Miss Bennet's attachment is real. And from what I saw of her this afternoon, I can doubt it no longer."

"You saw Miss Bennet! This afternoon?" His hands shook, and he set down the glass.

"I did. I expected to hear how she has been enjoying the season, but instead she spends her evenings at home." Darcy shook his head, marvelling that he could have been so wrong. "A woman desperately seeking a husband would not waste an opportunity like this."

Bingley jumped to his feet. "I must go to her at once."

"It is almost nine." Darcy doubted that the Gardiners kept town hours. Calling so late, unexpectedly, might well be regarded as an intrusion, and hurt Bingley's case.

Darcy rose. "Go in the morning."

"I shall not wait another moment! Are you coming with me, or must I make a fool of myself alone?"

For the second time that day, Darcy found himself being led toward the Gardiners' drawing room. At his side, Bingley was agitated, squaring his shoulders and fidgeting as if the servant could not walk fast enough.

With a little knock at the door, the maid announced the visitors' arrival to the family seated around the fire. At the sound of Bingley's name, Jane let out a little cry, then rushed to the window. She stood with her back to them, her face hidden, hand grasping the window frame as if for support.

Bingley, meanwhile, resembled a caged panther, muscles coiled for action. His eyes, wide and bright, kept darting toward Miss Bennet. Darcy had never seen such intensity in his normally light-hearted friend. The contrast was so stark, it was impossible not to be conscious of Bingley's pain.

"Mrs. Gardiner," Darcy said, "please forgive the lateness of the hour. This is my friend Charles Bingley. I have just told him of Miss Bennet's being in town, and he was most anxious to pay his respects."

"Yes, of course." Mrs. Gardiner rose and gestured toward her companion, a fit-looking gentleman in his forties. "This is my husband, Edward Gardiner."

Mr. Gardiner greeted his guests. After the briefest time courtesy allowed, Bingley bowed again and went to Jane's side. She flinched, and he gazed upon her as if mesmerized before speaking to her in low tones.

Respecting their privacy, Darcy took the offered seat next to Mrs. Gardiner. Though painfully conscious of the scene playing out at the window, he engaged her in conversation about their mutual acquaintances in Derbyshire. She was delightful—sharing humorous anecdotes about her old neighbours, yet never resorting to gossip. Under different circumstances, she would have held Darcy's undivided attention.

As it was, he could not keep his gaze from wandering to the two lovers. They leaned together, their words too muted to be heard, but every emotion was written on their faces.

Bingley, open by nature, was easy to read. Miss Bennet, by contrast, clearly struggled to keep her feelings in check. Bingley's eyes were imploring, hers teary. His looks moved from sorrow to contrition to happiness; hers from confusion to hurt to serenity.

Darcy now recognized her tranquil expression as a sign of quiet joy. How could he have been so blind?

The two young gentlemen stayed above an hour, and it would have been longer if Darcy had not called Bingley's attention to the time. As they departed, Jane looked more radiant than Darcy had ever seen her. She was an angel. A flush of shame rushed through him, thinking how he had hurt her.

But he had put things right, as he had promised he would. He was content with that. Even if Elizabeth never discovered that it was his doing.

Chapter 8

The party from the cottage dined at Rosings shortly after Darcy returned. When Lizzy spotted him in the drawing room before dinner, her stomach tumbled with anticipation.

Remembering her promise to Colonel Fitzwilliam, she endeavoured to keep an open mind. Yet the moment she allowed herself to think kindly of Mr. Darcy, she could not help noticing the appealing intensity of his dark eyes when they turned her way, or the set of his strong jaw.

He could be the ruin of her if she let herself like him overly much.

"Tell me, Mr. Darcy," Charlotte asked during the meal, "how do you intend to spend the summer? Will you go back to Pemberley?"

"My sister and I shall spend some time at Pemberley, and then visit my uncle's estate once Parliament is adjourned.

With the exception of Lady Catherine, most of my family lives in Derbyshire when they are not in London."

"Is Pemberley much like Rosings?" Charlotte queried.

"The parks are very different," Lady Catherine said. "Have you been to the Peak District, Mrs. Collins? The hills are quite pretty. The house at Pemberley is very well situated—the front faces a lake, which my sister Lady Anne Darcy adored. She used to take the children there for picnics in the summer, remember, Darcy?"

"I do remember—"

"The houses, though, are not so different," Lady Catherine continued. "They were built near the same time, so the architecture is similar."

Against her will, Lizzy found herself picturing the scene. Hills sloping down to the house built of limestone, surrounded by tall oaks and a grassy lawn, with a wide expanse of water below, shimmering in the sunlight.

"But surely," Mr. Collins said, "the house at Pemberley cannot compare to Rosings in size."

"It is difficult to say, of course, as they are laid out differently," Lady Catherine replied. "Pemberley might be the tiniest bit larger."

"Then Mr. Darcy," Charlotte said, "you *are* well situated." She gave Lizzy a look, which Lizzy steadfastly refused to return.

DARCY COMES TO ROSINGS

"Indeed I am," Darcy said. "One has a certain prejudice about one's own home, but to my mind, there is not a better favoured house in England."

"Then I hope I may travel to Derbyshire one day," Charlotte said, "that I might ride past and catch a glimpse."

Lady Catherine said, "The housekeeper there, Mrs. Reynolds, is most obliging. She will be happy to give you a tour. Just mention my name, and she will be sure to take care of you."

"Or you might mention mine," Darcy said without a hint of irony in his expression. "You are welcome at any time, Mrs. Collins."

"Do you think we might, Charlotte?" Maria said. "Derbyshire is so far, but I have heard wonderful things about the north. All the hills and lakes—like something out of a fairy story!"

"Perhaps we might, someday."

"My dear Charlotte," Mr. Collins said, "my responsibilities are such that I do not see how I could manage a trip so far."

"Miss Lucas," Colonel Fitzwilliam said, "perhaps when you marry, your husband could take you to the north for your honeymoon."

Maria beamed. "I would love that above all things!"

Of course she would. Lizzy gritted her teeth. Surely Colonel Fitzwilliam did not intend to encourage Maria, but the girl was smitten.

"And what about you, Eliza?" Charlotte asked. "Would not you be happy to travel to Derbyshire to see Pemberley?"

Lizzy nearly choked. She swallowed a quick sip of wine. "It sounds beautiful."

"It is." Darcy looked at her intently. "I would love to show it to you one day."

The expression in his eyes made her hot all over. To shake off the feeling, she quipped, "You yourself? Not Mrs. Reynolds?"

"We need not trouble her, I think. You must come when Georgiana is at home. She would be pleased to meet you."

His words silenced her. She struggled for a clever reply but could not manage one. Finally, she said, "If I ever travel that far north, I shall keep it in mind." She shot Charlotte a warning look, and Charlotte returned an almost imperceptible smile.

On her walk the next morning, Lizzy wandered far from her usual haunt. She had no desire to follow the route where she had twice encountered Darcy. In her hand was her latest letter from Jane, received just before Darcy's departure to London, a reminder of how ill her sister had been treated by the man who, for some inexplicable reason, seemed to seek Lizzy's favour. No, she would not bestow it, no matter how tempting his fine features or his grand estate might be.

Instead of Darcy, she happened again upon Colonel Fitzwilliam, who explained he was making his annual tour of the park. He had just finished, so they walked together toward the parsonage, where he had been planning to visit.

Their conversation was light-hearted, relating principally to the colonel's relative state of poverty, and his inability to marry where he chose. Elizabeth felt no pang for herself, but did feel one for her mama, who had mentioned the colonel in every letter to Lizzy since the man had arrived at Rosings.

The conversation then turned to his cousin Georgiana. To Lizzy's surprise, the colonel mentioned that he as well as Darcy served as her guardians, a role Lizzy assumed had fallen to Darcy alone.

Lizzy said, "She is a very great favourite with some ladies of my acquaintance—Mrs. Hurst and Miss Bingley. I think I have heard you say that you know them."

"I know them a little. Their brother is a pleasant, gentlemanlike man—he is a great friend of Darcy's."

"Oh, yes." Lizzy fought to keep the mockery out of her tone. "Mr. Darcy is uncommonly kind to Mr. Bingley, and takes prodigious good care of him."

"Care of him!—Yes, I believe Darcy *does* take care of him in those points where he most wants care."

"'Tis a pity he has not shown such care to Mr. Wickham."

The colonel stopped in his tracks, his face going pale. "You know Wickham?"

"His regiment has been stationed at Meryton for the winter, not three miles from my home."

"My dear Miss Bennet." The colonel took her gloved hand. "I beg you, do not be deceived in him. He is a genial man, to be sure, but not to be trusted. It pains me to say this, as we were childhood friends. His character is not as it ought to be."

She dropped her hand from his, disbelieving. Wickham had been nothing but attentive and kind to her. He seemed nothing like what the colonel described.

"I am surprised, sir. Mr. Wickham is well-liked in Meryton."

His brows furrowed, and his mouth pulled into a hard line. "Upon a brief acquaintance, he is charming to be sure. Unfortunately, my recent dealings with him have proven him to be a grasping, unscrupulous man."

Lizzy shrank from him, anger and confusion warring in her breast. She did not like to hear an unflattering word spoken about her friend, as she considered Wickham to be. Yet she could not allow her preference to blind her. As Charlotte had reminded her, she had no one to vouch for Wickham's good character but the man himself.

Surely Colonel Fitzwilliam was in a better position to evaluate Wickham's integrity than Lizzy was. She could easily imagine that a man who endeavoured to make himself amiable to the ladies of his acquaintance might reveal his true character to the gentlemen. And given the colonel's lifelong acquaintance with Wickham, he was unlikely to be deceived by superficialities.

Did she trust the colonel's motives? They had known one another a short time, but he had every appearance of being an honourable man.

Of course, Darcy might have misled the colonel about the rift between himself and Wickham. But if the colonel knew the man as well as Darcy did, then perhaps she had better listen to what he had to say.

"Forgive me, sir. You ask that I take your word against Mr. Wickham, when I have never known any harm of him. Might I inquire what you are accusing him of?"

He scowled, as if wondering whether to say more. "I do not like to tell tales, Miss Bennet. But it is best you know the truth, to protect you from his machinations. Wickham took advantage of a young lady—in truth, a girl little more than a child."

Lizzy gasped. Surely it could not be true! But the passion in the colonel's voice and the flush of his cheek bore witness to his sincerity.

No, it was not possible. Could she have been so wrong about Wickham? So willing to believe him because of his pleasing demeanour? So quick to accept his account of matters, and judge Darcy because of his coolness in company?

Her father had once complained of Wickham's penchant for recounting his misfortunes to others. And those misfortunes chiefly related to being misused by Darcy. Yet she had never heard Darcy speak a word against him. In fact, she had never heard Darcy speak ill of anyone.

She did not like the direction where her thoughts were headed. Wickham's words had turned her initial dislike of Darcy into an enduring contempt. Had that been calculated on Wickham's part? Had he disparaged Darcy to throw doubt on anything Darcy might say to discredit him?

Her head was reeling. She must know more of the story, so she could judge the truth for herself.

"Surely, Colonel, you cannot mean that Mr. Wickham compromised a young lady?"

"Thankfully, no. Rather, he preyed on a young woman of fortune, but her family discovered their plans to elope in time to prevent the catastrophe. She believed herself in love—whilst he had no interest in her beyond her thirty thousand pounds."

Horror flooded Lizzy's stomach as she thought of Miss King, and how Wickham's interest in her had not been piqued until he learned of her ten thousand pounds. He had even convinced Lizzy that his fortune-hunting was the product of necessity, rather than ignobility. How could she have been so blind?

DARCY COMES TO ROSINGS

She swallowed, pushing down the emotion that threatened to overwhelm her. If Wickham were truly such a man, could she believe any word he had spoken? She had trusted his vilifications of Darcy. Now, it seemed there might be more to the story that did not show Wickham in such a favourable light.

"I am in your debt," she said, her voice faltering. She swallowed. "I was utterly misled by Wickham's charm and flattery."

She breathed deeply to regain control of her wavering composure. She had counted herself too clever to be taken in by such attentions. Had she truly been such a fool?

"I am afraid, Colonel," she continued, "Mr. Wickham spread tales abroad that Mr. Darcy had ill-used him. Though it pains me to admit it, I allowed myself to believe them."

The colonel scoffed. "You mean the story about the living my uncle had promised him? Oh yes, Wickham loves to raise that old grievance to anyone who will listen." The colonel shook his head. "Never mind Wickham's refusal to take clerical orders, or the payment he received from Darcy in lieu of the living."

Lizzy's mouth fell open in astonishment. She stared, unable to speak, until a strangled cry escaped her throat.

The colonel approached and took her hands again. "Miss Bennet, are you well?"

She trembled, her cheeks growing cold. She had permitted herself to like the man more than she should have, when every word from his mouth had been a lie. No, it was worse than that; he had regaled her with half-truths designed to cast himself in the best light, with enough veracity to be utterly convincing.

The colonel squeezed her hands. "Dear lady, I fear this has been a greater shock to you than I imagined."

She looked up at him, and seeing the concern in his eyes, shook her head. "Oh no, nothing like that. I had no reason to feel any hope in that direction, as I had no wealth to tempt him." She dropped her hands and looked off in the distance at the leafy trees slanting down the hill. "I have been an utter fool."

"Do not blame yourself. He is an accomplished liar."

A liar indeed. He had utterly ensnared her. His intentions toward her could not have been honourable, as impoverished as she was. Could he have meant to...

No, she would not let herself think it. However corrupt the man might be, *she* would never have fallen that far.

She shivered. Looking toward the sky, she said, "It is growing cloudy. I hope it will not rain."

"Let us hurry to the parsonage."

As they made their way through the meadow, all sense of lightness left her. The glimpses of sunshine, the birdsong, the scent of violets beneath their feet could not break through her leaden mood. She had never been so happy in her life that her father's estate was entailed, and she had nothing more to offer a potential suitor than her share of her mother's five thousand pounds.

Colonel Fitzwilliam gave her a wan smile. "You must have believed Darcy to be quite the blackguard."

"Very near to it." She tried to laugh, but it came out as a whimper.

"I am glad I could disabuse you of that impression. Miss Bennet," he said with a sudden fervour in his voice. "Darcy is not just my cousin. He is one of my closest friends. He is not artful, nor eager to please. It is true that he ought to be more sociable. But he tries with you. More so than I have ever seen him."

A breeze tousled the colonel's hair, and he smoothed it with a gloved hand. "When Darcy is comfortable, as he is amongst family and friends, there is no better company than he. But with strangers—it takes him time to trust. You can understand that, can you not, Miss Bennet? How a man of his means could be a target for the unscrupulous?"

She had not considered that. "I...well, I suppose I can. If his goal is to repel everyone he meets from currying his favour, he has perfected that strategy. Indeed, not one Meryton mama pursued him as a possible match for her daughter."

The colonel let out a great laugh, and some of the heaviness left Lizzy. The more she thought about it, the more brilliant she considered Mr. Darcy's approach, even if it was accidentally so.

But as her thoughts turned back to Mr. Wickham, her initial shock and sorrow were replaced by anger. He had intentionally deceived her, and to what end? She had not fortune enough to tempt him. Why seek her friendship at all?

Had he been toying with her? Or had the move been calculated? Ingratiate himself with her, and gain access to all of Meryton society.

She had let him use her. For all her cleverness, she had been completely duped.

As she and the colonel fell into silence, she lost all sense of her surroundings. She had never felt such a fool. Her only comfort was that her infatuation had not progressed to love. That would have been a grief indeed.

What of the poor young woman he had deceived? Caught up in the rapture of his charms, believing him sincerely attached, only to discover his treachery? How heartsick she must have been! Had her family not rescued her, she would have been lost forever—

Miss Darcy. A wave of nausea washed over her, halting her steps. Wickham *must* have been the scoundrel Darcy had spoken of. An old and trusted family friend, he would have had the wherewithal to persuade the innocent girl of his true devotion.

Marching forward, Lizzy trembled in shock and anger. This same Mr. Wickham had had the temerity to spread lies about Darcy, after such abominable acts toward his sister! The man had no conscience, no shame—

Pain wrenched her ankle and she lurched forward, mind swimming as she struggled to regain her balance. An arm grabbed her, stopping her fall. She clutched the colonel's shoulders, looking up at him as she steadied herself.

"Are you all right?" he asked earnestly.

"I must have tripped on the uneven ground." She let go and gingerly put weight on the stricken leg, but nearly fell back into his arms. "Oh dear," she groaned as she leaned on him, the pain radiating outward from the joint. "I do not think I can walk alone."

Her thoughts had so distracted her, she had not attended where she was putting her feet. Wickham—good heavens! What harm she might have come to at his hand!

Now was not the time to think of that. Hunsford Cottage was still not in sight, and her ankle was utterly useless. She would have to impose on Colonel Fitzwilliam to help her home.

"Here, put your arm around me," he said. "Does that help? We have not much farther to go. Can you make it to the parsonage, or should I walk ahead to get you a conveyance?"

"Oh no, I could not trouble you so. With your kind assistance, I am sure I can hobble along."

"It is no trouble, madam. I shall carry you if need be." His eyes shone. If it were not for the pain, she would have enjoyed his gallantry.

"Thank you, but I can manage."

It was laughable how the two progressed together. Colonel Fitzwilliam was kind and witty and dashing. But she could not help noticing how his jaw was not quite so strong nor his cheekbones so high as his cousin's; how his eyes, though soft and teasing, lacked Darcy's acuteness. He was not quite so tall, nor his shoulders so broad. Colonel Fitzwilliam was a fine man in his own way, but Darcy was the handsomest Lizzy had ever seen.

And now Darcy had been acquitted of the worst of the accusations against him.

The thought struck her in the chest. In the past, it could do her no harm to think of Darcy as handsome, because it was impossible to like such a disagreeable man. But by the colonel's account, he was *not* disagreeable. He was proud, to be sure, and aloof. His manners were not at all endearing. But if his character was everything it ought to be, then perhaps she should give him a chance.

No, that would not do. Not after what he had done to Jane. Although if Lizzy and Darcy became engaged, Jane and Bingley...

She forced the thought out of her mind. She was not interested in Darcy. Was not, could not, must not be.

135

Chapter 9

Lizzy was sitting in the front parlour of the parsonage that afternoon as the sun settled ever closer to the horizon. The décor was the most fashionable in the house, both elegant and cheerful. The room was appointed in the Queen Anne style, the wood a dark cherry, the upholstery a broad gold and green stripe.

With her feet clad in silk slippers laced with ribbon, her injured leg rested on the couch. Her ankle throbbed, but as long as she endeavoured to keep it still, the pain was bearable.

The others from the parsonage had gone to take tea at Rosings, thankfully leaving her to her thoughts. She had so much to tell Charlotte. But she could not bear broaching the subject just yet. To have been so wrong about Wickham! It was humiliating to think how Lizzy had taken such a liking to him without any mutual acquaintances confirming his character.

Caroline Bingley had warned her, and Lizzy had utterly dismissed it. Not that Caroline *knew* Wickham. She had relayed only what she had heard from Darcy: that Wickham had behaved in an infamous manner.

Whatever else Lizzy might say about Caroline, she had put her trust in the right man—and Lizzy in the wrong one. That stung. If she ever saw Caroline again, she would have to apologize for reacting to the woman's kind attentions with disdain.

Fortunately, Lizzy was spared the necessity of dwelling on that thought. The housekeeper's knock provided a welcome interruption from her ruminations.

"Pardon me, ma'am. With all the excitement when you came home with your poor ankle, I neglected to bring you this earlier. My apologies." She offered Lizzy a letter on a silver tray, then curtsied before withdrawing.

Lizzy frowned in confusion. The handwriting on the envelope was Jane's, but the letter itself was flimsy—not like the long missives her sister usually sent. Lizzy's heart pounded as she tore it open. Had something happened? Did some emergency require Lizzy to return home at once?

As she read, Lizzy raised a hand to her heart. The words elicited an entirely different emotion than what she had feared.

Dearest Lizzy,

Please excuse the brevity of this note. The post comes any moment, and I cannot wait another day to tell you. The most wondrous thing has happened—I have seen him!

Your happiest of sisters,

Jane

A laugh escaped Lizzy's throat. She read and reread to ensure she understood the meaning. Tears prickled the corners of her eyes.

She could not doubt which "him" Jane referred to. But had they spoken? Had he renewed his addresses?

Her heart fluttered at the thought. Jane happy! Bingley restored to her! Could it be?

⁓⊗⁓

Darcy watched the clock with consternation. The report of Elizabeth's injury had disconcerted him, especially since it had prevented her from accompanying the Collinses to Rosings. He longed to see her, to ascertain her condition for himself. But his aunt would not forgive him if he departed in the middle of the repast.

"The colonel tells me he discovered some breaks in the hedgerow," Lady Catherine said to Mr. Collins. "I should like to think some animal responsible, rather than poachers."

"Indeed, your ladyship, I shudder to imagine that anyone would dare—"

"You must mention it in your next sermon," her ladyship proclaimed, and the obsequious Mr. Collins was certain to obey. "It is thievery, you know, if anyone should kill an animal on my property."

"Such a heinous act must be roundly condemned! I assure you, your ladyship—"

"Colonel, where did you say the break was?"

"On the western side, near to where Miss Bennet takes her walks."

Just the mention of her name sent Darcy into a spiral of worried impatience. Was his dearest love in pain? Did the servants attend to her? He pictured her alone and incapacitated, and thought himself a fool for staying put.

"Oh, Miss Bennet, the poor girl," Lady Catherine said. "Mrs. Collins, I must insist on sending the carriage to fetch her here. She cannot be happy suffering an injury alone."

"My dear aunt," Darcy said, "surely she is more comfortable nursing her injury at home, rather than travelling about the countryside, where every bump of the road would rattle her."

"She will not be travelling about. My barouche is quite comfortable. Certainly she can be better accommodated here for the afternoon, rather than at the cottage. I am quite worried for her health."

"Indeed, ma'am, in that case, I shall be happy to call on her to ensure that she is well." And before anyone could protest, Darcy departed with a bow.

He did not know what he was about. But once outside, he was certain he could bear this state of uncertainty no longer. It was torment that Elizabeth was in pain, and he could not be by her side every moment. He wanted to care for her, to make sure her needs were met.

He wanted her as his wife.

It was a fool's errand. The last time he had seen her, she had been furious with him. She knew not that he had effected a reconciliation between Bingley and her sister. And he was determined that she should *not* know.

Somehow, he would win her heart. If it took everything he had, he would make her his.

⁓♇⁓

At the desk in the front parlour, Lizzy sat composing a letter to Jane. She had already restarted twice. Her happiness regarding Bingley was easy to express—but her thoughts about Wickham were so jumbled she could hardly put them into words.

She was angry at him, yes, for deceiving her. At the same time, she was even more angry at herself. She had never felt such a fool in her life.

How vexing it was, that a man should not be everything he appeared! That Wickham should be so worthless, and Darcy of more merit than she had estimated! She had liked it better when she thought Darcy's good opinion not worth having.

If he was not a dishonourable man, then his attentions toward her held more value. A man of his station, with such...physical enticements, would likely never be in her power again. As much as she disliked him, could she really afford to dismiss him?

She still blamed Darcy for separating Bingley from Jane—but if they were reunited, it hardly signified. If Charlotte could make herself happy with Mr. Collins, ought Lizzy not to at least consider whether she could be happy with Darcy?

It was too much. Thinking about marrying him overwhelmed her. The first step was to discover whether she could like him.

In truth, she had never given him a chance. His insult on the night they met had so firmly fixed his character in her mind that she never looked for redeeming qualities.

Colonel Fitzwilliam—whom she liked so well—considered Darcy the best of men. Might Darcy not grow in her estimation upon greater acquaintance? She owed it to him—and for that matter, to herself and her family—to find out.

She set the letter aside, her mind too full to finish it coherently. She hobbled to the sofa and sat, her ankle still throbbing. The book she picked up could not hold her attention. She was staring out the side window, puzzling over her predicament, when the maid let in none other than the man who most vexingly occupied her thoughts.

Mr. Darcy bowed, and she nodded, forgoing to stand. She knew not what to make of his sudden appearance. Calling on her, when he knew her to be home alone but for the servants?

His eyes were bright, more intensely so than she had ever seen them, and his mouth grave. But the mask broke for a moment, the corners of his lips threatening to curve upward, before he schooled them again.

"Miss Bennet, I was troubled to hear of your injury. How is your ankle? I hope it does not cause you great pain."

She took a deep breath to quiet her agitation. Though trembling inside, she endeavoured to show a serene expression. "Not as much as it might. It is an inconvenience, but I expect it will be perfectly healed in a few days." She motioned for him to sit.

He chose the chair closest to her. "I am glad to hear it."

She thought about the last time she had seen him, and all that had transpired since then. With Jane's note foremost in her mind, she said, "I understand you were recently in town."

He stiffened. "Yes. I...received a letter. From a man. I had to take care of the business immediately."

She bit back the urge to laugh. "A letter. From a man."

"Yes," he said perfunctorily.

The reticence that had so annoyed her in Hertfordshire was back in full force. She would not be put off—the matter was too important. "Did you by chance see Mr. Bingley whilst you were there?"

He fell silent, not meeting her eyes. "Briefly."

Her lashes fluttered. "And how did you find him?"

"Quite well, I thank you." He said no more.

Impossible man! And yet, she suspected Darcy was the one deserving of thanks. He had said he intended to remedy the situation. Was that why he had gone into town so abruptly?

Or was her imagination running away with her?

She would not let that happen again. She could not jump to whatever conclusion most pleased her vanity. The facts were these: Mr. Darcy said he would remedy the situation. He went to London and briefly met with Bingley. Bingley saw Jane, and now Jane was happy again. Those events might be unconnected.

She shook her head. Of *course* they were connected. But she would let him have his charade.

If he had precipitated a reconciliation between Jane and Bingley, he obviously had no wish to speak of it. One way or another, Lizzy would find out. If Jane did not know the truth, Bingley surely did, and he lacked his friend's reserve.

Was this the sort of man Darcy was? One who would change all his plans at a moment's notice out of concern for a friend's happiness? Who would ride all the way to London when a letter would have sufficed? And would then refuse to take credit for his actions?

A thrill rose in her chest. She could fall in love with a man like that. Even now she felt it, a yearning building inside her, a sweetness toward him that could quickly grow to more. But she must not be hasty. No, she would wait until she had the truth of it all—until there could be no doubt.

The mantle clock struck the half-hour. She took a deep breath to slow the pounding of her heart. "I did not expect to see you. Your aunt must be jealous of your company, after your absence."

He gave Lizzy a half-smile. "My aunt threatened to send a conveyance to whisk you off to Rosings. She cannot fathom that under the circumstances you might prefer to spend the afternoon here alone. I hope you will pardon my interrupting your solitude. It was the only way I could see to make her easy about your condition."

She smoothed her fingers over the book in her lap. "I feel safe in saying you are always welcome here, Mr. Darcy." She turned her gaze from him. The words evoked an unexpected emotion in her, a realization that his presence was not only welcome but devoutly desired. How could her heart betray her thus? She gave it another stern warning to be circumspect.

"Have you forgiven me, then?" He spoke warmly, his eyes gazing at her intensely. "I fear I am a great blockhead."

She swallowed. So many thoughts occupied her mind, she could hardly decide which to speak first. "I shall forgive you, if you will forgive me."

He blinked, clearly puzzled by her words.

She set the book on the end table. "It seems I made a great error in judgment toward you regarding Mr. Wickham."

Darcy rose and turned from her. The fluttering in her heart increased. His profile accentuated his strong jaw and chin.

She hated to cause him pain, but she owed him the truth. He had a right to know that her animosity toward him was not entirely his fault. "Colonel Fitzwilliam told me that Mr. Wickham's account of your dealings with him have not been entirely truthful. I ought not to have believed the unkind things Wickham said without hearing your side of the story."

Darcy reddened. "Wickham disparages me to the world, does he? Well, I have no doubt his true nature will be revealed to the good people of Meryton in time. It is a wonder he has managed to stay out of debtor's prison."

"And I cannot help wondering..." But she thought better of mentioning Georgiana's name in this context. It could only increase his pain. "Never mind. I ought not speak of it."

"You can always speak honestly to me, madam."

She met his eyes. Again she had the feeling that he was seeing her intimately, as if she were wearing only her shift. This time, she felt no embarrassment. "You will forgive me, then. I shall never mention it to another soul, I assure you. But after what the colonel described of Wickham's behaviour, and what you so lately told me about your sister..."

His jaw worked. He walked to the window, his back to her.

"Pardon me," she said. "I have distressed you."

"No, I encouraged you to speak freely." He shook his head. "I am utterly ashamed. I should have taken better care of her. My sister is everything to me."

"Your affection does you credit, sir. I fear Mr. Wickham is a more dastardly man than I could have imagined—and I allowed myself to be used by him. I encouraged my family to believe his lies. If either of us ought to be ashamed, it is I."

Darcy came to her side. Pulling up a chair, he grasped her hand. The feel of his skin on hers was smooth and warm. With neither of them wearing gloves, she ought not to allow his touch. But he wore a stricken expression, his eyes so earnest she could not rebuke him.

"Do not torment yourself," Darcy said. "Wickham is a master of deception. It is how he survives. He preys on the goodwill of others. If the world knew the truth of him, he would be destitute."

She swallowed, unable to deny the magnetic pull between them. "I am sorry indeed, sir, that your past connection to him has brought such pain to your family."

"I begin to wonder if I shall ever be rid of him. He ingratiates himself to others, and portrays me as a blackguard."

"My apologies. I did not mean to trouble you. I shall not mention his name to you again."

Darcy stared straight ahead. "I have not his talent for making myself well-liked upon passing acquaintance."

A pang shot through Lizzy's heart. Had her careless words struck more deeply than she had imagined? The ability to fawn over young ladies at a dance was nothing compared to true strength of character.

"I have observed," she said, "that you are admired amongst those who know you best. Being able to make friends is less illustrative of a man's nature than being able to keep them."

"And what of you?" The passion in his voice was so powerful, his words were more command than question. "Do you think you could like me, upon knowing me better?"

Lizzy drew in a deep breath. Her heart pounded. She knew not how to answer. "That is a direct question, sir."

"It is. One I have no right to ask—yet I must know. You are not the sort of woman to trifle with me. Could you ever esteem me, or has my past behaviour turned you irreparably against me?"

Lizzy's mind was so full, she could scarcely think, much less speak. She had been wrestling with the same question on her own and had come to no conclusion. Or, rather, the conclusion she had reached was based more on the wish of her heart than on concrete facts she knew to be true.

She spoke carefully. "You once described yourself as having a resentful disposition. It is not a quality I share. I am not one to hold a grudge. I *prefer* friends who are imperfect—for otherwise I have no cause to tease them."

Darcy smiled, and it was a beauteous thing to be hold. He looked as carefree as a boy. Good heavens, what a burden it must be, to always present himself in a serious manner! She felt as though she were glimpsing the true Darcy for the first time, one unfettered by social constraints.

Her heart filled. The connection she felt to him was unlike anything she had experienced before. *This* was the man she wanted to know—the man behind the mask. The one who loved his sister and tortured himself over the fate that had nearly befallen her. The one whom Colonel Fitzwilliam praised to the high heavens. The one whom Bingley trusted so completely that he had left the woman he loved.

Had Darcy spoken the truth? Had he warned Bingley away from Jane because he truly believed she did not love him? Would not Lizzy have done the same, if she believed Bingley had not truly loved Jane?

The thought stunned her. Why had she not considered this before? Not once had she given Darcy the benefit of the doubt, but had viewed him in the worst possible light from the night they met.

For all the world, she would not wish Jane to marry except for the deepest, most enduring love. If Lizzy had believed Bingley indifferent, she would have admonished Jane to be careful, to be *certain* before giving herself to one who might not share her feelings.

Lizzy would have been more circumspect, of course. She would not have spoken with Darcy's brashness and self-confidence. But the content would have been much the same.

Oh, what torment this was, to know so little about a man who had all but professed his love for her! She had been deceived by Wickham—how could she be sure Darcy was trustworthy, apart from the reassurance of one of his closest relations?

She would have to be much more careful than she had been in the past. Knowing that only her poverty had kept Wickham from preying on her, destroying her peace of mind forever, was sobering. She would banish all romantic notions from her head, and think like Charlotte.

Darcy shifted in his chair, drawing her from her reverie. A quiet joy resided in his gaze. She felt it like a caress.

He rose. "I cannot express how gratifying your words are to me." He looked as if he was about to say more, but then crossed to the centre of the room.

Lizzy struggled to recall what she had said, that he had found so encouraging. Something to the effect that she forgave him? Yes, that must have been it.

Her thoughts were so jumbled, she barely noticed him pacing about the room. After a moment, he leaned against the mantle-piece, then paced again. Finally, he turned to Lizzy, his expression imploring.

"In vain I have struggled. It will not do. My feelings will not be repressed. You must allow me to tell you how ardently I admire and love you."

"Mr. Darcy!" she cried in disbelief, jumping to her feet. Pain immediately radiated from her ankle. She gasped and collapsed back onto the couch.

"Miss Bennet!" He rushed to her side, sitting next to her, grasping her hand again. "Are you well? Shall I fetch the maid?"

She exhaled a few times, allowing the pain to settle. What a stupid thing to do! Still, she did not believe she had damaged the ankle further. "I am fine, I think. In need of rest, nothing more."

"Of course. It was selfish of me to come here. I should not have excited you."

The expression on his face was so miserable, she forced herself to suppress the laugh that threatened to erupt from her chest. The man was berating himself for *telling her he loved her.*

How could she ever have thought him proud?

True, his bearing was regal, and the stiff angle of his cravat gave him a haughty look. He did not easily warm to strangers. He came from an aristocratic family, and possessed a superior mind.

Yet underneath that exterior was a man who loved his friends intensely, who desired to improve himself for her sake, and who—perhaps—had gone to Bingley and confessed that he was wrong.

All the humility he possessed, he kept out of sight.

Her heart ached at the dejection in his posture. She could not help leaning forward and planting a quick kiss on his cheek. "I am glad you came. I appreciate your kindness."

There was a slight trembling at his lips a moment as he sat in silence before saying, "I shall go at once and report to Lady Catherine that you are too ill to be disturbed." Yet he did not stir. He continued to hold her hand.

Lizzy found that she did not want him to go, nor to release her hand. No; rather, she was overwhelmed with the desire to feel her lips against his cheek again.

His gaze burned into her, and she was certain he would kiss her if she did not prevent it. She could not allow the situation to progress further. If he proposed, she was unsure what answer she would give.

She did not know him well enough to love him. His character was still a puzzle. The yearnings she felt had no bearing on it.

She withdrew her hand. "Mr. Darcy—"

"Yes, of course, forgive me. I have overstayed my welcome, and my aunt will wonder what became of me. I bid you good day." He rose and with a bow, he departed.

Lizzy watched after him for a long while. Something had shifted inside her, but she could not call it love. She had awoken that morning believing him the most disagreeable of men. She had been blind, but rushing headlong into the opposite opinion would be just as foolish.

In her own home, she had evidence daily of how a lack of marital felicity affected a family. A kernel of affection might still exist between her parents, but there was little kindness and no respect. She did not want to live out her days in the home of a man she barely tolerated, no matter how large and sumptuous that home might be.

She could not marry him until she was certain she could love him.

Chapter 10

Lizzy kept to her room the next day, the stairs an impediment. Walking up them with the aid of Mr. Collins and a manservant was a humiliation she did not care to repeat.

Charlotte came to her mid-morning and sat on the edge of the bed. "How are you feeling?"

"A great fool, and as useless as can be."

"You are injured. You must not be hard on yourself."

Lizzy shook her head. She had revealed none of the recent news to Charlotte, and it was time she did so. "Indeed I must, for I have been entirely deceived. You warned me to pay less regard to Mr. Wickham, and more to Mr. Darcy. I wish I had listened."

Charlotte straightened, her brows drawing together. "Has there been word from Meryton of Mr. Wickham?"

"Not from Meryton. From Colonel Fitzwilliam. It turns out Mr. Wickham could not have acceded to the living intended for him, for he refused to take orders."

Charlotte chuckled. "I cannot say that surprises me. He has nothing of the clergyman about him."

"It gets worse," Lizzy warned. "Mr. Darcy instead gave him a lump sum payment—which Wickham apparently squandered. Now that he is refused another penny, he maligns poor Mr. Darcy to anyone who will listen."

"Poor Mr. Darcy?" Charlotte asked with a coy smile.

Lizzy's cheeks heated. "You know what I mean."

"Yes, I believe I do."

Lizzy closed her eyes and shook her head. Her heart ached. She could not but grieve the loss of her favourite, the loss of the man she had *believed* Wickham to be. What a blow to her pride! The compliment he had paid her by singling her out was now worthless.

But it had been replaced by something better—the admiration of a man of intelligence and good breeding, one who was cultured and possessed the appearance of good character. Still, she did not *know* him.

"Oh Charlotte, I have never been more miserable."

Her friend grasped Lizzy's hands, lips parting as if in surprise. "But you said yourself, there was no understanding between you and Mr. Wickham."

"Indeed there was not. I never felt more than a passing infatuation."

"Then what troubles you? Surely a sprained ankle is not to blame."

Lizzy swallowed to loosen the emotion thickening her throat. "Mr. Darcy confessed his love last night."

Charlotte's eyelids fluttered, but she remained silent.

Lizzy pushed on. "I think he intended to propose. But his words startled me so that I jumped to my feet, forgetting about my ankle. That rather destroyed the mood, I am afraid."

"Dearest Eliza, that's wonderful!" Charlotte's bright expression quickly darkened. She rose and paced—well, to the degree that one could in such a small room.

"Yet you said you were miserable," Charlotte continued. "You cannot mean to refuse him!"

"Two days ago, I thought him insufferable. Now...I dare not say no, yet I cannot say yes."

Charlotte sat on the bed again, staring into her lap. She said in a small voice absent of emotion, "It is a woman's prerogative to change her mind."

Lizzy let out a huff of air. "Charlotte, you cannot...you would not...suggest that I accept the proposal, without committing in my heart to marry him!"

"Eliza, be realistic. If he is a man of honour, he will quickly follow up his confession of love with a proposal. If he does not,

I shall suspect him of trifling with you. You had better think about what answer you will give."

"But I barely know him!"

"Then I suggest you get to know him better, and quickly."

Lizzy's eyes grew hot. She had never imagined she would find herself in such a predicament. Nor could she see a way out.

Frustrated tears rolled down her cheeks. "How can I get to know him better, when I cannot get out of bed?"

Her friend patted her hand comfortingly, then gave her a sly smile.

"Charlotte!"

"No, no, you are quite right. Let me think a moment. There is a day bed in the small parlour. We can air out the room, put on some fresh linens, light a fire to chase away the damp. You can set up court there. And I shall make sure you are never alone with Mr. Darcy long enough for him to propose."

"Oh, that sounds perfect! You truly are my dearest friend. What would I do without you?"

⁓⁂⁓

By mid-afternoon, Lizzy was sitting comfortably in the small parlour. It had a lovely south-facing view across the garden to Rosings Park. Unfortunately the day was cloudy, and a mist settled over the landscape.

Charlotte had gone to visit a parishioner who had fallen ill, so Maria kept Lizzy company, chatting in her cheerful manner. Lizzy felt some alarm when Maria once again broached the subject of Colonel Fitzwilliam.

"When he first came to Hunsford," Maria said, "I thought he was rather plain. But now I think him the most dashing gentleman I ever met. He must look grand in his regimentals. Nothing can match a man in a red coat."

"Dashing indeed, and the son of an earl," Lizzy warned. "Were we not situated so close to Rosings, we could not hope to have a man of his station call on us so frequently."

"He is here nearly every day!"

"Yes, he pays us a great compliment in finding that the company here adds variety to that of Rosings."

Lizzy hoped her words would dampen some of Maria's enthusiasm, but the girl did not seem to catch the irony. Nor did the sound of hoof beats a few minutes later moderate her excitement.

The housekeeper knocked and showed the man himself into the room. Colonel Fitzwilliam did indeed look dashing in a red waistcoat, though his jacket was merely grey. His cousin accompanied him.

A thrill rose in Lizzy's stomach at the sight of Darcy. She berated herself for allowing him to affect her. No matter that the last time she had seen him, he had professed his love.

The advantages of his person sent a flush through her—now more than ever, since she no longer had reason to think him a scoundrel. Yet she was determined to keep her wits about her.

"You will pardon me for not rising," she said to the gentlemen, and gestured for them to take a seat. Darcy occupied the chair beside her, and the colonel sat next to Maria.

"You seem well accommodated here." Darcy looked about the room. "Mrs. Collins has taken care to ensure your comfort."

Charlotte had indeed been solicitous of her friend's needs. The daybed was topped with a cheerful wedding-ring quilt and an assortment of white throw pillows. The fireplace across the room blazed bright, and a vase of red-and-yellow-striped Rembrandt tulips sat atop the mantelpiece.

"She has been most attentive, and now I can avoid the stairs."

"I had hoped your pain would have subsided ere now. I am sorry it still troubles you."

She gave him a courteous smile. "Thank you. I expect it will be a few days before I can walk comfortably again. But at least here, I am no bother."

"I doubt anyone in this house would consider you a bother." He looked over at the colonel, then back to her again. "My cousin and I included."

Her cheeks warmed. "Your compliments are most kind."

It was ludicrous, how they were talking about everything except what mattered. He had confessed his love. What were either of them to do about that? A gentlemen in such circumstances ought to make an offer immediately. Yet she must prevent it for as long as possible.

The prospect of committing to marry him filled her with dread. In society's view, she would be lucky to have him. But what sort of husband would he be?

Though his manner was stiff, a deep affection stirred beneath that outer layer. She had glimpsed intense feeling toward herself, his sister, the colonel—even Mr. Bingley. But there was much of him she could *not* see.

Was Charlotte right? Was it impossible to truly know the person you were to marry until the vows had been taken? Was everything a mask until that point?

"I know little of your parents, sir," she said, hoping the subject might give her a hint of what his own bride could expect. "It must be difficult for your sister, growing up without them."

"It is indeed. She was but six years old when my mother died, and eleven when we lost my father." His lips tightened. "He was the best of men, Miss Bennet. Generous to all he knew, even those who did not deserve it." His throat worked, and Lizzy wondered if he was thinking of Wickham.

Darcy continued, "He and my mother both took an interest in improving the welfare of our servants and tenants, something I have tried to continue. My mother said that people are more productive when they are happy, so kindness is just good business."

His fond smile faded, and for a moment, the sadness in his eyes stole Lizzy's breath. The man had lost both his parents by the age of twenty-three and taken on the responsibility of caring for a much-younger sister. He loved his family above everything. Of that much she was certain.

She pictured him, just out of Cambridge—when many of his friends and peers would have been living carefree, sometimes dissolute lives—and he, instead, was running a great estate and seeing to his sister's education. How much that said about him!

Yet he seemed to feel no resentment about it. He cherished his responsibilities. He spoke with affection about Miss Darcy, and pride about Pemberley.

"I wish I could have known your parents," she said in a soft voice, an ache settling in her chest. "I am sure I would have admired them, if they were anything like you."

Something flickered in his eyes, and the line of his mouth softened.

If they had been natives of some far-distant land, freed from the strictures of English society, he would surely have kissed her in that moment. But they were not. Gentility had its demands. His mask quickly went back on.

No wonder two people could not know one another before marriage! They had to keep all their truest feelings hidden. Never before had she hated with such ferocity the restrictions that kept her from seeing into the heart of this most fascinating man.

She could not even suggest a quick turn in the garden so they could have a private conversation, because she could not walk. She cursed the stars that had put her into this predicament.

More than that, she cursed herself. She had known Darcy for months. Had stayed in the same house with him for three days last autumn during her sister's illness, and merely tolerated him. Why had she not sought him out—attempted to *know* him, before deciding she could feel no regard for him?

The answer brought heat to her cheeks. She thought he had felt no regard for *her*. Instead, all the time, he had been falling in love with her.

Now, she had but a few days to catch up, before honour would demand he make an offer. She could not put him off long.

She pictured herself as mistress of Pemberley, a place she had yet to see, yet felt equal to it. The housekeeper at Longbourn had been consulting her and Jane for years, to counter her mother's idiosyncrasies—like her refusal to understand that the cost of sugar in 1812 might differ from what it had been in 1792.

Moreover, Darcy was the sort of man she could turn to for advice in running the household. She imagined him as neither resenting her questions nor trying to dictate to her. Rather, he would be kind and attentive, a true partner.

Was she mad to picture him in that way? Was this purely the product of her own wishful presumptions? In the past few days, she had lost all confidence in her ability to judge a man's character.

Tears stung her eyes and she turned away. Darcy grasped her hand. He ought not, but she did not pull away.

"Dearest Miss Bennet, I beg you, what is disturbing you? I hope I have done nothing to—"

"Mr. Darcy, you are unutterably kind. The events of the past few days have overwhelmed me. I am ashamed to say I no longer trust myself. I have shown abominable judgment regarding yourself and...our mutual acquaintance, whose name I have promised never to mention to you."

"You were a victim. You are not to blame."

She shook her head. "I do not deserve your sympathy nor good opinion."

"On the contrary. I consider myself most fortunate that you are willing to look past my transgressions, and your own misapprehension, to give me a second chance. I want only to prove that I can be a man you esteem."

Elizabeth looked down at his hand, which still held hers. What was the rule when a gentleman had confessed his love but had not yet proposed? Might she admit his advances?

He settled the problem by letting go of her hand. "My apologies."

She gazed softly into his eyes. "You cannot doubt that if I objected, I would have made my feelings known."

"You have never been shy about expressing your opinion, that is true." The corner of his mouth turned up.

Even that bit of a smile turned her insides molten. Withholding something so delicious made it even more desirable. That hint of gaiety transformed his face. She could imagine the sweet looks he would give her when they—

No, she must not indulge in such thoughts until she and Darcy were promised to one another—until they were wed. She knew, rather than felt, that she desired him. She had managed thus far to keep her longings at bay. But the more she knew him, the more her control thinned.

Maria interrupted Lizzy's thoughts, her laughter ringing like silvery bells. Maria was a sweet, pretty girl who would make the right man a lovely wife. But that man was not Colonel Fitzwilliam.

Darcy must have seen the frown that crossed Lizzy's face, for he looked to the other couple a moment before saying to her, "You still fear for the welfare of the young lady?"

"Unfortunately, I do."

He nodded and said in a louder voice, "It would appear, Colonel, that it is raining in earnest. We may have to impose on our fair companions longer than expected. Perhaps a game of whist?"

"Splendid," the colonel replied.

"Miss Lucas," Darcy said, "I am afraid I have neglected you. Would you do me the honour of playing as my partner?"

Her eyelashes fluttered, and a blush rose in her cheek. "The honour is mine, sir."

A table was moved over, and a deck of cards fetched. They had not been playing long when Maria set down the ace of diamonds. The gentlemen followed suit, but Lizzy played the two of hearts. Maria went to claim the trick until Darcy reminded her, "Hearts trump diamonds."

The irony of the words struck Lizzy. They seemed like a window into his soul. She grinned at him. "Is that so, sir?"

His lips quirked up, and he returned in kind, "I am persuaded of it. The colonel might not agree, however."

"What say you, Colonel?" Lizzy asked. "Do you prefer diamonds to hearts? Or perhaps you simply have had more experience with diamonds."

"I confess that my experience with hearts is quite limited," the colonel said amiably.

"He prefers hearts when they are accompanied by diamonds," Darcy added.

Lizzy laughed, then countered, "I would rather guess that is a universal sentiment. The challenge comes when one must choose between them."

Maria gave them all a wondering look. "Which are trumps again? Did Eliza win the trick?"

"I beg your pardon," Darcy said. "The trick goes to Miss Bennet. Hearts are still trumps."

Maria nodded sadly. "I must be very dull that I cannot understand wit."

"You are not dull at all." Lizzy's chest tightened. She should not have made the joke in front of Maria. "I was using hearts as a metaphor for love, and diamonds as a metaphor for wealth."

Maria smiled. "Of course! Then I must agree, hearts trump diamonds. Though poor Charlotte, I do not think she was dealt any hearts. Instead, she plays spades. She encourages her husband to spend all his leisure time in the garden."

Lizzy struggled to subdue a laugh. "Oh, Maria, I never again want to hear you say you do not understand wit."

Once the rain cleared, the gentlemen prepared for their departure. Darcy sat next to Lizzy and said, "I hate to leave. You will always be my queen of hearts."

She gave him an arch look. "And you are my king of clubs."

He raised his brow, eyeing her cautiously. "How so?"

"I feel battered. It is not your fault. I think I must have misunderstood nearly every interaction between us. Whilst I was staying at Netherfield, sometimes I would see you looking at me. I thought you were finding fault."

He gave her an indulgent smile. "Perhaps I was trying to, and all I could see was your perfection."

"I am far from perfect."

"You are perfect to me."

She shook her head. Before she could speak, she had to swallow the knot in her throat. "Even after I believed the most dastardly lies about you?"

The muscles in his jaw worked. "Wickham sought you out. Ingratiated himself. Won your trust. I did none of those things. I made no effort to court your friendship the entire time I was in Hertfordshire. Of course you believed him. I gave you no reason to think myself anything other than what he portrayed me to be."

Her stomach dropped. The humility of his words astonished her. "Still, I should not have allowed myself to be misled."

"Perhaps, but then, I allowed it with my silence. I did not warn you against him. It is not my wish to ruin his life—to render him unemployable. The military could make him a better man. Yet I would not wish another young lady to suffer at his hand."

"Come, Darcy," the colonel said, "we had better go. My aunt will be cross that we have stayed away so long."

"We could not help the rain."

"She will say we should not have gone out when rain threatened."

Darcy nodded. He bowed to Lizzy. "May we call on you again tomorrow?"

"I shall be desolate if you do not."

A short time after the gentlemen departed, Charlotte returned home, damp but not bedraggled. She joined the ladies in the small parlour, warming by the fire.

Lizzy asked, "How is Mrs. Frasier?"

Charlotte shook her head. "Her daughter had been applying the poultices all wrong. I think I have set them straight, now."

"The parishioners are very lucky to have you."

Charlotte gave a soft smile. "I enjoy being of service. Now tell me, what did I miss? I believe I saw the gentlemen from Rosings riding away in the distance, as I approached."

"Oh, Charlotte, Colonel Fitzwilliam was so attentive!" Maria cried. "It was kind of Lizzy to distract Mr. Darcy so the colonel could talk to me alone."

Lizzy widened her eyes as she looked at Charlotte. Her friend took the hint.

"Maria, dearest," Charlotte said. "The colonel is far too grand for you to aspire to. I hope you will not break your heart over the man."

"I could break my heart over worse."

Charlotte looked at Lizzy, who shrugged. Maria had the right of it. All that remained was for the colonel to write her some terrible love poetry, and Maria would have a pretty story to tell indeed.

Chapter 11

The following day the sky cleared. Whilst Charlotte and Maria were in the garden that afternoon picking vegetables, Lizzy read quietly in the small parlour. She had not been alone long when Colonel Fitzwilliam and Mr. Darcy were shown in.

"My dear Miss Bennet," the colonel said, "how is your ankle today? I hope it is mending."

"It is no worse, at least, I thank you."

"You look well," Darcy said. "Has the apothecary sent something for the pain?"

"He stopped by with Lady Catherine's compliments. That was kind of her."

"My aunt takes great pleasure in being of use," the colonel said with a grin.

Lizzy motioned for them to sit, and they pulled up two wooden chairs. It seemed ridiculous for two strapping men to be seated in such a fashion, but it was the best she could offer

169

them. "Her ladyship seems to take great pleasure in your visit," Lizzy said to them.

"When we were boys," the colonel replied, "we spent a month here every summer. Although a month seemed like a year then, eh, Darcy?"

"We used to run through the meadows for hours, playing pirate or soldier..."

"And now I play soldier for real," the colonel said, a sad look in his eye.

"Will you be called to the continent, do you think?" Lizzy asked.

"It is only a matter of time. A man like Bonaparte will not stop until someone stops him."

A tortured expression crossed Darcy's face. "It is too beautiful a day for melancholy subjects." The forced lightness in his tone seemed to belie much deeper feelings.

"Quite right," the colonel said cheerfully. "Have you been outside today, Miss Bennet?"

"I could not possibly."

"Nonsense," Darcy declared, and before she even knew what was happening, he had scooped her up into his arms. Impulsively, she wrapped her arms around his neck, holding on for safety as he carried her through the cottage and out to the garden.

Lizzy had not been carried by a man since she was a child. As surprised as she was, she had to admit, it was exhilarating. Accustomed to the drawing room Darcy, she had not given much thought to how strong he was, showing no sign of exertion. After only a few moments, she felt utterly secure in his arms.

She could not be unaware of his masculine, woodsy scent, and it stirred something deep inside her. The womanly feelings were nothing like the infatuation of a schoolgirl. Yes, her heart fluttered with attraction, but she was drawn to him on a more profound level.

It was not love. Yet she could not deny that she would find pleasure in being his wife, in the intimacy a husband and wife shared. His nearness, the warmth of him, the sound of his breath—they all made it difficult to think of anything else. He intoxicated her.

"Good heavens!" Charlotte called when she saw them, calling Lizzy back from her musings. Lizzy understood the impropriety of the situation. Somehow, she could not find it in herself to rebuke him.

Gently, Darcy set her on a bench in the shade. He sat beside her, eyes gleaming. Then a serious expression fell over his face. His frown looked uncertain.

"That was most gallant of you, Mr. Darcy," she said to set him at ease. "Thank you. You were right—it is a beautiful day. I would have hated to have missed it."

He beamed like a schoolboy praised by his master.

Why, the man was utterly besotted! How had she missed that before? The idea of his disdain had grown so fixed in her mind that she had ignored every sign to the contrary.

"Miss Bennet, if I might be so bold— "

"You and Colonel Fitzwilliam both grew up in Derbyshire, I think?" It was not a very clever question, but it was the first thing she could think of to silence him from whatever else he was planning to say.

"Yes, we were nearly inseparable. Our fathers' estates were close to one another."

"He thinks highly of you."

He grinned wryly. "And you think highly of him."

She shrugged. "Perhaps I should not. I have recently learned that my first impressions are not to be trusted."

He took her hand, pressing it between both of his. "I hope you think more highly of me now than you did at first."

She arched her brows. "Given my original impression, you could hardly have sunk in my view."

He blinked. Then, his lips tightened into a grim line. "I see."

"Mr. Darcy, this is a poor start indeed. I tease you, and you take my words to heart."

"There is always truth in your teasing."

She looked up at him, captivated by that flash of vulnerability. "In this case, I am laughing as much at myself as at you. I was determined to dislike you, and self-satisfied at every perceived fault. Everything you did, I cast in the most unflattering light. It was horribly unfair and unkind of me. I am properly ashamed. It is now evident to me that you are a good man."

He squeezed her hand, looking at her with eyes full of hope and pain.

"I am not normally so petty," she said. "For the first time in my life, I met a man truly worth impressing, and I fell short. It was a blow indeed."

"But you have done more than impress me. You have my heart. I promise you, Elizabeth—"

She pulled her hand away, her whole body vibrating. She wanted his promises, his love. She could admit that much to herself. Yet the prospect of a sudden engagement overwhelmed her.

"I have stepped too far again," he said. "My apologies."

"Your words are not unwelcome. I find that...I am not yet ready to hear them. Can you give me time, Mr. Darcy?"

"Of course. I can only spend another fortnight at Rosings—"

"That will be enough."

She hated to put him off. She craved his company above anything. It was madness, and it was happening far too quickly. But she wished to know everything about Fitzwilliam Darcy, and whether it was safe to give him her heart.

Darcy hardly knew what had possessed him, carrying Elizabeth into the garden that way. He only knew that the sight of her in that stuffy room, when the day was so fine, was too much for him. She ought to be in the sunshine. Always.

When he got into bed that night, he could not forget the feel of her in his arms, the sweet scent of violets that had enveloped her. She inhabited every corner of his fevered brain—Elizabeth, *his* Elizabeth, as he had begun thinking of her. He rose, lit a candle, and took out a sheet of paper.

He wrote with no intention of giving her the letter, but only of pouring out his sentiments so he could be still and finally sleep. The words flowed from him without censor, expressing the true nature of his heart.

My dear Miss Bennet,

My every thought is of you. Your beauty in simple muslin surpasses that of the most fashionable lady in a sumptuous gown from the continent. The smiles you gave me today were as honey, your kind looks a tender balm.

I shall not be precipitous, since you have warned me against it, but the words of love on my lips ache to be spoken. When I think of how much time I wasted at Netherfield, when I should have been courting you properly! I was determined not to let a sly girl from a country town change me. Determined to go on with my life without you. But when I got to London and found how insipid the ladies had become, how they all paled next to you, I knew I was lost.

I let the difference in our situations persuade me that we were incompatible. Now I see that your lively mind is the perfect antidote to my serious nature. When I feel sullen, I need only think of you, and the world becomes a brilliant place. Your wit and intelligence hold me in your thrall.

Dearest, most beautiful Elizabeth! I long for you every moment we are apart. Over these past weeks, you have become as necessary to me as breath. I cannot sleep for thinking of you, hoping for the day when you say you shall be mine. I imagine you at Pemberley, managing the household in your kind way, acting as a friend and teacher to my sister Georgiana. She would benefit greatly from your guidance. She is a good girl, but too romantic and too easily influenced by others. With your sense and compassion, you would be the perfect companion for her.

But of course, I am running away with myself. You have not said you will be mine. I do hope that I can give you a happy life. I may be paltry company, compared to some you have known. But no man could respect or love you more. I daresay I shall become a better conversationalist once you know my character, and I am no longer under your scrutiny as you try to puzzle me out. I confess that your wit sometimes terrifies me, but it is a feeling I shall never tire of.

I fear this is a poor love letter, as dull and trite as any ever written. Mere words cannot capture what is in my heart. I hope ardently for the day when I might show you the depth of my devotion in a way words cannot. I love you, dearest Elizabeth, and I long to make you mine. You are the joy of my days, a beacon through my darkest night, my every thought of the future.

I am your humble servant to command at will.

Most sincerely and devotedly yours,

Fitzwilliam Darcy

Finding his signet ring, he took out a stick of wax in red vermillion. He folded and sealed the letter, certain no one had ever written a worse one. Perhaps it would be better to toss it into the fire. Although it might be amusing to look back on it one day when—if—he and Elizabeth were married. At any rate, he was tired. He would decide on the morrow.

"This came for you from Rosings, ma'am," the housekeeper said, stepping into the small parlour early the next morning and handing Lizzy a letter. Lizzy expressed her thanks, then squinted and broke the seal as the woman curtsied and withdrew.

Lizzy first checked the signature and wondered at Darcy's forwardness. When she perused the opening, she gasped. The more she read, the more astonished she became. He was normally so restrained, she would not have imagined he could express his feelings in such passionate terms.

She read a second time to ensure she had properly comprehended. There was no mistaking the meaning. He was declaring his intentions incontrovertibly.

Yet it was clear he had not done so with forethought. The expression was frenzied, not Darcy's usually deliberate words. Had he overindulged in his evening brandy? Could she lay stock in his declarations?

From her seat on the daybed, she looked out the window at the birds flitting through the cherry trees, their blossoms a haze of pink. How soon could she expect him to call? When he did, could she trust her impulses toward him?

Her feelings were changing rapidly. She felt comfortable with him, happy in his presence. She could admit it to herself—she had grown to like him very much.

His actions were those of a man trying to win her, showing her only the best part of himself. Still, she could not deny that he daily grew dearer to her. His words of love undid something in her chest and made it harder to breathe.

Apprehension snaked through her stomach. Could this be love? Or was she merely gratified by his attentions?

Marrying Darcy would mean taking a leap of faith. She had heard nothing to impeach his character, apart from Wickham's lies. She felt certain she could come to love him in time. What comfort her mother would feel! How much better her sisters' lives would be! Could she deny them that?

The sound of hoof beats drew her attention. Her window offered no view of the road, and it was not worth the risk to her injured ankle to peek out another. It was too early for Darcy at any rate.

She turned back to her letter, telling herself there was no point letting her anxiety rise at every visitor. Mr. Collins was not unpopular amongst his parishioners, who were forever dropping by to deliver a pair of handkerchiefs they had made him, or a bit of his favourite sweet.

But when Darcy's baritone cut through the air, she raised her eyes from her reading. A thrill rose inside her, an ache of longing in her breast. She had no time to reflect on what those sensations meant before the housekeeper let him into her room.

He bowed but did not smile. "Good morning, madam. I hope you are well."

"Yes, the throbbing in my ankle has gone down."

He nodded, but the apprehension in his features did not abate. "I am glad to hear it. I pray that is not my letter in your hand?"

The most awful dread washed over her. "I am sorry to say, sir, it is."

"You must forgive me. I wrote that in a fever last night. I had no intention of sending it, but I foolishly sealed it and addressed it to you. My valet had it delivered without consulting me."

The pain in Lizzy's chest at his words caught her by surprise. She had hardly imagined that these simple sheets of paper could have grown so dear to her in such a short time. Ought she to give them back? Did he truly regret his words?

"I am sorry you are distressed, sir. I hope it is not on my account. Your missive was not unwelcome."

He paced. "I was far too forward in my address, and my expression had all the sophistication of a love-struck schoolboy."

Was that the reason for his present mood? He was worried about the quality, not the meaning? "Oh, there is no question, it is a terrible letter. You did not spend nearly enough time searching for the perfect four-syllable words. But I have grown quite attached to the letter, and would like to keep it, unless you wish to withdraw the sentiments."

"Withdraw the sentiments!" He sat beside her on the daybed and took her hand. "Never, my dearest Miss Bennet."

"Oh, I am Miss Bennet now?" She looked at him slyly.

He coloured. "Indeed, I have presumed more than I ought."

"You have, and I should mind, but I do not. Does that make me very wicked, do you think?"

She expected her teasing to make him smile; instead, an intensity grew in his expression, his eyes darkening. In an instant, his lips were on hers.

Then just as quickly, before she could respond or even know what name to give the feelings that vibrated through her at that most tender touch, his lips were gone.

He continued to hold her hands, but he stared into his lap. "You must forgive me."

"Have you wronged me, sir?"

He looked at her with a pained expression in his eyes. "I cannot tell whether you are teasing me or encouraging me."

"I hardly know myself."

"It is taking all my strength to contain my words. If you wish to stop me, you must stop me now."

She gazed at him, feeling what a thing it was to be loved by a worthy man. Her heart filled, and she merely gave him a smile. He waited a moment, then rose and shut the door. An unexpected happiness flowed through her, and eager tears touched her cheeks.

Chapter 12

He let go of the knob and turned back to Elizabeth, stunned by the expression on her face. Her teasing smile was gone. The truest, clearest emotion radiated from her. And she looked happy.

He got down on one knee before her and took her hand. For a moment, he felt too much to say a word. But she laid her free hand on top of his, and his mind cleared.

"My dear Miss Bennet, I came to Rosings a man in love. I had to know whether I ought to prevail upon myself to forget you, or to make you the partner of my life. The first moment I saw you again, my apprehensions disappeared. Every argument against the match was countered by your own dear self."

He placed a quick kiss on each of her hands. "I shall not insult you with claims of what I can offer. I know that the only inducement that matters to you is love. I can promise to be a good husband, as doting and devoted as any who has ever lived, and I shall do everything in my power to secure your happiness if you will do me the honour of becoming my wife."

Heart in his throat, he gazed up at her, expecting her to tease him, perhaps evaluate his proposal. But she did not. Instead, she looked at him tenderly, her eyes glistening, her lips curving into a smile. In a wavering voice, she said, "Nothing could make me happier. Yes, Mr. Darcy, I shall marry you."

The flush of joy that rushed through him stopped all rational thought. His gaze locked on hers, and he drank in her sweet expression. Her cheeks glowed, and her eyes were positively luminous.

He rose and sat beside her. Taking her hands in his, he raised them to his lips, first one and then the other. His heart hammered in his chest. Engaged! At last, she would be his!

A vision of the future stretched out before him, she at his side at Pemberley, presiding over a dinner party or walking through the quiet of a spring wood. She playing at the piano whilst Georgiana accompanied her on the harp. She with a babe in her arms as he softly kissed them both.

All this he could have. It was not a mere dream. His chest filled as her fingers caressed his.

He gazed at her deeply, and a low growl escaped his throat. Before he knew he moved, his lips were on hers. This time, he did not resist her allure. She yielded to him, admitting his touch.

Nothing in his life had ever felt sweeter. Her lips were warm and soft, and the scent of violets clung to her. He longed to draw her close but dared not. His self-mastery wavered on a knife's edge.

He released her, and an aching moan hung in the air. He could not say whether it had come from her or from him—or perhaps that soft sound of regret had emanated from both of them in unison. All he knew for sure was that she was the loveliest creature he had ever beheld.

For a long time he could not speak. Words could not capture the depth of feeling in his heart. Then, the spell broke, and he recalled the actions a man ought to take in this situation.

He sat up and cleared his throat. "Shall I ride to Longbourn to speak to your father?"

"Longbourn? Oh!" The dreamy look in her eyes cleared, her mind apparently turning to practical matters. "My family will be quite astonished. Perhaps it would be better if I told them."

He puzzled a moment. Of course it was natural that she wanted to convey the news to her family herself, once he had secured her father's permission.

"If you wish. I could travel alongside you when you return to Hertfordshire...two weeks hence, I believe?"

"Yes, I think that is best. If it is not inconvenient."

DARCY COMES TO ROSINGS

He chuckled at that. "The only inconvenience is waiting before I can tell the world you are mine."

She knitted her brows, clearly troubled. Was she having second thoughts?

He pressed her hand. "Please, my love, you seem disquieted. How may I put your mind to rest?"

"I fear Lady Catherine will *not* find the news of our engagement felicitous."

He lifted his chin. "That need not be of any consequence to us."

"It may be of *one* consequence. She is benefactor to my host. Despite any filial attachment my cousin might feel for me, I would not wish to see his loyalties torn between his patroness and me."

Darcy saw her meaning. If Lady Catherine asked Mr. Collins to turn Elizabeth out, he would surely do so. Darcy would hate for Elizabeth to be forced to shorten her visit to her dear friend Mrs. Collins, all because of him.

"Yes, I see the impossibility of our announcing our engagement at the present time. Let us do this. I shall tell Colonel Fitzwilliam, and you shall tell Mrs. Collins. Then there can be no impropriety. We can rely on their discretion, I think."

"Yes, that will be satisfactory."

He gave her a wry smile. "Satisfactory? Is that how you find our current situation? Or perhaps tolerable would be a better word."

Her eyes flashed at him. "Already, you are teasing *me*? This is not a good start at all."

"I shall ever be your humble servant."

"Pretty words indeed."

He gazed at her as if nothing else in the world existed for him. "You do not doubt me, I hope?"

"I would not have accepted you if I did."

He swallowed the lump forming in his throat. "Are you happy, Elizabeth?"

"Of course! I am most happy."

"You spoke with more ardour when you were chiding me for my silence at the Netherfield ball."

She leaned toward him. "Darcy," she said, "you must allow for a lady to be in a contemplative mood upon the occasion of her engagement. A week ago, I would not have imagined this happening. In that small amount of time, I have come to recognize your worth, and you have grown very dear to me. But my head is spinning. I hope you do not mind?"

"I care only for your happiness."

"Then do not worry yourself. I am happy, truly I am."

He turned away, his glance travelling to the window where cherry blossoms floated in the breeze.

She touched his cheek, turning his eyes back to her. "I would not deceive you. I give myself to you freely, with my whole heart."

He nodded and smiled. She beamed at him. His chest lightened. With burgeoning emotions, he kissed her palms.

"We should open the door," she said, nodding in that direction, "before we raise suspicion."

"Not until I do this." He leaned toward her and kissed her mouth. She responded, rising into his embrace.

With his hand pressed to her cheek, he caressed the soft skin there, his lips still moulded to hers. It was decadent and lovely. How had he endured life without this? She was everything. Life, breath, sunshine, music—every good thing was joined together in her small frame.

She pressed her palms to his chest and let out a little moan. He wrapped an arm around her waist and pulled her closer. "Darcy," she murmured, and he kissed her again, harder this time, suckling and nipping at her lips.

Her ardour matched his own, and that was a revelation. Only yesterday she had asked him to give her time. But there was nothing tentative in her touch.

With a soft cry, she pulled herself away from him, her cheeks flushed, her eyes shining. She smiled at him. "The door."

"Yes. Of course." He rose, his body aching with the absence of her.

He turned the knob, and Mrs. Collins became visible in the corridor. She stopped short, mouth gaping but then closing just as quickly.

"Mr. Darcy, I did not realize you were here," she said with a tone of perfect calm. "Has anyone offered you refreshments? Mrs. Harold brought us some lovely shortbread biscuits yesterday."

"I thank you, but I should take my leave. My aunt will be wondering what has become of me—I have not paid her my respects yet this morning."

He turned and smiled at Elizabeth. "Delightful to have seen you, Miss Bennet. I am glad to hear that your ankle is healing."

"I am most gratified by your visit," she responded with an ironic smile.

He wanted to lift her into his arms and kiss her again, but that was impossible for the time being. Until Elizabeth was up and around, it would be difficult for them to meet together alone.

He bowed to Mrs. Collins and headed out the door. How would he keep this secret, when he wanted to declare it to the world? Yet he had no choice. If Lady Catherine found out, it would be a disaster.

187

Chapter 13

Once Darcy had gone, Charlotte arched her brows and scurried into the small parlour, closing the door behind her. "Tell me everything."

"Oh, Charlotte. We are to be married!"

Charlotte's mouth dropped open. "You made quick work of that."

"Do not say so. It was not contrived." Lizzy played with the gold cross on a chain around her neck. "I simply stopped resisting my natural feelings."

"And what feelings were those?"

"Charlotte! My affection for him, of course."

"Of course."

Lizzy clutched a pillow to her chest. "You must not tease me. My mind is aflutter. Married to Mr. Darcy! Mistress of Pemberley! Can such things come to pass? I have not even met his sister yet."

"He seems resolved to have you."

"Oh, but Charlotte, you must promise to tell no one. He will travel to Longbourn to speak to my father when Maria and I return home in a fortnight. Until then, we have agreed to keep the news a secret from everyone but you and Colonel Fitzwilliam."

Charlotte nodded. "I think that is wise. It will be better if Lady Catherine does not learn of it until you are safely in Hertfordshire."

"My thoughts precisely." Lizzy leaned back against the bedrail. "Do you think it will prove an impediment, if we do not have the approbation of his family?"

"You have the approbation of Colonel Fitzwilliam. You must not think that all his family stand on rank as she does."

Lizzy shook her head. "She has a strange sense of rank. Darcy has no title. For that matter, neither does Miss Anne de Bourgh. They are wealthy, to be sure, but I do not see that rank separates Darcy and me."

"Lady Catherine's brother is an earl."

"And Sir Lewis was only a knight. She married beneath her station. She can hardly hold it against Darcy for doing the same."

Charlotte smiled.

"What?" Lizzy asked.

"You seem quite comfortable calling him Darcy."

"Should not I?"

"Considering that you have been engaged mere minutes, and you have not called him anything but *Mr.* Darcy until now..." A bright smile came over Charlotte's face. "Eliza, I believe you *do* like him. I believe you have liked him all along. And *that* is why his insult the night you met was so cutting. That is why your professed *dislike* of him has been so passionate."

Lizzy waved her hand in surrender. "Believe it if you like, Charlotte. I am done arguing on the subject." She sighed happily. "You have proven yourself so wise, and I so blind, that you may well know my feelings better than I do."

A trickle of apprehension flowed through Lizzy's breast, interrupting her otherwise perfect happiness. She smoothed her skirts. "I should not have let this happen so swiftly. But when the moment came, I found I did not wish to stop him. He gave me the chance, but I did not take it." She grinned slyly. "He is so very much in love with me, you see."

"I have no doubt of it."

"He has utterly charmed me. I hate seeing him unhappy." Excitement carried her away. "We could be married barely a month from now! Two weeks until he talks to my father, then three weeks for the reading of the banns—"

"Unless he gets a special license."

The thought of being married even more quickly stopped her breath. "Charlotte, do not threaten me with a special license!"

⁓♨⁓

"Did you get it back?"

Entering the library at Rosings, Darcy looked at Richard in a daze. "What?"

"The letter." Richard set down his book and rose.

"Ah, that. No, Miss Bennet had already received it, and she refused to give it back."

"So it was not as bad as you thought, then."

Darcy squared his shoulders. "On the contrary, she agreed it was terrible, and said I obviously had not spent enough time coming up with four-syllable words. That was a joke Bingley had made when I was staying at Netherfield, so I think she was teasing. Perhaps I should ask her." He shook his head, grabbing the back of a chair to steady himself whilst he cleared the fog from his mind. "Sorry, I am rambling."

Richard gave him a wry smile. "Sounds like a waste of a morning, then."

"Not entirely. We are engaged."

Richard gaped. "You could have started with that."

Darcy could not help a jubilant smile from breaking out over his face. "You asked about the letter, and I got distracted."

"Perhaps you were already distracted."

"Perhaps I was."

Richard shook Darcy's hand and clapped his back. "Congratulations, old man. I wish you joy. I have no doubt you shall find it—you could not have chosen better."

Darcy blinked, still floating in a blissful stupor. "I hope you are not the only one in the family who believes so. I would hate to bring her into a situation where she feels uncomfortable."

"Not at all. My parents will adore her."

Darcy nodded, but he could not give Richard's words his full attention. He walked to the window, watching the robins scour the ground beneath a white-flowered hawthorn tree.

"She did not say she loved me," Darcy confessed at last. "She said she is happy, and I am dear to her. But if she loved me, she would have said so."

"Three days ago, she was railing against your treatment of Wickham. She did not even *like* you. If she claimed to love you now, I would suspect her words."

Darcy let that sentiment sink in. "I have never seen any hint of mercenary motives in her, but her future is uncertain if she does not marry well. Perhaps she felt she had no choice but to accept me."

"You must not think that way." Richard spoke gravely. "You insult her as much as you do yourself."

Darcy knew Elizabeth was not a frivolous woman. She would not have accepted him for the wrong reasons. He ought to be satisfied—he had got what he wanted with less resistance than he had imagined. But now that he had got it, he wanted more.

Her hand was not enough. He wanted her whole heart.

Later that morning, Lizzy was still sighing over the pages from Darcy when she received a letter from Jane. Lizzy expected it to be full of Bingley, but instead it was full of Wickham! She shook her head in disbelief as she read, dismayed that Jane had so thoroughly misunderstood the situation.

Dear Lizzy,

Your latest letter has distressed me more than I can say. I know how fond you were of W., and I find it nearly impossible to believe that a man so outwardly agreeable could be so black-hearted. Is it possible that there has been some misunderstanding? Perhaps he was truly in love with the lady in question. He ought not to have spoken to her of elopement, but love can blind one to practical considerations.

I know not what to think of the situation with the living at the rectory. I am glad, however, that your revelation shows D. in a happier light. He is of course one of B.'s dearest friends, and I should hate to have any reason to think ill of him. Perhaps we were all too hasty in considering him proud.

Oh, Lizzy! I pray you, do not give another thought to W. Whatever tenderness of feeling still remains for him will quickly pass, I am certain. He was pleasing, but he had not captured your heart. I never saw evidence of such a thing, and you would have told me if he had. You were disappointed that he was not at the Netherfield ball, but now I think it is clear why. It is much better in hindsight that you did not attach yourself to him any further.

It will be awkward, certainly, to see him again before the regiment removes to Brighton. I wish that circumstance could be avoided altogether, but perhaps you wish to say goodbye. I hope you will part from him without any reluctance. I think you must break off the acquaintance entirely. I hate to say so, because I know it must pain you, but in your heart, I believe you must know it is true.

Perhaps next year you will come to London with me for the season. This week alone, I have been to the theatre, the opera, and a musicale. Would you not enjoy that? I am determined you shall be happy, Lizzy. Only tell me what I must do to make you happy, and I shall do it.

Your loving and devoted sister,

Jane

Lizzy put her hand to her mouth, then laughed. Poor Jane! To be worried over nothing! Lizzy would have to disabuse her of her wrong impression immediately.

But what to say? She could hardly tell Jane about the engagement. It would seem too sudden—and indeed it was— but even more so for someone who had not seen events unfold.

Dearest Jane,

Please do not concern yourself with regard to my last letter. You suppose a greater attachment between W. and myself than existed. I liked him, yes; I am sorry he has turned out to be a wicked, deceitful sort of man. But I do not regret the loss of him. Indeed, if I ever had him, I lost him when he pursued Miss King. Good riddance to him.

You will be happy to hear that the discovery has proven felicitous by acquitting Mr. Darcy's character. You will not believe this, Jane, but he has been quite attentive to me, and I do not find him so disagreeable as I did before. In fact, I feel safe in saying I grow fonder of him daily. I assure you that I am being careful, though, and assuming no more than I ought.

I long to see you. We will have so much to discuss! I am counting the days until our return to Longbourn.

Yours, etc.

Elizabeth Darcy

When she saw how she had signed the letter, she at first thought of trying to blot it out, but then decided it would make a good joke. So she simply put a line through it, and signed *Lizzy Bennet* underneath.

Chapter 14

That evening, the sound of the barouche caught Darcy's ear as he awaited his aunt's dinner guests. He and Richard went outside to greet the party from the parsonage. As Richard took Charlotte's arm, and Mr. Collins followed behind with Maria, Darcy assisted Elizabeth out of the carriage, his hands at her waist as he lowered her until her feet gently touched the ground.

She beamed up at him, one hand on her bonnet as the wind tousled the escaping tendrils of dark curls. Her eyes danced, and the scent of violets enveloped her. His gaze landed on her soft, sweet lips, and he had to stop himself from kissing her.

"I have thought of you every moment," he said in her ear.

"And I you."

Her smile lifted his spirits. He had never seen her smile like that before—not at anyone. Finally, after all these months of yearning, she was his. And in a matter of weeks, she would belong to him in every way.

He lightly glided his fingers along her sides, knowing he should be discreet, but unwilling to let go. "Can you walk, or shall I carry you?"

"If I walk, we will proceed so slowly that we might have entire minutes alone together."

"A wise answer."

She entwined her arm in his. Hobbling along, her ankle appeared weak but mending. "It was kind of your aunt to send the carriage."

"She could hardly do otherwise. Although I believe she is truly concerned for your welfare. She will not stop fretting until she sees you." He helped Elizabeth up the stone stairs and into the foyer. Their footsteps echoed on the marble floor.

She looked around to make sure the footman could not overhear. "I wrote to Jane today," she said in low tones, "and you will not believe what I did. Without a thought, I signed it Elizabeth Darcy. I crossed it out of course, and signed it properly. But poor Jane! She shall be piqued with me."

Darcy thrilled at her words, yet did not know what to make of them. He was gratified that Elizabeth had eased so naturally into their engagement. He did not want to make too much of the incident—but did it not suggest love?

"Did you tell her about us?"

"I hinted at a warming in our friendship. I did not wish to give her an apoplexy by telling her the whole truth. She will not like my teasing about such a serious matter—she will worry that I am running away with myself."

"*Are* you running away with yourself?"

Elizabeth looked up at him, a dreamy expression in her eyes. "If I am already thinking of myself as bearing your name, then I would say so."

"Well, why not? I have run away with myself." Joy filled his heart. He ached to make this woman his wife. "If we are ever going to make fools of ourselves, it may as well be for love."

"Why Darcy, I never thought I would hear you say such a thing. But I completely agree."

The foyer narrowed into a hallway that led to the drawing room. "What think you of a June wedding?" he asked, speaking so only she could hear.

"The earlier in June, the better."

"I could get a special license." His mind whirred at the possibilities. She could be his wife in a week, with her father's permission. He tried not to picture it, Elizabeth in his bed, with nothing but a sheet draped over her beautiful body—

"No, do not trouble yourself," she said. "I have my wedding clothes to buy, which means a week in London at least. I cannot deny Mama the pleasure. And you have a honeymoon to plan."

He nodded, breathing deeply to cool his blood. "Is there anywhere in particular you would like to go?"

"I suppose Paris is out of the question," she teased.

He imagined them kissing as they floated in a boat along the Seine, sunlight reflecting off the water, Notre Dame cathedral rising in the background. But it could not be. "Given that we are at war with France, I would say not."

"Then what about the Cotswolds? You mentioned Miss Darcy travelling there."

"Please call her Georgiana. She will be your sister soon enough. But would not you prefer a holiday by the sea?"

"Perhaps it is silly of me," she said, "but I would not feel comfortable along the coast—not when there is a risk of invasion, however small."

"Then the Cotswolds it is."

"Only if you will be happy there," she insisted.

A pretty scene came to his mind: walking through the green countryside, stopping to look at the trees slanting down the rolling hills, with little villages and spires of churches below. "Yes, it will be quite picturesque. And most importantly, I shall be with you."

They stepped into the drawing room. He helped her onto the couch next to Mrs. Collins. Sitting on the chair closest to her, he rolled her words over in his mind—how without thinking she had signed her soon-to-be married name in a letter to her sister. That seemed to signify true happiness at their upcoming nuptials, even if she was still discovering his character.

Perhaps he should help that along.

At dinner, Lady Catherine had made a special place for Lizzy where she could rest her leg on a low stool—at the opposite end of the table from Darcy. The arrangement displeased Lizzy, not least of all because she was next to Mr. Collins.

"And I told Maria," said he, "that a young lady's coming out is a most auspicious occasion, to be smiled upon by Heaven, for it is good and right that she enter into the state of matrimony, like Adam and Eve, to be fruitful and multiply. And so we should not lament our sister Hannah's entry into Meryton society, even though we could not be there to share her good fortune. The debut of her youngest daughter must be a great comfort to Lady Lucas."

"But they might have waited two more weeks," Maria said gently, "so that I might have been there to share in it."

"My dear sister, we must not question your parents' judgment in this matter. A young lady such as yourself cannot be expected to understand the reasoning of her elders."

Lizzy said, "Poor Hannah. I can see why she wanted to make her debut on her sixteenth birthday, rather than waiting another two weeks. Things must be very dull for her with both you and Charlotte gone."

Maria nodded. "Hannah was not much pleased when Lydia came out at fifteen, but Mama insisted Hannah wait another year."

"Lydia begged my father daily, and persuaded my mother to take up her cause as well."

"It is an inversion of the natural order," Mr. Collins said, his voice rising, "when the child rules the parent. I shall advise my dear cousin—"

"I am certain my father would be most eager for your kind words of wisdom," Lizzy said. "But on this topic, with all his daughters grown, might not your time be put to better use? Many of your parishioners must be able to benefit from your guidance on this subject."

"Indeed, Cousin Elizabeth, you make a fine point. As I said to Miss de Bourgh just today—"

"Miss Bennet," Lady Catherine interrupted, "I understand the physician has been to see you. What says he about your ankle?"

"Your ladyship is all kindness for asking. He says it should be healed in a few days."

"That must be a great relief. Jenkinson has a cane she uses when her rheumatism troubles her. I am certain she would not mind lending it to you, would you, Jenkinson?"

"Oh, thank you, ma'am," Lizzy said quickly, noting the horror in the eyes of Mrs. Jenkinson, Miss de Bourgh's companion. "But one of Mr. Collins' parishioners has already been so kind. The cane belonged to her late mother. So there is no need to trouble Mrs. Jenkinson."

"It would be no trouble at all, would it, Jenkinson?"

The footman's arrival with a dessert of jam tarts distracted her ladyship and spared Jenkinson from replying.

After dinner, the ladies were not long in the drawing room when the gentlemen joined them. Darcy did not come to Lizzy's side at once, but first stopped to converse with Miss de Bourgh, then Maria. Maria had been quite terrified of him when they first met, but Lizzy could see that he was taking pains to put the girl at ease. It gratified Lizzy to see him so kind and attentive.

The colonel took the seat by Miss de Bourgh that Darcy had left. Lizzy observed something she had not noticed before: Miss de Bourgh's expression pinked quite prettily, and her grey eyes, usually dull, shone with light. Miss de Bourgh was normally quite listless, so the change in her was marked.

Did the colonel's attentions always affect her that way? Lizzy would have to watch and see. With Darcy now safe, Lizzy could look on Miss de Bourgh with compassion. Perhaps she was not the spoiled lapdog Lizzy had imagined. Perhaps she suffered under the tyranny of a mother whose love starved her of companionship and activity.

When at last Darcy came and sat by Lizzy's side, every other consideration fled. Her body awakened at his nearness. She had determined to ask him questions about things he knew, things he loved, to avoid the small talk he found excruciating.

"Tell me about Derbyshire," she said.

A fond smile spread over his face. "There is nothing like it in the south. The limestone plateaus offer beautiful vistas of the rivers and dales. Spring is my favourite time of year there. At Pemberley, the fields are covered with bluebells. The front of the house has a view of the lake, with hills and woodlands beyond. The trees must be just now coming into leaf, and to my eyes, there is no prettier sight in the world."

"You show the same prejudice toward Derbyshire as my Aunt Gardiner. She was raised there."

"Yes, she mentioned it when I saw her in London."

Lizzy eyed him a moment, leaning closer. Would he now confess all? "You met my aunt in London?"

His face paled, and he hesitated a moment. "Briefly. We were introduced by a mutual friend. I am sorry, I should have mentioned it to you."

"I am surprised *she* did not mention it."

"Perhaps she did not find me memorable."

Lizzy's eyes danced. If he was going to make up a story, he should not choose one so ridiculous. "I find that hard to believe."

His brows rose. "Why is that?"

Did he really not know? "You are an imposing figure, Darcy. It is difficult not to notice you, if for no reason other than your stature; but add to that your extremely pleasing features and your expertly tailored clothes, and you make an impression."

"But not always a good one."

She shook her head. Her mind fled back to the night they had met. "Darcy, do you not see! Your first introduction to Meryton society was a ball with a shortage of men, and you would not deign to dance! To most mamas, the purpose of a young man is to dance with her daughters; and the purpose of a young man of fortune is to propose to one of them. You did neither of those things."

He quirked his lips sardonically. "I did both of them, eventually."

Lizzy laughed gaily, unable to help herself. "And thanks to that, you may be forgiven. But you have much to make up for."

He leaned in close. "If I ask all the single woman in Meryton to dance with me at our wedding, will that do?"

"It will do quite well. Although once we are married, you will be of considerably less interest to the mamas of the world."

"I shall try to bear up under the strain."

She smiled at that, then groaned. "You are delightful. I wish I had known that six months ago, when I was staying at Netherfield. We would have had such fun together."

"I thought we did have fun."

She coughed back a laugh. "You and I have very different definitions of that word."

"Apparently your definition is dancing and chatting idly with strangers, which I find insupportable."

"Then we shall have to practice at it before the wedding."

He sat back. "Tell me then, what are safe subjects in Meryton society?" His tone suggested that he was truly interested yet incredibly annoyed.

"You might remark on how fine the calfskin gloves are at Wake's—"

"But they are not fine." He scowled at her, as if wondering what she was about. "They cannot compare to London."

She turned from him and looked heavenward. "Darcy, that is hardly the point."

"So I must not speak the truth, then?"

"You must be diplomatic. For instance, say you have never seen anything like them, even in London."

"I do not have your sense of irony, my love."

"You may develop one. It is a skill. You can speak the truth, but in a way that sounds like you mean the opposite."

He looked askance at her. "I shall never be easy now. I shall spend the rest of my days wondering if you are speaking ironically."

"With you I shall always be honest, except when I am teasing. I *do* believe you have learned to tell when I am teasing, have not you?"

"Most of the time." He looked at her intently, as if his thoughts had suddenly turned grave. "May I ask you a favour?"

"Of course."

He squared his jaw. "I hope you will not think it insulting."

She drew in a quick breath. With such a preface, there was a good chance she *would* find it insulting. "Oh, dear, this sounds concerning indeed."

He looked away. "Never mind. I do not wish to upset you."

Gently, she touched the back of his hand. "If you are troubled, I should like to ease your mind, if I can."

"Normally I enjoy your teasing. One topic, however, I shall find it difficult to laugh about, I think."

She waited for him to say more, but he did not. "Of course. What is it?"

"The suggestion that you accepted me because of my income."

She blinked a few times. "Is that what you believe?"

"Of course not." He fisted his hands. "A week ago you thought me beastly."

She hesitated a moment. "I was uncertain of your character. I confess that your wealth may have persuaded me to take pains to know you better. But in fairness, Darcy, you make yourself difficult to know."

He turned away a moment, as if ashamed, but she touched his arm to bring his attention back to herself.

"Fortunately," she said, "you are worth the effort. There is no man I admire more. I would not have accepted you otherwise."

He looked at her with an intensity in his eyes, as if her words were deeply gratifying.

Wanting to soothe any lingering doubts he might have, she continued, "I am marrying a man, not an estate in Derbyshire. I could be happy with someone of a thousand or two a year. I admit to finding comfort in the advantages you can offer my family, but they are far less important to me than *you* are."

He nodded slowly. "I had deluded myself for so long into thinking you not only liked me, but were hoping for my proposal. When I learned the truth, I did not do enough to earn your love and trust."

She swallowed, her heart aching. "Are you sorry to have proposed so soon?"

"Not at all." He shook his head. "I should not have questioned your motives. It was insulting."

"Someone who understood you less, who cared for you less, might have thought so. You must not think because I tease you, I do not truly care for you. If we were not in this close space, with so many ears listening, I would enumerate all the ways I admire you."

"It seems an eternity since I kissed you."

She gave him a sly smile. He was a man in need of kisses. How strange that she had never noticed before the sweet vulnerability that lay beneath his placid surface!

She said in a louder tone, "Mr. Darcy, I have just remembered that book you promised to show me in the library. Would now be convenient?"

He grinned at her. "Indeed it would." He rose and helped her to her feet.

Colonel Fitzwilliam stood and said, "Here, let me help you." He bowed to Miss de Bourgh and came to join them.

Supported by the arms of two strong men, she made her way into the hallway without much trouble. The colonel's attentions, whilst unexpected and not strictly necessary, were not unpleasant. Meanwhile, the closeness to Darcy set her heart fluttering. His touch filled her with longing.

Candles lit the passageway as they headed down the corridor. "I hope you do not mind," the colonel said. "If I had not offered, I feared Mr. Collins would have, and his presence might have interfered with this book the two of you are so interested in."

"That's quite enough, Richard," Darcy warned his cousin in that pleasant, teasing manner they had with one another.

"Ought I to be embarrassed?" Lizzy asked. "I am not in the least. I do believe I am quite wicked."

"You must stop saying so," Darcy scolded. "Nothing untoward has passed between us, nor will it."

"I fear you are right," she said. Darcy was such a consummate gentleman, it was difficult to imagine him engaging in unbecoming conduct. "Colonel Fitzwilliam, are we not the most boring engaged couple you have ever met?"

"Not at all, Miss Bennet, *you* are delightful under any circumstance."

"You are kind to say it," she replied. "I do believe my hobbling around in this manner makes me less so."

"If it gives me an excuse to hold your arm," Darcy said, "I shall not complain of it."

Lizzy smiled up at him, then turned to the colonel. "Is he not the sweetest suitor?"

"I confess, he is doing a better job of it than I might have thought."

"You give me too little credit, my friend." Darcy's smile at his cousin was comfortable and happy, an expression she too seldom saw on his face.

Their cheerful banter added to the bliss of her time with Darcy. Friendship with Colonel Fitzwilliam would be a welcome benefit of her marriage. She hoped the rest of his family were as pleasant as he.

As they approached the library, Darcy picked up a silver candlestick, the yellow flame glimmering against the polished metal. Opening the door, he said, "It is quite dark in here. It may take some time to find the book in question in such dim light." Looking through the shelves, he said, "Here, Colonel, is a book to keep you occupied. A military history of something. You had better read it out in the hallway, where the light is better."

Colonel Fitzwilliam bowed and exited with his book, closing the door behind him.

Chapter 15

"Nicely done," Lizzy said as Darcy set down the candle.

In an instant, he was upon her, clutching her face in his hands, his mouth devouring hers. For such a powerful man, his lips were delightfully smooth, yet probing and insistent. She matched his eagerness, a forbidden fire burning in her veins. An engaged man might take certain liberties, but she was determined to keep him in hand until their wedding night.

Her palms rested on the hard planes of his chest, his masculine scent enveloping her. She had never touched a man like this, never imagined it could be so intoxicating. She was not so swept away that she could not resist him if it became necessary. But how wonderful it would be, to give in to desire, to allow him to teach her all the ways of love!

"Do you like my kisses, sweet Elizabeth?" he breathed into her ear, hands roaming her back.

"More than is safe for a single young lady," she managed, though her throat was tight. "Perhaps you had better make haste to London for a special license after all."

"And what of your wedding clothes?" he asked, his lips gliding along the curve of her neck.

Her body vibrated with pleasure. "They can wait until after."

"And our honeymoon?"

"I hear the Cotswolds are beautiful in the autumn." She kissed along his jawline, enjoying the roughness of his razor stubble. She nipped at his earlobe. "We could summer at Pemberley. Georgiana could join us in June."

"And we could spend all of May in bed."

"That sounds delightful," she purred.

He cupped her face in his hands, looking at her intently. "You do not mind my speaking to you thus?"

"Should I?"

"I do not know," he confessed. "I have never been engaged before."

She giggled. "Nor have I. I have no desire to be missish with you. The whole purpose of our excursion to the library was so I could show you how dear you are to me."

He let out a growl. "I hate this limbo. You *were* joking about the special license, were not you?"

DARCY COMES TO ROSINGS

"I am afraid so. Five weeks is not so long, is it?"

He pressed his forehead to hers, then kissed her temple. "It will be a busy five weeks. And of course, we should give enough time for your ankle to heal."

She nodded. "I can just imagine myself hobbling down the aisle on my father's arm."

They both chuckled, but their breathing came heavily. Nothing in the world had ever felt so perfect as his arms around her like this, their bodies so close they could almost meld together. Lizzy now understood why a woman's virtue was so brittle. She was all too close to letting this go further than she ought.

"You shall be a beautiful bride, Elizabeth."

"And you a dashing groom." She stood on her tiptoes and kissed his lips. "But call me Lizzy. My family do, and now you are my family."

He caressed her cheek with his thumb. "I must admit, you are adapting to this engagement remarkably well."

"Charlotte thinks I have been in love with you all along, and that is why I was so put out because of your slight the night we met."

He drew in a breath. His eyes searched her face as if the secret to the holy grail was written there. "And what do you think?"

"I do not know what to think. But I know what I feel. I am happy and comfortable in your arms, and shall remain so for the rest of my life."

His fingers brushed against the curls that framed her forehead. "That is all I needed to hear." He kissed her again, with less ardour but more true, deep passion. It was absolute bliss, until a knock came on the door.

"Eliza, dearest," Charlotte's voice called, "I hope you have found your book. Lady Catherine is wondering where her nephews have gone off to."

Darcy looked away with a scowl, his brows heavy. He released Lizzy, leaving her bereft, and opened the door.

"You and the colonel should get back," Charlotte said. "I shall follow along with Eliza, even if my arm is not as strong as yours."

Darcy looked toward Lizzy.

She wanted to protest. She wanted to declare to the world that Darcy was hers. But the secret must only be kept for a little while longer. "Charlotte is right," Lizzy said at last.

He gazed at her a moment, then bowed and walked off with Colonel Fitzwilliam.

She would have been affronted by that perfunctory parting, had she not known him so well. Gestures she had once thought showed a lack of feeling, she now knew had been the opposite—the product of too *much* feeling. He kept his emotions in check by hiding them from the world.

Oh, how delicious to marry such a man, and draw every deep feeling out of him! To soothe his fears, to kiss away his sorrows, to bask in the light of his love. Five more weeks, and he would be hers.

Charlotte picked up the candle and led Lizzy out into the hallway. "Goodness, how dishevelled you are!" Charlotte set down the candle and straightened Lizzy's clothes. "I have never known reading to be such a strenuous activity."

Charlotte stepped back and eyed her.

"How do I look?" Lizzy asked.

"Like you have been thoroughly kissed. There is nothing to be done about your hair without taking it down entirely, and pinning it back up. But if we walk slowly, perhaps the flush on your cheek and the shine in your eyes will subside."

They walked slowly, and the increasing pain in Lizzy's ankle dulled her spirits nicely. Without Darcy's arms around her, she turned fretful. "Oh Charlotte, I fear I have been shockingly cruel to Darcy!"

Charlotte's brow wrinkled, and she met Lizzy's eyes, her expression concerned. "How do you mean, my dear?"

She gulped in air, feeling almost breathless. "Those days when Jane was ill, and I was at Netherfield, I would look up and find him staring at me. I assumed his looks were disapproving, but in fact he was falling in love! If I had been kind to him even a little, things might have progressed faster between us."

"You must not think like that. You are engaged now. All is well."

"When I tease him, he cannot always tell how I feel." Lizzy sighed in frustration. "Indeed, I have no idea myself sometimes. I like him exceedingly, Charlotte. I have never met anyone like him. It is an adjustment, getting to know his manners. But in truth, he is uncommonly kind and gentle. I worry I have made a muddle of things."

"Once you are married, it will be easier. Indeed, once the engagement is out in the open, it will be easier. You will not have to sneak off to the library on a pretext to have a private conversation."

Lizzy nodded. Charlotte was right, and the thought soothed her. Still, she was not entirely easy on the matter.

At last, they stepped back into the drawing room. The sight of so many people overwhelmed Lizzy. She could hardly keep her composure. The walk had done her ankle no good, and she could not help wincing.

Darcy jumped up from his seat. "Miss Bennet, you are unwell." He looked to the footman. "Have the groom ready my chaise."

"I am sure that is not necessary," Lady Catherine said. "We can make Miss Bennet comfortable here until the rest of the party is ready to return to the parsonage in my barouche. It will only be two or three hours."

Lizzy gritted her teeth, wanting to scream.

Darcy glowered at his aunt. "It is quite necessary, ma'am. She is in pain, and I shall see her returned safely home."

"But if you go, there will not be enough players for another table of whist. And I know how Mrs. Collins enjoys whist."

"Thank you for your solicitude on my behalf, ma'am," Charlotte said, "but I am quite happy to look over my husband's shoulder. Miss Bennet's comfort is my first concern."

"Yes, of course." Lady Catherine did not appear pleased at having been overruled.

When the servant announced the carriage, Darcy picked Lizzy up into his arms, carrying her out of the house amidst Lady Catherine's protests at his dramatic display. He paid her no heed. Lizzy was grateful for his gallantry, for her ankle was throbbing after so much exertion. She had not noticed it in the library. But when Darcy had released her, the pain came rushing back.

He helped her into the carriage and sat beside her, driving the horse in the open two-seater. She said, "I did not realize you had a carriage here."

"Yes, it is convenient for travelling with my man and a trunk or two. How are you feeling?"

"I quite exhausted myself, I am afraid. It struck me all at once. Thank you for taking care of me."

"You do not need to thank me. It is my duty now."

She smiled. "All the same, I am most appreciative."

"If you think anything gives me greater pleasure than taking care of you, dearest Lizzy, then you are mistaken."

A chuckle shook her frame. "Even so, it would mean a great deal to me if you would accept my thanks."

"I—yes, of course. You are quite welcome."

She entwined her arm in his. The air was cool and the sky moonless, the velvet blackness dotted with stars that sparkled like diamonds. She breathed the scent of honeysuckle wafting on the breeze.

She leaned into him, enjoying his warmth. "I feel as if you have done so much for me, and I so little for you."

"But that is absurd. This has been the happiest day of my life. Surely you know that."

She hesitated. "I had not thought about it that way. All I have to offer you is myself."

"That is all I need." His voice softened, rolling over her melodically like water over river stones. "You must not let the inequality of our fortunes trouble you. I wanted for nothing in the world until I met you. Then, I realized how empty my life would be without you. Your own sweet self is all I desire."

Lizzy mulled over his words. She understood the sentiment. She had never set her hopes on marrying a wealthy man—only on marrying a man she loved. She perfectly grasped that he wished for no more than herself. Yet she felt utterly unworthy.

She laid her head on his shoulder. "How can you care for me, when I have been so cruel to you?"

"Cruel to me! When have you ever shown me a moment's unkindness?"

"The way I have always teased you—"

"I love your teasing. Your wit is half the reason I fell in love with you."

She kissed the tiny patch of skin between his earlobe and his neck. "For so long I thought you had not the capacity for tender feeling—"

"Ah, I see what is troubling you. You forget that I had no idea what was in your heart. All the time you disliked me, I thought you were flirting with me."

She laughed. "And all the time you were flirting with me, I thought you disliked me."

Holding the reins with one hand, he entwined her fingers with the other. "I am glad we straightened that out."

"As am I." She sighed. "Oh, Darcy, is it truly this simple? That two people who like each other can marry and be happy?"

"Of course."

She shifted uncomfortably in her seat. "You have observed my parents. Can you imagine any two people more mismatched? And yet they were in love once."

"Were they?" He sounded startled.

"Oh yes, I have seen the letters my father wrote her. Quite beautiful."

"Better than the one I wrote you?" he joked.

Her mind conjured the aging sheets of paper, creased and fragile in a box in her mother's cedar chest. "My father's were more studied, more intentional, more lyrical. Yours was full of frantic passion. I shall treasure it above everything."

"I would rather you burned it," he said sardonically.

"Never!" she cried. "Were it not for that letter, we would not be engaged now."

"Then it was all my valet's doing?"

She pressed her shoulder to his. "I think we would have managed it in time."

He pulled up in front of the parsonage and helped her from the chaise. The housemaid met them as he carried Lizzy into the house and deposited her gently on the daybed in the small parlour. The maid turned up the lamp and added a log to the fire before withdrawing.

Darcy closed the door and stood looking at Lizzy from the middle of the room, setting down his hat. "Are you certain I cannot help you upstairs?"

She arched her brows. "Is that why you brought me home early? Was this all a ploy to be alone with me in my chamber?"

Shock crossed his face like a bolt of lightning. He stammered. "Of-of course not, madam. I would never—"

"My sweet Darcy!" She smiled up at him. "You are too easy. I love to tease you, but it will not work if you are forever taking me seriously."

He sat and removed her gloves, kissing both her hands. "I love your teasing, too. Do not stop just because I can be a dolt about it."

"You are not a dolt." She kissed his cheek. "You are the most intelligent man I know."

He gazed at her, his eyes dark and intense. "My beautiful Lizzy. Soon, you will be mine in every way."

She swallowed. It was dangerous, being close to him like this. His warm, masculine scent of wool and leather enticed her. His smooth skin and hard muscle begged to be touched. "I shall dream of you tonight."

He smiled. "I have dreamed of you every night for six months."

She sighed, wanting his kisses. The door could not remain closed long without inviting scandal. She stroked his hands. "I wish you could stay."

"I dare not, my love. I am human, after all."

"As am I." She met his eyes, which was a mistake. The directness of his gaze made her feel exposed—except now, instead of being unnerved by it, she liked the way it felt. She wanted to expose every part of herself to him. "Five weeks."

"Five weeks." In a sweet, tender embrace, he kissed her. The brush of lips deepened to the glide of tongues, and she pressed against his chest, her hand at the small of his back holding him to her. "Lizzy," he said gruffly, panting as he rested his forehead against her temple.

Want tightened in her belly. Vaguely she wondered how long it would take, if she gave herself to him, and whether they could finish before the maid would notice. But since she had very little notion of what went on between a man and woman, she could make no realistic assessment.

This was not a good start at all. They had been engaged one day, and already she was considering giving him her virtue before the wedding. No, not considering it, really. Just imagining it. But there was a very real awareness of her womanly desires, and how her body responded to him as a man.

"I must go," he murmured in her ear.

She forced herself to release him, and he rose in a quick motion. Then, after enjoining the maid to check on Lizzy every half hour, he took his leave. She missed him even before he closed the front door behind him.

Lizzy hugged a pillow to her chest. Had it really only been that morning that he had proposed? How much her life had changed in that short space of time! And yet, everything felt right and good.

She had always expected to marry a genial man, someone like Colonel Fitzwilliam. But Darcy, who required coaxing to express the sweetness in his heart... Somehow it made the sweetness more valuable, knowing it was only for her. Knowing that his secrets lay hidden from the rest of the world, and she was the only one who could peek inside.

And she had only begun to fathom his mysteries. What more would the morrow hold?

Chapter 16

When Darcy returned to Rosings, he could not face the others in the drawing room. He looked in long enough to show that he was back, and thus to stave off any suspicion of impropriety. Then, he headed to the salon and poured himself a brandy.

He sank into a chair and let the burning liquid roll over his tongue. The separation from Lizzy was a physical pain. Her signs of affection had been so unguarded, he could not doubt her sincerity. Yet he had never felt so vulnerable in his life.

He did not much like it.

In those moments when she smiled at him, colours became brighter, sounds richer. Yet his breathless love for her was accompanied by torturous passion. Even their happy moments were spoiled by the frustration of sensual desire.

He could feel it in her, too. That had been unexpected. Her responsiveness to his kisses held promise for their wedding night.

Surely, after that, things would get better? Once she was his wife in every sense of the word, his discontent would subside? He closed his eyes, annoyed. The haze of lust made it impossible to think.

Richard joined him presently and poured himself a glass. "Something troubling you?"

Darcy swirled his drink. A memory flickered forward in his mind. "When I was at Cambridge, there was a woman. I thought she cared for me until I found her in Wickham's arms. It was my inheritance that had interested her."

"Sorry, old man."

"My parents had warned me about fortune hunters, but until that moment, it had been theoretical. Ever since, it has been my greatest fear. Intellectually, I have no doubts about Lizzy. But a small part of me..."

He gulped down the remainder of his brandy. The embodiment of his dread had been in front of him ever since he had arrived at Rosings.

Mr. Collins adored his wife. It was not a sensible sort of love, because nothing about him was sensible, but it was clearly heartfelt. *Mrs.* Collins, for her part, was kind to him, and watched out for his interests. But she was not in love. Anyone looking at them from the outside could see that. Yet Collins himself seemed entirely ignorant of her indifference.

That was what Darcy feared. Being ridiculous. Being so besotted he could not see what the rest of the world knew.

Being in love with a wife who was happy to be Mrs. Darcy of Pemberley, but could never return his feelings.

Richard refilled Darcy's glass. "Does anything about Miss Bennet suggest to you she is a fortune hunter?"

"Nothing at all. Quite the opposite."

"I am inclined to agree with you. In fact, I observed that she was predisposed to dislike you, and fortune be damned."

"You have the gist of it."

Richard chuckled. "You are thinking too much, Darcy. If a man heading into battle worries about all that could go wrong, he will drive himself mad. Instead, he takes action. He prepares. He develops tactics. He plans contingencies. He does not sit by a fire brooding."

Darcy looked into his cousin's face and the fond smile he wore. Richard was right, of course. Wickham's betrayal had led Darcy to question his own judgment, but that was not rational. He had faith in Lizzy. What they had was new, but it was real. He would not let his baseless suspicions threaten their love.

⁓⊗⁓

The next morning, Lizzy awoke early and read over the letter she had written to Darcy the night before.

My darling,

Amid the crowd of people at Rosings, I was not at liberty to enumerate all the ways I admire you. Now

DARCY COMES TO ROSINGS

that I am alone, I wish to drive away forever any remaining doubts you may have about my affection for you. How things might have transpired differently between us if you were not a man of means, I cannot say. You are who you are. I can only tell you what is in my heart.

In the way you talk of your sister, I see so much of true devotion in you that I cannot help imagining what an excellent father you will make. More important than my own happiness is the happiness of any children God may bless us with. In this regard I have made an outstanding choice. That is the most important thing of all.

Your cousin, Colonel Fitzwilliam—who even upon a brief acquaintance is as fine a man as ever I met— speaks of you in superlatives, and only to compliment. In your dealings with him, I have seen the love of brothers, a bond of friendship that can never be broken. It is not only his words that have persuaded me of your worth, but every interaction between you. Your esteem for one another does both of you credit.

Then there is your kindness to your aunt. You are solicitous of her comfort and happiness, and she is besotted with you. When you insisted on taking me home in your chaise, you were firm with her but not cross. I am rather in awe of that.

Now, as to myself. I have never heard you speak an unkind word to me apart from the night we met, which I hope I shall never have occasion to think upon again. You were always civil to me when I was at Netherfield, no matter how much I teased you, and you have continued in the same way toward me here at Hunsford.

Indeed, with each day you have grown more patient and attentive and kind. Were I not a simpleton, I should have seen what your feelings were sooner, but I had persuaded myself that a great man like you could never care for a woman like me. I can still hardly believe it true.

As a fiancé, I dare anyone to name your rival. After one day, I count myself the most fortunate of women. You take care of those you love, and your loyalty is unsurpassed.

It seems rather trite to say it, since it is so obvious, but of course I admire your intellect. I have never known your equal. And in case you have any doubts (how could you have any doubts?) you are surely amongst the handsomest men on earth.

In a word, I am mad for you. Perhaps Charlotte is right, and part of me has been smitten with you all along—and it was only my persuasion that you could not care for me that kept me from falling sooner.

I pray that our past misunderstandings will not burden our future. I adore you, and I long to see you.

With deepest affection,

Your own Lizzy

The letter did not sound any worse in the light of day, so she sealed it and added the address: *Mr. Fitzwilliam Darcy, Rosings.*

She gave it to the houseboy with strict orders to place it directly into the hand of Mr. Darcy's valet and no other, saying there would be a shilling in it for the boy when he returned.

But the boy had barely come back when her misgivings began; Darcy's letter had been dear to her because it was full of the most passionate sentiment, and hers utterly lacked warmth. It was all wrong.

So she was relieved when he called mid-morning. Charlotte was sitting with her at the time, and Lizzy was restless. Being cooped up was most trying, but she could not risk walking outside. Her ankle was too unstable.

"How are you feeling, Miss Bennet?" Darcy greeted her.

His formality made her smile, but with the door open, Maria and the housekeeper were within hearing distance. "Like an invalid, sir."

"Then I have the antidote. You must be missing your morning walks. I have brought the chaise so we can take a ride."

"Oh!" The prospect was at that moment the most pleasant thing she could imagine. "How kind of you. I should like that very much."

Charlotte rose. "Let me get your bonnet and spencer."

"Thank you." Lizzy watched after her, then turned to Darcy. "She has been remarkably patient with me. I have realized since her marriage how much I have taken her calm nature for granted."

"She is an excellent woman."

"The very best."

Once Lizzy was dressed to go out-of-doors, Darcy carried her to the chaise. She felt she ought to object, for it really was not proper for a gentleman to get into the habit of carrying around a lady unrelated to him; but since they were engaged, and she truly was too unwell to walk without risking further injury, she allowed it.

And she enjoyed it entirely too much. His closeness, the heat of his body, the clean, masculine scent of him—she hoped the next few weeks would fly by, so at last she could be utterly his.

Once they got underway in the carriage, he said, "Thank you for your letter."

"Please do not thank me. I have been regretting it every moment since I sent it. You wanted ardour, and I sent you a list of well-reasoned arguments."

"I like your well-reasoned arguments."

"Would not you rather I had told you how I cannot sleep for thinking of you?"

He paused a moment, then said, "They were *your* words, from your heart. They were kind and complimentary, and full of concern for me. It was a letter that bore your own mix of earnestness and teasing, one that could not have been written by anyone else. And the signature filled me with joy. So you must not feel a moment's regret, my love. I shall cherish the letter and keep it until my dying day."

"Oh, Darcy!" She interwove her arm with his, her heart too full to speak.

The weather was cool but sunny, the trees greening up, the birds busy building their nests. With no breeze, it was quite pleasant as they travelled along the road around Rosings Park.

"This stretch of road reminds me of the approach to Meryton," she said.

"I hope you shall not miss Hertfordshire too much once we are married."

She pondered that a moment. Certainly, moving so far away from home would bring a certain amount of pain. Still, she would not be leaving forever. "We will have opportunities to visit when we are travelling to London. You spend a good part of the year in town, do you not?"

"Three months or so during the season. My uncle is of course there whilst the House of Lords is in session, so the family tend to gather there at that time."

Eager to learn more about him, she asked, "Is your uncle's family large?"

"The earl and countess have seven children, which makes up for the other branches being small. You will like him, Lizzy, and he you. Colonel Fitzwilliam is the most similar to him of all his sons, except my uncle is more jovial. You may find a worthy sparring partner in him."

The thought charmed her. "I shall take that as a challenge."

"Please do. You will endear yourself to him beyond anything if you can outmatch him."

"Outmatch a member of the House of Lords! Perhaps I aim too high."

"Do not deceive yourself. The House of Lords is filled with some of the most dreadful bores in the country. Some of them are outstanding men indeed, but they are notable for their rarity."

He slowed, and in another moment pulled the chaise off the side of the road under a chestnut tree, its spiky white flowers just starting to open.

"What are you doing?" she asked suspiciously.

He tied the horse and took a blanket from beneath the seat. "There is a pretty spot here where we can sit overlooking the stream. You will not have to walk far. I can carry you if you like."

"We are here for the scenery, then?"

"Of course. What else?"

She knew precisely why he had brought her there, but she was not going to complain. If Darcy had meant to take liberties, he had had every opportunity to do so the night before, after he had brought her home from Rosings. No, his motives were more innocent, and she did not object.

He helped her out of the carriage and down the hill to a flat piece of ground where he laid down the blanket. The trees and the slope hid the two of them from the road entirely, especially once they were seated.

Darcy untied her bonnet. Her heart raced, the act so intimate it startled her. Next he pulled off his gloves, followed by her own. She was trembling now. The man was undressing her, and if he reached for her spencer, she would have to stop him.

But he did not. He slipped a finger under her chin and gently kissed her.

"Oh, Darcy," she moaned. Nothing had ever felt so lovely as his kisses. His arms were quickly about her, her body engulfed in the heat of him. She had that feeling of madness again, of being unable to stop this if it went further.

Before she realized it, she was on her back, and Darcy on his side next to her. He kissed the hollow of her throat, and she thought she would melt. "We must not," she murmured, no strength behind the words.

"We will not." He kissed her fingers. "It is damnably difficult, but I shall control myself until our wedding night. But you had better be prepared, for I shall not hold back then."

"Why sir, I have no idea what you mean."

"Pleased to hear it," he replied, then kissed her fiercely. Her body went soft, utterly under his command. Her hands slid down his back and reached the waistband of his breeches. She ached to go lower but trusted neither of them to behave themselves if she did.

He sat up suddenly and pressed the heel of his hand to his forehead. "We should go."

"We should." She sat up beside him.

"If at any time you decide you want a special license, just say the word."

"But I take such delight in torturing you."

He turned and looked at her sideways, unamused.

"If we get a special license now," she said, "when our families have no inkling of our intentions, how will it look? And to be honest, I think my father would be loath to agree to it. Marriage in haste is unseemly in these circumstances."

He picked up a small branch and tapped it against the ground. "You are right, of course."

"I do not wish to be right. I wish to make you happy."

He tossed the stick away, then met her eyes. "I can be strong for your sake. I do not think I could do it for my own."

"No one cares if a man is a rake."

He stood and lifted her gingerly to her feet. "It was foolish to bring you here." He folded the blanket. "I put your reputation at risk. I am sorry."

"We are engaged, Darcy. Once we marry, no one will care."

She took his arm, leaning on it as he helped her back to the carriage. He did not speak, and she left him to his thoughts. This was untrodden territory for both of them—or at least she believed it was. He had said he had never been engaged.

Back in the carriage, they got underway again. The sun shone down, and she put her bonnet back on. Darcy seemed to have passed merely reflecting, and moved on to brooding. She would not have him blaming himself for wanting to kiss her. Time to distract him.

"How do you fill your days at Pemberley?" she asked. "I am trying to picture our life there."

His entire countenance lit up. "I spend my mornings meeting with the steward—you will of course meet with the housekeeper, Mrs. Reynolds—and then I catch up on my correspondence. If the day is fine, I may shoot or fish. Otherwise, I enjoy reading, or taking my favourite mare out for exercise."

She loved the picture he painted of a quiet country life. "I imagine there will be much for me to do, visiting the tenants, learning of their concerns."

"They will be happy to meet you. Georgiana can accompany you when she is at home."

Lizzy nodded. "I should like that. Who oversees her education?"

"Colonel Fitzwilliam and I. But we would benefit from a woman's advice."

Excitement blossomed in her chest. This was exactly what she had hoped for. Though she had not met Georgiana, she already felt as if she knew her, after all the girl had suffered.

Lizzy had long wished to serve as a guiding influence to her own sisters. But with parents who allowed them to spend their time in whatever nonsense they chose, it was hopeless. Georgiana perhaps would be different. Darcy had said she was an obedient girl.

It was not obedience, exactly, that Lizzy hoped for. Malleability, perhaps, or simply a desire to learn and improve. "Would you mind, then," she asked, "if I took an active part in her education? Perhaps we could find a good tutor, and keep her at home."

"That would please me very much. I have no idea how to educate girls—otherwise, I would not have sent her away." A look of consternation crossed his face.

Lizzy patted his hand. "You must not be hard on yourself. You are a good brother. You were deceived—it could have happened to anyone."

He continued looking straight ahead, watching the road, the muddy ruts of the last rain now hardened and turning to dust under the weight of the conveyance. His jaw set. "The fact unscrupulous people exist in the world, who would take advantage of a child—it is almost enough to make me lose faith in human nature."

Lizzy nodded, the hammering of a woodpecker echoing through the trees off to their right. She thought of the damage Wickham might have done to herself had she the dowry to tempt him—and how he might still harm another.

"I have been thinking," Lizzy said carefully, "I would like to write to my father and warn him of the character of...our mutual acquaintance. I would not give details, only say that I have learned more about the rift between him and yourself, and advise my father to keep a watchful eye on him."

Darcy did not speak at once. Only the sound of the carriage wheels and the horse's hooves broke the silence between them. It was agony, wondering what he was thinking, but she knew he needed time to contemplate her suggestion.

"I wish I could object," he said at last, "but of course you are right."

"It is possible the man is endeavouring to put his sins behind him. I would not like to ruin his reputation. But neither would I like to see another young lady caught up in his web."

"I trust you to convey the information to your father as you think best."

She nodded. "And of course, I shall forbid him to speak a word of it to my mother. Which he would not do anyway, until such time as would cause her the most vexation and inconvenience."

He smiled at last. "Your father is quite droll."

"Too droll for his own good. No one suffers more from my mother's poor nerves than he does." She shook her head, thinking about the folly of her family, and how they must seem to Darcy. "I am sorry."

"For what?" He glanced at her before turning his eyes back to the road. "For your parents? Do not give it another thought. I am marrying *you*, not them. Like your father, perhaps I shall learn to find humour in the situation."

A dove cooed mournfully from the crest of the trees. Lizzy's throat tightened. Hot tears of shame rolled down her cheek, and she sniffled.

He pulled the horse to a stop. Getting out a handkerchief, he wiped away her tears. "My love, you must not worry yourself. We all have relatives who embarrass us. Do you think less of me because of Lady Catherine?"

"Of course not. I think you are a saint for handling her as well as you do."

"And I think the same of you, for the way you handle the foibles of your own family. You and your sister Jane are two of the finest people I know. I look forward to calling her sister."

His words gratified Lizzy, but she could not be truly content. It had been months since he had seen her family. Perhaps he had forgotten how shocking they were.

The thought turned her blood to ice. What would he think once he saw them again? Would he regret his choice?

She told herself not to be ridiculous, but a pain lodged in her belly, one that refused to ease.

When Darcy returned Lizzy to the parsonage, his aunt's barouche was in the lane, with Anne inside. Richard was standing next to it with Mrs. Collins and Miss Lucas.

"Ah, Darcy," Richard said. "I convinced my aunt that whilst she was taking her morning constitutional, I would accompany Anne on a short drive. It is too fine a day to be indoors, do not you think?"

"Indeed it is." Darcy exited the chaise and helped Lizzy down, his hands at her waist. The feel of her reawakened his desire. Breaking that intimate contact cost him something, propriety once again winning out over his carnal inclination. The pain of waiting seemed unendurable, but now at least he had an end date.

They walked over and joined the other party. Lizzy's ankle seemed no worse for their excursion into the woods. In a few more days, it might be healed completely.

"Miss de Bourgh," said Mrs. Collins, "you are welcome to come into the house for tea. One of the parishioners brought Mr. Collins a lovely rhubarb pie."

"You are ever so kind," Anne said. "I wish I could accept, but my mother would be displeased if I exerted myself."

"Another time, then," Mrs. Collins said.

"I would like that."

They both spoke earnestly, even though it was a formality. The day would never come if Lady Catherine could help it. Pity, that. Darcy did not precisely understand the nature of his cousin's condition. She tired easily, but then, she never took any exercise. She was thin, but then, she barely ate. It was difficult to discern which was the cause and which the effect.

"I had better get her home," Richard said, but Darcy's chaise blocked the lane.

"Allow me to accompany Miss Bennet inside," Darcy said, "and then we can be on our way."

In the foyer, Lizzy took off her spencer and bonnet. Darcy eyed her, hat and gloves in his hand. He did not want to say goodbye. He wished he could spend the whole day with her.

But his aunt was already perplexed. *He* thought it logical that a man might wish to take a pretty young lady out in his chaise, when that lady was injured and could not take her usual morning walk. His aunt thought it giving Lizzy too much notice, and worried she might think he was courting her.

Well, he could not deny that much.

He would keep up the charade a while longer—even though he would have to spend less time with Lizzy than he would have liked. She would soon be his forever. In the future, these visits to Hunsford would happen just once a year. He did not wish to interfere in what little time she had with her dear friend Mrs. Collins.

"I wish you did not have to go," Lizzy said.

"I wish many things." He trailed his hand down her arm. "You are forcing me to wait, however, and I am your obedient servant." He gave her a teasing smile, which she returned. "I shall think of you every moment."

"And I you," she said.

Their privacy could not be assured, so he contented himself with kissing her palms, one then the other, until he could put off departing no longer. "My own Lizzy," he said, his voice rough, and opened the door.

"Yours always." Tears sprang to her eyes.

He forced himself to go, resenting every moment. He wished his aunt was a reasonable person, that the world was a reasonable place. Why should a man not marry the woman he loved, when they were as perfectly suited as he and Lizzy? Why should society put impediments in their way?

This was the last time. Never again would he be ruled by his aunt's caprices. He was a man of independent means, and it was time he asserted himself with her. No, he would not put Lizzy's visit with Mrs. Collins at risk. But Lady Catherine would know that the world did not answer to her.

Chapter 17

Lizzy sank into the daybed in the small parlour. She held a pillow to her chest and let her tears flow. She had watched until Darcy's chaise disappeared, and now, one minute later, she felt dreadfully alone.

Charlotte and Maria came to check on her, but they could not stay. The spring greens needed harvesting, along with the asparagus and early turnips. Lizzy offered to help, but Charlotte would not hear of it. So Lizzy put on a happy face and told her friends to go.

In their absence, she wrote the promised letter to her father. She considered her words carefully, since she had much to convey, but could say nothing directly.

Dear Papa,

I hope this letter finds you and the rest of my family well, and that you are bearing up during the absence of your two eldest daughters. I miss you all terribly.

Kent is lovely this time of year. The company here at the cottage and at Rosings Park is much as you would expect. You may have heard that Lady Catherine de Bourgh's nephews are visiting. They have increased the variety of our social circle most agreeably.

Colonel Fitzwilliam is quite the gentleman and as dashing as an officer should be. Mr. Darcy is as taciturn as ever, yet he is not quite so infuriating upon further acquaintance.

He was deeply chagrined at learning I overheard his slight of me on the night we met—especially as his opinion in that area has evolved. I have gone from tolerably pretty to somewhat pretty, and by tomorrow, perhaps on the very cusp of pretty. His opinion is changing at such a rate, I expect that before I return to Hertfordshire, he will have decided I am the most beautiful angel on earth.

You must be wondering how I can speak kindly of Mr. Darcy after the dreadful things Mr. Wickham recounted to us. I am sorry to say that after hearing Mr. Darcy's explanation, as corroborated by Colonel Fitzwilliam—a decorated officer and the son of an earl—Mr. Wickham is not what we thought him to be. Or rather, what I thought him to be, for you suspected all along that he was full of nonsense.

It is a story all too common, involving a young lady. Fortunately, her family was able to intervene before she was lost forever. His next victim may not be so lucky.

As you can imagine, for the sake of the lady and her family, the truth cannot be broadcast. And I truly hope for Mr. Wickham's sake that he is using this new opportunity in His Majesty's service to better himself. I must ask, therefore, that you share this information with no one except in the most dire of circumstances. Or perhaps you could call upon my uncle Philips for his discretion and vigilance, since he is likely to hear more quickly about the goings-on in Meryton.

It seems this letter ended far graver than it began. I hope my warnings are all for naught, and Mr. Wickham continues as agreeable as ever.

On a happier note, when I return to Hertfordshire, you can expect a young man of your acquaintance to call on you. I trust you will find his request amenable, as it reflects the dearest wish of my heart.

Lizzy thought a long time before posting the letter. Her father needed some forewarning, and certainly her hints were sufficient that he could not misunderstand her meaning. In the end, she concluded that the letter met her purpose, and set it in the tray by the front door, hoping for the best.

That afternoon at Rosings, Darcy was reading in the parlour, waiting for dinner to be served. Lady Catherine entered and sat by the fire, a footman adding a log to the glowing embers for her comfort, raising the scent of smoke.

Darcy gave his aunt a nod before returning to the newspaper. Or rather, returning to a pleasant daydream—involving Lizzy and a very private woodland walk—that made it impossible to focus on the written words.

"Darcy, do you not hear me?" Lady Catherine said, waking him from his reverie. He looked up to see her face lined with consternation. "My, you are distracted this visit," she said. "No trouble at Pemberley, I hope?"

"None at all. My distraction is more agreeable." He folded the paper. He might as well begin planting the seed. "I am thinking of marrying."

She grinned, her eyes the intensity of a cat about to pounce. "I quite agree. You know, it was the dearest wish of your mother that you and Anne should join the two great estates of Pemberley and Rosings Park—"

"I have heard you say so, though my mother never mentioned it."

"She did not get the chance, the poor dear thing. We lost her before you were of an age to marry."

The grief softening his aunt's features was real, but he could not say whether her claim about his mother's wish was the same. He believed it to be Lady Catherine's alone. He could not prove it, though, and had no desire to think ill of her, so he did not press the issue.

If his cousin Anne died without marrying, the estate would pass to her father's nearest kin, and out of the Fitzwilliam family. Perhaps Richard should marry her, as he was in need of a wife who could keep him in the style to which he was accustomed. That seemed like an arrangement to suit everyone.

"My dear aunt, you may not have noticed, but Anne shows no partiality for me. She should marry a man of high spirits who can keep her entertained." He set down the newspaper on the end table. "I fear she would find me deadly dull."

"But ever since she was in her cradle—"

"When she was in her cradle, you did not know the dispositions we would have as adults." He rose and stepped toward her. In a tender voice, he said, "Anne is dear to me, dear enough that I would not saddle her with a husband who could not make her happy. And I am certain I could not."

He bowed, leaving the room and brooking no further arguments from his aunt.

Finding Richard in the library, sitting in an easy chair with a book in his hand, Darcy closed the door and said, "What think you of marrying Anne?"

Richard scowled. Laying his book atop a table, he eyed his cousin suspiciously. "Marrying Anne? You do not mean me?"

"Lady Catherine has always hoped for *me* to marry Anne—you know that. She will be better pleased with my engagement to Lizzy, if Anne has another suitor."

"Ah." Richard nodded thoughtfully, his gaze unfocused. "So I should marry Anne to remove the burden from you."

Darcy smiled, though he was not entirely joking. "She is the heiress of Rosings Park, and fonder of you than she is of anyone."

"You are right." Richard stood and rounded the table. "The union would be most convenient. There is but one impediment—I am not in love with her."

"Come now, it has all the trappings of a great romantic tragedy. You will forge a family alliance, then fall madly in love. She will die in childbirth, you in the war, and Lady Catherine will be left with an orphan to raise. It would make a brilliant opera."

Richard laughed heartily. "But not a very persuasive argument."

"Never mind that. I shall suggest it to Lady Catherine at once. It will be a source of great comfort to her."

"You will do no such thing." Richard's eyes danced, but his body grew tense. A careless word to their aunt, even in jest, could make his life more difficult.

Darcy did not press him further. He did not wish to anger his cousin, and of course Richard was his own man. The scheme appealed to Darcy, but if Richard did not see the situation the same way, there was no point belabouring the subject.

Instead, Darcy turned and looked out the window at the darkening sky. He poured them both a brandy and handed one to Richard. "Today when Elizabeth and I were out in my chaise, we discussed our future. She will be an excellent wife, an excellent mistress of Pemberley. I could not have chosen better. Others may look at us and think me a fool, but she is perfect in every way that matters."

"Then Lady Catherine's opinion should be of no consequence."

"It should not."

"And yet, it is."

Darcy's jaw twitched. He swirled his glass, watching the amber liquid coat the crystal. "She has been kind to me my whole life. I see now that her attentiveness crosses a line into interference—but when I was a child, she was a doting aunt who showered me with love. I know my engagement will pain her, and I do not wish to cause her pain."

"I understand. That *does* seem like a good reason for me to marry Anne," Richard said lightly.

"You are thirty years old, and you have never been in love. You have no title, no income except for your colonel's pay and whatever your father sees fit to give you. Anne is your best option."

Richard shook his head and set down his drink. "I had better end this conversation now before you actually convince me." He quickly made his exit.

Darcy watched the retreating figure. He had given his cousin a much-needed push. It remained to be seen how far Richard would travel in that direction.

Chapter 18

To Lizzy's delight, Darcy called with his chaise the next two mornings. When she arrived home on the second day, a letter from her sister awaited on a sterling salver in the front parlour. She blushed to remember how she had signed her last letter to Jane, and tore open the envelope to see the response.

Dear Lizzy,

I am in such raptures, I hardly know what to think. Very little could please me more than your friendship with Mr. Darcy. Now that I know you are not grieving over your discovery about Mr. Wickham, I can relate my good news to you without worrying I am causing you pain.

A friend of Bingley's told him I was in town, and he came to me the moment he got the news. Though it was ever so late in the evening, I have never been happier to receive a visitor in my life.

He has called every day for the past week, and it is as if we were never apart. He is every bit as agreeable as before, and perfectly contrite for quitting Netherfield as he did. He said he was convinced by others that I did not care for him—including Caroline, who I thought was my friend.

It is distressing how her kindness ended where her self-interest began. She wants him to marry Georgiana Darcy, in the hope that a family alliance will help her secure Mr. Darcy for herself. But I see now, Mr. Darcy's affections lie elsewhere, with a woman who shall make him a better wife than Caroline ever could.

She lied to me, Lizzy—she told me outright that Bingley knew I was in town, when he did not. In time, I shall find the strength to forgive her, yet I shall never regard her again as I once did.

But I have no desire to think on such things. Despite Caroline's machinations, Bingley and I are friends again, and now you and Mr. Darcy are friends, too. I could not be happier. We shall have so much to discuss once we are back in Hertfordshire! Bingley has sent word to ready Netherfield for his return. One more week and we will all be home, and all shall be right with the world.

Lizzy read greedily, then went back and read again, focusing on each word. No, it was not her imagination—

though Jane did not say it outright, she referred to Mr. Bingley as *Bingley* several times. It could mean only one thing—they were engaged!

The letter was all the confirmation Lizzy needed. Darcy *must* have been the friend who told Bingley that Jane was in town. The dates aligned perfectly. And Darcy had met Mrs. Gardiner whilst there. Yet he had said nothing to Lizzy about it!

She could think of only one reason: he did not wish his actions to affect her feelings for him. But why should they not? He was certainly the dearest man on earth.

The next time she saw him, she would tease him mercilessly for it.

∽✤∾

That evening the group from the parsonage dined at Rosings. As they gathered in the parlour before the meal, Lizzy glanced slyly at Darcy before taking a seat by Colonel Fitzwilliam. He greeted her with his usual friendliness, then after a brief conversation rose with a bow.

He went and stood by the piano, where Miss de Bourgh turned pages as Maria played a Scottish air. Could Miss de Bourgh read music? She did not play, that much Lizzy knew, as Lady Catherine had said so.

Miss de Bourgh looked up at the colonel, and her cheeks pinked once more. Lizzy had not imagined it—Miss de Bourgh was in love with Colonel Fitzwilliam!

Darcy took the seat the colonel had vacated. He said to Lizzy, "You look beautiful. It is taking all my strength not to kiss you."

She smiled and smoothed her skirt. The pale blue of her gown was a good colour on her, and the fit flattered her figure. "Thank you. I would return the compliment, but since I have already said you are the handsomest man on earth, it seems redundant."

"Some things bear repeating."

"You take my breath away, Darcy. Always." She looked over at the pianoforte, then said in his ear, "But perhaps we are not the only lovers in the room. Do you not think your two cousins there might make an excellent match?"

He raised his brows, then gave her a single nod. "I do. I suggested as much to the colonel two days ago."

Her lips parted. "So you noticed it, too?"

He scowled. "Noticed what?"

"That Miss de Bourgh is in love with him."

"Not at all. I meant it as a joke. But in truth, it would be convenient for them both. Love might come in time." He eyed them curiously. "I admit, I have not noticed such a glow about her before."

"Perhaps boredom makes her listless. Even on the few occasions when she is allowed to go out, she cannot leave the carriage except at church."

He nodded, his expression thoughtful. "If only she had a stronger constitution, she might make him the perfect wife."

Lizzy did not think Miss de Bourgh's constitution was quite the impediment Darcy did. But he seemed content to let the subject drop, so she did not pursue it.

He squeezed her hand surreptitiously. "Are you feeling better, my love? How is your ankle?"

"My ankle is much improved, thank you. But I am feeling out of sorts. We agreed that we would be honest, and you have not been."

He blinked twice. "How so?"

She took a delicate sip of sherry, then set the tapered crystal glass down on the coffee table. Giving him a level look, she hid any hint of teasing from her voice. "You travelled to London last week and saw my aunt—"

"Ah." He looked away.

She gave him the opportunity to say more, but he did not. She continued, "When I asked you about it, you made no mention of also seeing my sister."

In a ragged voice, he said, "I had thought Miss Bennet would be more discreet."

"She has been quite discreet. The facts speak for themselves. You went to London and saw Bingley on the very day he learned she was in town. I pieced it together as soon as I heard she had seen him."

Darcy's eyes widened. "Before I proposed?"

"Of course before you proposed." She struggled to keep her voice low. In consternation, she rose and walked to the window. With twilight setting in, the trees had turned to shadows. Suddenly, this quarrel did not feel like teasing. It felt very real.

He followed. "I am sorry. I did not want my actions to influence your decision."

"Did you think it had no bearing?" Her voice turned pleading. She did not like being shut out from things that affected them both. "Why would you hide your goodness? How could you keep something from me, knowing it would make me happy?"

His face paled. "It had to be done in secret. I did not want you to think I had acted only to win your heart." He averted his eyes. "I wanted you to hear the news from your sister."

She knitted her brow, then pouted. How infuriating that he should act selflessly, and with the best of intentions! Reluctantly, she said, "That is a very good answer. You make it impossible to stay angry."

He gave her a tentative glance. "Then I am forgiven?"

She looked at him softly. "There was never anything to forgive. Truly, Darcy, I understand you are a private man. I respect that. But I cannot love you properly unless I know what is in your heart."

His eyes widened, surprise written on his face. He gave her a little nod.

"Oh, Darcy," she said on a sigh, pressing his hand. "The colonel said you were the best of men, and he was right. How could I ever deserve you?"

"I love you. I would be lost without you."

She nodded. "That is my saving grace, I suppose. I shall never give you reason to doubt me."

"And I shall endeavour to do the same."

"Darcy, promise me...you will not be one of those husbands who hides things to protect his wife, believing she is too fragile for the truth. I want to be a genuine partner to you. Anything less, and I shall be quite miserable."

He grasped her hand. "You are quite right. Any secrets would erode the trust between us. I should have told you about my trip to London, once you had accepted my proposal."

"And I should have told you my suspicions, instead of letting them hang between us."

He grinned. "You are far too clever for me to keep anything from you."

"I am," she teased. "And you would do well to remember it."

Before he could answer, dinner was announced. Without a word, he bowed, then took his place entering the dining room with Miss de Bourgh on his arm.

Lizzy followed, walking next to Maria and pondering Darcy's words. She thought about her parents, and the disdainful way her father treated her mother. The prospect of such a relationship made her shudder. If she could have a marriage of equals with anyone, it was with Darcy. He seemed to want that as much as she.

But was such a thing possible? Could he learn to be honest with her in all things, when he was by nature so private? His heart was open to her, but she would have to work to keep it that way. It would be all too easy for him to retreat inside.

Chapter 19

Later that week, Darcy and the colonel called early at the parsonage. As the morning wore on, rain threatened—so they cut their visit short. When they returned to Rosings, the sweet notes of Beethoven's "Moonlight Sonata" echoed through the halls.

The gentlemen headed toward the sound, which came from the drawing room. Darcy could not imagine the pianist to be anyone other than Mrs. Jenkinson, for no one else in the household could play. To his great shock, however, the musician was Anne!

He stopped short when he saw her, as Richard did behind him. They stared stupidly as she looked over and gave them a sly smile. When she released the final chord, she said, "The piano in Mrs. Jenkinson's room cannot do this piece justice. Sometimes I play it here whilst my mother is out taking her morning constitutional."

Darcy was too astonished to speak. Richard, however, managed to voice what they both were thinking. "How long have you been playing at the pianoforte?"

"Since Mrs. Jenkinson came to me when I was seven or eight. My mother did not want me to exert myself, but Mrs. Jenkinson could not stop me from plinking out little tunes on my own. So she decided she had better teach me, and it would be our little secret."

She shut the piano and rose. "I hope it can remain a secret?"

Darcy bit back a grin. Anne was a delicate thing, and could be peevish when feeling unwell. In the evenings, if she required laudanum to dull the pain, her mind grew hazy. But in the mornings, when she was alert, she showed herself intelligent and well-read.

He had never imagined, however, that she possessed this rebellious side. An accomplished pianist, and no one had any idea! What other secrets was she hiding?

"You have my word," Richard said. "My aunt shall not hear of it from me."

"And you, Darcy?"

"I would not dream of doing anything to incur your displeasure, madam."

She gave him a satisfied smile.

Darcy had often wondered whether Lady Catherine's oversight of Anne's condition might actually make it worse. His aunt was of such a confident disposition that she never allowed anyone's opinion but her own. Anne might fare better without her mother's influence.

It was impossible to say for certain. Lady Catherine had been carefully monitoring Anne her entire life, and perhaps did know best.

"How are you feeling this morning?" Darcy asked her.

"Quite well. In fact, I think I might be up to taking a turn in the garden, if the colonel would be so kind as to lend me his arm."

"I would be delighted."

Darcy smiled and watched them go. Over the past few days, Richard had indeed showed more attention to Anne than he had done previously. For as long as Darcy could remember, Richard had seemed better able to distract her from her illness than anyone. Perhaps Lizzy was right, and Anne had fallen in love with him.

With the growing prospect of being sent to the Continent, Richard might believe it time to think about an heir. Darcy would say nothing further on the subject, however. If Richard wished for Darcy's advice, he would ask. Richard had enough on his mind without Darcy tormenting him.

Darcy did not wish to think of how the war could change things forever. He loved Richard as a brother, and if he lost him, his life would be forever diminished. With their days at Rosings drawing to a close, Darcy often found himself thinking, *Perhaps this will be the last time...*

The last time they took turns letting Lady Catherine beat them at chess. The last time they raced their horses through the alley of oaks that opened into a broad field. The last time they argued over which of them had landed the killing shot that took down a twelve-point stag when Darcy was fifteen.

He pushed the morbid thought from his mind. It accomplished nothing—what would come, would come. Better to make the most of these pleasant days whilst they lasted.

Darcy picked up the newspaper, sitting and paging through it. A quarter hour later, Anne and Richard returned from the garden with Lady Catherine and Mrs. Jenkinson on their heels. Their voices in the hallway grew louder as they approached the drawing room.

"Anne, I do not think it wise for you to be out in this weather," Lady Catherine said. "It could rain any moment."

"I am sorry, Mama. We did stay close to the house, just in case."

"But the damp! It is affecting my rheumatism. It cannot be good for you, either."

"I appreciate your concern, but I feel no ill effects from it."

"My dear, your health—"

"I *am* of age now," Anne softly reminded. "You have been a saint, caring for me as you have all these years. But I know what I can tolerate, and what I cannot. A turn in the garden has never done me any harm."

Anne entered the drawing room, still on Richard's arm. Lady Catherine followed, helped by her cane, with Mrs. Jenkinson just behind.

"Darcy," his aunt said, "you must help me talk sense into my daughter."

"I do not see what I can say on the subject. Richard, did the walk seem to tire my fair cousin?"

"Not at all. If it had, I would have brought her inside at once. I would have thrown her over my shoulder if I'd had to."

Anne laughed at that. "Richard, I do not believe it will ever be necessary to take such drastic steps with me."

"You are as dear to me as anyone on earth," he insisted. "I shall take whatever steps are needed to protect you."

"Yes, well," said Lady Catherine, "I suppose I have no say whatever. I am only your mother."

"Of course you have a say." Anne kissed her cheek. "I rely on your experience and judgment. But I am no longer a child. I do hope I might be trusted to make my own decisions now and again."

That seemed to put Lady Catherine at ease, if it did not entirely satisfy her. She sat in her usual place by the fire, and

Mrs. Jenkinson settled a blanket over her ladyship's legs. Then Mrs. Jenkinson picked up her knitting whilst Anne and Richard sat on the couch.

"I am most displeased," Lady Catherine said, "that Miss Lucas and Miss Bennet will be returning to Hertfordshire so soon. Especially after I advised them to add a fortnight to their visit."

"I seem to recall their saying they are needed at home," Darcy reminded her, knowing it was fruitless.

"But there can be nothing for them at home that can compare to the delights of Rosings Park," Lady Catherine declared. "Miss Lucas, she is a sweet girl. Not as clever as her sister, but pretty. I daresay she shall marry respectably. A vicar, perhaps, or an officer."

"She is delightful," Richard said. "I know a captain or two who could do worse for themselves."

"I would be happy to make the introductions if I were ever in town," Lady Catherine said. "If you tell me their names, I shall raise the matter with the countess."

It was unclear why Richard could not raise the matter himself, as the countess in question was his own mother. But Darcy continued to scan the newspaper rather than questioning Lady Catherine's offer.

"Now, poor Miss Bennet," his aunt continued, "she is another matter, I am afraid. Whilst it is true that young ladies of beauty and wit have married well despite a lack of fortune, such an eventuality cannot be counted on. I like her uncommonly well. I shall be happy to make her a recommendation if necessary, though I hate to see any gentlewoman sunk to the position of governess."

Mrs. Jenkinson startled but did not raise her eyes from her knitting.

Darcy glared at his aunt, astonished that she should suggest such a thing. But before he could speak, Richard said in a fervent tone,

"Mrs. Jenkinson, might we have some music? What a dull place this would be without your talent."

The woman gave a little nod and walked quickly to the pianoforte. The colour in her cheeks and glisten in her eyes showed that Lady Catherine's words had stung.

Darcy set his jaw. No one knew better than he the importance of a governess in a girl's life. He had been completely deceived in the character of Mrs. Younge when he chose her as a companion for Georgiana. The woman might have done irreparable damage.

Mrs. Jenkinson, by contrast, had proven herself utterly devoted to Anne, despite the trials of illness and the officiousness of Lady Catherine. No one deserved his aunt's respect more. To suggest that working as a governess was beneath the dignity of a gentlewoman was insulting.

He set the newspaper aside, realizing uncomfortably that six months ago, he might have regarded the situation exactly as Lady Catherine had. Lizzy had taught him compassion toward those whom fate had not smiled on, as it had himself. The thought shamed him.

"Darcy," his aunt said, "I must admonish you to take care where Miss Bennet is concerned. I realize our society here is small, but you must not distinguish her with your attentions."

"What?" he asked, perfectly understanding her but offended that she should dare speak to him thus. Of course, no one had a greater right to. She was his mother's sister, and exactly the person who ought to act in his mother's stead if he were behaving improperly toward a young lady.

"Miss Bennet is a clever girl, and so she *ought* to recognize her own inferiority in regards to your position. But a young lady is not always as circumspect as she might be, when a young gentleman turns her head."

"I assure you, there is no misunderstanding between Miss Bennet and myself."

"Is that so?" Lady Catherine looked at him with narrowed eyes. "I hope matters will continue thus."

"Richard," Anne said, "will you sing a duet with me? Mrs. Jenkinson is playing one of my favourites."

"It would be my pleasure," he replied, as the pianist's fingers trilled over the notes of an Italian love song.

Darcy rose along with them, then bowed to his aunt. "If you will excuse me, I have some correspondence I must attend to."

He headed to his room, his thoughts muddled. His annoyance with his aunt was unfounded, at least with regards to Lizzy. Had they not been engaged, his behaviour would have been entirely too familiar.

He was not taking the care he ought, to safeguard her from his aunt's wrath. Lizzy still had another week in Kent. He would have to remain vigilant.

What annoyed him most of all, he realized, was that his aunt had been right about Lizzy's situation. If Mr. Bennet had passed away before Bingley had let Netherfield, the Bennet daughters—certainly the three eldest—would have been forced to take positions as governesses. It would have been the only option to keep their family out of poverty.

The thought crushed his heart. To picture Lizzy dressed in grey and blending into the background, suppressing all her exuberance, caused him physical pain.

He ought to have courted her whilst he was at Netherfield. He had wasted months, when they might have been happy together. By now, they might even have had a child on the way. He had allowed his filial pride to blind him, rather than seeing Lizzy as the jewel she was.

She had transformed him. With her clever mind and relentless teasing, she had shown him his own ridiculousness. She had forced him to become a better man if he wanted to win her. No woman was more deserving of his love.

Another week, and they would leave this place to begin their life together. He would not have to worry about subjecting her to his aunt's scorn, for Lizzy would be beyond Lady Catherine's reach. All differences between their stations would blur once he and Lizzy were wed.

He was determined. Their families would not serve as an impediment between them again.

"I am so out of sorts," Maria declared one evening during dinner at the parsonage. "Colonel Fitzwilliam has utterly thrown me over for Miss de Bourgh." She spoke with great cheerfulness, Lizzy observed, as if being thrown over by an earl's son in favour of his sickly heiress cousin was the most interesting thing that could happen to a person.

In truth, Lizzy surmised, it was likely the most interesting thing that would happen to Maria Lucas.

Charlotte stirred her soup, looking at Maria askance. "I warned you that you could not hope so high."

"I know." She sighed. "But he is so *very* dashing."

"My dear sister," Mr. Collins declared, "such a match as you suggest, between Miss de Bourgh and the esteemed colonel, cannot hope to take place. I have it on the authority of none other than Lady Catherine de Bourgh herself that her daughter is betrothed to her nephew Mr. Darcy."

"Perhaps someone ought to tell Mr. Darcy, then," Maria said. "For he is besotted with Eliza, and she with him. I shall be astonished if the banns are not read for them within a fortnight."

"Maria, you misapprehend the situation entirely," Mr. Collins said. "A man of Mr. Darcy's stature does not marry a woman entirely without fortune, as my cousin Elizabeth is. If my dear cousin her father had put aside a small sum for his daughters each year, as he ought to have done, it might have grown into a respectable dowry by now. But as he has been remiss, it is by no means certain that a gentleman shall ever offer for her again. No offense, cousin Elizabeth."

"None taken," Lizzy assured him.

She decided not to worry that Maria had found her and Darcy out. They were leaving for Hertfordshire in a few days. Maria was not wrong—the banns would be read within a fortnight. In truth, within a se'en-night. This very Sunday.

The thought terrified her but also made her indescribably happy. In a month, she would be Mrs. Fitzwilliam Darcy. And she could imagine nothing finer.

⁂

Darcy stood at the edge of a woodland on the Rosings property near Hunsford cottage. Now that Lizzy's ankle was fully healed, they had taken to meeting during her morning walks to avoid rousing his aunt's suspicions any further. Darcy always managed to arrive at the spot first, and now, as he looked down the slope to see Lizzy approaching, he could understand why.

Her happy, skipping steps were frequently interrupted with stops to admire a clump of wildflowers, or perhaps a butterfly taking a sip of nectar. The sight of her enjoying such simple things filled his chest with a happiness unlike anything he had experienced before. She took such pleasure in *being*, without having to *do* anything.

In small, careful steps, he was learning to do the same. He picked a daffodil from a clump that was growing wild. Sniffing it, he could detect only a hint of sweet scent. Still, the bright yellow colour and the soft, delicate petals evoked a smile.

As a boy, he had loved such simple things. When had that changed? When had this dark cynicism descended on him and cast a pall over every hope for happiness?

The loss of his parents had not helped, but he did not believe that was the cause of it. When he and Wickham had left for Cambridge, they had been friends—practically brothers. But as the months passed, Wickham's true nature became apparent. He developed such a debauched lifestyle at university, Darcy distanced himself for the preservation of his own reputation.

Wickham resented it—of course he did—even though it was not a rejection of Wickham's friendship, just his behaviour.

Wickham, however, did not see it that way. His treatment of Darcy turned angry and spiteful. Wickham became so bitter that he attempted to lure Georgiana into elopement—the ultimate revenge.

From that moment, Darcy was unable to experience happiness or even a moment of pleasure—until Lizzy came into his life. She had reaffirmed his belief in the goodness of the world. Her absence of artifice allowed him to trust again.

As she drew close, she untied the ribbons of her bonnet. They fluttered in the breeze as she removed it. Flinging it to the ground, she ran into his arms and he drew her close for a kiss.

She smelled like flowers and springtime and sweet morning air. He wanted to unpin her hair and brush his fingers through it, but it would not do for her to return to the parsonage in such disarray. So he contented himself with sliding his hands down her back and resting them at her waist.

"Darcy," she murmured against his lips, then kissed him hard. "Could anything be more perfect?"

"When we are married, it will be."

She entwined her fingers with his. "But do you not think that once we are married, such pleasures will grow so commonplace, we will forget to cherish them as we do now?"

He removed her gloves and kissed her fingertips. "All married couples do, I suppose, eventually."

"Then let us promise to never take each other for granted."

"I promise, my love, to cherish you every day."

"And I you." She beamed at him, a smile bright enough to rival the sun.

He kissed her again, suckling at her lips, flicking his tongue against her own. He resented every stitch of clothing on her body, every moment that remained until their wedding night. But Lizzy was right. There was pleasure even in this torment of longing—the pleasure of knowing acutely how precious she was to him.

They walked hand in hand for a while, leaving the woodland behind as they headed down the slope and into the grassy meadow from whence she had come.

"I have been thinking," Lizzy said, bonnet swaying in her hand, as the sky had clouded over. "After you have spoken to my father, perhaps you should stay with your family in London. You could return a few days before the wedding, instead of spending all that time in Hertfordshire."

Wearing a scowl, Darcy turned to her, slowing his pace. He could not account for such a sentiment. It seemed utterly at odds with what she had said about cherishing one another. "Is that what you want?"

"Once we are married, we shall have all the time in the world together." She gave him a fond smile. "Until then, you should enjoy your last days as a single man with your family."

"My uncle's family will return to Derbyshire four months hence, when the shooting season starts. It is not as if we will be separated long."

A line furrowed her forehead. "Yes, I suppose." She did not look happy.

A chill ran through him, though not from cold. He did not understand what she was about. A moment ago, she had been kissing him with great enthusiasm, but now she seemed distant.

"My love, you must tell me what is troubling you."

"Oh Darcy," she cried, stopping in the tall grass, tears filling her eyes. "I know how unhappy you were the last time you were in Hertfordshire."

He blinked, puzzled by that statement. "The last time I was in Hertfordshire, I met an enchanting woman and fell hopelessly in love."

"You were so desperate to leave the place, you followed Bingley to London in all possible haste, to convince him never to return."

Darcy grew silent. She was not wrong. Even worse, he had been eager to leave Hertfordshire because he wanted to forget about the woman he had fallen in love with. No wonder she did not want him to spend time there again.

"I was a blockhead."

"You made a perfectly logical decision. The thought of you or Bingley forming an alliance with my family mortified you. It is best that you spend as little time with them as possible."

He understood her perfectly now. Her reasoning was sound, but she had underestimated the change that love had wrought in him. He cupped her face in his hands. "On the contrary, I should get to know them, for they will be my family soon enough."

Her eyes softened, but he still saw fear in them.

He leaned in and kissed her. "My sweet Lizzy, it pains me to think of my arrogance last fall, unwilling as I was to look beyond the country manners of the good people of Meryton. I am utterly ashamed of myself. The fault lies not with your neighbours, but with my inexcusable pride. You have taught me to be a better man. Instead of looking to disapprove, I shall look to be pleased, as Bingley does."

The muscles in her jaw twitched. "I have accepted all that passed between us last fall, but I have no desire to relive it."

He lifted her soft fingers to his lips. "I promise, Lizzy, you will not. In London this winter, I witnessed as much folly amongst members of the *ton* as I had seen in Meryton society, and no more true goodness. I realized what a fool I had been."

She pressed a hand to his chest, then rested her cheek there. Drawing her close, he stroked the length of her back, grateful for the second chance she had given him, so utterly undeserved. He would spend the rest of his life proving he was the man he ought to be, thanks to her.

They walked together a while, talking about everything and nothing, enjoying the warm air and the soft earth beneath their feet. As they approached the parsonage, they stopped a moment behind the hedge, out of sight of the road and the windows. Brushing a wisp of hair from her face, he kissed her tenderly.

"In four days," he said, "I shall secure your father's permission, and we will no longer have to hide."

"At last." She arched a brow. "Assuming my father does not object. Will you whisk me off to Gretna Green if he does?"

"It would be more prudent to wait until you reach your majority."

She pondered that a moment, or pretended to. "It would be more expedient to tell him you have already taken my virtue."

Darcy nodded. "Whatever you think best."

She grinned. Tossing her bonnet onto the ground, she ran her hands up his chest and entwined her fingers at his nape. "We are very wicked."

"You have seen little of the world, if you think so." He kissed her forehead.

"Oh Darcy, I do not think I have ever been happier than I am at this moment."

"Nor I." He pressed his lips to hers one last time, savouring her softness, before accompanying her to the cottage.

He left her with a pang, but his joy did not abate as he headed back to Rosings. The thick grass smelled sweet under his feet, and a little creek gurgled and splashed as he crossed it at its narrowest point. These pathways recalled his boyhood, a time when he had been carefree. Lizzy had given him back that feeling.

He walked up the stone steps and into the foyer at Rosings. The clock struck the quarter hour—it was nigh unto eleven. He had not meant to stay away so long, but he could not regret it.

He headed for the stairs, but his aunt's voice stopped him. "Darcy, where have you been? I must speak with you at once."

He stepped into the doorway of the drawing room and bowed. "Forgive, me, ma'am. If I may be permitted to change—"

"At once, sir, or I shall be forced to expel you from my home."

He startled, and Anne let out a cry from her seat on the opposite end of the couch from her mother. "Mama!"

"Silence, girl, I am most displeased with you."

Anne glared and her cheeks reddened, but she said no more. Darcy looked between them in confusion.

"Sit," Lady Catherine said to him, as if he were a dog. He deigned to stand. Whatever Lady Catherine had to say, it ought to be interesting, at least.

He took a few steps into the room. "Have I done something to distress your ladyship?"

Her eyes narrowed. "I warned you not to trifle with that girl."

Darcy's face warmed. If he could placate his aunt for a few more days—

"Anne says she has seen you joining Miss Bennet in her morning walks from time to time. Do you deny it?"

"Not at all. I have occasionally happened upon her—"

"Do you take me for a fool? This morning, whilst Anne was out riding in the barouche with the colonel, she saw you kissing Miss Bennet. What say you to that?"

He stared at Anne. What was this? Why would she reveal such a thing to her mother?

"I am sorry," said Anne, flushed and trembling, tears staining her cheeks. "I thought it would convince her to forget this nonsense about you and me—"

"Silence! I shall not be disobeyed by you again! You knew of such happenings, and did not see fit to warn me. And now, things have progressed too far." She turned to Darcy and said in a lugubrious tone, "Tell me, Darcy, tell me you have not ruined her."

"Certainly not!" Fury filled his voice. Surely she did not think him capable of such a thing. "My behaviour toward Miss Bennet has been entirely honourable."

"Do you deny that you kissed her?"

"I do not deny it. When she leaves Kent, I shall travel to Hertfordshire to ask her father for her hand."

"What!" Lady Catherine cried. "You shall do nothing of the kind."

Richard rushed in, apparently concerned by the sound of raised voices. "Dear Lady Catherine, has something upset you?"

"Your cousin," she cried, pointing at Darcy dramatically, "my nephew, has forgotten all his filial responsibilities and aligned himself with a chit of no family and no fortune."

"Oh," Richard said. "That."

"You knew of this?" she demanded.

Richard looked at Darcy, then his aunt. "I knew he had made her an offer, yes."

It hardly seemed possible, but Lady Catherine's voice rose even higher, both in pitch and volume. "You have been staying under my roof, concealing something so momentous from me?"

"It cannot be broadcast until I speak with her father," Darcy insisted. "She is not of age."

"It will not be broadcast at all." Her ladyship sat with her back straight and said in a commanding tone, "You must end it with her."

"I shall do no such thing."

"You will explain that you are not at liberty to marry. That you did not fully comprehend the requirements of your father's will, and your duty to marry your cousin, Miss de Bourgh."

Darcy gazed at Anne, who sat turned away from her mother, her arms crossed, her cheeks ablaze. He set his jaw, waiting for his anger to settle before speaking. "My father's will held no such stipulation. I shall not lie to the woman I love, nor shall I end the engagement."

"Bah, love. You barely know the girl."

"I have known her for eight months. We spent considerable time together in Hertfordshire, and seeing her again here in Hunsford removed any uncertainty I had about my choice."

"Be reasonable, Darcy," Lady Catherine argued. "Not only does she have no fortune, she can bring no honour to the Fitzwilliam name. Have you so little understanding of your duty?"

He clenched his fists at his side. "Madam, I have a duty to God, to my king, and to my sister, but I have no duty whatever to the Fitzwilliam name. If you are embarrassed by my choice, so be it. I shall not betray my fiancée for your sake."

"Mama, do you not see?" Anne cried. "Darcy does not love me, nor I him. A marriage between us is impossible. He is sworn to another. His honour is at stake."

"Five thousand pounds would buy her silence."

280

"The devil!" the colonel cried. "Aunt, you cannot mean to compromise Darcy's integrity. He is promised to Miss Bennet. She has given him her heart."

"If she has not given him her maidenhead, then all is not lost."

"Mama!" Anne cried. "What a dreadful thing to say."

Darcy was too angry for words. He paced about the room, thinking it best to absent himself at once. But where would he go? If he packed quickly, he could be in London before dark.

To his aunt, he said, "Madam, this conversation is over. I have nothing more to say on the matter."

"Nor I," Anne agreed. "I would not marry Darcy at Miss Bennet's expense, even if I were in love with him, which I am not."

Lady Catherine's face reddened. "Uniting the great properties of Pemberley and Rosings Park was the dearest wish of his mother and yours from the time you were in your cradle—"

"And why should that signify?" Anne asked. "Why should Darcy and I be tied to some dream you and Lady Anne had twenty years ago?"

"If Darcy does not marry you, then who will?" Lady Catherine cried. "How shall you possibly find a husband?"

The rest of the room fell into a stunned silence, the insult hanging in the air.

DARCY COMES TO ROSINGS

"I have done my best for you," her ladyship continued, "but you have not the constitution for a London season. There are no gentlemen your equal in the parish. You must marry, Anne, or Rosings Park will pass out of the Fitzwilliam family. It will go to that toad Archibald de Bourgh, or one of his worthless sons." She raised her head high and said dramatically, "Is that what you wish? For me to be forced from my home by one of those creatures?"

Darcy could not find voice to speak. His mind whirled as if he were drunk. *This* was why his aunt wished him to marry Anne? So she herself could continue to live at Rosings if Anne *died*?

Lady Catherine looked away as sobs wracked Anne's delicate frame. Richard ran to Anne's side and knelt before her, taking her in his arms.

Struggling to maintain what was left of his composure, Darcy strode to the window. The clouds had darkened and a sudden breeze whipped the trees. The abuse his aunt had lobbed at Lizzy and himself was mild compared to the devastation her words had wrought on her daughter. Had the woman no conscience?

It had not occurred to Darcy before, but—now that Anne had reached her majority, *she* was mistress of Rosings Park. Lady Catherine was dependent on her daughter. A daughter she had just humiliated.

Mrs. Bennet had nothing on Lady Catherine.

Never before had Darcy witnessed anything as crass as that tirade. Poor Anne! To be dismissed in such a way by her own mother! Who else could Anne rely on to look out for her interests?

He turned back to the room and startled as his gaze fell on his fair cousin. Richard's comforting caresses had turned into passionate kisses. Anne pulled back, but Richard's gaze remained fixed on her.

"My darling." He caressed her hand. "Dearest Anne. We will go to London for a special license, and be married within the week. Yes?"

Anne nodded violently, joy sounding in her voice. "Yes."

Richard looked at Lady Catherine, pure hatred crossing his features. "You may remain in the house, for now. But you will not see your daughter again until *I* determine her health can endure it."

Lady Catherine stared straight ahead and said nothing.

The colonel rang for the footman. When the man appeared, Richard said, "Tell Mrs. Jenkinson she is going to London. She must pack Miss de Bourgh's things. We leave within the hour."

Chapter 20

"**L**ondon!" Lizzy cried, jumping to her feet when Darcy told her the news. They were in the front parlour of the parsonage, where she had been catching up on correspondence whilst Charlotte and Maria tended the poultry. Lizzy rubbed the heel of her hand, mind whirling at this sudden turn of events. "You are leaving today?"

"As soon as possible," said Darcy, standing next to her. "With any luck, when you come to town in three days' time, I can travel on to Hertfordshire with you. I cannot miss the colonel's wedding. He is the closest thing I have to a brother."

Lizzy nodded. Of course he could not miss the wedding. She would not want him to. How odd it would be, staying in Hunsford after he and the colonel had gone! She suspected Lady Catherine would be unbearable, which meant Mr. Collins would be as well.

Obviously, though, Darcy had to go. "I shall miss you," she said with a pout.

"And I you, my love." He took her hands, looking around. "I only pray Lady Catherine does not take out her ire on you. It was our engagement that precipitated the debacle."

Lizzy tilted her head, the situation mystifying her. "Her daughter is marrying a Fitzwilliam. Surely that is enough for her."

Darcy's jaw worked. "I have no idea whether she will see that as a triumph or a tragedy."

Lizzy stared, her gaze unfocused. Could Lady Catherine be that unreasonable? If so, things could be even worse than Lizzy had imagined. Wringing her hands, she paced.

"I think I must go as well," she said at last. "Mr. Collins is my cousin. Charlotte is my friend. If I am here, and Lady Catherine visits her anger on me, it may affect them. If I am gone, then perhaps the connection will be less forward in her mind."

Darcy's brow furrowed, a pensive expression clouding his eyes. "You do not think she would..."

"Deprive Mr. Collins of his place? It is conceivable that she would try, is it not?"

"After what I witnessed this morning..." Darcy gave his head a slight shake, the muscles of his face taut. "Anything is possible."

She looked out the window at the pleasant prospect before her, the cherry trees pregnant with tiny green fruit that would soon blush red. "I never thought I would say this, but

Charlotte is happy here. I would never forgive myself if I cost my friend that contentment."

Lizzy swallowed, berating herself for her careless behaviour. She and Darcy had known that Lady Catherine would not approve of the match. They should have been more circumspect.

Darcy nodded. "Of course. You can travel with us. There will be room in the coach with Anne and Mrs. Jenkinson. How quickly can you pack?"

Fortunately, she had already started filling her trunk in preparation for her departure. She had three days' worth of clothing still to add, plus her notions and other personal items. "Half an hour?"

"That will do. I shall tell the colonel. Once we are in town, I am sure the countess can find a room for you—"

"I was thinking I would stay with the Gardiners."

"If you prefer." He gave her a sly smile and clasped her hands. "I wish I could invite you to stay at Darcy House."

She gazed at him archly. "We must think of appearances. Sleeping under the same roof would in no way prove a temptation, but others might question our virtue."

"Naturally." He trailed kisses along the curve of her neck.

A shiver ran through her, blocking all conscious thought. For a moment, she allowed herself to revel in his touch. Then, she pulled away. She could not dawdle. Lady Catherine might appear at any moment to visit her wrath on Lizzy.

She scowled as another consideration came to mind. Everything was happening too fast! "What of Maria? My uncle Gardiner planned to send a chaise for us in three days' time. Must she come with us instead? I would hate for her to lose the time with her sister."

Darcy looked at her thoughtfully. "I can send my own carriage to bring her to London in three days. She can then return to Hertfordshire with you and Jane as planned."

Lizzy smiled, a lump forming in her throat. "That is kind of you."

He cupped her face in his hands, his fingers smooth and soothing. "In a month, I shall be your husband. When I attend to your concerns, it is not a kindness. It is my duty and my pleasure." He kissed her. "Besides, it is the least I can do. If I had not brought down my aunt's anger on us, none of this would have happened."

She leaned into him, resting her head on his shoulder. He smelled of wool and his own masculine scent. She revelled in his warmth. "You could not have imagined this. It is madness."

The sound of wheels and horses' hooves caught their attention. Lizzy looked out the window to see the colonel helping his new fiancée out of a coach, his arms around her waist as he set her on the ground. The two beamed at one another.

Lizzy grinned wryly. Now that she was out from under her mother's control, Miss de Bourgh might get to see the inside of the parsonage after all.

"I must pack at once," Lizzy said.

He nodded, a faraway look in his eyes. Lizzy ached for the sadness he must feel at this rift in his family, but there was no time for sorrow. They must leave Hunsford with all possible haste.

Lizzy and Darcy arrived at Gracechurch Street as the last rays of twilight faded. The rest of the party was settling in at his uncle's home. Darcy had decided to sojourn there as well, rather than opening up his own residence for the short stay.

"I hope my aunt does not mind the extra company," Lizzy said as they exited his chaise. She appreciated his driving her across London after the long journey, instead of sending a servant. "I can sleep on a pallet in Jane's room if necessary."

"Nonsense. I shall set you up at Darcy House if it comes to that. The future mistress of Pemberley will sleep in a comfortable bed tonight."

"Ordering me about already?" She led him up the brick steps to her aunt and uncle Gardiner's home, the red-painted door sporting a cheerful spring wreath.

"It is my responsibility to ensure your welfare. I shall be most diligent, I assure you."

She gave him an arch look, then rang the bell.

The maid led them to the drawing room, where the lady of the house sat alone, wax candles burning brightly. Mrs. Gardiner gave them an astonished look. "Why, Lizzy, what a wonderful surprise! And Mr. Darcy, too!"

The next moment, she clamped her lips together, a look of consternation wrinkling her forehead.

For a moment, Lizzy wondered at her aunt's expression. Then, she remembered that Darcy had apparently sworn everyone to secrecy about his previous visit. "Do not fret," Lizzy said. "Darcy told me he had met you when last in London."

"Indeed!" Her aunt looked between them but said nothing more. The maid brought coffee and little raspberry cakes.

"Is Jane at home?" Lizzy asked.

"She is," Mrs. Gardiner replied. Then, her eyes widened as she seemed to comprehend Lizzy's meaning. "That is to say, Jane is at home at Longbourn."

Now it was Lizzy's turn to be astonished. It took several minutes for the necessary explanations to be made. As they sat on the couch, with Darcy in an adjacent chair, Lizzy revealed her own predicament, and asked if she was welcome to remain at the Gardiner's home until the planned trip to Meryton.

"Of course!" her aunt replied. "I would appreciate the company, especially with your uncle gone. He had business in the country, and so took Jane with him. She was eager to be back in Hertfordshire, now that Mr. Bingley has gone to Netherfield."

"Mr. Bingley is at Netherfield!"

"Yes." Mrs. Gardiner shifted uncomfortably, looking between them. "I do not like to gossip, but since Mr. Darcy is his intimate friend, I think it is safe to speak freely."

Mrs. Gardiner gathered her shawl around her and said in a mild tone, "Mr. Bingley and his sisters have had a falling out. It is no secret amongst the present company, I believe—Mr. Bingley was distressed to learn that his sisters had known Jane was in town, and hid it from him."

"But that was weeks ago, surely," Lizzy said.

"Yes, well, he had planned a trip to Hertfordshire in any case. His sisters hastened his travel. I do not know the details, nor do I wish to. It is an unfortunate business. I feel sorry for Mr. Bingley, and for Jane as well. He is such a kind and amiable man—'tis a pity he has such relations."

Lizzy looked askance at Darcy, who had the grace to turn red at that comment.

"Oh dear!" cried Mrs. Gardiner, covering her mouth with her hand. "Mr. Darcy, please forgive me. If you are friends with—"

290

"Do not distress yourself, madam. Miss Bingley and Mrs. Hurst deceived me as to the strength of Jane's regard for their brother. I no longer count them as my friends."

"Darcy's good opinion, once lost, is lost forever," Lizzy teased, repeating words he had once spoken to her at Netherfield.

He smiled at her sheepishly, his eyes alight.

Picking up his hat and gloves, he turned to Mrs. Gardiner. "I am afraid I must get back to my uncle's home. Much as I would prefer to spend the evening here, my cousins have a wedding to plan, and I must assist if I can. I imagine they will secure the special license tomorrow and marry the day after."

Lizzy could not help laughing at the haste of it. She and Darcy had spent the time since their engagement longing for one another, denying themselves the pleasures of married life when it all might have been accomplished so quickly. And they still had weeks to go.

"Is a special license so easy to procure?" Lizzy asked.

"If you are the son of an earl."

"What if you are the nephew?"

A smile brightened his face. "Perhaps. But Anne is of age, and you are not. A visit to Longbourn would be necessary, at least."

She returned his smile, unable to look on anything but him. The desire that pulsed through her—not mere carnality, though that was part of it—had transfixed her, as if the house around her, the ground beneath, and the sky above had ceased to exist, and there was only the two of them, an unseen force joining them.

She gulped a breath of air, breaking the spell. She smoothed her skirts and met her aunt's eyes a moment before looking away.

"I had better be off," Darcy said.

"Yes, you had," Lizzy added in a firm voice. He bowed, and her aunt accompanied him to the door.

Lizzy felt broken in half, as if the best part of herself were getting into a carriage to travel back to Mayfair. She did not want to wait for the banns to be read. She no longer trusted herself to be alone with him.

But wait they would. Too many now knew they had been secretly engaged, and to marry in haste would look as if something untoward had happened. Three weeks was not such a very long time. She could endure it.

But she must keep her distance from Darcy.

Images floated through her mind of sneaking out of Longbourn to meet in the woods under the moonlight, with no one at all to stop them from giving themselves to each other. It was a dreamy, romantic fantasy, and immensely appealing. But she would not risk her reputation when she was so near to taking her vows.

She woke from her reverie to see her aunt looking at her. Lizzy said, "He will accompany Maria and me to Hertfordshire so he can speak to my father."

"Of course. That's wonderful news. But you look sad, my dear."

Tears fell onto Lizzy's cheek. "Parting is such sweet sorrow." Her throat thickened, and she swallowed. "Was it like that for you and my uncle?"

"It still is, sometimes. When he left this morning, my heart broke a little, as it always does. Being in love is a fine thing, but the ache of separation is never easy."

Lizzy dried her eyes with a handkerchief. "I am the luckiest woman on earth. I have never met a finer man." A sudden thought struck her. "You have seen Pemberley, have you not?"

"Oh, yes, I used to ride through the park there when I was a girl. There is no place finer in England, I would wager."

"No place finer," Lizzy repeated, the words not truly registering. She could not care about Pemberley. She could only care about Darcy. If he were a pauper, she would marry him and still count herself the happiest of women.

"You will visit me there?" Lizzy asked.

Mrs. Gardiner smiled brightly. "Nothing could please me more."

Lizzy shook her head in confusion. "I ought to be happy, but instead I am horribly sad."

"That is the way of brides-to-be. Once you see Jane, you will feel better. The two of you can commiserate."

Lizzy smiled at that. "Is not Bingley the kindest man?"

"The very best. The two of you have chosen well."

"But that is the miracle of it. Darcy chose *me*, and forced me to fall in love against my will. I thought him proud, but indeed, he has no improper pride. He is aloof, but once you know him, he is...sweet." She shook her head. "He has been gone five minutes, and I feel as if he has been gone five years."

Her aunt embraced her. "That is a symptom of new love. As time goes on, it will mature into something less desperate, more enduring. If love always felt this way, no one would get any work done."

Lizzy laughed and blinked back tears. Then she turned serious, knowing she might never have this opportunity again. She certainly could not expect coherent advice from her mother. "What is it like, being married? The wedding night, I mean?"

Mrs. Gardiner rose and looked about the hallway, then closed the door. She sat beside Lizzy on the sofa. "If the husband is loving, it is the most rapturous thing in the world, sharing the intimacies of the marriage bed. You must not be ashamed or embarrassed, because it is perfectly natural, and how children are made."

"I am afraid of disappointing him. I will not know what I am doing."

Her aunt squeezed Lizzy's hand. "Listen to the responses of your body. Tell him what you like, and what you do not. When you touch and caress each other, and join as one, it is pure bliss—not something to fear."

Lizzy nodded, grateful for those words. She would discover the rest soon enough. And truly, she did not want to know all the details. There were some things she wanted to learn from her husband, and her husband alone.

Darcy called the following afternoon, sitting with Lizzy whilst Mrs. Gardiner worked on her needlepoint at the window. The drawing room was cheerful at this time of day, soft light streaming in, and a low fire chasing away the damp. The maid brought in tea and lemon biscuits.

Darcy remembered how Miss Bingley had once scoffed about Mr. Gardiner being in trade—but the French provincial furnishings were as comfortable and elegant as any in Mayfair. There was no grandeur, to be sure. But the Gardiners' fashion and taste could not be in doubt.

Darcy intertwined his hands with Lizzy's and shared news of Anne and Richard's upcoming nuptials. "They have got the special license," he said, rubbing his thumb across Lizzy's knuckles, enjoying the softness there. "They could not reserve the church on such short notice, so the wedding will be held at home in the ballroom tomorrow afternoon. Anne is having some lace added to her best gown, and the colonel will wear his regimentals, of course."

"All very simple and tidy," Lizzy noted.

"Yes." He scowled. "I must say, a week ago, I did not expect Richard to be married before me."

Lizzy laughed gaily. "I doubt he did, either." Her expression turned serious. "Is he in love with her, do you think?"

Darcy contemplated a moment. He had never heard a romantic word cross his cousin's lips, yet knew his feelings to run deep. No man had ever shown more loyalty to his family.

"Richard is a man of action," Darcy said, "always has been. He has claimed Anne for his own, and is fiercely protective of her. That is perhaps his definition of love, rather than some poetic sentiment. It would perhaps not satisfy you, but it is precisely what Anne wants. She is radiant. Even after the long carriage ride yesterday, she refused the laudanum Mrs. Jenkinson offered her."

"Then I am happy for them both." A soft smile settled on her lips.

The affection she showed for his cousins warmed him. A thrill rose in his chest, her goodness reminding him of the wisdom of his choice. He was more certain than ever that she would fit seamlessly into his family, despite the differences in their situations.

He hated to disturb her good mood, but knew he must broach a subject he wished he could avoid.

Warily, he said, "I have been wondering about the propriety...that is, since our engagement has not yet been sanctioned by your father, I have not told my uncle's family about it. I think Richard and Anne would be very happy to have you at the wedding as my fiancée, but it would seem odd without some formal announcement."

"Oh!" she cried. "I had not considered the possibility of attending. Of course I would love to. But as you say, given the timing, it does not seem proper."

"You must know I *want* you there..." Consternation thickened his throat, cutting off his words. Secrecy had made sense when they first got engaged, but in retrospect, it was badly done. In three days' time, though, he would call at Longbourn, and at last they could be easy.

He did not stay long after that, reluctant as he was to go. He was to stand up with Richard the next day, and had preparations to make. Lizzy understood.

That evening, his uncle's household had just finished dinner when the doorbell rang. A sinking feeling gripped Darcy's chest, even before Lady Catherine's voice resounded through the front hall.

To no one's surprise, she demanded to attend the wedding. Richard objected strenuously, but his father, his mother, and his bride convinced him to relent. Anne was her only child. Once tempers had cooled, Richard would regret denying her this, everyone said. He realized they were probably right.

Though still furious with her, Darcy could not disagree with Richard's decision. Lady Catherine was family. She had damaged her relationship with her daughter and nephews irreparably, but that was no reason to be cruel.

The following afternoon, the ballroom was decorated with fruit trees from the orangerie. Anne, dressed in silver, carried a bouquet of white roses trailing long strands of satin ribbon. Following the ceremony, she let her mother kiss her cheek before Richard, in his red coat, swept her off in his carriage.

They would visit the spa at Cheltenham, stopping for a few days to take the waters before he rejoined his regiment—at which time he would trade his commission in the regulars for one in the militia, so he could stay close to Anne. He was now master of Rosings Park, and no longer had to make his fortune.

Darcy was pleased with the outcome. Or, more precisely, he was overjoyed. Relieved of the fear of Richard's being sent to the continent, he could now look forward to his own wedding with true contentment.

He did not fear his upcoming sojourn at Netherfield. His initial shock at the country manners of Meryton society had worn off months ago. He would conduct himself with Lizzy's neighbours in a way that made her proud. He would prove that for her sake, he would endure anything.

Chapter 21

Maria Lucas arrived in Gracechurch Street wearing her usual wide-eyed, cheerful expression. "Oh, Eliza, I have never been so happy to leave a place in my life!"

Lizzy could well imagine that. She fought back a smile as she and Maria sat in the front parlour whilst Mrs. Gardiner was out shopping.

Maria squeezed the juice of a lemon slice into her tea. "Mr. Collins does nothing but wander about and sigh as if the world were coming to an end. And he blames you for all of it. If you had not been so insistent on rising above your station," Maria said, mocking Mr. Collins tone, "Mr. Darcy would have married Miss de Bourgh as Lady Catherine had wished, and all would be well."

Lizzy arched her brows. "Perhaps for Lady Catherine, but not for Mr. Darcy nor Miss de Bourgh."

"Oh, but that does not signify, because he is not indebted to *them* for his living."

Lizzy considered a moment. "Mr. Collins seems confused," she suggested. "Since coming of age, Miss de Bourgh—that is, Mrs. Fitzwilliam—has come into her full rights as mistress of Rosings Park. The living is now in her husband's keeping, not her mother's."

"Oh!" Maria wrinkled her forehead prettily. A smile broke out over her face, no hint of malice in it, only joy at the change of circumstances. "That is quite a different matter, is it not? The colonel is a sensible man."

"He is, and fond of your sister. I think he can be counted on to support Mr. Collins' place in Hunsford."

"That *is* a relief."

Lizzy had to agree with that. She counted her blessings that her own foolish behaviour had not harmed Charlotte in any material way.

Early the following day, they made the journey to Hertfordshire—Darcy on horseback, whilst Lizzy and Maria rode in the chaise, his manservant driving. Darcy parted ways with them when they reached the lane leading to Netherfield. The driver then dropped off Maria at Lucas Lodge before delivering Lizzy to Longbourn.

Her heart rose when the manor house came into view. As the carriage approached, a flock of starlings rose from the lawn. Sheep lowed in the distance.

Under the bright afternoon sun, white and pink damask roses, just coming into bloom, sent a heady fragrance into the air. Each foot of the lane and slant of the trees was as familiar as her own hands. How much dearer the place was to her now, when she was so soon to leave it!

Her family came out to greet her, her mother leading the way, her father standing aloof as usual. But she hugged him tightly and kissed his cheek anyway. "Here you are, Lizzy," he said. "You are welcome, my dear. I had not heard a word of sense in your absence, until Jane came home a few days ago." He stepped back and appraised her. "You look well."

"I am well, Papa." Love filled her heart. Her father was near fifty, his hair turning a soft white. She had missed his sardonic smile and the soft blue eyes that shone bright behind his spectacles.

"Oh, Lizzy!" Her mother gathered her into a rose-scented embrace. Mama's golden-brown hair, styled in tight curls, was now laced with silver, more so than Lizzy remembered. Tears pricked Lizzy's eyes. Despite the differences between them, her mother's face beamed with love, and Lizzy beamed back.

"We have had so many changes here since you were gone," Mama said. "The regiment is heading to Brighton for the summer, and what do you think? Lydia and Kitty have been begging your father to take us all there, and he will not hear of it. It has been dreadfully trying on my poor nerves."

"I am sorry, Mama. Perhaps the officers will be back next winter."

"Yes, perhaps they might!" The thought seemed to cheer her, though Lizzy knew it was nonsense.

Lizzy stepped out of her mother's arms, then took Jane's hands and kissed her cheek. Lizzy's tears flowed freely now. "How good to see you smiling."

"I have so much to tell you!" Jane cried in her soft voice, as beautiful to Lizzy as the sweetest music.

"Oh!" their mother cried, "I forgot to say that Mr. Bingley is back at Netherfield, and he has been calling on Jane every day! Now, I am not one to tell tales, but I have it on good authority that he plans to stay at least a month. And if that is not enough time for Jane to secure him—oh, but he told us last night that Mr. Darcy shall be coming to stay with him again. I do not know why Mr. Bingley must have such a disagreeable friend."

"It is unfortunate indeed," Lizzy said, too happy at seeing her family again to be irritated by her mother's words, "that Mr. Darcy is ill-at-ease in company. I have found, though, during my visits to Rosings, that if one has the good fortune to engage him in a tête-à-tête, he is a fine conversationalist."

"Oh, lord!" cried Lydia when Lizzy hugged her. The youngest of the sisters, just turned sixteen, she was as dangerously pretty as any girl in the county. "You do not mean that you have become friends with Mr. *Darcy*?" Lydia spoke his name as if referring to a clod of mud on her shoe.

"Great friends, in fact." Lizzy embraced the rest of her sisters. She entered the house and took off her spencer and bonnet, as the others processed in along with her.

They gathered in the parlour, and her eyes roamed over the room to reacquaint her with the familiar sights. It was a stately house, nothing to compare with Rosings, but spacious even for a family of five daughters. Atop sturdy, unpretentious wood furniture, fresh-cut blooms overflowed their vases. The aroma of baking bread emanated from the kitchen.

"Lizzy," cried Mary, the middle sister, studious and philosophical in nature, but passionate in her morality, "when he was last in Hertfordshire, we observed Mr. Darcy to be consumed with pride, one of the seven deadly sins. Are you certain it is safe for you to be often in the company of a such a man?"

"I am afraid we judged him too harshly—upon too brief an acquaintance." Lizzy kept her tone steady. "It is my fault for taking offense at his words the night we met. He was out of temper due to concern for his sister, to whom he is quite devoted."

"Out of temper indeed!" her mother cried. "To insult my daughter upon no acquaintance at all. It was most ungentlemanly."

"He has acknowledged the fault, Mama, and could not have been more apologetic. These past weeks at Hunsford, he was nothing but kindness. He has proven himself every bit the gentleman he should be."

"Why, Lizzy," said Kitty, her youngest sister but one—a pretty girl, and amiable except when vexed by Lydia, which was much of the time. "It sounds as if you are in love with him!"

"Oh, lord!" cried Lydia. "Lizzy in love with Mr. Darcy! What a good joke that is!"

Kitty giggled. "Did you often meet him in the woods at first light for a secret assignation?"

"Did you let him kiss you?" Lydia teased.

"That is quite enough, girls," their father scolded.

"Oh, Papa, we are only having fun," Lydia replied. "We know Mr. Darcy would never kiss Lizzy, for then he would have to marry her. And Lizzy is far too poor for a man like Mr. Darcy."

"A man like Mr. Darcy does not care about money," their mother said. "He has ten thousand a year. What does he need of a fine dowry?"

"Lizzy," said Jane, "you must be tired after your long journey. Perhaps you would like to go to your room and rest?"

"That is a splendid idea," Lizzy said, grateful. Impatient as she was with her family for their notions about Darcy, she had no one to blame but herself. It was her dislike of Darcy, as much as anyone's, that had fixed their belief that he was proud. Just as it had been her easy acceptance of Wickham, on no more evidence than his pleasant demeanour, that had helped convince them that he was a fine gentleman.

The two sisters headed upstairs. Behind the closed bedroom door, Jane asked, "Well, did you?"

"Did I what?"

"Go on walks in the woods and let Mr. Darcy kiss you."

Lizzy laughed gaily. She warmed to think of the pleasant hours they had spent together enjoying the countryside. "Yes on both counts."

Jane squealed and hugged her. "You are engaged?"

"Yes. And if I am not mistaken, so are you and Bingley."

Jane's cheeks pinked. "You will not believe it, Lizzy. He proposed the very day after I first saw him again in London. And I was on tenterhooks, because I could tell no one but my aunt and uncle Gardiner, until he spoke with my father. But I asked Papa to keep the information to himself until you had returned."

Lizzy raised her brows. "My poor mother! I worry how her heart will handle the news—not of your engagement, which she has been expecting since before she laid eyes on Bingley—but of mine. He is still 'that disagreeable Mr. Darcy' to her."

"Given his fortune, she will adjust to calling him 'my dear son Darcy' soon enough."

Lizzy nodded. "I tried to soften her perception in my letters, but you know she only half reads them. If it were not for Mary keeping track of things, I am certain there would have been no horses waiting for us today when it came time to change."

Jane took Lizzy's hands, and they sat on the bed. "How soon are you planning to marry?"

A thrill rose in Lizzy's chest. It hardly seemed real. Yet in a few weeks, she would be Mrs. Darcy. "As soon as the banns are read."

"We should have a double ceremony, then. What say you?"

Lizzy's lips parted. She herself had had the same idea, but she had not wished to suggest it, for fear of drawing attention away from Jane on her special day. "Nothing in the world would give me more pleasure. Marrying my dear Darcy, at the same time you marry your dear Bingley, is as great a happiness as I can imagine."

"I pinch myself every morning when I wake, to make sure it is not a dream."

Lizzy's chest tightened at Jane's words. For though Lizzy was happy, she could not say she shared Jane's effusive joy. Lizzy had not endured what Jane had. She had not lost the man she loved and mourned him, only to get him back months later.

Three weeks ago, Lizzy had despised Darcy.

Or at least, she had despised the man she had thought him to be. A sudden chill coursed through her veins. She believed herself in love, but the change had come on so suddenly. Could she trust these feelings now?

She pushed the thought from her mind. Sometimes the course of true love *did* run smooth. It was not necessary to suffer as Jane and Bingley had, in order to be certain of love. Her aunt Gardiner had once said she had fallen in love the first time she met her husband.

Lizzy smiled at that, reminding herself of her aunt's reassuring words a few days earlier. Doubts were natural in a bride-to-be. Lizzy would not let them spoil her happiness.

When Lizzy and Jane descended the stairs, their father called Lizzy into his study. She gave Jane a nervous smile, which her sister returned. Apprehension twisting in her stomach, she entered her father's haven.

The room was lined with shelves of dark wood, and the well-worn leather of his cognac-coloured desk chair added an earthy scent to the air. Lizzy eyed the untidy stacks of books, her father's most treasured possessions, with great affection. The happiest moments of her childhood had been spent in this room.

Her father had doted on her, and let her borrow books from it without restriction. Of course, she had only had access to the books she could reach. She suspected the highest shelves might hold tomes unsuitable for gentle young ladies.

"Well, well, my dear," her father teased, "it seems you have something to tell me."

"About Mr. Wickham, you mean?" she asked with an innocent smile.

"If you tell me Wickham is a worthless young man, I am happy to take your word for it. I have seen no evidence to the contrary. I understand Bingley will bring Mr. Darcy to dinner this evening. Does the gentleman wish to speak with me in private?"

"He does." Lizzy could hold back no longer. "Oh, Papa, he makes me very happy, I promise you. He is the finest young man I know."

"That is quite a change."

Tears fell to her cheeks. "It is. But as I said, I made a quick judgment. I was dreadfully mistaken. I shall be very happy with him, I am certain of it."

"Well, now. You are not a silly young woman, and I trust you would not enter into marriage hastily, without giving it the proper consideration."

Lizzy shook her head, contemplating the events of recent weeks, and how they had transformed her feelings for Darcy. "I have thought of nothing else since my first inkling of Darcy's affection. This is a marriage of two minds." With a coquettish smile, she added, "I do not deny that I am mad for him, but I also respect and admire him—and of course, his great estate at Pemberley."

He eyed her sardonically. "Your mother does not care for him."

"She will like his ten thousand a year well enough."

He nodded. "As you say. I must congratulate you, Lizzy. You and Jane have done well for yourselves—certainly better than your mother and I did for you, much to my shame. It is no less than you deserve. I wish you great joy."

"Thank you, Papa." Lizzy smiled, certain she had already found it. She counted down the hours until she could tell her family.

Lizzy watched nervously when Darcy stepped into her father's study shortly after his arrival at Longbourn. She settled her apprehension by greeting Bingley, whose spirits were even higher than they had been the last time she had seen him, back in November, before he and Jane had parted. His curly mop of light brown hair was as insouciant as ever, but his blue eyes positively beamed with joy.

"I could not be more pleased to see you again, dearest Bingley," she greeted in low tones.

"And I you, Elizabeth," he replied, speaking with the same familiarity as she had. "I owe you a debt of gratitude, I am sure. Darcy is much changed since November, and has entirely altered his view of what will constitute my happiness."

"You put great stock in his opinions."

Bingley hesitated before saying, "Perhaps some would fault me for that. I reached my independence early in life. I have neither father, mother, nor brother to guide me. Darcy has been the best friend I can imagine. He erred on this one point, but he acted out of concern for my happiness. I find it difficult to blame him for that."

"As it has all ended so happily, and he endeavoured to make things right, I shall not blame him, either." Nor would she fault Bingley. His inconstancy to Jane was more understandable to Lizzy when seen from his perspective. And in his heart, he had not been inconstant at all. He was devoted to her, and had been since the night they met.

After Darcy and her father exited the study, dinner was announced. Bingley naturally took the place of honour to Mrs. Bennet's right, and she was all smiles. Her face fell, however, when Darcy took the seat to her left.

As the soup dishes were cleared, Mr. Bennet said from his place at the foot of the table, "Well, Mrs. Bennet, I must congratulate you. For when you said that Netherfield was let, and in due course would bring joy to one of our daughters, you showed remarkable foresight. In fact, Netherfield has brought joy to *two* of our daughters."

"Mr. Bennet, what nonsense do you speak?" the lady asked her husband, irritation in her voice. "How could I imagine that Mr. Bingley's letting Netherfield would be of consequence to our daughters? Not that I am anything but delighted that a friendship has developed between our two families—"

"That is a fine thing, my dear, as Mr. Bingley will soon be your son-in-law."

"Oh!" Mrs. Bennet cried out, her raptures beyond anything that had been seen at Longbourn in all the generations of Bennets that had lived there. "My dear Bingley, nothing could please me more! How happy my Jane must be! And you, sir, could not have chosen better, I am sure, though I say it myself. Jane has such a sweet disposition, she cannot fail to make you a most agreeable wife. What a celebration we shall have! And of course you must buy Netherfield outright once you are wed—"

"Indeed, Mrs. Bennet," her husband interrupted, "I am certain Bingley will give careful consideration as to where he and Jane will settle once married. But I have more news. As I said, Netherfield has brought joy to *two* of our daughters. Mr. Darcy there will also be your son-in-law."

Mrs. Bennet turned stony silent. "What are you about?" she said at last, glaring as if her husband were making a joke at her expense. "Mr. Darcy, my son-in-law? How could that be?"

Mr. Bennet raised his brows. "I would think that obvious, unless you suppose he has been courting Mary, Kitty, or Lydia by correspondence these six months."

Lizzy smiled. "Mama, Darcy and I are engaged. You must wish us joy."

Mrs. Bennet's mouth twisted. "You engaged to Mr. Darcy! Impossible. You must be mistaken."

Lizzy fell back against her chair. Did her mother esteem her so little? Did she truly believe Lizzy to be deluded, with Darcy sitting *right there*?

"I assure you there is no mistake, madam," Darcy said in an even tone. "I have made her an offer, and she has accepted. We are to be married as soon as the banns are read. I suggested a special license, but she wanted time to order her wedding clothes."

"Oh, the wedding clothes!" Mrs. Bennet's amazement seemed to abate at the mention of shopping.

Darcy continued, "Lizzy is hoping you can take her to London with all due haste. I imagine Jane would like to go, too?"

"Indeed I would," Jane said. "We have decided on a double wedding here in the church at Meryton in early June."

"In June, you say!" For perhaps the first time in her life, Mrs. Bennet sat speechless. It was unclear whether her surprise stemmed from the fact that Lizzy had been able to find a husband of superior station to Mr. Collins, or that her daughters had made such strides in planning their wedding before she had learnt of their engagement. But the news, however astonishing, was undoubtedly the best she had heard in her life, and she could not be expected to stay silent for long.

"Why, Jane! We must go to London at once. I know all the best warehouses, and indeed you must have the finest clothes money can buy. A double wedding! Oh, what a celebration that will be. All of Hertfordshire society will turn out."

She looked to Jane's fiancé. "Mr. Bingley, I welcome you most humbly to the family. I knew the first time I saw you and Jane together that you were destined for one another. No two people could be more perfectly matched. And so handsome together! You must have a portrait done, I insist upon it. I may insist, now that I am to be your mother-in-law. How well it will look above the mantelpiece in the great room at Netherfield!" She hesitated a moment, then turned to her other son-in-law-to-be. "And Mr. Darcy, you are welcome, too."

Lizzy shot a merry yet apologetic glance at her beloved, who did not look at all distressed. Perhaps, as he had said, he was learning to find humour in the situation.

"Lizzy is engaged to Mr. Darcy?" Lydia said in astonishment. "Then perhaps husbands are not to be found at Brighton after all. Perhaps they are all at Netherfield. Bingley, once you and Jane are back from your honeymoon, you must hold a house party, and invite all your friends from London."

"Perhaps I shall," Bingley cried with enthusiasm, and Lydia gave him her most coquettish smile.

Chapter 22

In late May, the streets of London were dusty and dirty, and not at all to Lizzy's liking. She much preferred the countryside, with its clean air and open spaces. But Lizzy did find certain recompense during the sojourn in town. The shops with their sumptuous fabrics and the latest accessories from the Continent were ever so appealing.

Darcy and Bingley had followed their fiancées to London, a blow to Meryton society that was soon to be followed by the removal of the officers to the coast. Mr. Bennet was steadfastly refusing to let Lydia travel to Brighton, despite an invitation from Colonel Forster's young wife. With the wedding approaching, Lydia was required at home.

Lizzy felt a bit sorry for Lydia, so many admirers being taken from her at once. The Bennet girls all had beauty—it was true that Mary was often viewed as plain, but she did nothing to highlight her natural attributes, and indeed her sullen expression and severe style of dress could only detract—but

Lydia was the prettiest of all, except perhaps for Jane. Jane had beauty in her stillness, and Lydia in her animation.

Lizzy could well remember how she had felt at Lydia's age, just discovering her womanly nature, and constantly hungry for attention from the opposite sex. No matter how she had tried to set her mind on serious pursuits, a word from a young gentleman would send her heart racing and her flesh burning. Lydia, meanwhile, had no use for serious pursuits, and was in danger of becoming one of the most accomplished flirts in England. Despite her youth, it would be better if she married as soon as possible.

Though Lydia was the same age as Darcy's sister Georgiana, the two could not have been more different—as Lizzy soon discovered. When Darcy arrived in London, he sent for his sister to stay with him and act as his hostess.

Lizzy was eager to meet her, but also a bit intimidated when Georgiana invited the Bennets and Gardiners to dine.

"But Lizzy," Jane said as the two readied for bed that evening in one of the spare rooms in the Gardiners' home, "Miss Darcy is but sixteen."

"Perhaps, but I cannot help thinking about how Caroline Bingley described her. Unequalled for beauty, her performance on the pianoforte exquisite—"

"Every word from Caroline was flattery designed to win Darcy for herself. I am sure you shall find Miss Darcy flesh and bone like the rest of us."

"What if she does not like me?"

A pretty scowl settled on Jane's brow. "Why should she not like you?"

Lizzy fumed in silence. "Miss Bingley does not like me."

"She recognized you as a rival almost from the beginning. Besides, from all I have heard, Miss Darcy is a dutiful sister who defers to her brother's superior wisdom. As long as you are kind to her, which of course you shall be—"

"Of course!"

"Then she will like you exceedingly well."

Lizzy shook her head. "She is more accomplished than me."

"You are already engaged, Lizzy. No one cares how accomplished you are anymore."

"Too true."

Jane's words eased some of Lizzy's apprehension. Still, she would be happy once the initial meeting was behind them. Her fears would not abate until then.

❧

Darcy worried all day over how Georgiana would acquit herself upon meeting Lizzy for the first time. The girl was too eager to please, and fretted that she would make some sort of mistake, offending Lizzy. Her brother had done his best to reassure her. "Lizzy does not stand on ceremony. She is disposed to love you, Giana."

"And I her! Is not that more reason to worry?"

Darcy placed his hands on his sister's shoulders and kissed her forehead. "Not at all. Now, I have warned you that Mrs. Bennet is an ill-bred woman who will likely shock you more than once in the course of the evening. If you overlook the mother's faults, you will go far in endearing yourself to the daughter."

Giana gave him a fond smile. "I have never been troubled by country manners, as you are. The poor woman cannot help the society where she has lived all her life. But her daughters— they must be very fine indeed if you and Mr. Bingley wish to marry them."

"That is true. But you may be easy on that score, dear sister. You are the natural heir of Lady Anne Darcy. All her grace and dignity show in your bearing, without your even thinking about it. You make me proud every day."

Giana's eyes misted, and she blinked away tears. Darcy kissed her forehead once again. Then, he left her in the company of the housekeeper, to continue preparing for the evening's festivities.

Darcy was not as confident as his words had suggested, however. Despite her natural poise, Giana's nervousness might undo her. But when the guests arrived, she was all graciousness.

When he introduced her, she put aside her shyness to make them feel at home. In her soft voice, she declared to

Lizzy, "I have been wanting to meet you. My brother has told me so many things about you. I confess I am rather afraid of your wit."

Bingley stepped in behind them, Jane at his side. "Lizzy only uses her wit against those who deserve it," he said, "like your brother. You, my dear Miss Darcy, are perfection." He kissed her hand.

"That is kind of you, but I am far from it, as Miss Elizabeth will learn soon enough."

Lizzy touched Giana's shoulder and said with a sweet smile, "Please call me Lizzy."

"And you must call me Giana, like a true sister."

Tears shone in Lizzy's eyes as she took the girl's hands. A lump formed in Darcy's throat. He had not realized until that moment how dearly he had hoped for a friendship to form between these two people he loved most in the world.

Ever since the near catastrophe with Wickham, he had doubted his ability to give his sister the guidance she needed. But Lizzy could. More than that, she *wanted* to. He could see that in Lizzy's eyes—in the way they sparkled with curiosity and kindness when she looked at Giana.

As they waited for dinner to be announced, he spoke with Mr. Gardiner but watched with a gratified smile as Lizzy endeavoured to put Giana at ease. Lizzy's natural vivacity smoothed over his sister's awkward silences. Before long, the two ladies were laughing as if they had known each other for years.

As they headed into the dining room, Lizzy took his arm and asked him, "Would you mind if I sat next to your sister? There is a surfeit of women, and it would give me a chance to know her better."

"I would be delighted." He pressed her hand. She took the spot to Gianna's left, with Gardiner across from her in the place of honour.

Once or twice during the meal, Darcy noted that Giana seemed a bit unsure in the role of hostess. Lizzy gently prompted her, in such a way as to inspire gratitude rather than embarrassment. He berated himself for ever hesitating to court this woman. Lizzy was everything he had hoped she would be, and more.

On occasion, his eyes met Lizzy's across the table. Her glances seemed wary. Mrs. Bennet, at his right, was babbling in her usual way, which appeared to make Lizzy anxious.

"Oh, my poor Lydia, she is quite desolate now that the officers are leaving for the coast. Perhaps after the wedding, we will convince Mr. Bennet to take us to Brighton at last. Some sea bathing would do us all good, I daresay. And the officers are so fond of Lydia. No less than Mrs. Forster herself invited her to come, but Mr. Bennet would not hear of it. It is all quite vexing."

Darcy had no idea how to respond to this, but soon realized no response was required. Mrs. Bennet immediately launched into raptures about the lace they had found for Jane's gown. Unlike Lizzy, Mrs. Bennet did not require him to speak in turns. She was happy to carry the conversation for both of them.

This was a most fortuitous discovery. He had only to nod occasionally whilst stealing glances at his fiancée. She wore a brocade of pale pink silk, the cut of the bodice more daring than he had seen on her before. He stared, and knew he stared, but could not seem to stop himself. He imagined all the things he would like to do to her, growing more eager for their wedding night with each passing moment.

He stored away enough wicked thoughts to fill their entire honeymoon.

He pictured them in the bedroom where he had stayed at Netherfield, the room dark except for a few candles. She wore only a chemise, the fabric so sheer he could see every delectable curve. Her hair hung long over her shoulders, dark curls contrasting with the white fabric.

He approached, and she looked up at him, lips parting. With one hand at her waist, he cupped her cheek with the other, stroking the softness there. He pulled her into a kiss, his palm roving downward to the fullness of her rear...

"Is that not so, Darcy?"

He blinked, Mrs. Bennet's shrill voice pulling him out of his reverie.

Drawing his brows in an effort to appear thoughtful, he gave a little nod, then cleared his throat. "Indeed," he ventured, wondering what he had just agreed to.

He looked over at Lizzy again. She was talking to Giana in low tones, the two looking conspiratorial. He sipped his wine to quell his desire.

Two weeks. Then she would be his.

After dinner, the ladies retired to the drawing room. A quick glass of port later, he, Bingley, and Gardiner re-joined them. Darcy sat next to Lizzy and took her hand. She looked up at him and smiled warmly. It was a pleasure to be open in his affection toward her, after so many weeks of secrecy.

Yet, her manner toward him was not as effusive as it had been during their stolen moments in Kent. The change troubled him—but perhaps it was due to her mother's scrutiny. Mrs. Bennet was quick to scold, sometimes for no logical reason. She took offense at the impertinence in Lizzy's nature that *he* found so delightful. He would be glad to remove Lizzy from that situation.

Once they were at last alone together as husband and wife, she would be herself again. His own Lizzy. So he told himself, and so he tried to believe.

Lizzy sat with Darcy in the grandeur of his drawing room, unable to believe that she would soon be mistress of this fine home. Watered silk wallpaper, a marble fireplace, a Persian carpet three times the size of the largest room at Longbourn. She could not even fathom the wealth that he took for granted.

She told herself not to let it intimidate her. Surely she would adjust to the opulence of the place in no time. She need not feel unequal to the situation—Darcy loved her, and that was what mattered.

Sitting close to him, she could not help thinking how near his bedroom must be, perhaps one flight above, and what joy it would be to steal away with him. With the marriage contract signed, it seemed ludicrous that they must maintain this decorum. Her mother's eyes were ever upon her, though, and Lizzy could not let down her guard for a moment.

Thankfully, her frustrated yearnings were interrupted when a footman entered. He brought lemon cream petits fours to accompany the coffee, and Lizzy's mouth watered. The citrus scent was heavenly. The tiny sweets were the perfect size to enjoy after a scrumptious meal.

She looked over at Georgiana. After all Lizzy's worrying, Giana had turned out to be a demure girl no more than Lizzy's height with slender shoulders, wispy blond hair, and a nervous smile. She was lovely—hardly the imposing figure Lizzy had expected.

That Wickham could have harmed this sweet, innocent girl showed him to be even more of a blackguard than Lizzy had thought. Affection for Giana filled her heart, more so than she could have imagined at this first meeting. Already, Lizzy felt fiercely protective.

She saw in Giana something she had never encountered in her own younger sisters: a heart and mind eager to learn. Lizzy was not so bold as to think she could take a mother's place in Giana's heart, but she could be counsellor and friend. And Giana could ease the pain of Lizzy's separation from her sisters, especially dear Jane, once the Darcys had retired to Pemberley.

Bingley spoke up so that his voice might carry across the room. "I say, Darcy, do you know of any properties for sale? With Jane and me marrying, it is time I had my own house in town."

Jane's expression changed almost imperceptibly to one of surprise and muted joy. What a relief it would be for her, Lizzy thought, if she did not have to share a home with Bingley's sisters!

Darcy scowled, though, tapping a finger on the arm of the couch. "I thought you were saving your capital for a country estate."

"I am. Thankfully, one of my investments has proven more fortuitous than expected. I do not wish to rely indefinitely on Hurst's generosity in staying at his house on Grosvenor Street."

"Come now, Bingley," Darcy said. "You and I shall be brothers soon enough. You must consider this house as your own. I think I am safe in speaking for Lizzy on this point—nothing could give us more joy than hosting you and Jane here, as well as any little Bingleys who might come along."

Jane blushed at that but smiled happily.

"Of course!" Lizzy added.

"Unless," Darcy said, "Georgiana has some objection."

"I?" The girl raised her brows, looking at Darcy. "Surely not! I appreciate your condescension, but Mr. Bingley is as dear as a brother to me. I have no doubt that I shall soon think of Jane as a beloved sister." She and Jane shared affectionate glances.

"Naturally," Mrs. Bennet said, "I would think Lizzy's family would always be welcome at her husband's home. Why, we must make preparations for Kitty and Lydia to be presented at court. I am sure, Darcy, that your aunt the countess would be happy to sponsor them. Mary, too," she added as an afterthought, "if she desires."

The room descended into silence. The scheme was mad. The cost of a gown to present *one* of his daughters at court would exceed Mr. Bennet's annual income. Presenting *three* daughters would ruin him.

It would not do to tell her mother so. Instead, Lizzy said, "Perhaps one of my younger sisters would wish to come to London for the season next year."

That seemed to satisfy Mrs. Bennet. Still, Lizzy's good humour had been hampered by her mother's nonsense. What must Darcy think? She could not meet his eye.

The sooner they married and removed to Pemberley, the happier they would be.

Chapter 23

Darcy and Bingley called the next day, later than usual. Bingley seemed in a foul mood, frowning and speaking in a sharp tone, his sentences clipped. He was so unlike himself that Lizzy could not help looking at him in wonder. She said nothing, only watched after him as he took Jane outside for a turn in the garden.

Lizzy did not raise the question with Darcy, nor did he offer comment. Instead, he said as they sat together on the couch, "My aunt and uncle are planning a dinner to welcome you to the family. You can expect the invitation today."

She swallowed and smoothed her skirt, contemplating her reply. She knew this would happen eventually. But after Lady Catherine's reaction, she hardly wished to subject herself to more scorn.

Darcy took her hand. "You must not be nervous, love."

She met his eyes. "I am conscious of the honour they do me, but surely, they must have hoped for more for you."

He reddened. "I shall not countenance this, Lizzy. There is no *more*. No one in England—nay, the world—is a better match for me than you. I shall not hear anyone say otherwise, not even you."

She smiled and kissed his cheek, grateful for his reassurance. It calmed her somewhat, but she could not help feeling anxious at meeting a peer, who was also her fiancé's uncle. She would be on display, and could only hope to make a good impression.

They talked quietly a while, tones low enough that they could not be overheard by her mother and her aunt Gardiner, sitting at the other side of the room. Tension roiled in her stomach. How could she have been so much more at ease with him at Rosings, than here in her uncle's home?

Perhaps something about her visit to Hunsford had seemed unreal, a place out of time. In these familiar surroundings, she could not hide. Her mother's foolishness was on display every moment. Lizzy wanted to sink through the floor.

Darcy seemed in a good enough mood, though, and eyed her whilst wearing a sweet smile. She wanted to sink into his arms and forget the rest of the world existed. His soft words and tender gaze eased her worries, at least for a little while.

Jane and Bingley stepped back inside. His anger seemed to have eased, but his manner was still brusque. He mentioned an appointment, and he and Darcy soon took their leave.

Once they had gone, Lizzy said to Jane, "I hope all is well with Bingley."

Jane looked over at their mother and aunt, then drew Lizzy out into the garden. Jane pressed her lips together a moment, a look of consternation adding a hard edge to her usually docile features. Then, she said, "I hate to gossip, but this cannot be kept secret, at least not within the family. Bingley and Mr. Hurst had a row this morning—"

"A row? Mr. Hurst?" Lizzy struggled to keep the merriment out of her voice. "The man is so indolent, I wonder he found the energy."

Jane tilted her head a moment. "To be honest, I am not sure he did. The passion may all have been on Bingley's side." Jane's gaze travelled over the little plot of land, espaliered apple trees a leafy green against the red brick wall that surrounded the property.

Lizzy took her hand, waiting for her sister's thoughts to settle. Jane had a strong sense of propriety, and doubtless was wondering how much she could reveal without compromising Bingley's private family concerns.

"I know I can trust you, dearest Lizzy, so I shall tell you all. You will guess most of it anyway, once you learn the heart of it."

"Anything you tell me in confidence, I shall take to my grave."

Jane squeezed her sister's hands. "You know that Mr. Hurst travels in Beau Brummell's circle. He insists on wearing the latest fashions, and using the same tailors as the Prince Regent."

Lizzy nodded. If the rumours were true, the Regent had racked up enormous debts with his tailors. She wondered how they managed to stay in business. They must be loath to extend much credit to their other customers.

Jane continued, "It seems that in order to pay for one set of bills, Mr. Hurst has fallen into arrears on another—namely, the lease for the house on Grosvenor Street."

"Good heavens!" Lizzy cried, her thoughts swimming. He would pay for fashionable clothes before a roof over his wife's head? Lizzy would think him wicked, but she did not consider him clever enough for that. So she could only think him a fool.

"This morning," Jane continued, "he let Bingley know they were all on the verge of eviction, and asked Bingley to pay what was owed. Bingley does not mind paying, of course, as he and Caroline have been living there these six months. But Lizzy, it is the principle of it. Hurst overextended himself, and did not have the decency to let Bingley know until the situation had reached a crisis."

A sudden thought tore through Lizzy like a thunderbolt. "Tell me Mr. Hurst has not squandered his wife's entire fortune!"

"Oh, no. Apparently, Bingley's father had concerns in that area. He established a trust. Hurst receives the interest but cannot touch the principle."

"That is a relief, at least."

Jane shook her head, blond curls bobbing. "Bingley is determined it shall not happen again. That house is Louisa's only home. He has contacted the landlord about buying it outright."

Lizzy placed her hands in her lap. "He *was* talking about buying a house in town..."

"Yes, but for the two of us, so we could live *apart* from his sisters." Jane's eyes brimmed with tears. "I should not allow myself to be upset about it. They are his family, after all."

"They schemed to separate him from you. And very nearly succeeded. Of course you are not eager to share a house with them."

"There is Netherfield." Jane stood taller a moment, then, her shoulders fell again. "But I would not be surprised if his sisters want to remove there for the summer."

"As Darcy said, you are always welcome to stay with us."

Jane gave her an affectionate smile. "You are very kind, and of course I would love to visit you. But I would like to be mistress of my own home, without his sisters sniping at me or whispering behind my back."

Lizzy laid a comforting hand on Jane's shoulder. She hated seeing her sister distressed, and contemplated how she might ease some of Jane's burden. Nothing came to her, but she would not give up. Her kind-hearted sister deserved nothing less than perfect happiness.

That evening, Darcy dined with Bingley's family at the house on Grosvenor Street. The furnishings throughout had been culled back considerably since his visit a month earlier. The house now looked elegant rather than ostentatious.

After the meal—three courses this time, rather than five—he and Bingley once again retreated to the study to take their brandy, leaving Hurst snoring in the dining room.

"Thank you for coming tonight," Bingley said. "I do not know if I would have been able to keep my temper otherwise."

"My pleasure. You are welcome to stay at Darcy House, if that would be easier for you."

Bingley considered that a moment. "It would be easier in the short term, but I am the head of this family. I shall not allow my sisters to run roughshod over me again. If I am the one to put a roof over their heads, I shall not let them drive me out of my own home."

"Quite right. Still, it is not an easy path."

Bingley nodded thoughtfully. "What would you do in my position?"

"Ban the Hursts from Netherfield and marry off your other sister as quickly as possible."

Bingley chuckled. "You have given this some thought already. But it is not a bad plan."

Darcy set his glass on the coffee table. "What sort of husband is Miss Bingley looking for?"

"I believe you know the answer to that."

Darcy gave him a wry grin. "If I had to guess, I would say social standing is more important to her than wealth. An impoverished viscount might suit her."

"She would rather have a flush one."

Staring at the bookshelves with unfocused eyes, Darcy contemplated a moment. "Would one of our old friends from Cambridge suit?"

"Possibly." Bingley sat forward. "I hate to think in these terms. Louisa has already made a disastrous match. I was hoping for more from Caroline—that she would want love. But when she looked at you and saw opportunity, that settled the matter for her. Now..." Bingley shook his head. "She is miserable, and making everyone around her miserable. If anything, she seems even more mercenary than before."

"She has all the attributes to attract a man of quality. Surely she can find one she liked better than me."

"Perhaps she has lost her confidence. She did everything in her power, yet lost you to a woman who was not even trying."

Darcy looked at him askance. "Your sister and I were ill-suited. She would have realized that, if she had considered the essentials." He picked up his glass. "I hope I can teach Georgiana to value a man only so far as he values her. I do not want her to rush toward marriage. Look at Jane. She has the maturity and self-possession to know what is important in a husband—something a younger woman might not."

"And what of Lizzy?" Bingley asked.

Darcy sipped his brandy. "She is perhaps more romantic than she should be. Otherwise she might have had the good sense to put me off longer." He grinned sardonically. "I made poor work of courting her, and she accepted me anyway."

"You would not have liked her if she played the coquette."

"True enough. She is leading with her heart rather than her head. I am not sure she knows her own mind. She only had a few days to get used to the idea before accepting my proposal. Although I've every reason to believe her feelings sincere, she is struggling to overcome certain misgivings."

Bingley looked at him in concern. "Such as?"

"She seems terrified of meeting my uncle."

"I must confess," Bingley interjected, "I was rather terrified of meeting him, too."

"It is more than that. She is worried about the disparity in our fortunes. Which I admit I was troubled by at first—but not for the same reasons she is. I was concerned she might accept me for my income rather than for love. Now I know she would not consider that. But she worries I shall think less of her, which is absurd."

Bingley swallowed the last of his brandy. "Jane does not seem to have that problem."

"Of course not. She knows she is far too good for you, and accepted you anyway."

"It is true! She is a perfect angel. And I abandoned her. I ought to have been flagellated for that, and instead she forgave me almost instantly."

"The two of you will be very happy."

"So will you and Lizzy. I've no doubt at all."

In truth, neither did Darcy. But the change in Lizzy since leaving Rosings was palpable. Once they were settled at Pemberley, he trusted she would be herself again. But he would not be at ease until he had made her his wife.

⁓§⁓

If Lizzy never again saw the interior of a modiste's shop, she thought she would die a very happy woman. Then she realized that as Mrs. Darcy, the modistes would likely come to her. Her one consolation was that she did not have to travel to Paris for her trousseau, owing to the war.

She gazed into the mirror as the seamstress pinned and pulled, fitting the gown perfectly to her curves. The ivory silk with the gold fleur-de-lis pattern was the most sumptuous fabric ever to touch her body. She could not imagine spending so much on a wedding gown if her new station did not require it. But she was determined to economize as best she could.

She knew she was lucky. Yet social expectation weighed on her. She comforted herself with thoughts of Pemberley's tenants. She would visit each family to introduce herself, bringing them baskets of indulgences and necessities alike. Surely Darcy treated them well, but he had not a woman's sensibility about what was needed to run a household.

She looked into the mirror, seeing how grand she looked in the fine gown, as if she were of noble birth. A wave of shame brought colour to her cheeks, or rather those of her reflection. She seemed somehow disconnected from the lady in the mirror, as if it were another person. Lizzy Bennet could not deserve such fine things.

She was being silly, of course. An accident of birth separated a commoner from a queen. Lizzy did not believe that members of the aristocracy were inherently better than labourers. And if she *had* believed that, six weeks in the company of Lady Catherine de Bourgh would have knocked that idea out of her head.

She had won the heart and hand of a man who happened to be wealthy. That was not in itself an evil. She could waste his fortune on clothes and frivolous things, or she could better the lives of others.

That thought freed something inside her. Her role as mistress of Pemberley would bring duties as well as delights. She could find great satisfaction in that life, in raising their children according to the values she and Darcy shared. Generosity and humility. Honesty and kindness.

And a good bit of irony and teasing, too.

The magnitude of it terrified her. But with Darcy at her side, she was equal to it. His wisdom and strength would guide her—and his love.

Underneath her fine gown beat the heart of a flesh-and-blood woman. One who responded to him as a flesh-and-blood man. Her skin warmed at the thought of the intimacy they would share as a married couple.

When he touched her, when he kissed her, she wanted more—more of something she could not name or completely fathom. But he would know, and he would teach her. She looked forward to that knowing. She wanted it with all her heart.

Even now, with the banns to be read for the second time on Sunday, some dark part of her feared he would reject her. Feared the ending of this unexpected fairy tale. She blinked at her reflection. That was how she looked in the mirror, like a princess in a fairy tale. Like she was not real.

What if this blush of infatuation faded, and they became objects of consternation to one another, as her parents had? She had never met a man she admired so much. To lose Darcy's love would devastate her.

Unbidden tears fell onto her cheeks. The seamstress patted her arm softly, then gave her a handkerchief. "'Tis normal for a bride to be nervous, ma'am."

"Of course." That was all this was. Nerves. She would be herself once the wedding was over.

Once it was too late for either of them to change their mind.

Yet, she did not want their marriage to be Darcy's prison. Oh, why had she listened to Charlotte? Why had Lizzy not insisted on a proper courtship rather than rushing into an engagement, so these fears would not be troubling her now?

She could not deny the powerful attraction between them. She admired his character and took pleasure in his company. But was that love? In the past week, she had become a tangled bundle of doubt, too fragile to think or joke or laugh.

Yet when she thought of being alone with him in a quiet bedchamber sparkling with candlelight, her doubts quieted. Perhaps that, in the end, was what marriage was. Not the public appearances, not the running of a household or a grand estate, but two people alone in that quiet knowing.

The thought brought a smile to her lips. Darcy was her touchstone. In two weeks, he would belong to her.

Chapter 24

Lizzy, Jane, and their mother returned to the Gardiners' home after a long day of shopping to find a missive had come for them. Miss Bingley had invited them, along with Mr. and Mrs. Gardiner, to dine the following evening.

Jane's face changed to pale white, then to deep red, as their mother read aloud. "Oh, my dears," Mrs. Bennet cried, "how lovely it will be to see Miss Bingley and Mrs. Hurst again. And Jane, how they will welcome you as their sister! Miss Bingley always was so fond of you—she must rejoice at your engagement to her brother."

Jane stood silent. Lizzy ached for her and the pain their mother's utter misapprehension must be causing. "Yes, we are all to be one happy family," Jane said at last.

It was awful to see Jane, who never had an unkind word for anyone, put in this position. She would forebear, and Miss Bingley would be all civility. They would pretend they were friends, ignoring the grievous wrong Miss Bingley had done her.

Yet this meeting could surely be no more comfortable for Miss Bingley than for the Bennet sisters. All her machinations had been for naught. She had sacrificed Jane's friendship in hopes of winning Mr. Darcy, and had lost him anyway.

Lizzy almost felt sorry for her. She resolved to be kind to Miss Bingley for Jane's sake, to help heal over the wound. Perhaps that would help put Jane's mind at ease and create a more harmonious home for her.

Moreover, Lizzy had no desire to lord her victory over Caroline Bingley. The woman had been humiliated enough. Darcy was the only prize Lizzy desired.

The following evening at the house on Grosvenor Street, the butler led them into the parlour where the rest of the party were gathered. The house was furnished in elegant simplicity, silver candlesticks atop dark wood furniture, and Rococo paintings of wood nymphs and pleasure gardens adorning the walls.

Miss Bingley approached, dressed in gold silk. Mrs. Bennet introduced her to Mr. and Mrs. Gardiner. After greeting the others, Miss Bingley finally turned her attention to Lizzy.

"Dear Miss Bingley." Kissing her cheek, Lizzy breathed in the scent of gardenia. She was determined to show as much genuine kindness as she could muster. "We have missed you in Hertfordshire."

Miss Bingley blinked twice. "Miss Elizabeth Bennet, how lovely to have you in our home at last."

"Please, you must call me Eliza, now that we are to be sisters-in-law."

"Of a sort." Miss Bingley's head tilted to one side as she eyed Lizzy, assessing her, seeming unable to reach a conclusion. "And you must call me Caroline."

"With pleasure."

The next moment, Darcy was at Lizzy's side, apparently too impatient to wait for the niceties to conclude. "How beautiful you look." He deposited a kiss atop her gloved hand.

"Yes," Caroline said drily, "Mr. Darcy always did admire your fine eyes."

"You are too kind," Lizzy said.

Bowing to Caroline, Darcy led his fiancée away to a window seat, which offered a view of the garden. The yews were formed into elaborate topiaries with nary a bloom to be seen. Still, it was a pretty vista, and the spot was as private as one could hope for in a crowded parlour.

"How is the shopping?" he asked.

"Nearly done. Just a few small things that Mama says we must have. It is to be a wedding unlike any Hertfordshire has seen."

He gave her a wry smile. "Or perhaps Meryton."

Of that much Lizzy had no doubt. Certainly nothing in living memory could match it. She hated to be at the centre of such a circumstance, but she would have to get used to it. As Mrs. Darcy, she would be a prominent personage, at least in their corner of Derbyshire.

She scanned the room. "Poor Caroline. She looks under a strain. This must be trying for her."

Darcy cocked his head. "I cannot tell whether you are teasing."

"Not at all." Heaviness gathered in Lizzy's chest. "I feel sorry for her. What she did to Jane was awful, but in the end, she is the one suffering for it."

"She will get over it." His voice was even, unperturbed.

Worry tightened Lizzy's stomach. "Or she might spend the rest of her life viewing Jane and me as villains for thwarting her plans. If we meet her with overtures of friendship, offering forgiveness before it is asked...perhaps all can be smoothed over."

His eyes surveyed her from below a furrowed brow. "That is Christian of you."

"It is also practical," Lizzy insisted. "She and Jane will be sisters. Would it not be better if they were also friends?"

He took her hand. "You are right, of course. But I do not wish to discuss Miss Bingley."

She smiled at him, affection rising in her breast. "Let us change the subject, then. How did you spend your day?"

"Bingley and I went to the club and got in a bit a fencing."

"Who won?"

"It is not a question of winning or losing. It is about developing strategy and skill—"

"Bingley, then," she teased.

He grinned, eyes shining. "I have never met a man who shows more agility with a sabre. But fencing with him makes me better, so I ought not to complain."

She leaned in and said in a low voice, "I do not suppose we dare risk taking a turn out in the garden. It is dreadfully tedious being in a room full of people when I would rather be alone with you."

"It is only for two more weeks, and then we can be alone together as often as we like."

She gave him an arch look. "You are remarkably patient."

"I am trying to be."

She sighed, feeling as distracted and foolish as a young lover had ever been. There was no contentment in this waiting. She was constantly on edge, and she suspected Darcy was as well.

She pressed her palm to his. "Are you happy?"

"Do I not seem happy?"

ANDREA DAVID

"You seem restless." She pressed her lips together pensively. "Which I suppose every prospective groom must feel."

He nodded. "Are you not restless?"

She looked out the window into the waning sunlight. "I wish I could kiss you."

"Perhaps it is better you cannot, because I would not want to stop at kissing."

She whimpered at that, an unbidden desire flaming low in her belly. Her body tingled for his touch. "I am having the most wicked thoughts."

"I have wicked thoughts every moment I am with you. And most moments when I am not."

His dark, heavy-lidded eyes pinned her where she sat. She could not move or even breathe. Everything was Darcy. Nothing else existed for her.

Sudden laughter across the room pulled her out of the spell. "It will not do to discuss such things," she said to him reluctantly. With a wave of her hand, she added, "Tell me something I do not know about you."

He considered a moment. "Bingley may be better at fencing, but I am better at billiards. Now tell me something about you."

"I cannot ride a horse. I break out in hives if I touch one."

"That is unfortunate." He smoothed a curl behind her ear. "Riding is one of the great pleasures of my life."

She nodded absently. "I wish I could learn to ride with you, but it is out of the question."

He gazed at her a moment with his intelligent eyes. "It is good for us to have solitary pursuits, is it not?"

Lizzy tilted her head and looked up at him. "You are right, of course. I suspect you are right most of the time, and unused to anyone disagreeing with you."

"I hope you will disagree from time to time, especially when I am wrong."

She laughed gaily. "I shall be most happy to oblige."

They walked over to Jane and Bingley, who were standing by the fireplace. It was sealed for the summer by a fireboard painted with pink hydrangea blooms. "Bingley," Lizzy said, "you look almost sullen. I have never seen such an expression on you."

He gave her a weak smile. "Forgive me. It is not *your* company, I assure you. If we were not going back to Hertfordshire so soon, I would take Darcy up on his offer to stay with him."

"Have you decided yet where you will live after the wedding?" Lizzy asked.

"Netherfield for now," Jane said, "until we find something else."

"You must buy an estate in Derbyshire," Lizzy cried. "I cannot bear to be separated from you, Jane. What say you, Bingley? Would Derbyshire suit?"

"It is the prettiest place I have ever seen," he said affably. "If it will please Jane, then nothing could make me happier."

"It would please me very much!" Jane said.

"It is settled, then," Darcy said. "I shall make inquiries on your behalf."

"Splendid!"

Lizzy shook her head. "You will have the most agreeable husband, Jane."

"And why not?" Bingley asked. "I shall have the wisest wife."

Lizzy clutched her chest, happiness for Jane welling there. "I cannot argue with that."

Whilst Jane and Darcy chatted, Lizzy drew Bingley off to one side. "How is Caroline?"

"That is not my concern," Bingley said. "She is my hostess for now, and therefore is giving this dinner at my request, whatever her own feelings. She will have a home with me for as long as she needs one, but it will be some time before I can forgive my sisters for conspiring to separate Jane and me."

Lizzy touched his arm. "You have forgiven Darcy."

"Darcy is not the most perceptive when it comes to the feelings of others. He genuinely believed Jane indifferent. My sisters, on the other hand, were Jane's confidantes. Do you truly believe they viewed her as a fortune hunter with no real regard for me?"

Lizzy bit her lip. No, she could not believe that. The only fortune hunter involved was Caroline. The obsequiousness she had shown toward Darcy had not borne the look of love.

"Caroline knows she has wronged you. She must feel it every moment. I hope the wedding will be a chance to put any bad feelings behind you—for Jane's sake?"

Bingley pressed her hands. "I shall try."

The butler soon called them to dinner. Due to a persistent shortage of gentlemen, Lizzy was seated beside Caroline. As the footman served the white soup, fragrant with chicken and almonds, Lizzy scoured her brain for something kind to say.

Silver scraped on china, filling the uncomfortable silence.

Caroline, a hostess smile plastered on her face, said something cheery and meaningless. Her voice was too loud and her eyes too bright. She glanced over at Jane a few times, and her fingers seemed to fidget. This was not the cool, composed woman Lizzy was used to. Caroline was distressed.

She was so unlike herself, Lizzy could not help but take pity. She turned to Caroline and laid a gentle hand on her forearm. "Last fall, you gave me some good advice about Mr. Wickham. Instead of thanking you for your kindness, I dismissed it. I wish now I had listened to you. I am sorry I was not more gracious."

Caroline's face crumbled—lips trembling, eyes filling with tears. Quickly she rose. Excusing herself, she fled the room.

Bingley stared after her a moment, his face like stone. "More wine," he called to the footman, then stood. "Excuse me."

"Allow me," Lizzy said, and went out into the hallway. Her chest tightened. She had meant to help, but had only made things worse.

She found Caroline standing by the staircase with one hand on the railing, and the other drying her tears with a handkerchief. She looked so distraught, Lizzy wanted to embrace her. Unsure how such a gesture might be received, she held back.

Caroline looked up, her cheeks pale. "How can you be kind to me, after what I have done?"

Lizzy took a tentative step forward. "In the past year, I have learned some uncomfortable things about myself. I trusted George Wickham and believed his lies against Darcy. If I had had any fortune at all, that trust might have cost me dearly. I thought myself clever, when in fact I was a complete fool. So I have decided that I shall not judge a person's character until I at least attempt to know their heart."

Caroline trembled. "Charles will never forgive me, and neither will Jane."

Lizzy pondered that a moment, then shook her head. "I defy you to find two people with larger hearts than Jane and

Bingley. They are about to be married and are happier than they have ever been. If you are truly contrite, they will forgive you."

"I do not know how this went so wrong." She folded her handkerchief and put it away. "Charles has been a trusting soul his whole life. Louisa and I considered it our duty to protect him from fortune hunters. Until Jane, every time we have separated him from one of his infatuations, he has got over her in a week or two."

Gently, Lizzy said, "This was not an infatuation."

Caroline shook her head sadly. "When Jane came to town...I should not have deceived my brother. I only wanted the best for him."

"You wanted him to marry Georgiana, so you could get closer to Darcy."

Caroline startled, her lips parting. Then, a dry laugh escaped her throat. "I am completely transparent. I can lie to myself, but not to you."

"You do not love Darcy."

Caroline blinked a few times, then gave a curt nod.

Lizzy looked hard at her, fighting down the ire in her breast. "He deserves a wife who feels for him everything that she ought. I am not marrying Pemberley—I am marrying a man."

348

Caroline did not meet her eyes. "Jane and I were friends once. Do you think she could give me a second chance?"

Lizzy considered the question. "Jane is far more hurt than angry. She wants harmony in the family, but you must admit your mistakes and apologize. Do not pretend everything is fine, as you did when we arrived this evening."

Caroline met Lizzy's eyes at last, chin held high. "I stayed silent when Louisa married Hurst, and I have regretted it every day since. He is a fop who spends half his day dressing and the other half playing at cards. She threw herself away." A look of scorn crossed Caroline's features, but she quickly schooled it. "I want the very best for Charles."

"Jane *is* the very best." Emotion rose from deep inside Lizzy, her gut clenching at everything her poor sister had suffered at this woman's hands. But if Caroline had repented, it was Lizzy's Christian duty to forgive her.

"You are right, of course. Jane is an angel," Caroline conceded without emotion. "I only hope I shall find the same felicity she has one day."

"You are a woman of means—beautiful, intelligent, and accomplished. If love is what you want, you will find it. But it cannot be forced."

Caroline's gaze fixed on some distant point. "My entire education was centred on pleasing a man. It turned out to be utterly worthless."

"Not utterly so. Let the world see *yourself*, not a china doll."

Caroline dabbed her eyes and laughed drily. "I must look a mess."

"On the contrary, you are a natural beauty."

Caroline allowed herself a smile.

They went back into the dining room together. Jane gave them a pensive look, but did not seem displeased. On the way to her own chair, Lizzy brushed a soothing hand across Jane's shoulder.

After dinner, in the drawing room, Caroline took Jane aside. The two spoke earnestly. Lizzy sat with Mrs. Hurst— Louisa—hoping to extend an olive branch.

"I see you and Caroline are friends now," Louisa remarked.

"I hope we are becoming friends," Lizzy said warily. Louisa's tone held no warmth.

"How magnanimous of the future Mrs. Darcy to take notice of us poor Bingleys."

Lizzy stared into her lap. "My change in circumstances must have come as a shock to you."

"A shock to everyone, I daresay. Pray what does his uncle the earl think of the match?"

Deep breaths. Lizzy reminded herself that this woman would soon be Jane's sister. Lizzy could endure a little

ANDREA DAVID

unkindness for Jane's sake. "I shall have the honour of meeting the earl and countess at dinner tomorrow."

"I expect it will be a most entertaining evening."

Lizzy ignored the barb. "I expect so. I have become great friends with their son, Colonel Fitzwilliam. I understand he and his father are much alike."

"How much the colonel is like his father, I cannot say. I have noticed that the colonel regularly shares Darcy's opinions, especially as Darcy is so generous with him, whilst he must subsist on a colonel's pay."

Ire rose in Lizzy's chest, but she endeavoured to push it down. "You have heard of the colonel's marriage, I assume? His opinions are all his own now."

"Yes, and once he is returned from his honeymoon, we should have a better idea of what they are."

To calm herself, Lizzy lifted a cup of tea to her lips and sipped, letting it warm her before she swallowed. "Tell me, Mrs. Hurst, where are you and Mr. Hurst planning to live after your brother's marriage? Will you continue to stay here, once Jane is mistress of this house?"

Louisa looked at her tartly, mouth pinched. "We will be quite pleased by the addition of Jane to our household."

"You mean your brother's household, I believe? As I understand it, you do not have a household. We both know how generous your brother is, but also how easily persuaded to change his mind."

Louisa's eyes narrowed, and the next moment she rose. "Excuse me."

Lizzy sighed. She should not have mentioned that recent humiliation—it was beneath her. But perhaps Louisa needed the hint. She was used to leading her brother, but those days were behind her. Even if she did not realize it yet.

Emotionally exhausted, Lizzy and Jane approached their mother soon after the gentlemen rejoined them. In hushed tones, they persuaded her to make an early night of it. Darcy expressed regret at seeing Lizzy go, but he understood that it had been a trying evening.

Back at Gracechurch Street, after dressing for bed in the guest room they shared, the sisters talked a while. Jane was grateful for the thaw in her relationship with Caroline. It would not be quick and it would not be easy, but Lizzy hoped that one day the two could be friends again.

Chapter 25

"Now girls," said Mrs. Bennet in the carriage on the way to the town home of the Earl and Countess of Matlock, "I am sure you will be quite frightened in the company of so grand a person as an earl, as well you should be. Therefore, you must let me do the talking. I have more experience at this sort of thing than you, and I know what is best."

Lizzy gritted her teeth. Her mother had never in her life met an earl, and appeared more frightened than either Lizzy or Jane. Lizzy carefully considered her reply. "Dear Mama, you are right of course. Darcy assures me his uncle is a jovial man who enjoys a battle of wits—"

"Elizabeth Bennet, you will present yourself with the utmost modesty. I insist upon it." Her mother's shrill voice made Lizzy wince. Mrs. Bennet continued, "This is the most important night of your life—of all our lives. What if you embarrass Darcy, and he changes his mind about marrying

353

you? Hmm? Then where will you be? You will not find another man of ten thousand a year, I promise you."

Lizzy turned silent. She had never seen her mother like this. Mrs. Bennet's disposition was irritable on the best of days, but this meeting had clearly put her under a strain.

Already nervous, Lizzy was desperate to make a good impression on Darcy's family. She had no doubt Lady Catherine had filled her brother's head with insults about Darcy's intended. Add to that her mother's erratic nature, and Lizzy well knew the evening could end in disaster.

Everything depended on this night. It could set her reputation amongst Darcy's family forever.

In truth, Darcy was not at liberty to jilt Lizzy now. Not only was he honour-bound—they had a marriage contract. But if the earl and countess despised her, and Darcy's feelings changed, would she hold him to his promise? No, she could not marry a man who did not love her. It was unthinkable.

As they were led into the reception hall, Lizzy marvelled at the opulence of it. Great crystal chandeliers, intricate mouldings, and paintings of clouds and cherubs on the ceiling were hallmarks of conspicuous wealth. Lizzy had promised herself to remain calm, but she was losing her resolve.

She searched the room for Darcy, but apparently he had not yet arrived. Surely he would have planned to be early, for her sake? It was all the more odd, since her mother had insisted on being fashionably late.

The footman announced them, and an elegant couple of about sixty greeted them. His lordship was tall, his features still bearing the mark of the handsome man he must have been in his youth. His style of dress was contemporary and refined.

Her ladyship, her face bearing the lines of a lifetime of cheerful smiles, wore a lilac brocade threaded with gold, her headpiece a simple velvet ribbon that sported an ostrich feather.

"Mrs. Bennet," the earl greeted Lizzy's mother, "a pleasure to meet you at last. My nephew has told me much about you and your family."

Lizzy cringed to think what Darcy had told them about her mother—her country manners, her unrefined mind, her inexplicable *hauteur* toward him?

Mrs. Bennet's words drew Lizzy from her musings. "You do me a great honour, my lord. May I present my eldest daughter Jane, lately engaged to Mr. Charles Bingley. I believe you know him?"

"Yes," the countess said, "he is a great friend of Darcy's. Pleased to meet you, Miss Bennet."

"And you, your ladyship," Jane said with a curtsey.

"And this is my second daughter, Elizabeth."

"The lady herself," the earl said, "the one who has stolen my nephew's heart."

"Welcome to our home, Miss Elizabeth," the countess said. "Darcy has long been a favourite of ours. He is quite the prize."

"Indeed, ma'am," Mrs. Bennet said, "and I assure you, no one could be a more dutiful mistress of Pemberley than my Lizzy shall be."

"Mama, you forget yourself," Lizzy said quickly. "The earl and countess are not as familiar with your wit as Jane and me. The countess of course means that Darcy himself is the prize, not his estate at Pemberley."

"Yes, naturally," Mrs. Bennet said. "He will find my Lizzy to be most amenable. She is as docile as a lamb!"

The earl scowled. "Indeed? Darcy promised me she had the liveliest mind of any girl he had met, and would prove a challenge in a battle of wits."

"Once I take the last name Darcy, I shall be happy to do so," Lizzy said. "But as long as I bear the last name Bennet, I must obey my mama."

"Quite right," the earl said. "Perhaps your skills at diplomacy will be of use to me, Miss Elizabeth."

The footman announced Darcy, and Lizzy felt a weight lift from her. She had not recognized how tense she was until she saw his face, and the sensation eased.

Good heavens, her mother was not making things easy! Would the entire evening go like this, Lizzy forced to come up with clever replies to smooth over her mother's blunders?

To cheer herself, Lizzy approached her fiancé, who was greeting his aunt and uncle. After bowing to them, he took Lizzy's hands and kissed her cheek. "Sorry to be delayed. An oxcart had overturned in the street. I intended to be here before you arrived."

"Nothing *too* humiliating has happened so far," she said brightly, "but the night is young."

He squeezed her hand, then greeted her mother. Before Lizzy had a chance to speak with him again, though, they were whisked into the dining room.

Lizzy tensed up again. She wanted Darcy with her, as a crutch or a talisman—something to drive away the panic freezing her brain. Seated to the right of the earl, she found herself at a loss. Whether owing to her own nerves, or her mother's admonitions, she could not think of a single sensible thing to say.

She suddenly felt sympathy for Darcy, and how out of sorts he must have felt at that first ball in Hertfordshire. He had nothing in common with the party there, just as she had nothing in common with the earl.

Except Darcy.

Stirring her Lorraine soup, enjoying the aroma of veal and parsley, she said, "Pray you, sir, I am most eager to know what Darcy was like as a child. He tells me very little."

"A serious boy, as you might expect," his lordship said with a fond smile. "He and Richard were inseparable. Richard was a wild bull from the beginning, and he and Will used to run and play for a whole day together. They would be up before dawn, get a parcel of bread and cheese from the cook, and come back at sunset, dirty as vagrants."

Lizzy smiled. "I can picture them—they must have been adorable."

He nodded. "The groundskeepers kept an eye on them, and as they were sensible boys, we did not worry. Well, old Darcy and I did not worry. Their mothers wanted to coddle them more, especially Anne. Her son was her whole world, at least until Georgiana came along." His expression turned grave.

An ache settled on her heart. "You must miss your sister terribly."

"Georgiana is so like her, the very image of her. Whenever I think of Anne, I think of her at Giana's age—or a bit older, just before she married. When I look at Giana these days, I feel a little pang, as if I am looking back in time."

Lizzy placed a hand on her heart.

When the next course was served, Lizzy turned to the man on her right. Dr. Peter Fitzwilliam was the second-youngest son of the earl and countess, a physician of Darcy's age, or perhaps a bit younger. Rather plain with a slim build, he had blond hair and blue eyes, a trait he must have inherited from his mother. His angular countenance bore a studious air.

It was unusual for the son of a peer to choose medicine as a profession, but Dr. Fitzwilliam spoke animatedly about the latest discoveries in his field. Lizzy inferred that he was driven by a passion for healing, and cared little about what others thought of his choice. His independent nature appealed to her.

During a lull in conversation, she asked him, "What do you recommend for a nervous complaint? We are in the midst of planning a double wedding, and I am afraid that Jane and I are putting a great strain on our mother."

"I can give you the recipe for a lavender poultice. It is most efficacious, especially if used whilst lying down for thirty minutes."

With a straight face but a little flutter of her lashes, Lizzy asked, "And what if the patient were to lie down for thirty minutes, without using the poultice?"

Dr. Fitzwilliam scowled. "Rest on its own can be helpful, but the lavender does have therapeutic effects."

"Pardon me, sir," she said, heat rising in her cheeks, "I was making a little joke, and apparently a poor one."

He sighed. "You will find that wit is lost on me. I can never tell whether my father is being serious."

"I shall endeavour to be plain, then, and save my teasing for Darcy."

His expression did not change. Had she offended him? His brooding silence reminded her a bit of Darcy, which should have comforted her, but somehow did not.

She could not escape the feeling that she was making a muddle of this. She looked at Darcy, seated at the opposite end of the table, to the right of the countess. She wanted his guidance, his reassurance—yet with all the intervening conversations, neither could hear a word the other spoke.

When the dishes were cleared and the next course brought, Lizzy turned to the earl when he asked, "What do you think of this situation with Boney, my dear? What shall we do to put a stop to him?"

She might have thought he was patronizing her, but he wore an acute expression, as if truly interested. The situation on the continent concerned her very much, but she was hardly in a position to play general.

"I have little to share that would be of interest to you," she said. "All my opinions have been formed from talking to Colonel Fitzwilliam. You will find I think as he does." She turned quiet a moment. "I am pleased that his new position in the militia will keep him closer to home."

The earl patted her hand. "I must agree with you there. A great weight has been lifted from me, I assure you."

"And Darcy as well. He thinks of his cousin more as a brother, a sentiment I am coming to share." Warmth blossomed in her breast at thoughts of the colonel. She met the earl's eyes, and he gave her a genial smile.

Diagonal to her at the table, her mother's voice carried in Lizzy's direction. "We quite expect our dear Bingley to buy

Netherfield outright, so Jane will be settled ever so close to Longbourn. Such an amiable man, not one to think himself above his company. The first night we met him, he was ever so kind, and danced with all the young ladies. Unlike *some* people. The insult my poor Lizzy suffered—"

"Mrs. Bennet loves to tease me on that score," Darcy said in a loud voice, cutting off whatever she was preparing to say. "Fortunately for me, Miss Elizabeth Bennet has done me the kindness of forgiving my careless words."

"Now you have piqued our curiosity," the earl said. "You must tell us what you said."

"I am ashamed to repeat it."

Lizzy grinned. "He said I was not pretty enough to tempt him to dance."

"Darcy!" the countess cried, her face frozen in shock. "That is not like you!"

"He meant no harm," Lizzy said. "He was speaking privately to Bingley. Perhaps a lull in the music permitted me to overhear."

The countess continued to stare at him with wide eyes. "But to say such a thing aloud—and about such a pretty girl!"

"Perhaps it only shows how disinclined he was to dance," Jane teased.

"He *is* a very reluctant dancer," Lizzy said.

"I have never known him to be," the countess scolded. "Darcy, what a dull fellow you must have been whilst you were in Hertfordshire!"

"I am afraid I was. After that unpleasantness with Wickham, I was determined to be displeased with the world."

"You do not mean Mr. *George* Wickham!" Mrs. Bennet cried. "Such an amiable fellow, and he turned Lizzy's head, I can tell you. I had some hopes there, but then he got engaged to Miss King for a time—"

"His brief engagement to Miss King followed very shortly after her inheritance of ten thousand pounds," Lizzy said, her cheeks flaming. Good heavens, could her mother have exposed Lizzy any more thoroughly, than by revealing her initial partiality for that scoundrel?

"His motives were quite clear, Mama," she continued. "And it is not the first time he has behaved in that manner. He is able to make himself pleasing—but I am afraid he has managed to alienate all his friends of quality."

"Why, Lizzy! How can you say such a thing about dear Wickham?"

"I daresay he is not dear in *this* house, Mama," Jane intervened. "He has behaved quite badly to Darcy's family. Darcy did not wish to embarrass him by saying so in Hertfordshire, in case Mr. Wickham meant to better himself."

"It is a painful history," Lizzy said, grateful beyond words that Georgiana was not amongst the company, "and it is best if we do not distress Darcy further by discussing it. I am sorry, Mama, I ought to have told you."

"The fault is mine," Darcy said, "for bringing up his name. Indeed, madam," he said to Mrs. Bennet, "do not distress yourself. You could not have known."

"I can hardly believe Mr. Wickham is so bad. Perhaps there has been some mistake—"

"There has been no mistake."

At the sharp tone of Darcy's voice, tears sprang to Lizzy's eyes. His lordship patted her hand kindly.

Jane came to the rescue. "Mama, you must consider. Darcy grew up with Mr. Wickham and knows him better than any of us. The man betrayed him. I daresay we have all been deceived in his character—it is upsetting, but it is beyond dispute."

Mrs. Bennet shifted in her chair, looking uncomfortable.

"Until Colonel Fitzwilliam told me the truth of him," Lizzy said, "I was too willing to believe his favourable reports of himself—and his disparaging remarks about Darcy." She felt a sudden pang in her heart, like the prick of a needle, at the prejudice she had shown toward her fiancé. "One man had all the goodness, and the other all the appearance of it. Darcy is so modest, he does not wish the world to know how noble he is."

The countess nodded. "That is very true. I recall a time when we witnessed an accident in the street—a runaway carriage knocked down a tradesman. Darcy hurried out of the coach and stayed with the man until the surgeon arrived, covering the costs of the man's treatment. Darcy refused to give the tradesman his name, but the man recognized our livery. When he recovered, he brought us a beautiful wooden angel he had carved for Darcy. I believe the carving is at Pemberley now, in a place of honour."

Darcy coloured but did not reply, gaze fixed on the table top.

Lizzy startled, realizing why he had been so late arriving after he came upon the overturned oxcart. He had stayed to help. Emotion gathered in her throat.

She watched him with a smile full of love and admiration. Lifting his head, he met her eyes, his embarrassment clearing. He smiled back.

Her mind wandered to wicked thoughts of how she might express her admiration.

⁓⟡⁓

In the drawing room, the countess motioned for Lizzy to sit next to her. "I am so happy to finally meet you, my dear. When Darcy was here at Christmas, he could not stop talking about you."

"Indeed?" Lizzy cried, astonished.

"Oh, yes. He always turned the conversation to you. When literature was the topic, he mentioned the books you had read to your sister during her illness at Netherfield. When my daughter invited him for a turn in the garden, he mentioned the long walks you took each morning, and how they lent a sparkle to your eye."

She chuckled, her face warming. "He must have bored you all to tears."

"He was clearly in love, and nothing could have pleased us more. Richard's letters from Rosings assured us that you were a most genteel woman, and Darcy's equal in every way."

Lizzy blinked at that. "I am...flattered." Heat rose in her neck and face at the countess's kindness.

"You must not think anyone in *this* house regards the situation as Lady Catherine does. My husband loves his sister, but it is a trial, having a family member who is not what she ought to be." She patted Lizzy's hand.

Lizzy could not speak. She was stunned by the countess's words, and even more by her implication. She was reassuring Lizzy that she need not worry about her own embarrassing relatives, for she would be judged on her own merits. Or even that she would not be judged at all, for Darcy's family had already accepted her.

Could it be that simple?

She pondered a moment, knowing how respected Darcy was by his family. It stood to reason they would trust his choice of wife. Lizzy would remain cautious—but some of her nerves subsided.

The countess excused herself to serve the tea and coffee. When the gentlemen joined the ladies in the drawing room,

Darcy took a seat by Lizzy's side. Her heart sank at his expression. He showed no pleasure upon seeing her, but instead looked distracted, as if his mind was miles away.

She wondered at the cause. She wanted to apologize for her mother's insensitivity regarding Wickham, but in this close space she risked being overheard. Instead, she took a different tack, and hoped it would ease his mind rather than adding to his distress.

"Tell me what happened with the oxcart. Was anyone gravely injured?"

He stared a moment, recalled from his brooding, then looked at her acutely. "The driver took a bad fall but appeared to have suffered no serious harm. The beast, however, had to be destroyed. The cart fell on top of him and broke his back."

"How awful!"

"It was, truly—seeing a creature in such distress. The driver was disconsolate at the loss of the animal. It was his livelihood, as well as his companion."

Lizzy squeezed his hand. "So you did what you could."

"Yes, of course." He said nothing further.

In that moment, the silence she had so teased him for became the dearest thing in the world to her. She did not need to hear the words to know that he had saved a man from destitution. Doing good was its own reward, and he would be mortified if the truth were broadcast.

She had never esteemed a man so much. How could she ever make amends for his sacrifices in choosing her? Georgiana had a fortune of thirty thousand pounds, which had doubtless come from her mother. How was Darcy to save up such an amount if they had a daughter—or daughters?

And if they had more than one son, they would need to set up the younger ones in a profession. Ten thousand pounds a year sounded like a grand sum, until one considered the costs of running an estate like Pemberley, and setting aside the funds needed to secure the future of their children.

She would have to economize. It was unthinkable to allow the estate to be diminished because of her. No; Darcy would live as a man of his means ought, and she would spend only enough to be a credit to him as his wife.

Why had she not thought of this before? His income had seemed so enormous, she had not considered how easy it would be to exhaust it under the circumstances.

She estimated how much her father spent on her a year. Surely twice that ought to be enough to maintain her as Mrs. Darcy. She might need a bit more during the season. But last year's gowns could be updated to this year's fashions. Jewellery could be reset. Had any of Lady Anne's jewellery been reserved for her, or had it all gone to Georgiana?

She felt sick at the thought of Darcy spending money on jewellery for her. It might well be necessary, though. It could not look as though they were struggling financially. His social circle must feel confident of his solvency.

"You are quiet, my love," Darcy said, interrupting her thoughts.

"I am thinking how little I deserve you."

He scowled. "We cannot have that. Is something in particular troubling you?"

"Oh, Darcy, it is everything," she cried. "I am overwhelmed by your goodness. You are of far more consequence than me—"

"No one is of more consequence than you. Not in my eyes."

Her heart filled, and she swallowed the emotion in her throat. "But how? I have nothing to offer you."

"I have seen the world, Lizzy. Until I met you, no woman had tempted me to marry. You were designed for me. I might not have recognized it instantly, but I did soon after we met. Why do you doubt yourself?"

"Look around!" she cried, incredulous. "This house is the most magnificent thing I've ever seen—it is like a palace to me. To you, it is your uncle's house in town."

"Then I shall endeavour to see it through your eyes, so I can better appreciate it."

She smiled and shook her head. "You are the kindest man I ever met."

"My own Lizzy." He kissed her hand. "Can you doubt I cherish you?"

"I do not doubt it, but neither do I understand it."

"Well, then, I must spend my lifetime showing you." A sweet smile spread across his face.

She could not continue in this vein. It was unkind to constantly need his reassurance. She owed him the courtesy of believing he knew his own mind.

"I promise, I shall make you a good wife, and do everything in my power to deserve you."

"Just be your own sweet self. That is all I ask."

As Lizzy and Jane readied themselves for sleep that night, Lizzy sat on the side of the bed and said in a low voice, "I cannot help thinking Darcy must be wishing he had not proposed to me."

Her voice a low panic, Jane asked, "What did he say?"

"Nothing at all. In fact, he was quite encouraging. But the things Mama said about Wickham—"

"You must not fret about that!" Jane's relief was evident in her soft features. "Darcy himself acknowledged that *he* was the one who raised the subject. In this case at least, Mama cannot be blamed for her ignorance—you are I were just as incredulous at first. She had the misfortune to be in Darcy's company when she learned the truth. She is not at fault."

Lizzy nodded, persuaded by Jane's words. "But poor Darcy was so distressed."

"Once the officers are removed to Brighton, Darcy and Wickham need never encounter one another again. Perhaps this painful business can be put behind them."

"I hope so."

Jane eyed her carefully, then said in a gentle tone, "Lizzy, you seem rather too worried about Darcy's state of mind. He is not a fragile person."

"I hate to see him suffer on my account." Lizzy could not stop the tears that sprang to her eyes.

Jane encircled Lizzy in her arms. "Your lives will be joined together as one. It is natural and even desirable for a husband and wife to share each other's joys and pains." Jane sat back, her eyebrows drawing together. "Lizzy, are you intimidated by his fortune? You never were before."

"I never esteemed him before as I do now. He deserves a woman who is his equal."

"He is a gentleman, and you a gentleman's daughter. And if he is anything like Bingley, the difference in fortune is as nothing to him. You must not let it blind you to his love. If you start measuring your worth to him in pounds and shillings, you will make both of you miserable."

"Oh, Jane, I am as hopelessly in love as a woman has ever been! And that should make me happy, but it only makes me wish I could give Darcy more."

Jane patted Lizzy's hand, then rose and sat at the vanity. She brushed out her hair, a faraway look in her eye. "Being in love is not unadulterated joy. But when a man and woman are well suited for one another, like Bingley and me, or like you and Darcy, they are in the best possible situation for happiness. Love and respect will go far in helping them through the challenges of their lives."

Lizzy tried to believe that. And indeed, some part of her knew it to be true. But she also knew they were starting out with a strike against them. The earl and countess had been kind, but that was no promise they would consider her one of them. Would anyone? Or would Darcy's circle always treat her like an outsider? Treat him as if he had come down in the world by marrying her?

She did not know. And that was the worst part. She had no idea how she would be received once she was Mrs. Darcy.

Chapter 26

The group returned to Hertfordshire the next day. The gentlemen settled in at Netherfield, and the ladies at Longbourn. Lizzy was suddenly aware that these were the last days Longbourn would be her home. The realization made her weepy, and more appreciative of the joys it held.

The familiar woods had never been so dear. She spent hours walking in them, whether alone or with a companion. She grew more patient of her sisters and her mother, more attentive toward her father. Though she was happy—eager, even—to begin her life with Darcy, she could not but feel sorrow at what she was leaving behind.

But all her time could not be spent in reflection, for there was the wedding breakfast to be planned. Whilst her mother and Hill, the housekeeper, did the bulk of the work, she did like to give an opinion every now and again.

Yet her favourite part of the day was still the visits from Darcy, promptly at eleven each morning. If the weather was fair, they generally took a turn through one of her favourite haunts, a cheerful wood or beloved hillside where she had spent some of the pleasantest moments of her childhood.

One evening, Darcy and Bingley dined at Longbourn. Before the soup had cooled, Lydia complained, "I do not see why we could not have some of the officers to dine with us. They will only be here another se'en-night. And if it had not been for Jane and Lizzy getting married, I could have gone to Brighton as Harriet Forster's guest. Can you imagine, the wife of the commanding officer, inviting me to be her travelling companion! And I had to turn her down because of the wedding."

"That's quite enough," her father said. "You are very fortunate to have Darcy and Bingley joining the family. When I am dead, Mr. Collins will toss you out to live amongst the hedgerows. You will be happy then to have brothers to care for you."

Lydia glared at him but said no more.

"Have you renewed the lease on Netherfield?" Mrs. Bennet asked Bingley.

"Yes, for another year at least. That should give Jane and me time enough to decide where to settle."

"But why should you settle anywhere else? You are happy at Netherfield, and Jane is so comfortably situated near her family."

Bingley's eyes shifted between Jane and Mrs. Bennet. "Except that Lizzy will be settled in Derbyshire."

"Oh, that should not signify," Mrs. Bennet insisted. "You may stay at Pemberley any time you like, whilst Darcy and Lizzy may of course visit you here."

"It is something to consider." Bingley brought his glass of wine to his lips, then turned to the master of the house. "I say, Bennet, this is a fine vintage. A hint of cherry, yet not oversweet."

Lizzy smiled at Bingley's talent for getting himself out of uncomfortable situations. Darcy met her approving glance. She knew her mother would not be persuaded that Jane and Bingley would settle anywhere but Netherfield—not until they had actually moved out and departed the local environs. Her mother would be convinced until the last moment that her will would prevail.

"Bingley, you cannot leave us," Lydia moaned. "Meryton will be the dullest place in the world once the officers go to Brighton."

Lizzy winced, certain they were about to be treated to a fresh bout of whining from her youngest sister.

Darcy spoke up. "I hope you will all come to Pemberley for a few weeks during the shooting season. We will be sure to give a ball to introduce my fair sisters to the people of Derbyshire."

"Oh, how I adore a ball!" Lydia cried. "Can we, Papa? The society here will be unbearable. "

Mr. Bennet cocked a brow. "That sounds like a fine scheme, but Derbyshire is a considerable distance."

"It is," Darcy said, though Lizzy knew he did not speak from his heart. When one had a comfortable conveyance, the money for inns, and the leisure to travel, the miles between Hertfordshire and Derbyshire were of little consequence. But for most people, it was a formidable distance.

Darcy continued, "I can recommend the best places to stay during the trip. If you mention my name, they will take excellent care of you. Come, six weeks in the Peak District, when the autumn colours are at their finest—surely you will not deny us?"

Mr. Bennet smiled lightly. "It is not the worst scheme I ever heard."

"And we could sojourn at Bath on the way home," Mrs. Bennet suggested.

"Bath is by no means on the way back from Derbyshire," her husband declared. Then, however, another thought seemed to cross his mind. "But if you and the girls wish to go, perhaps we could manage it, now that there are only three of them."

"Oh, could we, Papa?" Kitty cried. "I love Bath above all places."

Mr. Bennet looked at his youngest daughter but one, seeming surprised by her vehemence. "Do you, Kitty? I cannot promise any officers will be there."

"I am not as enamoured of officers as Lydia. At Bath there will be all sorts of people."

"That there will," Mr. Bennet agreed. "If you and Lydia promise to be good girls, I shall consider it."

"Oh, thank you, Papa!" Lydia cried, all thoughts of the departing regiment apparently forgotten.

Lizzy was pleased with the proposed scheme. That Darcy had been so magnanimous as to invite her family for a long stay—that had surprised her. And the side trip to Bath would give Kitty and Lydia the opportunity to dance until they became sick of balls. That might make them more bearable once they returned to Longbourn and rejoined her father.

She only hoped Darcy did not come to regret his generosity.

After the ladies withdrew, the gentlemen took their time with their port. "Are you quite sure, Darcy," Bennet asked, "that you wish my gaggle of girls to descend on you for six weeks?"

"Lizzy will miss her family. I want to make the transition as easy for her as possible."

"You are right about that," Bennet said, "and the loss of her will hardly be bearable for me. I am grateful that Bingley is taking Jane only three miles. But I suspect," he said, turning to Bingley, "you will whisk her off to a new home in Derbyshire soon enough."

"Jane and Lizzy absolutely demand it of me," Bingley said. "Who am I to refuse them?"

Bennet chuckled. "They are good girls, both of them. You are taking away the best of me."

"But your other daughters are charming girls," Bingley insisted. "Lydia is very pretty, and vivacious, too. The men at Bath will fall over themselves to dance with her."

Bennet clucked. "She has too much of her mother in her."

Darcy's jaw clenched. That was no way for a man to speak about his wife and daughter, even in front of his future sons-in-law.

"Lydia is but sixteen," Darcy said. "She will outgrow her high spirits. And if she could be persuaded to pick up a book now and again, I think she would prove herself quite a clever girl."

"Perhaps." Bennet sipped his port.

"And Kitty," Darcy continued, "she is always in her sister's shadow. I would like to see how she fared, without Lydia's influence. Perhaps she could stay with us in Mayfair during the season next year."

"You would invite Kitty, but not Lydia!" Bennet gave him a sardonic smile. "You will not be forgiven for that."

"I am not afraid of a sixteen-year-old girl. Lydia will have her chance."

"I admire your insouciance," Bennet said. "I wonder if you will find it misplaced. Have you much experience with the younger members of the fair sex?"

"I am guardian of my sixteen-year-old sister."

Bennet nodded. "Does she give you much trouble?"

Darcy chose his words carefully. "Not usually. I made an unfortunate choice of companion for her last year, and the woman quite neglected her duties. Fortunately, Georgiana is an obedient girl, and I was able to prevent any lasting harm from coming to her."

"Georgiana is the sweetest creature in the world," Bingley said brightly. "Except for Jane, of course."

"They are of a similar disposition," Darcy said.

"Ah," Bennet replied. "Jane was the easiest of my daughters to raise. Lizzy was more headstrong, of course, and gave her mother fits. But she was a clever and kind-hearted child, and her chatter brightened my darkest days. I shall miss her dearly."

Darcy could not fault him for that. "I shall not apologize for taking her away from you. Fortunately, you will still have three daughters at home, and they will benefit from getting more of your attention."

Bennet raised his brows but said nothing. Eventually, he nodded.

Bingley, as usual, broke the silence. "I understand Sir William and Lady Lucas are giving an assembly next week. The girls must be happy about it."

"It gives them something to look forward to, now that the officers are leaving. I shall be glad to be rid of that lot."

"Darcy will be pleased to see Wickham's back, I daresay," Bingley joked.

Bennet sat up straighter and met Darcy's eye. "My wife prattled some nonsense about that. To listen to her, the man might be a murderer."

"Nothing so exciting," Darcy replied. "A gambler, a reprobate, and a seducer."

"Lizzy's letter hinted at that much." Bennet sounded at once sardonic and bored. "And all these months, he has been welcomed into the company of gentlemen's daughters. You might have said something sooner, Darcy."

"Perhaps I should have," Darcy admitted. "I wished to give him the benefit of the doubt. His joining the militia seems to show a willingness to better himself."

Even as he said the words, Darcy did not believe them. He was certain Wickham's newfound patriotism was a matter of necessity, and reflected a desperate need for currency. But Darcy could hardly reveal Wickham's true character to the world without risking Georgiana's reputation.

The less said about it the better.

"Do you know anything of Denny?" Bennet asked.

Darcy shook his head. "Nothing at all."

"He has been a great favourite of my youngest daughter. I hope he has been deceived about Wickham's character, just as the rest of us have been. I would hate to think he had knowingly brought a wolf into our midst."

"I cannot say," Darcy confessed. "I wish I could."

"Ah, well. They will be gone soon enough. Good riddance to them."

It occurred to Darcy that a man with five unmarried daughters, with no means of providing for them after his death, ought to have made more of the opportunity to find one or two of them a respectable husband from amongst the gentlemen of the militia during their stay.

It was true that militia pay was abominable, barely enough to keep a man, much less a wife. But surely some of these men came from good families, and might be a desirable match for a young woman a heartbeat away from destitution.

Darcy realized, in a way he never had before, that it was up to himself and Bingley to be proper brothers to the younger Bennet girls, for Mr. Bennet himself would never be a proper father. He was not a bad man, but a careless one who could not seem to fathom the dangers his daughters faced.

It took Darcy but a moment to see how it might play out. Mary could benefit from the company of Bingley's sisters, if the man could threaten them into treating her kindly. Kitty and Lydia would benefit from Georgiana's influence, and she from their greater sociability. Her sweetness would soothe Kitty's irritability, and her grace would prove a good example to Lydia.

Rather than feeling put upon by this new responsibility, he felt in his heart what a privilege it was. These girls needed him. Their future depended on the right guidance, the right introductions, and he could give them those things.

His engagement to Lizzy had expanded his mind outside the narrow world where he had always lived. To be sure, he had cared for his tenants and made certain none of them were left wanting. But he had not thought much about those in Lizzy's position, who were on a knife's edge between gentility and poverty.

He had seen men gamble away fortunes, seen men of promise turn into dissolute rakes. He had thought himself not so much blessed as morally superior in avoiding their fate. But now he recognized how little women could do to protect themselves from misfortune brought on them by irresponsible husbands, fathers, and brothers.

He would not forget again. Lizzy had taught him a level of compassion that had previously escaped him. He would be forever grateful to her for making him a better man. Each day brought a new reason for him to look forward to making her his wife at last.

The next morning, when Lizzy welcomed Darcy to Longbourn, he shared the happy news that Georgiana would arrive at Netherfield in a few days. Lizzy longed to see her, and for the Bennet family to get the chance to know her. It was Lizzy's dear wish that Kitty and Lydia might benefit from Giana's example, and learn what it meant to be a poised young lady.

Whilst Lizzy and Darcy flirted on the couch, she embroidered handkerchiefs for her trousseau. So distracted did she become, that she had to tear the stitches out of one of them, and start over. "It is a good thing you are not marrying me for my skills as a seamstress," she said to him. "You would be sorely disappointed."

"Why, Lizzy," her mother interrupted, "do not be so modest. I assure you, Darcy, Lizzy has created some of the finest handiwork in the county."

"Only a mother's love could convince anyone of that opinion," Lizzy replied. "Mary and Kitty both have a great talent with a needle. Lydia would be the best of all of us if she applied herself. Jane works carefully and acquits herself admirably. I am happy if I can make the seams line up."

"Such false humility is entirely unnecessary, my dear," her mother persisted. "We are all family here."

The tension rose in Lizzy's scalp. Her mother's games grew more tiresome each day. Did she think Darcy would break the engagement upon learning that her sewing skills were lacking? "Mama, it will do no good to deceive Darcy about it now. He will learn the truth of it soon enough once we are married."

Her mother's squinting eyes and tight lips expressed all the disapproval she could not speak aloud.

"I assure you, Mrs. Bennet," Darcy said, "we have seamstresses enough at Pemberley that my dear Lizzy never need exert herself if she chooses not to."

"Well. Yes. I am sure you do," her mother said, not looking at all placated.

Lizzy sighed. She would never please her mother, but soon her days of trying would be over. She would dedicate herself to Darcy and the good people of Pemberley, which seemed like activity enough to keep her busy.

To clear her head, she invited Darcy to join her for a turn in the garden. The sun shone bright among fluffy white clouds, and a slight breeze touched the leaves of the black alders growing downhill from the flower beds.

"I have been thinking about your invitation to my family, to visit in the fall," she said. "It is generous of you, but do not you worry that six weeks will be too long?"

He eyed her cautiously, wearing a frown. "Do *you* think it is too long?"

"Not for myself. But I cannot help thinking how eager you must be to leave Hertfordshire and the country manners in such evidence here."

His eyes widened. "I am sorry indeed if I have led you to believe that. I do not deny an eagerness to leave the county, but that is because I shall be taking you with me as my wife." His dancing eyes brought a blush to her cheek.

He continued, "The more I get to know your family, the more I respect them. We all have our foibles—I am certainly not immune, as you well know. But you must understand, my love, that your family is dear to me, because you are dear to me."

He pressed her hand, and tears sprang to her eyes. As the days to the wedding wound down, she grew weepy at the slightest provocation. She knew it was nerves, yet could not escape the misgivings that filled her mind.

A lingering fear washed through her that she was fettering Darcy. Once they were married, there could be no escape for him—at least, not a respectable one. What if he realized, too late, that he had made a horrible mistake?

As finches flitted among the daisies, Darcy said in a slow, deliberate voice, "You seem unhappy, love."

"We come from different worlds." Her chest tightened. Every day with her family brought a new humiliation. She wanted to be his helpmate, and yet it seemed she only made his life harder.

"And yet we are made for one another," he insisted.

She looked up at him and smiled. When she gazed into his loving eyes, it was easy to see that her fears were not rational. Darcy did not believe he was throwing himself away on her.

He had praised her in every possible way. It would wound him if she did not trust in his esteem for her. She forced the worries from her mind. She must not let her silly thoughts spoil their time together.

"You seem distracted, my friend," Bingley said to Darcy that night as they took brandy by the low fire. Though it was summer, the old house was draughty and a bit damp at this time of year. The crackle, the glowing flames, and the light scent of smoke created a pleasant ambiance.

He met Bingley's eyes. "Lizzy has been dispirited lately. Quieter. She hardly ever teases me."

"Odd," Bingley said. "My Jane is usually reserved, yet she talks nonstop these days. I have never seen her in such a tizzy as she is over the wedding plans. I daresay things will return to normal once the ceremony is over."

Darcy nodded thoughtfully at that. He *had* noticed a giddiness in Jane that had not been there before. "You are right, of course. The wedding is putting a strain on them, and their mama."

Lizzy, he had noticed, seemed to be in agonies over Mrs. Bennet's behaviour. She was forced to navigate her mother's expectations of proper courtship behaviour, which were often rather silly. At the same time, Lizzy exhausted her mental faculties covering up any slights Mrs. Bennet made toward him.

He had told Lizzy not to bother—he had learned to ignore them—but poor Lizzy could not seem to help herself.

Darcy was offering Lizzy a better life than the one she had now—yet it was natural she would have some misgivings. Marriage would mean leaving all she knew behind to start a new life with him. Some degree of sorrow was expected.

Once Lizzy was at Pemberley, she would blossom. Of that he had no doubt. She would have free reign over the house, and she would enjoy the liberty it offered her.

He did, however, expect they would make most decisions together, both in his sphere and in hers. Her opinions were cheerfully given with an eye toward influencing, but not dictating. He looked forward to her gentle counsel as one of the pleasantest prospects of married life.

Was that not one of the holy purposes of marriage? Having a helpmate to guide one through difficult decisions? He hoped that she would never lose her spirit, that she would continue to challenge him. He did not want a deferential wife. He wanted a true partner.

He sank inside himself a moment. Usually, he played the role of counsellor to Bingley, due in part to the difference in their ages and experience. But in this case, he needed

Bingley's advice. Bingley was better skilled with people, and with women in particular.

"Lizzy frets constantly that I disapprove of her family, despite my reassurances. I do not know how to put her mind at ease."

Bingley turned thoughtful a moment, then said, "Jane has mentioned that since meeting your family, Lizzy is more...cognizant of your place in the world. Perhaps she does not feel up to the task of being your wife. She is but twenty, and has seen little of the world. To suddenly be thrown into the best society must be a strain."

A frisson of panic rose in his breast. "But Jane does not think Lizzy is unhappy?"

"Not at all. It is likely nothing but nerves about the wedding. These past few days, Jane has been weepy at the prospect of leaving Longbourn behind, but that does not mean she is sorry to go. And she is only moving three miles, at least until we decide where to settle."

"You are welcome to stay at Pemberley whilst you look for a property."

Bingley nodded, wearing a pensive look. "That would be hard on Caroline."

"It might be good for her to see in Jane and Lizzy what a man values in a wife, rather than the artifice she was taught at school. Unless you want another brother-in-law like Hurst."

"I used to think him droll. Now I realize he is every bit as superficial as he appears."

"Pity. Louisa could have done better."

"She did not want to do better," Bingley said sharply. "He is a man easily led."

Darcy smiled at the truth of his friend's words. "Is it not better to find a true partner, than to seek a mate one can dominate?"

"I think so. Why would I want to dominate Jane? She is perfection."

Darcy grinned slyly. "She is too forgiving. She took you back far too easily."

"You can hardly expect me to find fault with that," Bingley said, wearing a smile.

"You will be a happy man."

"As will you. I am certain of it." Bingley sat forward. "Rest assured, once Lizzy is settled in at Pemberley, she will be herself again."

Darcy wished he could believe that.

Chapter 27

The following afternoon, at Lydia's insistence, some of the officers came to Longbourn for tea and a final farewell. Thankfully, Wickham and Denny were not among them. Lizzy suspected her father had warned them off. She knew of no proof that Denny was as profligate as his companion, but she nevertheless did not want him near her younger sisters. That was courting trouble.

After the men had gone, she engaged Darcy in a game of chess. He was clearly distracted—she took his queen far too easily. She sighed. "Darcy, if you do not tell me what is troubling you, I shall end up speculating that it is something awful. Are you having second thoughts about the wedding?"

He looked at her with wide eyes, his face blanching. "Of course not." His voice carried a jagged tone. "Are you?"

"You are the one brooding," she reminded him. He did not respond.

DARCY COMES TO ROSINGS

Suddenly, all her worries flowed back. Did Darcy regret their engagement? Was he finally seeing the madness of it all?

Even after he and Bingley returned to Netherfield that afternoon, she could not shake the feeling that something was very wrong. Of course, Darcy in a sullen mood had not been unusual before their engagement. She had grown accustomed to the happy Darcy, and the contrast seemed significant. Perhaps it was no more than a passing mood.

Late that night, when the house was quiet and these disconcerting thoughts troubled Lizzy's mind, she wandered into her father's study. He was sitting at his desk, which was well-lit by an iron candelabra. How many times had she seen him thus? With a pang in her heart, she realized that the comforts and routines of Longbourn were about to become memories.

He looked up at her and smiled. Taking off his spectacles, he asked, "Something I can do for you, my dear?"

She closed the door and sat at the chair opposite him. "Whilst I was in London, I understood for the first time how very wealthy Darcy is. And I wonder if he has realized yet...how very poor I am."

Her father raised his brows and gave her a satirical look. "For a man of his means, that can be of no consequence."

"But it can, Papa. Miss Darcy's dowry is thirty thousand pounds—the fortune inherited from her mother. Thanks to the entail, I can bring nothing to the marriage nor to any children Darcy and I may have."

Her father tapped a pen on the desk. "Clearly, the man cherishes you more than the fortune he might have gained by marrying another. Otherwise he would not have proposed. That speaks well to your prospects for happiness."

"Does it?" she asked in frustration. "A year from now, he may count himself the greatest fool in England. Many men of his stature have fallen out of love with their wives but have contented themselves with the capital she brought them. Darcy will not even have that."

Her father sat back, his eyes searching her. "Where is this coming from? The man is besotted."

"Precisely. His choice is not rational."

Her father rose and walked around the desk, pulling up a chair beside her. "My dear, no one is better acquainted than I with the symptoms of a nervous condition. Your mother drives herself to distraction worrying about all the terrible things that could come to pass, but likely will not. In my experience, brides-to-be put considerable energy into the same exercise."

He took her hand and pressed it between his own. "Darcy is one of the most sober young men I have ever encountered. Had he proposed last fall, I might have thought his actions rash. But he has clearly given this match considerable reflection. I can only conclude that he knows what he is about, and is certain you will bring him happiness."

Her heart ached. She wanted to agree, yet could not ignore the anxiety coursing through her. "What if he is wrong? I cannot bear the idea that he will wake up every morning for the rest of our lives, wishing he had not married me. I cannot bear for him to think of me the way you—" She broke off, realizing she had stepped too far.

Her father sat back and eyed her placidly. "Ah, I see what this is about. It may surprise you, Lizzy, to know that my fellows still congratulate me on having won the hand of the prettiest girl in Meryton, all those years ago. My marriage to your mother does have its conciliations, even if you are not privy to them."

Lizzy's face burned. Surely he could not mean... Oh, heavens, she could not even think about it!

"It is true, I delight in vexing her," he continued, "and she in being vexed. We would not be treated daily to her histrionics if she did not enjoy working herself into a frenzy and creating as much inconvenience as possible for those who attend her. I daresay it must seem an odd arrangement to others. But I get my way most of the time with very little trouble, so I cannot complain of it. I have my privacy and my books, and she the run of the rest of the house."

Lizzy stared, wondering how much of her father's statement was teasing and how much the truth. One could never tell with him. Regardless, she was in no way comforted.

"I thank you for your kind advice." She rose, the blood heating in her veins. "If I perceive that Darcy is tiring of me, I now know what to do. I shall let him have his way and avoid his company. Better yet, I could suggest he move to the house in town and take a mistress, whilst I stay at Pemberley and comfort myself with the stable master. That is what the fashionable couples do, is it not?"

Standing at her side, her father patted her shoulder. "My dear, you are worrying over nothing."

"Or perhaps I am the only one seeing the situation clearly."

A headache gripped her. Her father, she realized, was the last person on earth who could give her sensible marriage advice. Even her mother would be a better counsellor. Fanny Gardiner had done well for herself in marrying Thomas Bennet, the richest man in town, with little but her beauty to recommend her.

And her mother had been right about Netherfield. Lizzy would grant her that.

The only person who could allay her fears was Darcy. She would have a serious talk with him on the morrow. Then, she could enter the married state with a clear conscience.

※

The next day was fair, so Jane and Bingley joined Lizzy and Darcy on a walk through the countryside. Robins twittered their cheerful song, flitting from tree to tree. At the woodland's edge, wild roses were coming into bloom. A brook cut through the meadow, gurgling and sparkling in the sunlight.

"I am so looking forward to our trip to the Lake District!" Jane said, holding on to Bingley's arm as they walked. "My aunt Gardiner says it is like a fairyland."

"I can think of no better place for our honeymoon," he agreed.

Lizzy smiled at them, pleased for her sister. She and Bingley would be deliriously happy. Had two people ever been better suited for one another?

Then she looked up at Darcy, and her stomach dipped with excitement. Surely no man could be better suited to her than he.

It seemed odd to her now, that it had taken her so long to realize they seemed made for each other. She had once called him taciturn, and certainly conversation did not come easily to him. Nor had she made any effort to draw him out when he had been at Netherfield the previous fall. They might have gone their whole lives without discovering how well they fit together.

So in a sense, she must be grateful to Lady Catherine. Had it not been for her, Lizzy and Darcy might not otherwise have found themselves in company together again so soon—or perhaps ever. So she had cause to feel grateful to the woman who, through no intention of her own, had indirectly brought Lizzy the happiness she had found.

Yet Lizzy's mind was still troubled by her thoughts of the night before. She wondered if broaching the subject would displease Darcy. Still, her mind was in turmoil. She could not rest until she discussed it with him.

Bingley had stopped to pick Jane a bouquet of cornflowers and daisies, so Lizzy and Darcy walked ahead, arm in arm.

She said to him, "I wish to speak to you about a delicate matter. I hope you will not be angry."

"What is it, my love?"

She chose her words carefully, cognizant of the offense they might give. "I recognize that my lack of fortune has placed any children we may have at a disadvantage. I am happy to economize so we may save for a dowry for our daughters, and a living for our sons. I could be quite content limiting myself to a hundred pounds a year for my personal expenses, if that would please you."

He stopped and stared at her. "Why would that please me?"

"The cost to maintain an estate the size of Pemberley must be enormous. I would not wish to see the estate diminished in any way because of me."

He lifted her hand and pressed it between his own. "Tell me, do you think me a reckless man?"

She blinked, taken aback by the question. "Of course not!"

"Then let me assure you, I have the means to secure our children's future. Mrs. Darcy shall not have to live on a hundred pounds a year."

She eyed him a moment, then nodded. "Whatever you think best, of course."

"My darling, I do not wish for you to believe, on a daily basis, that you must deprive yourself for the sake of our family. I wish to take care of you, Lizzy, to ensure your needs are met. That is my duty, as well as my heart's desire."

He entwined her arm in his and patted her hand. "We will discuss these things together once we are married. I shall not keep you in the dark about our finances—I value your insight. Whilst I am not averse to eliminating unnecessary expenses, I did not propose to you so you could live like a pauper as retribution for the size of your fortune."

A thrill rose in her chest. "I hope you will not scold me for thinking of pecuniary matters."

"Never." He shook his head. "Lizzy, you underestimate by far how much I love you."

"Not at all. I simply recognize how much you have given up for me."

"But you do not recognize how much I have gained." He untied her bonnet and tossed it onto the soft grass. Then, he drew her close and kissed her. "You are worth more to me than money, more even than Pemberley. If I had to choose, I would choose you."

She drew in a quick breath, and her eyelids fluttered. "You cannot mean that."

"I do mean it. I love you, dearest Lizzy, and I cannot wait to make you my wife."

Emotion swelled her throat. She could not speak. This man was dearer to her than life itself. How could she deserve him, when he was superior to her in every way? And yet, he indisputably wanted her as his wife. She could not deny him that on the basis of unfounded fears.

No, she would have faith in him, and in the words of others more experienced than herself. She was nervous about the wedding, nothing more. Darcy loved her. She would take him at his word.

꩜

The next morning, Darcy and Bingley arrived at Longbourn at their usual time. As rain threatened, the group did not venture out of doors, but instead gathered in the breakfast room for cards. To Lizzy's astonishment, Darcy insisted on playing at Mrs. Bennet's table, along with Bingley and Kitty. Jane, Lizzy, Mary, and Lydia played at the other.

"My dear Mrs. Bennet," Darcy said, "I hope you received the pheasant I sent over?"

"I did, sir, most kind of you."

"I remembered your saying you preferred pheasant, so I shot it especially for you."

DARCY COMES TO ROSINGS

"Did you, indeed? What fine sons-in-law I shall have!"

Lydia looked over at them, wearing a scowl. "And why should Kitty be Darcy's partner at whist? None of the officers like her so well as me."

"Perhaps that is why," Lizzy said. "You are always the centre of attention. Darcy would like to get to know Kitty, too."

"What is there to know? She is a dull, irritable thing."

Jane laid down a jack of trumps to win the hand. "She is perfectly amiable when you are not tormenting her. For heaven's sake, Lydia, allow your sister to have some notice. It costs you nothing for her to play at cards with Bingley and Darcy. They are already spoken for."

Lydia pouted. "I do not understand why the regiment must go to Brighton rather than staying here."

"To defend the coast," Jane said. "We are at war with France."

Lydia rolled her eyes.

"At such a time as this," Mary said, "we ought to think of our brave military men as autumn leaves that may fall at any moment. Glorious as they may be, their time is fleeting."

"Oh, lord." Lydia scowled. "'Tis a pity Colonel Fitzwilliam married before I got a chance to meet him."

Jane shook her head. "It is foolish to aspire to someone of his rank."

"I do not see why. Lizzy is marrying his cousin."

"The colonel is the son of an earl," Lizzy said. "His rank is higher than Darcy's, yet his fortune smaller. He had to marry a wealthy wife. And you, Lydia, are quite poor indeed."

"Cannot Darcy give me a dowry?"

Lizzy's jaw dropped, but she quickly closed it again. "Darcy will be busy saving up for our daughters, since I can contribute almost nothing."

"I thought he was very rich."

"He is. But that does not make *you* very rich. If you behave yourself, perhaps he will introduce you to some ancient country squire seeking his third wife, who shall not mind that you are poor."

"Lizzy!"

"She is teasing you," Jane said. "If you behave yourself, you may in fact marry well, Lydia. You are a pretty, lively girl. But it would not hurt you to open a book now and again, or to practice at the pianoforte. If you have not money to recommend you, you ought to at least have some accomplishments."

"I can fix up a bonnet better than anyone."

"That is not an accomplishment a man looks for in a wife," Jane warned.

"The officers do not think I need any accomplishments. Mr. Denny is ever so fond of me."

"Have the officers come making offers of marriage?" Lizzy asked. "Or are they whiling away the time with you whilst they are stationed in a sleepy country town? There is an enormous difference between a man liking you and a man wanting to marry you."

"I thought so, too, after Bingley jilted Jane, but now he is back."

"The officers will not be back, Lydia," Jane said sharply. "They are leaving for Brighton tomorrow, and you should not expect to see them again. And it is just as well. During their time here, they have been looking for entertainment, and you are entertaining. To win the serious interest of a worthy man requires more than high spirits and a pretty face. You are an idle, careless girl. If you want men of Bingley and Darcy's circle to take notice of you, then you must endeavour to cultivate your mind."

"Kitty does not cultivate her mind, and yet Darcy chose her as his partner."

"For a round of whist!" Jane said. "You have an excellent chance in front of you, Lydia, to join the best society. If you behave like a jealous, peevish girl, it shall all be wasted on you. You might steal the heart of some young baronet if you put some effort into it. But you will need the education of a lady, not some wild country girl."

Lydia threw her cards onto the table. "I shall not sit here and be spoken to like this." Her chair screeched against the floor as she jumped to her feet.

Lizzy rose. "Lydia, sit down."

Lydia glared at her.

"Do not think that because our guests are soon to be family," Lizzy said, "that you can behave like a spoiled child. A lady does not stomp off when she is annoyed. A lady behaves in a graceful and dignified manner. You were desperate to come out into society the day you turned fifteen—you owe it to your mother and father to act like a woman and not a little girl. Sit down, Lydia. I insist upon it."

Lydia gaped for a moment, but obeyed. After a moment, she began quietly crying, but continued to play.

Bingley came over and knelt on one knee beside her, taking out his handkerchief and handing it to her. "Now, no more of that. Perhaps if the weather clears, we can all walk to Meryton, and I can buy you that book by Mr. Wordsworth that everyone is talking about."

"Oh, but there is the prettiest pair of gloves—"

"Lydia," Jane warned.

The girl lowered her eyes. "Yes, thank you, Bingley, a book of poetry would be lovely."

The weather *did* clear. The rain never came, and they headed to Meryton on dry roads. Lizzy and Darcy lagged behind the others. "I am sorry about that display with Lydia this morning. I hope you are not too cross with me."

DARCY COMES TO ROSINGS

Darcy looked at her with a furrowed brow. "Why would I be? A girl Lydia's age needs supervision—if she is left to her own devices, heaven knows what will happen to her."

She smiled at him. "I could not hear your conversation with Kitty this morning. I hope you did not find her too dull."

"No, to be honest, I quite like Kitty when she is not under Lydia's influence. Perhaps she could stay with us in Mayfair for the season. It would be good for Giana to have a companion."

"That would be splendid! Poor Mary, though, with no one for company but Lydia."

"Perhaps they will bring out the best in each other."

"Or the worst." Lizzy sighed and looked off into the distance, where the chimneys of Meryton were just coming into view. "I wish I had done more for my sisters whilst they were growing up."

"My dear, you are barely grown up yourself. Mary is only a year younger than you, Kitty two. And Lydia has only just come out. What more could you have done?"

"I confess that being the future Mrs. Darcy does give me a sense of authority over them I did not have before."

"As well it should. They need more guidance than they have had in the past. If your mother is unable and your father is unwilling, then it naturally falls to you and Jane."

She gazed into his eyes. "I am glad I have your approval. I ought not to have lost my temper this morning—"

"You did not. Lydia needs some firmness. If I had been firmer with Giana... Well, no point thinking about that. Fifteen-year-old girls are easy prey for an unscrupulous man if they are not properly supervised. My great regret is trusting in Mrs. Younge. I cannot say how relieved I am that you will be taking over Giana's education."

"I am pleased, too."

They reached the main street running through Meryton and soon arrived at Wake's General Store. Instead of the promised volume by Wordsworth, Lydia convinced Bingley to get her Blake's *Songs of Innocence and Experience*. It seemed fitting, and Lizzy was pleased with the choice.

As they left the shop, two officers in red coats turned the corner, heading toward them. Lizzy's heart seized when she recognized them as Mr. Denny and Mr. Wickham. Darcy stiffened, and Lizzy clutched his arm harder.

It was too late to cross the street and avoid them, for Lydia cried out, "Why, Denny! Where have you been hiding yourself? And Wickham, too. I do not think Lizzy has seen you at all since she returned from Kent. It is naughty of you to stay away so."

Wickham bowed in Lizzy's direction. "Miss Elizabeth has found a companion who is no doubt more pleasing." He gave her an appraising glance. "I must congratulate your fortunate fiancé. Your circumstances are much changed since we last met."

"I am most happy indeed," Lizzy said, her manner as detached as she could make it without a direct snub.

"I must confess to being surprised when I heard the news. You were not always as kindly disposed toward my old friend Darcy as you now are."

Her blood warmed. "I hardly knew him then. He improves on acquaintance."

"Does he? Others have not always found that to be the case. But your reaction is understandable. You and I have been in much the same circumstances when it comes to our prospects for marriage."

With a great effort, she managed to keep her composure. "I believe our circumstances differ in that regard. You have indicated your necessity of marrying for advantage, whereas I can only imagine marrying for love. Now I pray you must excuse me, sir. My mother expects us all home for dinner."

As she moved quickly away, her hand on Darcy's arm, her mortification was complete. That Darcy should be humiliated in such a way, entirely on her account, by a man a fraction of his worth! Darcy was all goodness, and Wickham petty and vindictive.

It was easy to see now who was the better man.

Lizzy's cheeks burned with shame. Darcy's chin was set in indignation, and he stared hard ahead of him. Tears burned her eyes, thinking of how easily duped she had been, how her carelessness had brought him this embarrassment now.

They walked swiftly toward Longbourn, breaking ahead of the others, both of them eager to put distance between themselves and Wickham. At last, Darcy broke his stony silence. "If that man ever speaks to you that way again, I shall be sorely tempted to put a fist to his jaw. Only the presence of your younger sisters restrained me this time."

Lizzy let out an inadvertent chuckle. She had not imagined that his thoughts had headed in that direction. "I blame myself, for being misled by him."

"You must not, Lizzy. In fact, I forbid it. The man is a master manipulator. We were at Cambridge for two years before I finally saw him for what he is. I clung to our boyhood friendship. I did not want to believe he was as bad as he seemed."

His Adam's apple bobbed, and she laid a hand on his arm. "Dearest Darcy, how painful that must have been."

"It is of no consequence now," he said, though the hurt in his voice showed that the wound still rankled. "He resents me because I refuse to finance his dissolute behaviour. Were he my own brother, I would do no more for him than I have already done, as long as he persisted in that lifestyle. He has made his choices, and I must make mine."

Her heart ached for him. For Darcy to have done so much for the man, and then to have been so viciously betrayed! She could only hope that his trouble with Wickham was behind him.

Chapter 28

After they returned from Meryton, the gentlemen went to Netherfield to dress for dinner. Georgiana, travelling with her maid, was expected that afternoon as well. When the group arrived to pass the evening at Longbourn, however, they had another surprise in store. Colonel and Mrs. Fitzwilliam had also joined them!

"Please, call me Anne," said the former Miss de Bourgh, greeting Lizzy with a kiss to her cheek. "We will be cousins in a few days."

Squeezing her hands, Lizzy smiled and said, "We were not expecting you until the day before the wedding."

"We have news to share that will not keep." She looked up at Richard and gave him a smile.

"I've resigned my commission," he said, "instead of joining the militia. It was a difficult decision, but now that I am master of Rosings Park, Anne has convinced me that it is time to proceed with the serious business of siring heirs."

Anne blushed red, and Lizzy cried, "How scandalous!"

"I knew you would say so, dear Lizzy," Richard replied. "We will ever be of one mind, I think."

She pressed his hand, delighted by his news and his company. "Perhaps we will differ on who is the happiest married couple."

"Perhaps we shall."

Anne beamed. "I for one highly recommend the married state. I have never felt healthier in my life."

"You look radiant," Lizzy said.

"We left in such a hurry, Mrs. Jenkinson forgot to pack my tonic. As it turns out, I am better off without it."

"Fresh air and sunshine are all she needs," Richard said.

"I would not go that far," Anne said. "I still have pain. But exercise makes me feel better, not worse."

The sound of laughter rose from the other side of the room. Lydia was showing Giana the latest bonnet she had pulled apart and redesigned, and modelling it in different poses.

"I do not think I've ever heard Giana laugh that way," Richard said. "Perhaps she has not been enough around girls her own age."

Darcy looked at Richard with furrowed brows. "I consider sober company best for her. Do not you?"

"No, I do not. And I still have a fifty percent say in her guardianship. I suggest she spend at least one quarter of the year in the company of Miss Lydia Bennet."

Lizzy startled. "I think Kitty would be a better companion for her."

"The two of them together, then," Richard suggested.

Lizzy turned to Darcy. "What do you think, my dear?"

"The two of them, yes—but not necessarily together," Darcy said. "For Kitty's sake. Time away from Lydia would benefit her."

"I do not think they would appreciate our making plans without consulting them," Lizzy suggested, "but I agree with you. And if Lydia has to turn to Mary for companionship, it might force Mary to put down her books on occasion."

Dinner was announced, and it turned into a boisterous affair. The colonel's typical good humour helped Mrs. Bennet forget he was the son of an earl. She was all gentility toward him, rather than being awed by his presence.

Lydia was in her element, enticing Giana into friendship. They whispered and giggled more than was strictly dignified. Lizzy was not entirely at ease about it, but since Darcy made no objection, she let it pass.

When the ladies withdrew after dinner, Jane engaged Anne in conversation. Lizzy enjoyed seeing the natural rapport that developed between them. Both were naturally quiet, but seemed unselfconscious in each other's presence.

Lizzy was proud for Anne to see that Lizzy's relations were not as base as Lady Catherine had seemed to imagine.

Upon finishing an air on the pianoforte, Mary came and sat by Lizzy's side. She said in low tones, "Lizzy, I hope you can relieve my distress. I could not help overhearing some of Mrs. Fitzwilliam's conversation with Jane. I fear I must have misunderstood. Is it true that Mrs. Fitzwilliam did not secure her mother's permission before marrying? Surely that cannot be!"

Lizzy looked at her sister in confusion. "Anne is of age. Her mother's permission was not required."

"But she would not have married against her mother's wishes!"

Lizzy scowled, wondering what Mary was about. "Her mother wished her to marry Darcy. You cannot expect *me* to think they should have made the match just to please Lady Catherine."

"But a match should never be made in defiance of one's parents."

"Her mother was at the wedding. To my knowledge, she did not disapprove." Lizzy shook her head. "Mary, this sort of gossip is unbecoming. As is eavesdropping. This does not concern you."

"In a spirit of Christian love, we must all be concerned for the souls of our companions."

ANDREA DAVID

"You are not responsible for Mrs. Fitzwilliam's salvation. I pray you, do not interfere with Darcy's relations. You will make no friends that way."

Mary gave her a prim look, then rose and walked away. Lizzy shook her head. Somehow Mary seemed to have inherited the worst of both her parents, pursuing gossip as if it were an intellectual exercise.

Lizzy gazed at the clock. The addition of Colonel Fitzwilliam to the party of gentlemen appeared to keep them at their port longer than usual. Lizzy was pleased for her father to get to know the colonel. And she knew Darcy could not be happier than to spend time with his cousin again.

How relieved he must be that the colonel had resigned his commission! She knew that Richard took his duty seriously, but now he had new responsibilities. Darcy could rest easy, no longer worrying about his cousin being on the battle lines to defend against invasion.

At last the gentlemen rejoined the ladies in the drawing room. They appeared in good spirits, or perhaps it would be more accurate to say in fine port. Her father's wine cellar was one of his favourite indulgences.

They settled into the available seats, Darcy beside Giana on the couch, whilst Lizzy was in a chair cattycorner to them.

"Mama, I forgot to tell you!" Lydia cried from the other side of the room. "Who do you think we saw in Meryton today?"

DARCY COMES TO ROSINGS

"Good heavens, Lydia," Lizzy said quickly, schooling her glance to avoid Georgiana's eye. "Surely there must be a more interesting topic of conversation than the comings and goings of the officers. I for one shall be glad when they are removed to Brighton."

"I do not see what it is to you, as you shall be married soon," Lydia said. "And besides, you are only cross because you had a fight with Wickham. Is it not strange, Lizzy, that Wickham did not call on you after you returned from Hunsford? You were a favourite of his."

Mortification washed over her, chilling her blood. "I was no favourite—just one to while away the time with."

"He *did* turn his attentions to Miss King easily enough, once she came into her fortune. I was surprised when she jilted him. It is a good thing she is rich, because she is certainly not pretty."

"Lydia, that is enough!" Lizzy cried.

Darcy put his arm around Georgiana, whose eyes had filled with tears.

Lydia paled. "Oh lord, I forgot, you know Wickham!" Coming to sit on the arm of the couch, she took Georgiana's hand. "Did he hurt you?"

Georgiana said nothing, but her expression spoke all that needed to be said.

412

"I shall never mention him again," Lydia insisted. "He must be a great cad to have hurt my sweet Giana. You do not mind my calling you Giana, I hope? We will be sisters soon."

"I would like that." Georgiana gave her a soft smile.

The weight on Lizzy's chest lifted, her heart warming at Lydia's kindness to her new friend. After all, Lydia had had no way of knowing how her words might affect Giana. Still, Lydia ought not to have spoken so freely, gossiping in that careless way and exposing her vulgarity to all assembled.

Lydia played with her necklace, sliding the gold cross along the chain. "How strange it must be to have no sisters!" she exclaimed to Georgiana. "And now you will have five. No man will dare hurt you again whilst we are watching over you." She patted Giana's shoulder. "We will find you someone much better than a lieutenant in the militia. An earl perhaps, or even a marquess."

Giana's lips parted. "I would never aim so high!"

"Why ever not? I intend to marry a baronet. With your fortune, you should at least be a countess."

Georgiana giggled. Lydia rose and took her hand, and the two walked off together.

Lizzy turned her gaze to Darcy, whose eyes followed the girls, his jaw set tight.

That night, as Lizzy was readying for sleep, a knock came on her door and Lydia entered. The girl sat next to Lizzy on the bed. "What sort of man must Wickham be," Lydia asked, "that he hurt Giana? Do you think he is *very* bad?"

Lizzy gave her a sad smile. In many ways, Lydia was still innocent, still ignorant of the evil in the world. "Yes, I am afraid he is. As agreeable as he may seem, he is the basest sort of scoundrel."

A look of pain crossed her features. "Poor Denny—how he must be deceived! He would never be friends with him, if he knew the truth."

Lizzy sighed and stroked her sister's hair. "I understand that you enjoyed Mr. Denny's company during his time here. The truth is, we know very little about him, just as we did about Wickham."

Ire flared in Lydia's eyes. "*You* may know little about him, but Denny has been my dear friend these seven months! He says he cannot marry me, because I am too young—even though I am the same age Harriet was when she married Colonel Forster. But I am quite certain of Denny's character. If he knew Wickham was capable of hurting a young lady, he would not be friends with him."

Lizzy squeezed Lydia's hand. "I hope that's true. But the officers are leaving tomorrow. You must forget about them."

Chapter 29

The Earl and Countess of Matlock descended on Netherfield a few days later. To Lizzy's relief, her mother bore up better upon the second meeting than she had the first. Mr. Bennet, for his part, acquitted himself admirably, extending an effort to display the polished elegance he was capable of when the mood suited him.

Fortunately for all involved, Kitty and Lydia displayed less excitement than they might have upon meeting a peer of the realm. They were too preoccupied with the ball the Lucases were holding the following day at the Meryton assembly hall. With the officers en route to Brighton, the youngest Bennet girls were hoping that Bingley's and Darcy's relations would offset the surfeit of ladies that constantly plagued Meryton social events.

When the appointed evening arrived, Lizzy entered the assembly hall with a fluttering in her stomach, eyes searching for Darcy. It was in these very rooms that the two had met.

415

Her mind could not help travelling back to that night, and the emotions that had risen in her breast.

Upon first seeing the man, she had been startled by the strong handsome features of his face, the intelligent dark eyes. She might have developed a hopeless infatuation for him if it had not been for his slight. But she could not mourn the events of that evening, nor the winding road that had led them to their current destination.

As she scanned the ballroom, her chest fell when she did not spot him. If he were arriving with the earl and countess, they might well be fashionably late. But her spirits were soon restored when she caught sight of Charlotte.

Lizzy immediately headed toward her, and the two kissed in greeting. "How well you look, Eliza!" Charlotte said, beaming. "Your impending marriage agrees with you."

"How is life in Hunsford since I left? I confess I was not expecting such a look of gaiety about you." Lowering her voice, she added, "I imagined that Lady Catherine would be in a frightful mood, and making everyone around her miserable."

"Oh, she is. I am required to attend on her at Rosings daily—I have all but moved in there. She was put out at my coming to Hertfordshire, but I explained the absolute necessity of my attending the ball tonight. It pleases her to think that *that* is the reason for my coming, and not the wedding of my dearest friend in the world."

Mr. Collins approached and paid his respects to Lizzy in a most perfunctory manner, before moving on to give his regards to her mother. Lizzy watched him go, then said to Charlotte, "I believe that is the shortest conversation I have ever had with your husband."

"Oh, yes. He is quite put out with you. Not only did you defy Lady Catherine, you managed to avoid the fate of living out your life as an old maid after refusing him." Charlotte said this with the sound of unadulterated pleasure in her tone.

"I am sorry to have visited so much sorrow upon the people of Kent."

Charlotte twittered with laughter. "I deserve a little of the blame, at least. I may not have made Mr. Darcy fall in love with you, but I like to believe I helped things along."

"Indeed you did. What would Mr. Collins and Lady Catherine think of that?"

Charlotte was spared the necessity of a reply by the servant announcing the arrival of the party from Netherfield: the Earl and Countess of Matlock, Colonel and Mrs. Fitzwilliam, Mr. Darcy, Miss Darcy, Mr. Bingley, Mr. and Mrs. Hurst, and Miss Bingley.

Lizzy looked over. The sight of Darcy stopped her breath. He was every bit as handsome and magnetic as when she had first seen him, except now he appeared contented. The stiffness in his bearing was gone. Rather than steeling himself against his surroundings, he looked as if he belonged.

He greeted his hosts, then came over to pay his respects to Charlotte. "Mrs. Collins, lovely to see you again. It was kind of your parents to host this event."

"My sisters were ever so sorry to see the officers depart. The prospect of a ball lifted their spirits."

Darcy looked pensive. "Do you think Miss Lucas would care to visit us in town during the season? She is a sweet, unassuming girl, and pleasant company."

Lizzy laughed. "My fiancé is so generous, I fear I shall be chaperoning half a dozen girls this season when he is finished with his invitations."

He scowled at her. "Georgiana, Kitty, and Miss Lucas. That is not half a dozen. Are not Kitty and Miss Lucas particular friends?"

"They are. I am surprised you noticed."

"Tell me, Mrs. Collins," Darcy said to Charlotte, "should I feel wounded that my own Lizzy believes me indifferent to her family?"

"I believe, sir, that the change she has affected in you is so sudden, her mind has not yet caught up."

"That may be true," Darcy conceded. "Do you know, I have spent the past week thinking how much prettier Hertfordshire is in the spring than it was in the fall. But perhaps the difference is in me, rather than the countryside."

"I suspect you will be a most happy bridegroom, Mr. Darcy."

"I am certain of that." He smiled and placed a hand at the small of Lizzy's back. She warmed at the touch.

Charlotte curtsied and gave the couple their privacy.

He kissed Lizzy's gloved hand. Eyes dancing, he said, "Three days."

Joy bubbled inside her chest and rushed over her. "Are all the arrangements complete for our honeymoon?"

"Do you doubt me?"

"Never." She sighed. "I keep worrying that something could go wrong to spoil the wedding."

"What could go wrong? As long as the vicar pronounces us man and wife, that will be enough for me."

"If you are not careful, Mr. Darcy," she said in low tones, "I shall begin to wonder whether you are anticipating the marriage, or merely the wedding night."

"I am anticipating both. Is that not permitted?"

She gave him an indulgent smile. "I shall allow it."

He rested his hands at her waist. "There are far too many people in this room. Is there somewhere we can go, just for a moment?"

His suggestion tempted her, awakening her feminine desires. "If we steal out, we are sure to be noticed, and to set tongues wagging. To be honest, this close to the wedding, I do not trust myself."

"That admission, madam," he said with a wry smile, "is far less of a deterrent than you might think."

She laughed gaily. "Three days."

He closed his eyes and let out a long sigh. Then, he gazed at her and placed a quick kiss on her lips.

"Be good," she insisted, hands pressed to his lapel. "All of Meryton is watching, and your aunt and uncle, too."

"My uncle would be disappointed if I did *not* steal a kiss." His words sent a thrill through her.

She took his arm and went to greet Richard and Anne. "How do you find our little country town?" she asked them.

"Most amiable," Richard said. "Except for *one* lieutenant in the militia, who hurriedly crossed to the other side of the street when he saw me the day I arrived."

"Fortunately, you shall not have to suffer than insult again," Lizzy said. "Watching that parade as the militia marched out of town was one of the happiest moments of my life."

Remembering herself, she added, "I am grateful for their service, of course. Their effect on the single ladies of the town is not all I might have wished. And some of the tradespeople complained to my father, as magistrate, of officers leaving without settling their accounts."

"Understood," Richard said. "In truth, I think they were quartered here too long. It makes a man soft, especially the officers. Too much leisure time."

"Speaking of leisure time," Darcy said, "what are your plans after the wedding?"

"We might do some sea-bathing, before heading home to Rosings," Anne said. "I have never been to the coast, and all this talk of Brighton has me longing to go."

"Do not let Lydia overhear you say that," Lizzy said, "or she will beg to go along."

Anne beamed. "Why, that is a splendid idea! What think you, Richard?"

He gave her a broad smile. "I think you have been far too sheltered, and would benefit from the company of a spirited girl like Miss Lydia Bennet."

"But I hardly think—" Lizzy sputtered, "that is to say, I am not certain my father could be persuaded of such a scheme! Lydia is far too young."

"She is sixteen, is she not?" Anne said. "And Mrs. Jenkinson will never let her eye off her for a moment."

"Well…" Lizzy pondered that suggestion. This was not at all the outcome she had hoped for.

"We will take good care of her, I promise," Richard assured her.

DARCY COMES TO ROSINGS

Lizzy knew how it would go. Once Lydia got to Brighton, she would take advantage of Mrs. Forster's invitation, and end up staying the entire summer. Lizzy had no doubt that the Fitzwilliams would be excellent chaperones, but Mrs. Forster was barely older than Lydia and had no more sense.

Darcy interjected, "Mr. Bennet is sure to have strong opinions on this. Discuss the idea with him before raising it with Miss Lydia."

"Of course!" Anne replied. "We would not think of doing otherwise."

Lizzy wanted to protest, but Darcy drew her away. "Do not fret, my dear. I shall ask Georgiana to talk to Lydia before she embarks on a trip to Brighton. Lydia may not listen to a parent or older sister, but she will listen to Giana. Unfortunately, my sister knows all too well how duplicitous a worthless young man can be."

Lizzy considered his words, then nodded. She still thought it was a terrible idea for Lydia to go to Brighton. But if it came to pass, Lydia would do better if she understood the danger a man could pose to a woman's reputation.

The dancing began, and Darcy made good on his promise to stand up with the young women of Meryton. Lizzy, for her part, joined most of the dances. To her relief, she was not forced to suffer the awkwardness of Mr. Collins' missteps as she had been at the Netherfield ball the previous autumn. Not only did he not ask her to dance, he was barely civil to her if they passed one another when walking about the room. She was not distressed at his slight of her, but it did feel odd, as solicitous as he had always been.

Lizzy did not desire the goodwill of Mr. Collins. But since he had neither sense, manners, nor dignity, winning the sort of profound disapprobation he was showing to her that evening did not bode well. She could not escape the feeling that becoming an enemy of Mr. Collins was even a worse fate than being regarded as a friend.

Darcy did not much enjoy dancing as a rule, and dancing with strangers was torment to him. But he had promised Lizzy to make himself pleasing to the good people of Meryton, so that was what he did.

He stepped into the card room between dances to find his uncle engaged in a hand of whist with Bennet, Philips, and Mr. Robinson. They were conversing about the wisdom of investing in steam power. Darcy was perhaps more surprised than he should have been at how well-versed Bennet was in the technology. The man had a keen intellect—Lizzy was her father's daughter in that regard—but he so rarely showed the depth of his knowledge in company that any proof of it was unexpected.

Stepping back into the ballroom, he spotted Lizzy looking downcast as her mother scolded her. He moved instantly to his fiancée's side and placed his hand at the small of her back. "Dear Mrs. Bennet, is something amiss?"

"I thank you, sir. Lizzy and I were just discussing the possibility of Lydia going to Brighton with Colonel and Mrs. Fitzwilliam."

Good heavens, how had *that* news gotten about so quickly? This was why he never spoke at balls—they were nothing but gossip mills. "It is not at all certain my cousins will go to Brighton. I think it far more likely they will return to Rosings. All this travelling cannot be good for Anne's health."

"Lizzy does not think Lydia should go with them. To be under the care of an earl's son, and the heiress of a great house like Rosings! Why, I have it on good authority that the chimney-piece there alone cost eight hundred pounds! Why should Lizzy not wish to share her good fortune with her sisters?"

"She is sixteen," Lizzy protested. "You would expose a girl of that age to an entire encampment of soldiers?"

"I do not see what harm could come of it."

Lizzy turned to Darcy, mouth open but no words escaping.

He ran his hand soothingly along her back. Turning to Mrs. Bennet, he said, "Perhaps it would be best to discuss this with Mr. Bennet, if an invitation is issued. There is no point ruining tonight's festivities over something that may not come to pass."

"True enough," Mrs. Bennet said. "But I am most displeased with you, Lizzy. Only think of your poor sisters, and how all their pleasures have been taken away now that the officers are gone!"

She stormed off, and Lizzy stared ahead, looking dazed.

Darcy kissed her temple. "I am sorry, my love."

Lizzy turned to him and said, "What *harm* could come of it?"

He looked into her stunned expression, then broke into a laugh. She joined him a moment later. "Oh, Darcy," she said at last, "it is a wonder we were not all carried off by vagrants as children!" Tears of mirth escaped the corners of her eyes, and he wiped them away with a gloved finger.

Dear heaven, he loved this woman! If only they could make it through the next few days, he would ensure she never had to suffer under Mrs. Bennet's scolding again.

~⚬✄⚬~

As the supper hour approached, Lizzy thought to herself that balls were where the Bennet family went to expose themselves. She prayed that no one had overheard her mother, but of course that was a futile effort. Given the dimensions of the room and the number of revellers, of course her mother had been overheard. So Lizzy turned instead to praying for Lydia's safety.

What a comfort it was to have Darcy to share her troubles with! She could not have imagined laughing so hard with anyone else over her mother's foibles, not even Jane. Poor

Jane would feel guilty and put a stop to it. Not so Darcy. She could laugh with him as much as she liked.

Her eyes fell on Anne standing across the room, looking cornered. Mary was leaning toward her, speaking with an intent expression on her face, whilst Anne's eyes wandered as if searching for an escape route.

Lizzy and Darcy headed toward them. Mary could be heard saying, "Honouring thy mother is like unto honouring God. As Fordyce reminds us in his sermons, the only child of a widow is her sole hope and joy, the last repository of the sense and probity of a much loved and lamented spouse—"

"Mary," Lizzy said, heat rising in her cheeks, "I believe my mother is looking for you."

Her sister turned to her with a stricken look on her face. "Can it not wait? Mrs. Fitzwilliam and I are discussing the importance of—"

"Please do not worry about me, Miss Mary," Anne interrupted. "As you say, honouring your mother is akin to honouring God."

Lizzy took Mary's arm and led her away whilst Darcy remained with Anne. "Mary, I really must implore you, do not discuss Anne's mother with her. The situation is complicated, and you cannot begin to understand it."

"According to Mr. Collins, Lady Catherine is horribly aggrieved by the loss of her daughter—her only child, whom she has devoted her life to! Is that not ingratitude?"

"Lady Catherine has not lost her daughter. Anne is on her honeymoon, and will return to Rosings later this summer. This is none of your concern, Mary. Your heart may be in the right place, but you can only make the situation worse."

They approached Mrs. Bennet. "Mama," said Lizzy, "I believe you wanted to speak to Mary?"

"Yes, my dear. Mary, you are soon to be the eldest sister unmarried—which means we must put serious thought into finding a husband for you. 'Tis a pity that Charlotte Lucas stole Mr. Collins away, when he was so well disposed to marry one of my girls. That would have been a fine match for you. And whilst it is true that you are not so pretty as your sisters, you are pretty enough, or would be if you put in an effort. These grey frocks you like will not do. We can add some brocade and ribbon in pink or purple, something to put some colour into your cheek—"

"Mama," Lizzy objected, cheeks burning on Mary's behalf, "do you not think it best to have this conversation at home?"

"Perhaps you are right, my dear, but mark my words, first thing tomorrow, we will begin making over Mary's wardrobe."

Lizzy patted her sister's arm comfortingly. Then, her gaze wandered across the room, and she caught sight of Anne crying. As Darcy soothed her, Richard flew to her side. Lizzy headed in that direction.

Leaving Anne in her husband's care, Darcy walked up to Lizzy and said in low tones, "Do not trouble yourself, my love.

Anne is fine. Upset about her mother, but that is Lady Catherine's doing and no one else's."

"I am sorry, Darcy! If Mary had not interfered—"

"It is not Mary's fault, or even Collins'. Lady Catherine is painting herself as the martyr, and making a good argument of it. If you had heard her speak to Anne, you would understand the machinations she would stoop to."

"And my family members are her willing dupes."

He shook his head fervently. "Do not do this, my love. Do not blame yourself."

She took a deep, uneven breath. Tears prickled at the corners of her eyes. Poor Anne! She had been a victim of her mother's overbearing nature her whole life. Even now, when she was out of her mother's control, she was still paying the price.

As they gathered for supper, Lizzy was relieved to see that Anne was all smiles again. Richard had that effect on her. How strange to think they had been cousins all their lives, and in a short space of time, their relationship had utterly changed!

In truth, however, Richard had spent most of his time in Derbyshire or London, and Anne in Kent. They had probably seen one another no more the one month out of a year. And he *was* almost a decade her senior. Perhaps it was not so strange after all—and once she had reached her majority, they had begun looking at each other with new eyes.

Whilst her neighbours took their chairs, Lizzy allowed herself a moment to appreciate the joy of this night. She had known these people all her life—had shared in their celebrations as well as their sorrows. They were dear to her, and she would miss them once she left for her new home.

But Lizzy's poignant musings were interrupted when her gaze landed on a sight that chilled her blood. Her mother, wearing an intent expression, accosted Lady Matlock.

Chapter 30

Mrs. Bennet spoke in a voice that surely everyone at the assembly could hear. With Darcy in tow, Lizzy moved toward her, hoping to intervene, but she could not get there in time.

"Your ladyship is most gracious with your compliments toward my daughters," her mother began. "But if I may say so, the middle girl, Mary, is the most accomplished of them all. She sings and plays all day long. Her embroidery—oh! Such tiny, straight stitches. Quite pretty, if I do say so, even though I am her mother. And you will not find a more pious girl in all of Meryton. Our cousin Mr. Collins, the rector at Hunsford, praises her knowledge and her studiousness. If she were presented at court, I am certain she would—"

"Poor Queen Charlotte," the countess said in a sad tone. "She is despondent over her husband's illness, and hardly ever holds drawing rooms anymore. The one in April was the first in two years, and who knows when the next might be. The earl and I are quite resigned that our youngest daughter might not be presented until after she marries."

Darcy looked at Lizzy with laughing eyes, but *she* wished she could turn into a vapour and disappear through the cracks in the floor. She shook her head and said to him in low tones, "Your aunt is the most gracious woman I know. How she can keep her countenance..."

"Lady Catherine uses her rank to intimidate, and the countess to put people at ease," he observed.

"She is truly noble," Lizzy agreed. "But what she must think! My mother has not the least concept of the cost of presenting a girl at court. It is an expense I would happily waive for our daughters."

"I am glad we are of the same mind about that." Darcy smiled and pressed her hands. "I would rather put the assets toward their dowries to secure their future."

"Better than squandering the funds on a few seconds of curtseying to the queen." She looked up into his eyes. It comforted her that Darcy was generous without being extravagant. She felt more certain than ever that they would be of one mind when it came to finances.

At supper, Lizzy and Darcy sat apart—Lizzy with Charlotte, and Darcy with Kitty and Maria Lucas. They were not far into the meal when Charlotte's eyes widened and she quickly rose.

Lizzy turned to see Mr. Collins approaching the Earl of Matlock. "Have they been introduced?" she asked Charlotte.

But Charlotte was already moving in her husband's direction, presumably to keep him from making the same faux pas he had with Darcy at the Netherfield ball.

"Your lordship, if I may be so bold," Mr. Collins began, but fortunately, Richard arrived at his side the next moment.

"Collins, old man, I have been remiss. Allow me to introduce you to my father, Lord Matlock." Richard turned to his father. "Mr. Collins is rector at the church in Hunsford, and the happy recipient of Lady Catherine's patronage."

"Good to meet you, sir!" the earl said graciously, rising and shaking Mr. Collins' hand.

"And you as well," Mr. Collins declared. "I am happy indeed, for your honoured sister has been uncommonly kind to me and my wife. I always say that Lady Catherine de Bourgh is the very image of nobility and grace. You will be pleased to know, sir, that I dined with her just last evening, and she was in excellent health."

"I am gratified to hear it."

"But I must lament that she was not in the best of spirits, and has not been since my fair cousin left the humble parsonage at Hunsford."

Lizzy's stomach lurched at that. What was Mr. Collins about?

"Your cousin?" the earl asked in confusion. "Ah, I understand. You refer to Miss Elizabeth Bennet. I remember hearing that she was staying at the parsonage whilst Darcy courted her."

"I can assure you, sir, that if I had known such goings-on were occurring under my roof, I would have put a stop to them. I am of one mind with Lady Catherine in this matter, and am shocked at my cousin's raising herself above her station. I avow that my branch of the family understands right behaviour, and when I am master of Longbourn—"

"What nonsense is this?" Matlock bellowed, his face becoming a deeper shade of red as each moment passed. Watching this disaster transpire, Lizzy felt the blood drain from her face at her cousin's impudent insults. She was certain everyone in the room could hear him.

"As I say, your lordship," the fool continued, "I told my honoured patroness that under the circumstances, she was quite right to decline to attend the wedding of Mr. Darcy and Miss Elizabeth Bennet."

The earl stared, shock written on his features. He said in a booming voice, "My sister Lady Catherine de Bourgh is prevented by her *rheumatism* from travelling here for the wedding. But I assure you, sir, she has sent her regards for the couple's happiness and prosperity. Her daughter Mrs. Fitzwilliam is here representing the de Bourgh branch of the family. And I am amazed, sir, that you would disparage your own cousin in this unseemly manner. Miss Elizabeth Bennet is the epitome of a gentlewoman, and a most welcome addition to the Darcy and Fitzwilliam families."

Lizzy grabbed the table to steady herself. Head spinning, she reached fruitlessly for her chair. Darcy's strong arms encircled her before she was even aware of his approach, and he lowered her into her seat. "That blackguard," he whispered under his breath, holding Lizzy's hand.

Darcy had never seen Lizzy so pale. As much as he wanted to challenge Collins to pistols at dawn for insulting his fiancée, he dared not leave her side. Collins was already cowering under Lord Matlock's rebuke, and by the expression on Richard's face, the worst was yet to come.

But Lizzy's dear friend Mrs. Collins asserted herself into the situation, saying, "My lord, Colonel Fitzwilliam, you both have my deepest apologies. My husband rarely indulges in strong drink, as we live a quiet country life. I fear he has partaken of brandy this evening, believing it was wine, and now has lost his head."

"Dear Mrs. Collins," Richard said, "I thank you for your astute assessment of the situation. I hope you will remind your husband, once he comes to his senses, that I am now master of Rosings, and his living is in my power. I shall not hear my soon-to-be cousin Miss Elizabeth Bennet spoken of in such a disrespectful manner again."

A gratified smile curved Darcy's lips—until he heard a strangled sob. "Please, Darcy," Lizzy said in a trembling voice, "can we get some air?"

"Of course." He helped her to her feet and whisked her outside. The gravel crunched as they walked under the moonlit sky. Once they were safely out of sight of others, she came to a stop, drinking in deep breaths.

"My love, are you well? Can I get you something?"

She collapsed into his arms and wept. He held her tightly, soothing her until she was spent. Rage gathered in his chest. Fool or no, Collins would pay for this.

"I have never been so humiliated," she said. "In front of my family and everyone in Meryton—and your family, too."

"You were not humiliated. Collins humiliated himself."

"Oh, Darcy, can you not see? Your uncle and cousin were most kind to defend me, but Mr. Collins was right. I aspired above my station, and that is what everyone who knows us will think of me for the rest of my life."

He pressed his cheek to her temple. "That is utter nonsense. This is not my Lizzy talking. This is nothing but wedding nerves. *My* Lizzy knows she is every inch a gentlewoman, and will make a fine mistress of Pemberley." He held her face in his hands and kissed her. "No one could be more perfect for me than you are. And that is all that matters."

"I cannot go back in there. I can never show my face in Meryton again. Please, can we elope? We have the license. We can be married at Pemberley, in your parish. It will be perfectly legal that way."

He dropped tender kisses along the curve of her neck. "Would you do that to Jane? Abandon her on her wedding day? Marry without her by your side?"

She sniffled. "I cannot stand up in church three days hence. I simply cannot."

The sound of footsteps on the gravel behind them turned Darcy's head. In the light of the moon, he could see Bennet approaching them.

"Ah, there you are, my dear," Lizzy's father said to her. "Your mother is quite worried for your reputation. Going off alone with your fiancé three days before your wedding? What will the neighbours think?"

"They already think I am an utter fool," she said. Darcy's chest ached at her suffering.

Bennet wrapped his arms around her. "None of that, my dear. No one who knows you believes you to be a fool. They believe Collins a fool, and did so even before that display. The Lucases are mortified. But Charlotte has the situation in hand. She is brilliant at managing him, just as Lady Lucas is brilliant at managing Sir William."

Lizzy gasped. "Surely you are not comparing Sir William to Mr. Collins!"

Bennet nodded thoughtfully. "Sir William lacks my cousin's intellectual deficiencies, I'll grant you. But they are not so different in character—only in degree. I daresay Charlotte knew what she was getting into, when she married

Collins. She is a good wife for him, though better than he deserves."

"*Far* better!" Lizzy cried.

"Yes, yes, Lizzy. But does it not gratify you a little that Charlotte will have the running of Longbourn when I am gone? Would you have your beloved woods fall under the care of Mr. Collins and a woman equal to him in every way?"

She let out a long sigh. "I suppose you are right about that much, at least."

"Let us hope her children inherit her nature," Bennet said, "and that she has a houseful of boys to remove the entail."

Beneath the light of the moon, Lizzy shook her head. "I wanted so much more for her."

"But she is happy, my dear. It is not a life that would have made *you* happy, but you are not Charlotte." He kissed her forehead. "You could not have married for anything less than love, or chosen a man who lacked a keen intellect and an upright character. And you will be every bit as happy as you deserve, because you had the sense to choose well."

Some of the heaviness in Darcy's chest dissipated. To hear himself praised in that way gratified him more than he had thought it could. He had expected Bennet's approbation on no more merit than his fortune alone. Now he realized how mercenary that thought had been.

Bennet respected Lizzy above nearly anyone on earth. For him to place her in Darcy's care with such equanimity was a profound compliment—one that Darcy had not properly appreciated until that moment.

"Come now," Bennet said, hands on her shoulders, "we had better get back before your mother begins to suspect that Darcy has killed me in a duel over your honour."

"Oh, Papa," Lizzy said in a light tone.

Darcy entwined Lizzy's arm in his own as they headed back toward the building, walking beside her father. The full moon shone in a clear sky, stars twinkling. The soft breeze caressed him like the sound of Lizzy's sighs.

Once they stepped back into the ballroom, the countess came immediately to Lizzy's side and kissed her cheek. "Pay no attention to that man's nonsense, my dear," she said in low tones. "We could not be more pleased that you are joining our family. Any fool could see how happy you make Darcy."

"Your ladyship is all kindness," she said in a voice taut with emotion. Darcy was proud that one aunt, at least, not only recognized Lizzy's value but had the compassion to soothe her spirit as well.

He helped Lizzy back to her chair. Then, he found Collins. The man cowered, which seemed ridiculous. Had he not realized Darcy had been in the room, and heard every word the man had said? Did he think he could make such comments with impunity?

"Tomorrow," Darcy growled, "you will apologize to my fiancée. Tonight, you will stay as far from her as possible. Do you understand me?"

"Yes, sir. My apologies. I misjudged."

"You did not simply misjudge. You all but called me a fool for choosing her as my bride. Is that what you think, Mr. Collins? Am I a fool?"

"Of course not, Mr. Darcy—far from it! You are renowned for your intellect—"

"It is a good thing for your sake that I am not a violent man, or I would be tempted to flatten you. But I can hurt you in other ways. If my fiancée sheds one more tear over you, you will answer for it. Are we clear on that?"

"Quite clear."

Darcy stalked back to the table, blood still raging, hoping they would have no more unpleasant surprises that evening.

⁓⊶❦⊷⁓

As supper broke up, Lizzy looked about the room. It seemed things had returned to normal, the ugly scene put behind them—at least as much as it could be. She doubted anyone present would forget this night, nor Mr. Collins' insufferable behaviour.

At least for now, the company was laughing and talking in the ordinary way of things: Jane and Bingley gazed at one another with happy smiles and longing glances, Lydia and

Georgiana giggled and whispered conspiratorially, Caroline chatted with Anne wearing her usual polite, disinterested expression.

When the dancing began again, Lizzy stood up for the next reel with the eldest son of the Long family, a young man she had known all her life. Their rapport was comfortable and they joked together easily. For that half-hour, she forgot her cares. But when the dance ended, a strange sensation fell over her.

Something was wrong. She looked about the room, and her stomach dipped. Lydia and Georgiana were nowhere in sight.

Pushing down her fear, she peeked into the card room. She was met only by the sight of middle-aged men and the odour of cheroot smoke.

Back in the ballroom, she spied Darcy and hurried to him. He had not seen the girls, either. They checked with Jane and Kitty, but without success. Lizzy told herself not to panic.

"I shall look outside," Darcy said. As he headed for the door, Lizzy took a deep breath. He was right. They had probably gone out for air.

He had been gone perhaps a minute when her heart crashed at the sound of angry voices on the stairs. *Lydia.* But who was that with her? Surely it could not be—

"Stay away from her, Wickham."

"My dear Miss Bennet, Miss Darcy is my old friend."

Georgiana came rushing into the room, eyes wide and cheeks pale. Colonel Fitzwilliam bolted toward her and drew her deeper inside, his face red and fists clenched.

Lydia bounded inside with Wickham on her heels. "Take a care, sir," the girl said in a tone of primal anger that Lizzy had never heard from her before, "I shall not let you hurt her again."

"I am wounded, madam. Surely you cannot think I would ever lay a hand on her." Wickham startled as he suddenly took in his surroundings, all eyes on him. He bowed and said, "Forgive me, friends. I did not mean to interrupt the party."

Darcy came up behind him. "Wearing your sword to a ball, sir?" he asked, confiscating the weapon. "That simply is not *done*."

Lizzy filled her lungs in relief. The girls were safe, and Darcy, too. But what on earth was Wickham doing there, dressed in his red coat, as if coming to join the dance? She had gone to the parade specifically to watch him march out of town—and out of her life, she thought, forever. Why was he back two days later?

"Why, Darcy, my old friend." Wickham bowed. "Forgive me. You are correct, of course. I did not recognize that a ball was underway."

From the corner of her eye, Lizzy noticed her father speaking to the eldest of the Philips boys, who quickly took off down the stairs. Her father then rounded up Bingley and

Colonel Fitzwilliam, and walked with them toward Wickham. Darcy positioned himself between the scoundrel and the exit.

Wickham looked around at them like the caged animal he was. Darcy unsheathed the sword. Lizzy's heart jumped to her throat.

"Now, now, there is no cause for violence," her father said in a calm tone, but did not admonish Darcy to put away the weapon. "Mr. Wickham, so kind of you to join us. I assume you are here to pay back the debts you owe the merchants of Meryton?"

A stunned look crossed his features. Apparently he had not thought through that part of his adventure. "Of-of course I intend to pay every penny I owe," Wickham stammered. "I do not have sufficient c-coin with me at the moment—"

Her father silenced him with a gesture of his hand. "Of course. No need to explain here. My nephew is fetching the constable, and we can have this conversation in private."

Wickham looked like he might grab for the sword but seemed to realize how poor his odds were. All fight left him, and his shoulders slumped.

Lizzy went to Georgiana, who cried in the countess's arms. "Oh, Lizzy!" the girl exclaimed. "We meant no harm. We just stepped outside for air. Then Wickham approached, and Lydia told me to run inside."

"You did the right thing," Lizzy said.

ANDREA DAVID

"There, there, child." The countess stroked Georgiana's hair, which had fallen from her chignon and hung about her shoulders. "I am sure he only wanted to talk to you."

"He still thinks I am a stupid girl who will believe his lies and run off with him."

Was that why Wickham had come? Was he really so desperate, Lizzy wondered, that he would try to seduce the same girl a second time, after he had failed the first?

The sound of boots on the stairs caught her attention. When the door swung open, she expected to see the constable. Instead, it was Lt. Denny!

Cutting a dashing figure in his red coat, Lt. Denny scanned the room. Lizzy looked on with astonishment as Denny caught sight of Wickham and exclaimed, "Thank heavens you have caught the blackguard." To Darcy, he said, "Is Miss Darcy well?"

Lydia flung herself into his arms. "Oh, Denny, you have come to save her!"

Lt. Denny let out a rush of air, eyes wide at the greeting. He placed his hands on the girl's shoulders and stepped back. "Where is Miss Darcy?"

Lydia pointed over to Georgiana, then turned back to him. "She is fine, now. Oh, Denny, it was awful. We were outside when a man approached us. He was wearing his regimentals, so I recognized he was an officer. I was not the least bit afraid.

But then I saw his face, and I just knew he meant to hurt Georgiana. If Darcy had not come—"

"All is well now, my girl," Lt. Denny soothed. "No need to fret."

"Oh, Lydia!" Mrs. Bennet cried, coming to her daughter's side and taking her in her arms.

"It was so exciting, Mama!" Lydia cried as her mother led her away. "I thought Darcy would have to fight Wickham. But Wickham had a sword, and Darcy was unarmed—I was sure Darcy would be killed!"

Lizzy's insides grew cold. Darcy, however, looked down at the sword in his hand, and gave Wickham a wry grin.

The next time the door opened, it was in fact the constable. Wickham was marched off in the company of several sturdy men, including Darcy, Richard, and Lt. Denny. As magistrate, her father went along.

Before too many minutes had passed, Anne and the countess took Georgiana back to Netherfield. Exhausted, Lizzy suggested to her mother that their family return home as well. Her mother seemed to consider a moment, as if weighing the odds of finding Mary a husband that night if they stayed, but at last relented.

In the coach on the way to Longbourn, with her head on Jane's shoulder and her arm around Lydia, Lizzy dozed off for a few moments. Vague images of the night's strange events flitted through her brain. But when she roused, all she could think about was Darcy and how magnificent he had been.

The appearance of Mr. Wickham had been odd, and of Lt. Denny odder still. But she knew she would not be able to stay awake until her father returned to tell them the whole story. That would have to wait until the morrow.

Chapter 31

Lizzy did not wake until the sun was well-risen the next morning. Drained by the late night, she joined the rest of the family in the breakfast room at half-past ten. The sideboard was set with plates of plum cake, rolls, butter, and preserves, and pots of tea or chocolate.

When all were settled at the table, her father shared the news of Wickham's fate. In sorrowful tones, he said, "Wickham had several warrants against him for funds owed to local merchants. His next destination is debtor's prison. With no resources, and likely no friends willing to pay his creditors, he may stay there for a while."

A solemn silence stretched out. Lizzy could not help but feel sad for what Wickham might have become if he had not chosen a dark path. "What did Mr. Denny have to say?"

"Apparently, ever since Wickham had encountered you and Darcy in Meryton, he talked of nothing but Georgiana. He was convinced that without her brother's interference, he could persuade her to elope with him. Rumour reached him on the road to Brighton that she was in Meryton for the wedding. When Denny discovered him missing, he guessed where the man had gone. Colonel Forster gave permission for Denny to ride here and seek him out."

Lydia looked pointedly at Lizzy. "You see? I said Denny was a good man, and must have been deceived in Wickham."

"You did," Lizzy conceded, giving her sister a fond smile. "And I am very glad you were right."

Lydia smiled back at her, but then, a dreamy look fell over her eyes. Lizzy could not help speculating that Lydia's interest in Denny was more than the girl had let on. Nothing could come of it, of course. He was probably on his way back to Brighton that very moment.

Lizzy did not allow the business with Wickham to cast a pall over her last days as a single woman. She enjoyed every pleasure that Meryton, the countryside, and the companionship of her family had to offer. Already, Darcy and Bingley were ensconced, their presence at Longbourn as natural as anyone's.

She had been astonished to see how easily Darcy had made the change. An outsider would never have thought he belonged with her family. She could hardly believe it herself. But he belonged with Lizzy—and that had made all the difference.

On the day of the wedding, the church was every bit as full as even Mrs. Bennet had hoped it would be. Meryton had never seen the likes of it. Two open carriages, each pulled by a team of four white horses and decorated with bouquets of roses and lilies, waited outside the church for the bridal couples to emerge as husbands and wives.

Lizzy, though deliriously happy, spent the entire double ceremony half-worried that Lady Catherine might burst through the doors at any moment, stating her objection. But nothing so dramatic happened. By the time Lizzy finally relaxed, the vicar said *man and wife*, and she was married.

Darcy leaned in for the expected kiss, but she was too overwhelmed to respond. His lips brushed hers gently, the sweetest kiss of her life, because it was her husband's.

The wedding breakfast went by in a blur. A few people toasted her, and a few called her Mrs. Darcy. The next thing she knew, she was being led to the carriage for the ride to Netherfield, where she and Darcy would stay the night before leaving the next morning for their honeymoon. They would stop overnight half the distance to Swindon, and Darcy had not wanted their wedding night to be spent at an inn.

The Netherfield foyer was full of trunks and servants, the family members set to depart so the two couples could have their privacy. The butler led the Darcys and the Bingleys to the breakfast room, where sparkling wine awaited. When the man withdrew, the two couples stood looking at each other. Neither gentleman made a move to open the bottle.

"I say," Bingley declared finally, breaking the tension, "it has been a deuced tiring morning. Perhaps we should retire until dinner."

The other three responded in unison with an audible sigh of relief. "Splendid," Darcy said, and took Lizzy's hand. She could not meet Jane's eyes as Darcy led her to his rooms in one wing of the house, whilst Bingley took Jane to the master suite in the other.

Darcy took off his jacket and waistcoat. Lizzy looked about the room with its massive four-poster bed of carved oak. "Should I call for my maid?" she asked. For the first time in her life, she had a lady's maid all to herself, instead of having to share with her sisters.

"That will not be necessary," he said, untying his cravat.

Her breaths came fast and thick. Seeing her husband in his shirtsleeves made her light-headed. She could not work out exactly what she was supposed to do. So she waited for his instruction.

She did not have to wait long.

Tossing aside his neckcloth, he took her in his arms. With one hand at the small of her back and the other at her nape, he drew her against him. His mouth found hers.

His kisses were deep and needy, tasting and exploring as if she were the sweetest delicacy. His urgency matched her own, and yet her nerves made her limbs heavy. Her hands hung limp at her side a moment, until she tentatively rested them at his waist.

The heat of his body through the linen of his shirt awakened something inside her. As she ran her hands along the plane of his back, a strange tension gripped her, low and hot. She breathed in his clean, masculine scent, like wool and bay rum soap.

Deft fingers unlaced her gown. She leaned into him to give him better access, her mouth suckling his earlobe. Her hands slid lower, discovering more of him than she had ever dared before.

He pushed her beautiful silk gown to the floor, and she stepped out of it. Gazing at her, his eyes grew dark and hooded. She let him look his fill, unplagued by embarrassment. She wanted to give him every pleasure he desired.

She drew closer to unbutton his shirt. Her hands trembled, but his kisses soothed her, and she managed the task. Her mouth found the hollow of his throat, then moved across his collarbone to the smooth arc of his shoulder.

He made quick work of her corset and petticoats. She climbed onto the bed in her shift whilst he unfastened his breeches. She averted her eyes, cheeks burning.

He slid under the covers next to her, and she remained on top of the quilt, hugging herself protectively. He slid close and unpinned her hair, letting it fall loose at her shoulders. She could not look at him.

"You are quiet, love," he said at last, no rebuke in his tone.

"And you are naked," she countered.

He chuckled. "Does that worry you?"

"A bit."

He ran his hand along her back, and she rested her head on his shoulder. She risked a glance at him, at his broad chest and thickly muscled arms. Her belly tightened with want.

Climbing under the covers, she allowed him to gently coax the shift off her. He gazed at her as she had never seen him do before, eyes alight with happiness and desire. His kisses, tender at first, grew insistent. An ache rose inside her, a breathless longing that enflamed her skin and penetrated deep into her core.

Their bodies melded in perfect passion. She surrendered herself utterly to him, and he gave her a bliss like nothing she had ever known. As their bodies disentwined, she curved into him and sighed in joy and satisfaction.

After a long while, she said, "Promise me it will always be like this."

"It will be better," Darcy said, "for every day I shall love you more."

In a soft voice, she cooed, "Then surely I shall die of happiness."

"No, my Lizzy. We will grow old together and fill Pemberley with grandchildren."

"That sounds lovely." She snuggled against his chest.

He kissed the top of her head and drew his arms around her. In that moment of quiet knowing, she understood the true meaning of love.

Epilogue

Lizzy had been at Pemberley two months when a letter arrived from Lydia. The new Mrs. Darcy had settled into a comfortable routine during the day: meeting with the housekeeper, visiting the tenants, overseeing Georgiana's education. Evenings were dedicated to books and music. Once Georgiana retired for the night, Mr. and Mrs. Darcy took to their bed and endeavoured with great alacrity to fulfil their duty of producing an heir.

From the window in the bedroom where she read Lydia's letter, Lizzy could see Darcy riding through the property with his steward. She loved watching him, waiting for him to come home and share his latest concerns about the running of the estate. He was a wise and generous master, as she had known he would be, and the people of Pemberley and the surrounding village held him in high regard.

She opened her sister's letter, expecting it to be filled with tales of balls and clothes. When the sense of it became clear, though, she sat forward—shocked to her core.

Dear Lizzy,

Harriet has bid me send this letter, so you hear the news from me. I am sure Kitty will write you straightaway. She can never bear to keep a good bit of gossip to herself.

You will not believe it—I hardly believe it myself! But I knew that if I came to Brighton, I would secure a husband, and so I have. You must not suppose me married—though I am to be, just as soon as the banns are read. Denny rode to Longbourn once it was settled between us, and Papa has given his permission.

You must not suppose that I showed myself eager to have him, though I have been in love with him these six months. I forced him to court me. He wrote me some pretty poems, and whilst I tell him they are nothing to Blake's, in truth I treasure them more.

You may wonder how this came to pass, when he has been telling me I am too young. Well, it turns out he was embarrassed to say he could not afford a wife. Now, with the death of his poor cousin, Denny is heir to a baronet. His uncle is offering him an allowance that will keep us quite comfortable. Can you imagine, Lizzy, me married to a peer of the realm!

(Well, Harriet tells me baronets are not peers, but you know what I mean. We will live in an actual castle! Even if it is a small one.)

Oh! I had better post this now. Me and Harriet are going to watch the regiment march and do their drills. They are so droll, always parading about and firing their rifles.

Denny will sell his commission once we are settled. I shall be sorry to leave Brighton, but—oh Lizzy! I am so happy! I shall be an actual lady, and have precedence over you all.

Your happiest of sisters,

Lydia Bennet

Lizzy read and re-read to be sure she was not imagining things. Lydia to marry Denny! And Denny the heir to a baronet! Lizzy laughed aloud at the irony of Jane's pronouncement. Lydia had pursued Jane's vision of the future, and brought it to pass.

When Lizzy told Darcy and Georgiana at dinner, he wrinkled his brow. After a moment, he said, "It is good news, I think. A girl with her high spirits is best married as soon as possible, do not you agree?"

Lizzy recalled having come to the same conclusion herself, but now felt wistful about it. Lydia was so very young. And yet, she was a clever, resourceful girl, despite her lack of proper education.

"It is a happy thing," Georgiana said, "that Anne and Richard took her to Brighton. I know you worried about it,

Lizzy, especially once your father allowed her to stay there with the Forsters."

Lizzy was not sure how happy it was, but she hoped that in time, she could learn to be content for Lydia. The girl had made a good match for herself, and fancied herself in love. Maybe that was enough. Perhaps not everyone was formed to have the kind of spiritual connection Lizzy shared with Darcy.

Late that night, as she lay wrapped in her husband's arms, floating in a state of bliss, she said, "I do not think I realized until today how very lucky I am. I wanted to marry for love, and I found the one man on earth best suited to make me happy. What we have is rare, Darcy. I do not think I knew before *how* rare."

"True, my love. And yet, in my experience, what people find in life depends largely on what they seek. You and I, and Jane and Bingley, refused to settle for anything less than love."

She kissed him, then snuggled against his shoulder. The fire crackled and gave off a soft glow. How much her life had changed since Darcy had come to Rosings! And yet, it was not her new home nor sumptuous clothes that made each moment a delight. It was only this man, her Darcy, who had looked inside her soul, and loved her for what he found there.

The End

About the Author

Andrea David is a Regency romance author in Raleigh, North Carolina. When she's not reading or writing, she enjoys gardening, scuba diving, and hiking active volcanoes with her husband. To learn more about her books, visit her website at www.AndreaDavidAuthor.com.

More by Andrea David

The Darcys' First Christmas: The Disappearance

After a blissful honeymoon, Elizabeth Darcy from Jane Austen's *Pride and Prejudice* is thrilled to see her sister Jane again as the two prepare to spend their first Christmas with their new husbands. But when distressing news arrives from their family at Longbourn, it overthrows their plans. With the shame of her sister Lydia's elopement still fresh in her mind, Elizabeth fears the worst—and worries that this new proof of her family's folly will test Darcy's attachment to her. Can their love endure this new challenge? Or will their first Christmas together be their last?

This is a clean and wholesome Regency novella with a happy ending and no cliffhanger.

Made in the USA
Coppell, TX
10 August 2023

20198199R00268